THE ONIS

THE PROPHECY

From the Series:
REIGN OF THE ANCIENTS
PART 1

By: R.E. DAVIES

TABLE OF CONTENTS

This book is dedicated to my family, who have supported and encouraged me to make this long-overdue dream a reality. And also to all who have endured my tales of this land and its inhabitants for the last 25 years or so. Believe in yourself and anything is possible.

"It is not the mountain we conquer, but ourselves."
~Sir Edmund Hillary

PROLOGUE

*T*urathyl closed her eyes and deeply inhaled the morning air as the cold wind of the mountaintop blew strongly across her face. Digging her claws into the rock beneath her feet, she stretched out her long neck and pointed her nose toward the sky, smelling for telltale signs of what was to come. Below her, Turathyl's kin grew restless on the rocks as they swayed back and forth in the wind, their wings spread slightly open, ready to take flight at any moment. She grew uneasy from the silence as the sun reached mid-morning, her scout having been gone since dawn. Shifting her weight, the slate-gray ledge below her feet crumbled and cracked in protest, large pebbles breaking free and tumbling down the mountainside, echoing their fall through the air.

Turathyl and her kin were part of the Silver dragon clan, named for the beautiful reflective silver scales that were an ample form of armor covering most of their body. Broad impenetrable white scales took dominance over their underbelly. The dragons' nearly translucent-white wing membranes were veined with silver-blue streaks. A pair of long horns protruded high on their heads, followed by stiff quills atop flat, scaly scalps, cascading down their spines to the tips of lengthy, muscular tails. The Silvers' maturity could be deciphered from the accumulation and loftiness of these quills, with Turathyl's outnumbering her accompanying Silvers by at least double as they feathered and diverged from her spine. They were "Masters of the Sky," dominating the winds and storms, manipulating the atmosphere to their command, and flight for them was effortless.

'*The caravan is due south of you, Elder,*' Turathyl sensed her scout mind-speak to her. Scouts were chosen for their agility and youth, making them more stunted than the elders, which helped them remain inconspicuous to onlookers.

Closing her eyes, Turathyl connected with the scout, stretching her mind open, reaching out for the familiarity of his own. Sending her thoughts south, she sensed him in the skies and grasped onto his semblance. Their link strengthened as she located him, and the bond was formed, their minds coalescing into a unified thought. Opening her eyes, she was no longer seeing from her platform on the Gorén Mountain ledge but was now flying elevated through the sky above the trees.

As the scout lowered his gaze to the trees beneath, Turathyl saw through his eyes to a company of elves traveling along a concealed path within the Emerald Forest. She tallied a dozen mounted guards. They wore brown leather armor and beheld small wooden bucklers rimmed with steel, portraying their king's emblem on the exterior. Long sovereign swords were sheathed at the elves' sides and a longbow with quiver strapped against their backs. They equally surrounded a caravan with four preceding, four pursuing closely, and two on either side. The horses were colossal, bred for strength to carry armored soldiers, caravans, and long journeys. Elegant braids adorned their manes and tails, but they were slow and ungainly due to their mass and stout legs.

The caravan was embellished eccentrically with golden hues glittering in the sunlight, piercing through the foliage overhead, unwittingly making them fairly easy to spot from above. Brown silken tassels danced in unison with the carriage's motion from the laborious path. The coachman was a seasoned elf with thick leather gloves and a green cloth cape, his large hood drawn over his head. He was hunched over as he thrashed the reins of two strong gray war-horses, keeping them at a steady trot.

The scout looked at the surrounding area, and Turathyl recognized it as being halfway between the two elven cities of Má Lyndor and Othsuda Theora, with a small clearing to the east and a river to the west. At the pace they were going, the travelers had a two-day expedition to Othsuda Theora, but—unbeknownst to them—they would never again see the great city in the trees.

Closing her eyes, Turathyl touched the scout's mind with thankful affection and quietly severed the link between them. As her thoughts returned to her body back on the mountain ledge most southeasterly of the Gorén Mountains, she inflated her lungs, rumbling the brisk air down her throat. Opening her large jaws, she exhaled a bellowing war cry before heightening her immense wings to take flight. She unleashed a series of prolonged, roaring cries, causing the dragons beneath her to beat their wings in an uproar, leaping from the perches and echoing her chorus with their own. Including Turathyl and the scout, they formed a band of seven Silvers, which were more than capable for this task. However, the Great Aeris never underestimated the elves and always sent her forces out in mass to show the elves whom they were dealing with and dissuade their attacks.

Aeris was the monarch of the Silver dragons, the eldest of them, and by far the strongest, with Turathyl as her successor should anything happen to her. Although anxious of her destiny, Turathyl would see to it for that day not to come. Aeris was an honorable leader, very esteemed among all the dragons, and it would be tragic if anything were to befall her, causing an unnatural demise.

As Turathyl headed south, the others maneuvered in behind her like birds of prey. They were elevated enough that their forms would be seen as a flock of large gulls or a small mass of clouds until the moment was befitting their descent. Hours passed, and they were finally getting close. Turathyl beat her wings viciously, hastening her party, while she searched the trees ahead for signs of the caravan. Her heart began to pound with excitement. *This attack will not be taken lightly for either side*, she anticipated proudly to herself.

The sun had reached high noon, but the heat below did not bother the Silvers as the clouds' frigid winds rushed over them. Turathyl's keen glare caught the reflected sparkle of the sun hitting the caravan through the forest canopy, and she signaled the location to her army telepathically. *'Wait for it!'* she mind-spoke to them. When the caravan cleared the trees and came to an opening, Turathyl roared loudly into the air, 'NOW!!!'

She tilted toward the earth and folded her wings against her body, diving faster and faster toward the caravan below, each Silver following her command and diving in unison after her. She saw the elves' alert below as their horses reared, and they raised their bows to the sky. *Oh, no you don't!* She summoned her power from within, directing it toward the winds surrounding the elves, and hurled a great gale against them. Several fumbled as the wind slammed into them with brilliant intensity, and two of them lost grasp of their bows as they flew off in the distance. Curses and sneers came from the elves as the horses faltered, eyes broad with fear, ears tucked back on their heads, and they pranced backward, eager to bolt. The soldiers pulled at the reins to hold them firmly in place.

With a great roar, Turathyl swept down toward one of the riders, feeling arrows fly by her flank. Preparing for the collision, the elf drew his sword and aimed it toward her but did not brace himself swiftly enough. As more arrows were shot, deflecting off her scale-armored hide, she grabbed hold of the rider with her great jaws. Her hind legs braced against the dirt, kicking up a cloud as she landed and lifted the elf into the air with her powerful jaws, crunching him between her teeth. The elf's sword dropped from his blood-soaked grasp, clanging on the rocky dirt below. She heard his puny bones break, and then his body fell limp. She would not ingest these creatures nor any other intelligent life form. Some dragons were afraid that the souls would haunt them for eternity, and Turathyl was not a monster—just a knight in a never-ending game of chess; her companions, the pawns.

Abruptly, Turathyl felt an arrow rip through her left wing. She winced and growled in annoyance, thrashing her tail to deflect another arrow from hitting her vulnerable wings. Dragons did not have many vulnerable places with their hard scale armor, but their wings were an easy target for arrows. Thankfully for them, they were also quick to heal.

She tossed aside the lifeless elf and turned her head to the shooter. Then, with a strong beat of her wings, she leapt forward and landed a few paces from him. Her onyx-black eyes bore into his soul, entrancing him, putting up a shell around his mind. She disabled him from moving, locking his sight with hers. Another Silver came down from the sky, toppling onto the elf with his talons, crushing him and his horse, sending them both flailing to the ground.

The other Silvers were quick to the attack on the riders, swooping down from the sky, arrows repelling off their scaly flanks as they swarmed their enemies, filling the air with monstrous roars, instilling fear into the tiny two-leggeds.

Turathyl heard a commotion from the caravan behind her. She turned and saw an elven female running for the trees, a small parcel tucked in her arms. *Lady Leona*, Turathyl huffed. The Silvers were killing off the mounted elves rather effortlessly and crippling their horses. They obtained only minor wounds from the arrows and sword befalling them as they slashed at the elves and crushed them between their teeth.

Turathyl turned and pounced off toward the trees where Lady Leona, the mission's target, was escaping. She slowed while she approached Lady Leona cowering against a rock, shielding her eyes from Turathyl's sight with a raised hand, whimpering in elvish, "Areta... Areta naiht..." *Please... Please no...* Turathyl strode proudly up to her, growling softly, head raised high in sheer mockery. "Suliath Ono... Areta..." *Great One... Please...*

The frail creature shook beneath Turathyl's magnificence. Her golden hair was strung around her slender face in large ringlets embedded with a distinguished platinum tiara containing several sparkling gems that gleamed in the sun's rays. Crystal-blue eyes blinked in fear as she tried to guard them against the entrancing blackness of Turathyl's glare.

For a moment, Turathyl nearly felt pity for the feeble creature beneath her, but her orders were absolute. She rumbled and stretched her jaw, and then with one swift motion and an unholy scream from the elf, Turathyl crunched down around the slender body of Leona, picking her up and crushing her bones between her molars. Disgorging the mangled remains on the ground by the rock, Turathyl would leave Lady Leona for the elves to find but first nudged the corpse with her nose to make sure there was no way the elven healers could revive her.

As she was about to leave, an abrupt high-pitched wailing came from the hollow of a nearby tree. She had never heard such a noise, and although it bothered her ears, it breached within the boundaries of her mind and astonished her. Cautiously, she tramped over to the tree's hollow and glimpsed inside. There, within the tree, was the parcel Turathyl had seen Leona carrying when she fled the caravan. Miniature elven limbs were reaching from a soft brown cloth, waving around in the air. The hands were in tiny fists, and its feet were flailing around with its toes curled up while it continued wailing its displeasure. *An elf cub!* Turathyl blinked in bewilderment. *How unexpected!*

Not knowing what to do, she intuitively purred softly to the cub, clicking air at the back of her throat, and nuzzled it with her snout to hush its cries. The cub's discord softened as it touched Turathyl's chin with its itty bitty hands and soon was quiet and content.

'Elder, the elves have been defeated. We are awaiting your order,' came the mind voice of one of the Silvers. Startled, Turathyl raised her head, knocking her snout on the mouth of the tree hollow, then pulled it out of the hole and looked at the Silvers who were beginning to assemble around her.

'Good,' she replied. *'Head back to Aeris and give her the news. I will join you soon.'*

The Silvers opened their great wings, beckoned the air around them, and thrashed several times, lifting them higher and higher into the sky.

The dragons of Onis have an extra set of lungs filled with gasses formed by the acidic digestion of food. Each dragon species uses the additional lung for diversified mastery, adapting to the various terrains they inhabit. The Silvers pressurize their lungs to form helium, giving them added lift into the sky to carry their large masses. Other clans can all fly, but none with the mastery, speed, and height of the Silvers.

Turathyl watched them as they gained in altitude and headed north towards the mountains. Then, she looked back at the cub and contemplated what to do with it. *I suppose I should destroy it. It would not survive on its own, and the last thing we need is another elf being raised to hate our kind and bring more war to the dragons. I could not possibly take care of it. Even if I got it to the lair, it would be destroyed for sure when discovered. Yes,* she decided, *I must kill it.*

Turathyl gently grasped the cloth around the cub with her teeth, pulled it from the camouflage of the tree, and then lowered it to the ground. Looking down on it one last time, she sighed heavily before closing her eyes and opening her jaw, slowly descending her head towards the cub. However, something stopped her.

Opening her eyes again, she gawked down at the cub. It lay on its back, tangled in the cloth, calmly looking up at her with its veneer remaining expressionless as it fixated its large glistening-blue eyes on hers without blinking. She felt a warm aura emanating from the small figure, and while observing it, she felt tenderness penetrate into her mind, caressing her thoughts soothingly with love. Turathyl closed her eyes and purred, her head swaying gently side-to-side as the strange mind-touch nestled against her thoughts like a newborn Silver. Jostled by the likeness of the touch, Turathyl opened her eyes in alarm and looked back down at the elven cub staring up at her.

Trickery! Turathyl gasped in anger and confusion. Her foreclaws clutched the earth, supporting her as her body tensed. Looking down at the cub staring back at her so peacefully and innocently, she suddenly felt foolish and looked around to ensure they were still, in fact, alone.

No, she realized and relaxed her flanks, *there is something...special about this cub, something different.* To look at the cub, it did not resemble anything extraordinary with its round body, portly digits, slightly pointed ears, and a golden tuft of hair upon its crown. She investigated the vicinity to make certain she was void from all attention, large or small, and then delicately guarded the cub in her foreclaws.

Opening her mighty wings, Turathyl summoned gusts of wind to take her into the skies. *I must take it to a safe place. To someone who I know will watch over it and guard it.* As she took flight and gained altitude, she felt no distress coming from the little one in her paw and smiled. *Lupé Caelis,* she thought optimistically, *she will know what to do.*

Tilting her great form, she veered to the left and destined south toward the Sacred Forest. It was a few more hours from the battlefield before she spotted the river where Lupé Caelis could be encountered by those who knew where to search. She spotted two wolves by the riverbank, lapping up water in the glowing sun, and began to descend gracefully. The wolves gazed up at her alarmed, baring their sharp canines, and watched her perch on a small mound by the riverbank overlooking them.

Turathyl hobbled closer to them on three paws, keeping the young one elevated with her fourth, and reached out her mind to the wolves before they could bolt into the forest. They lowered their aggression toward her as she soothed their minds with her own. Their matted fur of varying shades of gray rustled in the light breeze brought down by Turathyl's landing. They were very muscular under their thinning fur from the warm climate. The larger of the two took a few small paces toward her, bowing its head in homage and salutation. Turathyl mind-touched the imminent wolf gently, sending feelings of benevolence and warmth, then conveyed an image of their mother, Lupé Caelis, and an under-stood request for her audience. Any animal could be mind-touched with thoughts and feelings if one were strong enough in the gift—as all dragons were.

The wolves were a proud pack due to the confidence instilled in them from being part of Lupé Caelis' pack and did not startle easily, foreboding rarely. But, they were wolves and nothing more, not magical nor more intelligent than any other wolves of the forest. They could only receive simple communications, such as feelings and pictures with no words. The same could not be said for their den mother, however, for she was a great, magical beast, much older than Turathyl, wiser than the dragons, and much larger than any wolf. *She will know what to do with the cub,* Turathyl reassured herself.

As Turathyl broke the mind-link with the wolf, it raised its pointed head to the sky and howled a long, throaty call. After the call ended, the wolf turned its back to Turathyl and pounced off into the forest, disappearing into the shrubbery with the other wolf close behind.

Curling her tail around her, Turathyl lowered her flank and lay on the warm earth beneath, tucking her free forepaw under her breast. She opened her paw with the cub in it and looked at the strange creature with bewilderment. The cub had been resting but opened its eyes drowsily as the sun was exposed and then returned Turathyl's gaze with its large, glistening eyes. Turathyl purred and nuzzled the cub with her nose again. Feeling it grasp its little fingers over her snout, it tickled her nose, causing her to snort, jostling the delicate strands of hair atop the cub's head. Letting out a gurgling sound of dragon laughter, Turathyl smiled down at the cub and cradled it in her paw.

A limb snapped on the forest floor near the opening by the river, and Turathyl looked up to see Lupé Caelis standing proudly at the base of a large tree, observing her with the cub. Her stance was strong for one so old, and she held her head high with her large white mane framing her bold face. She was taller than any man or elf at her shoulder, and her coat was thick, despite the heat. It was a brilliant shade of white with no gray or black markings of any kind. The only other colors the wolf sported were her ice-blue eyes and ebony nose and lips. Her tail was lustrous and velvety, as was her entire integument, flowing smoothly in the gentle breeze.

Her eyes were the only indication of her age as they showed a wisdom and soul, both great of power. Turathyl could see the anguish and trials in the wolf's eyes of battles and descendants lost, but they had the warmth found in any mother who has known a love stronger than any other.

Turathyl bowed her head to the Great Wolf and sent a mind-touch of good intention and graciousness for her presence.

'You have woken me from my afternoon nap, dragon. Say why it is you have come,' bellowed Lupé Caelis' mighty and unmistakable mind-voice to Turathyl.

'Great Lupé Caelis,' Turathyl began, 'I have come to you out of desperation for your help. I have come across a cub unlike any other and fear for its safety. I seek your wisdom and your guidance.'

Lupé Caelis glanced unmasked at the elf cub in Turathyl's claws. 'You waste my time, dragon. I have no interest in your trials and wars with the elves. Now, leave me be.' The Great Wolf slowly turned her back to Turathyl and took a step toward the forest. Instinctively, Turathyl growled her displeasure, instantly regretting it.

Snarling ferociously, Lupé Caelis took one leap from the forest entrance and landed on Turathyl. Her jaws snapped on Turathyl's snout, piercing through her thick hide and drawing cold dark-blue blood that trickled down her lips. Turathyl screeched in pain, falling on her side from the impact of the Great Wolf.

'You disturb me in my home and dare threaten me, dragon?!' Lupé Caelis boomed into Turathyl's mind while continuing to clasp her snout shut. 'You want to know what to do with the cub? Kill it! Drown it! Drop it off a mountain for all I care! It is your war and your problem! Now take that feeble thing and leave my home before I bring your kind a new war by killing you!'

There was no mistake in Turathyl's mind of how serious Lupé Caelis was and how humiliated Turathyl felt for neglecting her reverence for the Great Wolf God, even for a moment. *'My apologies, Great One! My intent was not to threaten, but this is no ordinary elf cub! Please! I beg of you to see for yourself. I guarantee you will understand why I believed it necessary to disturb you!'*

Lupé Caelis hesitantly released her hold on Turathyl's snout and looked at her coldly. *'For your sake, you had better be right.'* But instead of looking to the cub, the Great Wolf bore into Turathyl's mind. Her cerebrum was tormented as she sensed Lupé Caelis reach into and around her memories, stealing what information she desired. Turathyl knew better than to block her, so she clenched her eyes, wincing as the memories poured out of her mind into the Great Wolf. The intensity in which Lupé Caelis bore into her mind was excruciatingly painful and would have killed a lesser being, but the Great Wolf God knew dragons' limits and was uninterested in pacing herself to spare the dishonorable dragon some pain.

Visions of Aeris's orders for the attack on the elves swirled around in her head, followed by the attack itself and the discovery of the cub. Turathyl could see the memories as they were stolen, but it was all so fast that it made her dizzy. She moaned in disgrace as the memory of nearly slaughtering the cub left her but eased as the rest of the events leading to her decision to spare the cub followed. Turathyl opened her eyes as she felt the tension on her mind ease up and withdraw, then looked back to Lupé Caelis with humility.

The Great Wolf put her massive paw on Turathyl's raised claw with the cub inside, pulling her talons down toward the earth so she could see the cub for herself. Lupé Caelis sniffed the cub several times without causing it to stir and stared into its eyes for several moments. *'I understand,'* came Lupé Caelis' mind-voice, soft and gentle this time. *'Yo have no idea what you have found, do you?'*

Turathyl gaped at the Great Wolf, shaking her head bewildered. Before she could say anything, Lupé Caelis swept up the cub in her jaws, grasping onto the material encompassing it, carrying the cub as one of her own firmly in her mouth, and trotted back to the forest wall. '*Return to Aeris and tell her nothing of the cub, for it will only anger her, and she will seek to destroy it. I will raise the elf cub as my own. I will care for her until she is strong and grown, but you must promise me something in return.*'

Turathyl rose to attention, nodding curiously at the Great Wolf, and replied, '*Anything.*'

Lupé Caelis turned her head, looking back to the dragon, the bundle dangling beneath her chin, and said, '*Good. You are to forget the cub and put her from your thoughts. I do not need any unwanted attention; from your kind or any other. There will come a day when I will call on you. You must do as I tell you and be mine to summon. You do not know it yet, but someday you will realize the significance of your obedience to me. Do you understand?*'

Turathyl's heart sank as she nodded mournfully, wondering if she'd ever get to see the cub again, ever get to feel that strange— yet familiar—connection again. '*Yes, Great One, I understand, and you have my word.*'

'*Remember,*' Lupé Caelis sternly mind-sent, '*tell NO ONE!*' Then, she turned to the forest and gracefully disappeared into its foliage, leaving the dragon alone by the river clearing.

Stretching her wings to the sky, Turathyl sighed somberly and whispered toward the forest, *Goodbye, wolf child.* She did not understand why she felt such a strange affection for the cub, but she perceived it would be safeguarded here. With that, she summoned the surrounding air, plummeted her wings toward the earth, and launched into the heavens, back to Aeris and her kin.

CHAPTER ONE

GRADUATION

*I*t was an afternoon like any other in the land of Onis, but, for a select few in a human city to the south, it was just a little bit more special. Many were gathered in a great room, waiting anxiously for their shining moment on the stage. However, there was one boy that was not looking to the stage awaiting as anxiously as the others for his name to be called. Davion was seated with his fellow classmates but didn't hear a word that was being said by the Dean. Instead, he was busy searching for his Uncle Hort in the stadium seating that had been set up on either side for family and guests. He hadn't seen him arrive prior to the commencement of the ceremony and was beginning to worry that he wouldn't be there. Hort wasn't blood—not even the same race—but he was all that Davion had left in the world. Squirming in his chair, he looked all around at each side of the audience, trying to catch even a glimpse of his uncle's scruffy face.

Davion, like most of those around him, was human. He wore the same drab-brown mage robe as those of the same rank and class and was average height with a slender build—definitely not designed for physical tasks, such as the guard or farming. Like his eyes, his hair was light brown and was cut short around the sides with a finger comb of wavy locks on top. By no means was he the most handsome man in the room but was still considered rather attractive.

The great room had white-marble columns reaching all the way to the highly elevated ceiling. Dragons, Orcs, Elves, Drow, Dwarves, and Man artfully danced around in the mural above, looking down over the audience as they acted out a scene of war, lighted with blasts of magic and swirls of color all around. If you concentrated, you would see the characters moving in action, fighting with one another in a great battle.

The stadium seating on either side was only three rows high, and wooden folding chairs had been placed in the center for the thirty-two graduates, all robed in the same drab brown for their newly-graduating skill level. The room was much too large for the occupants, creating an echo with each word from the Dean, but it all fell on deaf ears as Davion continued to hunt for his uncle. He assumed the Dean was just reciting a generic speech about how proud he was of all the students and what great progress they had made, etcetera, etcetera, which was a very accurate assumption.

"And without further delay, let us begin," called out the Dean. The first row of students stood and began walking single-file up to the stage as they were instructed. "Alan Artrue, Earth Magic," he said as the first student went to receive his diploma.

After a few more names were called out, Davion's row stood to join the first row in line. His heart sank as he continued to search for Hort to no avail. It somehow didn't mean much to him being here if there was no one to see it, supporting him and acknowledging his achievement. He should have been booming with pride. Not only had he been accepted to the prestigious mage school, Silex Valley Magi Academy, but believed he had really excelled at it, and here he was finally graduating. He closed his eyes, took a deep breath, and thought of his mother. He hoped in the back of his mind that maybe, just maybe, she was watching him

CHAPTER 1

now from the beyond, smiling with pride. He pictured her wavy scarlet-red hair and ruby lips with her sparkling green eyes. Of course, in his memory, everything was brighter and cheerier than it probably had been in real life, but he liked to remember her this way. It had also become harder for him to hold onto the actual memories of her with each passing year. Nearly twelve years had passed since he last saw her face, twelve very long years.

Shuffling along with each name called, Davion made his way inch by inch towards the stage. As he took the first step up onto the platform, he hung his head, no longer caring, just ready for it to be over with.

"Davion Collins, Fire Magic," called the Dean.

Davion lifted his hand towards the Dean to accept his diploma when he heard very clearly a deep husky voice screaming, "DAVION!!! ME BOY!!!"

Suddenly Davion smiled and blushed with embarrassment and excitement all at the same time. He'd know that voice anywhere; his uncle had made it after all. He held up his diploma and fist to the ceiling and looked again for Hort but still couldn't find him amongst the sea of faces. It didn't bother him anymore, though, because he knew he had made it, and that was all that mattered.

Heading back to his seat, Davion was much more elated than he had been on the way to the podium. Davion was just about to retake his seat when, in the audience to his right, he noticed his uncle's face pushing through between two large women happily cheering for someone else. He spotted his large round nose peeking out over a thick brown beard masquerading around several silver hairs and recognized his two beady eyes with thick brows just below the brim of a wobbly helmet. He had an unmistakable scar along his left temple down his cheek. The top of his head was only at the level of the ladies' chests, and Davion could see through the thick whiskers of his uncle's long beard the biggest smile that he had ever seen, and it made him smile too.

His uncle removed his helmet, tucking it under his arm as he made eye contact with Davion. Although sweaty from the helmet and a bit disheveled, Davion was surprised to see him looking so dapper. His brown hair had been combed and slicked to the side, and his beard groomed with thick braids, something he had never seen. He knew how much his uncle hated to gussy up for anything, which made it mean that much more to Davion, no matter how unusual a dwarf with slicked hair and a groomed beard looked. The closest he had seen him look that prim and primed was back home in Lochlann for Hort's first date with the handsome dwarf, Glondora.

The rest of the ceremony went rather quickly with only thirty-two graduates, and Davion was excited for it to be over, for it to finally be official. He was a Silex Valley Magi Academy Graduate!

"Congratulations, graduates!" yelled the Dean as everyone stood. "Always remember..."

Every graduate and faculty raised their right fist to the air and yelled together, "HONOR! RESPECT! FREEDOM! FOR ONIS!"

The rest of the audience raised their right fists as well and repeated, "FOR ONIS!" The voices echoed through the grand room, followed by complete silence as everyone bowed their heads. They clasped their fist in front of their chest with their other hand; elbows bowed out to the sides. The only sound Davion could hear was the heavy breathing from the portly boy next to him.

One of the head fire magic professors raised her hands high above her head, sending sparks and fireworks raining down from the ceiling, breaking the silence with bangs and crackles. Everyone cheered and embraced in exhilaration. It was a magnificent display of both beauty and power. Davion watched the dazzling display in awe, knowing that it required great strength and control. He only hoped he could be as great as the academy's professors one day. The fireworks then fizzled into silver rain, showering down over them as it slowly disappeared, and everyone cheered in an uproar again. They had finally graduated!

Immediately following the ceremony's conclusion, Davion pushed past his classmates to get to his uncle, who was already making his way to him as well. The room was booming and echoing with commotion from the attendees and their shuffling of chairs to get to the ones they loved.

"Uncle Hort!" Davion called out, barely audible amongst the crowd. He waved his hand at him, hoping not to lose sight of each other. When at last they finally met, Hort held his arms out wide, and Davion bent over to give his uncle a welcoming hug. "I thought you weren't going to make it," he told him honestly. "When did you arrive?"

"Shortly aft' it began. I snuck in through the side," Hort replied, leading Davion toward the side exit where he had come in through. "You know I wouldna' missed this, me boy. I'm so proud of ye." He smiled again and punched him gently—for a dwarf—in the arm. Davion rubbed his arm and smiled.

Looking back at all the guests and graduates, Davion smiled nostalgically one last time. He spotted one of his study partners looking his way and gave him a friendly wave before letting Hort know he was ready to go. He never made any close friends, preferring to keep to himself, so he saw no point in waiting around, but he was still going to miss the academy. The feeling of safety from being surrounded by protectors, of working towards something greater than himself, of harnessing his powers around those who understood and held the same dreams as he, were all things he would greatly miss.

The world beyond those giant solid doors was anything but safe and secure, full of war and destruction, with so many unknown variables of what his future would hold. However, now was the time for him to show what he had learned, to be tested among actual foes and not just sparring with classmates. It all felt a little too overwhelming and frightening, but he also felt ready to show what he was capable of; to others and to himself.

"Ye sure yer ready?" Hort asked, confused. "No one ye'd like me ta meet?" he said, nudging him suggestively.

"No, Uncle," Davion replied, "no one special."

Hort sighed in disappointment. He worried about Davion not finding anyone fitting for himself, as it was difficult and unlikely for him to meet anyone compatible back in Lochlann. As charming as dwarf women tended to be with their aggressive, brutally honest attitudes and their bushy faces, legs, and backs, Davion just didn't find himself attracted to any of them.

"What about offers? Did a mighty wizard come and snatch ye up?" Hort inquired.

"The army was the only recruiter I'm afraid, Uncle." Davion frowned. "I'm sorry," he added, disappointed in himself.

Only the academy's top graduates were given special opportunities to be placed in apprenticeships with great mages, a very prestigious offer to receive. Those lucky few were exempt from the drafts, so the army could not claim their lives, where they would then be piled together and sent off to battle with no further training. Davion was lucky to have a loophole by not belonging to the human cities, or he too would have little choice in his future. So, instead of a forced draft, he was lucky to receive only a recruitment. Even though Davion's advantage of not being a citizen enabled him to bypass the forced mage drafts, the costs were seen by the holes made in his uncle's pockets. Steep prices were set for foreigners to have the honor of attending the Magi Academy since it would receive no benefits from the kingdom for their training. They also only accepted students every four years after a series of highly intense testing sessions to determine each applicant's depth of magic. Magic wasn't very common among humans like it was with the elven races. It was believed to be caused by a blending with the elven race long ago that magic entered the human soul at all.

"Right. So let's be off then," Hort huffed, and they started to walk. "I do have a gift fer ye," he remembered as he pushed open the side door. "It isna' much, but ye be needin' 'er."

Hort gestured across the alley to a horse at a hitching post. It was a stunning brown mare with a mane and tail that were nearly pure white, and she appeared to be in decent health and vigor. Turning her head as they approached, Davion reached out his hand to stroke the bridge of her nose. On her forehead, she sported a white diamond-shaped spot and looked calmly at him with bright blue eyes, bowing her nose acceptingly to him.

"Thank you, Uncle," Davion said sincerely. "What's her name?" he asked while softly rubbing the white spot on her forehead.

"She doesna' 'ave one yet," Hort replied.

Searching his brain, all Davion could muster up was the word for horse in the elvish tongue. "Helna," he said aloud to see how it felt and nodded satisfied.

Hort went and grabbed his okullo, Orbek, from the other side of the post. Okullos were a favorite among the dwarves due to their short and sturdy stature. They were about half the height of a typical horse and had buffalo-style horns lying on top of their heads with a long-bearded chin and furry hind legs. Their front legs and all four feet were striped like a zebra, and they had white patches around their eyes, while the rest of their head and body was a deep dark brown. They weren't quite as fast as a horse but were strong and superior in battles, and Hort loved and cared for his okullo as though he were family.

"We'll 'ead back ta the inn and 'ave a little celebration of our own, then leave first light for Mira," Hort said as he mounted his saddle.

"Is it safe?" Davion asked. "I heard rumors that things have become worse."

"Aye," Hort nodded. "Things have become much worse since ye been 'ere. But nothin' me and me axe canna 'andle!" he said, smiling smugly and tapping the handle of his weapon as he took it from Orbek and strapped it to his back with his shield.

The two, at a slow walk, led their mounts to the main road. It was early evening, and the city was still in a bustle, surrounded by its tall stone walls offering adequate defenses. Roco, the capital human city, was always busy and crowded. Davion hadn't spent much time out of the academy, but he was familiar enough with the main roads.

The streets were paved with large flat stones of red and cream, and the city was alive with people rushing to and from places, trying to sell their wares to passers-by, all very assertively. Every so often, there would be a forcedly planted tree or other vegetation along the side of the street that needed a lot of maintenance and magic to be kept alive due to the dryness of the land.

There were entertainers dancing and singing or performing basic magic tricks, hopeful for coin. He saw a fire mage making flames dance like a ballerina from one candle to the next and then across the sky back to the first flame. A water mage was using a pot of water to make a beautiful fountain, which shot up past the rooftops at times. All were child's play tricks for any beginner mage but still amusing to the public.

It was rumored that Silex Valley, where the human towns were located, had once been full of lush greenery with bushes and flowers nearly 1,000 years ago, but now it was mostly just bare, dry, rocky terrain south of the Miran River.

The elves owned the forest laying north of the river, believed to be kept abundant and thriving due to their magics. So, humans made the best they could of their barren lands and traded what they could for the rest. Most water and earth mages were scooped up by the king to work farms since they could manipulate those elements to help keep harvests going, leaving the fire and air mages as favored recruits for the army.

Hort turned down a side road towards Raven's Inn, which featured a wooden sign with a carved raven over the door. It was a quiet little inn with only a few rooms and a small tavern as you walked in. After Hort and Davion tied up their mounts outside, Hort went in and obtained them a room for the night. They weren't wealthy, but they weren't exactly poor either, and their accommodations suited them just fine.

After locking their sacks in the room, they went to the tavern and ordered their meals along with some ale from the innkeeper's daughter, a young, fair-looking girl of about fifteen, who flirted a little-too-much with Davion for it to be subtle.

"I'm Lira if you need anything else," she said to Davion as she leaned over to place his plate before him, trying to enhance her petite bosom, then hovered for a moment, gazing at him. He smiled uncomfortably and nodded to her, letting her know that she could leave. He watched as she walked away, overly swaying her hips to make her skirt swish back and forth as she went.

Davion took a sip of his ale, and Hort laughed as he watched the two of them. "Perhaps I shoulda' got two rooms?" he teased.

Davion snorted his ale a little out of his nose as Hort caught him off guard. "Uncle!" he whined, embarrassed. "Not at all," he said after putting down his mug.

Davion was used to the attention of youthful naïve girls. Aside from his moderate good looks, his mage garb made him an easy target for admiring eyes. It was similar to wearing an army uniform in Roco in that it gave a sense of protection, and that was something in high demand around here. However, Davion was modest and didn't let the attentions of fantastical young women get to his head. He was more interested in his magic and avenging his family. There wasn't much else that took his attention away from that.

CHAPTER I

CHAPTER TWO

TRAINING

*S*cratching behind Lupé Caelis' ears, Pavula embraced her mother and mind-touched warmly, '*Good morning, Mother.*'

It was dark inside the concealed cavern and had the pungent smell of the wolves, but it was home to Pavula, and the aroma had become delightfully intoxicating to her, causing her to feel safe and loved. She loved her family immensely and often forgot that she was not actually one of them. Nevertheless, she would forever consider herself so.

'*Good morning, Lupé Pavula,*' Lupé Caelis whispered while nuzzling her and giving her a quick love-lick on her cheek. '*You must have been tired from yesterday's hunt. You did very well.*' Pavula smiled proudly into her mother's mane. She became more skillful at hunting with every chase, and her confidence enhanced through each kill. Not that she favored killing, but she understood her obligation to the survival of her pack. For a long time, Pavula was unsuccessful, lacking claws to retain the prey and fangs to slay it. However, over time she acquired different techniques with forged rudimentary weapons and soon brought back the equivalent of the best hunters in her pack.

Pavula stretched her limbs and then crawled through the tunnel, out of the dark cavern. The sun beamed in her eyes, and she winced against the daylight, her sight adjusting to its brilliance. Birds were singing their morning songs far up in the trees. A scrawny squirrel darted across branches between two trees and then up the backside of a slender trunk. The Sacred Forest was flourishing as all the critters bustled about with their early routines.

Frolicking playfully, Pavula headed south along the invisible path that directed her in her usual morning stroll. She encountered her brethren by the river and took a plunge to freshen up. Her stomach ached on account of the feast from the night before still swimming around unhappily in her belly. The raw rabbit meat never sat well with her. Even though she was educated on how to cook over fire by her mother, she was not permitted to light fires at night in fear of giving away their location. So, only on very successful hunts, when they returned before dusk, was she permitted to enjoy the bliss of the roasted rabbit.

Splashing water at her brethren, Pavula laughed as the wolves pranced around the riverbank, wagging their tails joyfully. They growled and barked playfully back at her. When she finished bathing, she wrung out her long golden locks, letting them fall loosely over her petite bare breasts, the tips of her pointed ears poking out just beyond the thick tresses. She shook the excess water from her body, letting the water drip freely from her swine-skin loincloth. Her skin was sun-kissed to a golden bronze, and her crystal blue eyes shone brightly against her tanned face. Even through her unkempt hair, scratched-up skin, and mud-covered feet, her beauty was still undeniable, but she was also still very young and naïve in many respects.

Sauntering off towards a great oak by the river, Pavula felt a wolf cub nipping at her heels friskily with each step. She laughed and ran backward for a ways, the wolf cub bounding after her clumsily and barking happily. Pavula tripped over a tree's roots and fell backward, landing on her rump, her loincloth absorbing some of the impact. Giggling, she fell back into the grass as the mischievous cub tackled her, running up onto Pavula's chest, and then licked her nose repeatedly while wagging its tail. "Good morning to you too, little sister," she laughed.

Pavula picked her up, snuggling the cub in her arm like a baby, and scratched under its chin with her free hand while she went and lounged by the oak. After a few moments, the cub decided it had obtained enough attention for now and tottered off after a butterfly.

It was blossoming into another beautiful summer day in the Sacred Forest. Zephyr was sweeping through the trees, rustling the leaves in calming measure. The trickling river water's soothing sound added its harmonious effects to the forest, and the sun was partially blocked by the occasional marshmallow cloud. Pavula stretched out under the great oak in its shade, soaking in all the glory of the day.

The sun was reaching midday while Pavula lay and played with blades of grass. Pressing them between her thumbs, she blew on them carefully to create buzzing noises that would tickle her lips and make her giggle. She had been in this wonderful place with her "family" for sixteen years but was still very much a child at heart with very few responsibilities.

Out of the many rules that Lupé Caelis insisted upon, at the top of the list was: "Stay near the den always, never leave the confines of the territory." Pavula understood her rule but would never cease her daydreams about the wonders of the world outside; the creatures she'd encounter, the regions she'd discover, the events she'd witness. Her mother discouraged conversations about what was out there, leaving most things to her imagination. She pictured gardens abundant with large purple flowers towering around her, and she would run through them, becoming lost in their scent. She fabricated cities made of marble and castles in the sky, white waterfalls with hidden entrances, trees that walked and talked. Often, she thought of what it would be like to be one of the dragons she would occasionally spot overhead, soaring above everything, investigating the world beneath. *What would the realm look like from way up there?*

Lupé Caelis always took commendable care of Pavula and treated her more precious than any of her own children. Sometimes Pavula would notice jealousy from her kin due to the attention and love bestowed upon her by their mother, but it was never hateful or resentful in any way.

'*Lupé Pavula, it is time for your lesson,*' Pavula heard Lupé Caelis mind touch.

'*Yes, Mother. I'm coming,*' Pavula responded. She jumped to her feet in excitement, then ran back through the forest to the den. It was quite close to the river, only being a few minutes walk, but was very well disguised. No one, to Pavula's knowledge, had ever discovered it that wasn't meant to. It was surrounded by brush and trees, and the angle of the opening, unless standing just perfectly, blended into the mound it inhabited. The wolf clan was always patrolling the perimeter, intimidating anyone or anything who got within range, and Pavula could sense a magic barrier surrounding the edge of their territory that their mother had put up long ago.

Pavula often wanted to patrol beyond the border, but her mother would never allow it, telling her that others might not understand what an elven girl was doing surrounded by wolves. They would condemn her and their family by spreading allegations concerning her, intriguing more people to come in search of the "Wolf Child." She declared Pavula must never leave the confines of the wolf territory and, in doing so, must never be seen by man. At times it made her lonely, longing to be amongst others like her, but

CHAPTER 2

she cherished her family more than anything and would never purposely put them in danger.

As Pavula neared the den, she saw Lupé Caelis resting outside, sprawled out in the shade of the trees, grooming her front paw. "I'm here, Mother!" she said aloud.

Licking her paw and then grooming her face with it, Lupé Caelis responded, '*Yes, I know. You are as quiet as a herd of elkah on a stampede.*' She paused, resting her paw back down, and looked into Pavula's eyes. '*What was lesson number three?*'

'*I'm sorry, Mother,*' Pavula replied silently, resting her head on her knees as she squatted on the ground. '*I just look forward to my less...*'

'*What was it?*' Lupé Caelis persisted.

Trying to recall, Pavula squinted off to the side and counted out the lessons in her head. '*Always remain hidden,*' she managed to respond; correctly.

'*And how do we do that?*'

'*We...um, blend into our surroundings, and...*' Pavula fumbled for the exact words, '*stay silent like the wind.*'

Lupé Caelis stood and stretched, reaching her front paws out before her, chest low to the ground, hindquarters and tail high in the air. Taking a step forward, she stretched her hind legs in sequence and then turned to Pavula, sitting proudly before her as her tail danced back and forth in the grass. '*I teach you these things to be safe, Lupé Pavula. You must never forget them, no matter where you are. Lesson Two: Always be aware of your surroundings. One day you will know when it is time to be seen and when you must remain scarce. I love you and fear for your safety.*' Before continuing, she shook her head and rustled her mane in the gentle breeze, then let out a yawn, with a quick jaw-snap at the end. '*Now, today, I will teach you more earth magic. You have been doing well so far with it, but it is time to go to the* next level. For this lesson, I need you to take your hands and place them in the dirt.'

Pavula obeyed, kneeling and digging her fingers into the soil, and then looked up for her next command. 'Now, close your eyes, and search with your mind. Find the seeds in the earth and focus on them.'

Opening her mind, Pavula reached her thoughts down through her fingers into the dirt, feeling her arms and hands tingling as her energy surged through them. She pushed her thoughts further out until she could feel the small life forces of some nearby insects that tickled her mind-touch like a feather on the back of her neck. Striving not to lose her concentration, she quested past the arthropods and sought the tiny life sources of nearby seedlings. Once she grasped onto one, the others came more rapidly. She could feel and recognize the aura that each one emitted, distilling the spirits of several dozen seedlings at once. She became excited at the volume that was amassing in the grasp of her mind-touch. 'Focus on the seeds and ask the earth spirit to give them life. Give your energy over to the spirits and let your life force flow into them.'

Pavula held onto the seedlings' essences and tried to imagine them sprouting to life, pushing her magic into the seeds, but she felt nothing happen, even after several attempts. She could see them all in her mind, she could feel the energy leaving her and flowing toward them, but they all just lingered there in the dirt, oblivious to her demands. Their life sources began to dim from her grasp, and one-by-one, they fell away. Finally, in frustration, she raised her hands over her head and shouted, "Nothing's happening! Mother, I can't do it!" Sulking, Pavula fell back onto her buttocks, wrapped her arms around her legs, and then stared at the rustled dirt. "Why can't we do more with the water? I'm good at water."

CHAPTER 2

Lupé Caelis emitted a low growl in the back of her throat, but her mind-voice came sincere and patient in Pavula's thoughts. *'Of course, you are, my child. The water spirit has taken to you easily and was your first, but you can harness so much more than that. You have the power for all four spirits and even more beyond that. You must learn to harness them. You must learn to be patient. Now,'* she insisted, *'try again. Reach deeper into yourself than when you did the water magic. Find the spirit of the earth within you.'*

Returning to her stance, Pavula tried to shake off the failed attempts. Lupé Caelis seemed to have much more faith in Pavula's abilities than she had in herself, or cared to. When it came to her lessons, they were more like a game to her, and the game lacked luster when she wasn't "winning." She had yet to understand the importance of these sessions. With her fingers firmly in the dirt, Pavula tried again: collecting the seeds, forcing her energy, and losing them all over again.

On the fifth try, she pulled with her mind more adamantly than ever before. She found a sparkling light similar to the ones she had seen when she discovered her blue water spirit and white air spirit, except this one was gold. She grasped onto the little golden light, entwining it in her thoughts, and pulled from it with all of her strength. At first, there was great resistance, more than the others had given her, but she refused to let go of it. The golden light flickered and then flared brilliantly, succumbing to her demands.

Pavula could feel the light filling her entire being, spreading from the tips of her fingers, down through her toes, and up her neck. It overflowed her head with hundreds of images of lands from all over Onis, places she couldn't have ever fantasized. To the north were large mountains with their peaks hidden amongst the clouds and a magnificent waterfall dropping hundreds of feet into a lake below. Her abundant forest stretched much further than she had been permitted to explore, all the way along the eastern shoreline of Onis. There was a large desert to her west so dry that the dirt was hard and cracked. Beyond the desert was a forest so barren and dead, not a single tree bore one leaf, and the land was dark and gray. And, to the south, was a rock-covered land along the shore of a vast ocean with small mountains to the far southeast. The images filled her mind and soul, and she gasped at them in astonishment. Even though it was all so expansive, it was as though she was holding it all in the palm of her hand.

'*Focus!*' Lupé Caelis mind touched, but it was so faint that Pavula almost didn't hear it. However, she did hear it and pulled back from the visions dolefully, without letting go of the force.

Harnessing the earth spirit, Pavula pushed it toward the seedlings in the soil, down and out through her fingertips. It was more intense than even the water spirit had been. Her hands started shaking, the tiny hairs on her arms all stood on ends, and perspiration dripped down her brow and back as she strained to maintain control. The ground began to tremble underneath her, and earthquake rumblings surrounded her. The pebbles rattled on the ground, and birds flew frantically away in droves. All around her, green sprouts began protruding out of the earth, growing rapidly and blossoming into flowers and plants of various shapes and sizes. They formed a perfect circle around her, wreathing her with their scents and glory. Each flower bloomed toward her, facing her like the sun that would normally have given them life, thanking her for waking them from their slumber.

Pavula could feel the garden that was maturing around her but kept her fingers in the earth and her concentration in check. She clenched her eyes tighter and continued passing her energy into the ground. More plants developed in abundance surrounding her. When one seedling had grown, she gathered another and kept gathering every one she encountered that encompassed her. Slowly,

CHAPTER 2

and without realizing it, she began to feel weak, and her arms started trembling aggressively.

Lupé Caelis saw Pavula passing an excessive amount of energy into the soil and tried to caution her to terminate her actions, but something was blocking her mind-touch. Pavula had unconsciously put up a mind resistance, blocking off all contact as she harnessed the earth magic—a trick that Lupé Caelis had warned her not to use when in lessons. The more Pavula became drained, the more hostile Lupé Caelis' attacks became, slashing at the wall, trying to expose its weakness. She growled and barked loudly, stomping her feet on the ground, but Pavula did not move nor acknowledge her. After searching the wall and testing its barrier, she noticed a section crumble at her touch. Lupé Caelis propelled all her concentration towards breaking it down.

'STOP!' Pavula heard her mother scream into her mind. Blinking her eyes wide, she came out of her trance as the barrier dropped around her thoughts.

As her hands released from the earth, Pavula felt a painful rush strike into her head, as though being bashed with a club. She fell backward into the garden she had created, her chest rising and falling rapidly as she caught her breath. She was nearly depleted of all energy, extremely light-headed, and on the verge of blacking out. Her head felt as heavy as a boulder. Pain pounded through her temples, scorning her for her actions. She lay there, twitching in the garden. Her heart pounded fiercely in her chest, working overtime, not only to get her blood flowing properly again but to recreate the energy she had lost. She was barely conscious and felt an urgency to hold on to something real to keep from disappearing into the noise within her head.

With what strength she could muster, Pavula dug her dirty hands back into the soil by her sides, grasping it, feeling its chill between her fingers. A shaking and numbing sensation ran through her fingers, along her hands, passing her wrists and continuously flowing up her arms and neck. She relaxed her hold of the dirt as the tingling numbness surrounded her mind, enveloping, and cooling all her thoughts. It lasted less than a minute before fading away, leaving her now-still body lying out on the ground. With the numbness gone, her senses returned little by little, and she began to ease her body, mind, and spirit.

Lupé Caelis stood by her, watching intently, observing what was happening. All around Pavula, the garden was now dead; nothing was left but withered, brown plants. Not a blade of grass was living within at least three feet encompassing her. Pavula, without knowledge nor training, had taken life from the earth to save her own. Lupé Caelis stood there in awe of her young pupil, baffled at her strength and self-discovery.

The shallow, breathless words distracted Lupé Caelis as Pavula feebly elevated a hand to her and uttered, "Sorry, Mother, I didn't know I made a wall." Her hand fell down across her chest, and her breathing softened.

Lupé Caelis licked Pavula's cheek and nuzzled her neck with her nose. '*Are you alright?*'

Pavula weakly nodded. "A little tired. I could probably use a nap."

The Great Wolf sat back on her haunches and stared at the young elf. Pavula had no idea the strength that she possessed, the powers that flowed through her soul. Lupé Caelis wished she could tell her everything she knew, but it had to be discovered. Pavula wasn't ready, not yet. She was still too young and ignorant to the world and to her powers. There was much to be done before she would be ready, and Lupé Caelis just hoped that her teachings would be enough.

Even though there was a great deal to master, Lupé Caelis marveled at the young one's capability, not surprised so much, but

CHAPTER 2

enthralled. The amount of force she sent into the earth would have killed anyone else. She had created a garden around her, and, without even meaning to, she had poured her energy into the surrounding forest. The trees were more abundant, the grass greener, there was life in places where none existed before, and several dormant plants were now grown prematurely, all in addition to the garden she made encompassing her. As if that weren't enough, she unconsciously withdrew enough energy to keep herself alive. Lupé Caelis had never predicted even Pavula could be that strong—not so soon. If she was capable of accomplishing all this so early into her earth magic lessons, when Lupé Caelis had only hoped to see one or two plants bloom, what more was she capable of? Was there anything this child couldn't do?

Stretching out in the now-dead flowers surrounding her, Pavula closed her eyes and inhaled the beautiful aroma of those still thriving. "Did I do well, Mother?"

Lupé Caelis smiled and lay beside her in the garden. '*You did very well, Lupé Pavula.*' She thought it best not to tell Pavula how much more she actually did, believing she still had much more to learn, particularly with her control. '*When you feel up to it, we can continue with another lesson. But, for now, get some rest.*'

Pavula fell asleep right where she lay without saying another word, and Lupé Caelis licked her on the cheek before laying next to her protectively, watching over her mysterious cub. '*Sleep well, my child,*' she thought gently to Pavula, who was already sound asleep. '*You will need your strength sooner than I imagined, I fear.*'

CHAPTER THREE

FIENDS

*I*n the morning following graduation, Davion gathered some provisions for the trip ahead while Hort prepared Orbek and Helna, securing their place with the caravan that was to accompany them as far as the city of Mira. It was a long way back to the Gorén Mountains, even by horseback, and would take them a few weeks—at best—to reach their home, Lochlann.

The caravan gathered at the closed city gates at the crack of dawn with a parade of wagons and travelers; the livestock and travelers alike anxious about the upcoming trip. Joining them, adorned in navy blue and light gray armor, were half a dozen armed guards—a provision that King Lyson, ruler of the human cities, had implemented for safety; one of the few things implemented by the king that no one objected to. The roads continued to become more dangerous with wildlife, orcs, trolls, and the occasional drow. So, having armed, trained fighters along for the ride was always a welcomed blessing.

Davion had prepared just enough victuals to get them to Mira, a typically eight-day journey, where they intended to restock again. There was an outpost along the way for safety and supplies, but there was no guarantee it would still be there when they arrived.

The sun had just crested over the horizon, and the horses were growing more restless, disquieted by the journey ahead. It was a cool morning with a light breeze making its way through the city streets, and the sky appeared almost bereft of clouds. It was a good morning for traveling.

Hort was clad in his battle armor, wobbly helmet and all, ready for anything, while he helped Davion pack the saddlebags strapped across Orbek and Helna. Fully equipped, they mounted up and positioned themselves for departure with the caravan. The carts and wagons rocked and creaked in anticipation as the coachmen steadied their horses and oxen. There were two mounted soldiers at the front of the line, near the still-closed gates, and four more were tiredly joining the party at the rear. Hort and Davion also stayed at the back, knowing it was the most vulnerable to attacks, Hort always ready for action. It was a good-sized group that morning of roughly twenty people and eight horse-drawn vehicles, mostly with goods for trading. One of the wagons was being led by a middle-aged couple with their children, a boy about Davion's age, and three younger daughters.

"WALK ON!" a guard at the front of the party announced as the gates began to open. Everyone followed suit; flicking reins and whipping oxen; carts and wagons jolting into motion, beginning their journey.

Davion was looking forward to getting back to Lochlann, although he wasn't quite sure what would be next for him. He had submitted requests to fire masters for an apprenticeship and figured he could use his fire magic to help out in the foundries in the meantime while still honing his skills. The dwarves mostly kept to themselves and out of the wars of the races. They enjoyed their solitude and their strong mead, usually venturing out only to trade.

There were, however, a few that wanted more than a sedentary life. Hort was one of those few who craved the battles, particularly defeating orc invaders and drow scum. That being said, they still tried to avoid the dragons. They held great respect for the dragons as the legend's keepers of the land, and they didn't want any part of the raging war between the dragons and the elves. The Silver dragons also lived on the Gorén Mountains, where the dwarves tunneled their cities into, and they would be fools to start a war so close to home.

Passing through the massive stone gateway, Davion looked back to Roco one last time. This place had been his home for a few years now, and it would be strange not to see so many of his own kind again for who-knows-how-long. He let out a sigh, a little sad to see it go, then turned back to face the road ahead, excited about what the trip would bring, albeit a little scared too.

Hours passed, and the band was going along the path at a steady rate. The guards kept them going with no plans to stop until they needed to eat and rest. Everyone surveyed the barren hills around them, keeping an eye out for any danger.

Davion rode silently as Hort droned on about everything that he had been missing back in Lochlann since he left for his final years of schooling. "...and then Orga says ta Stantul that he should be leadin' the mines, but Stantul wouldna be goin' 'gainst Thorgru, but Orga 'ad told Thorgru already that Stantul is gonna take 'em over, so now there's all these meetin's and yellin' 'bout who should be doin' what. So Rundo gave Stantul the mines fer a fortnight and, wouldn't ye know it, they be spittin' out Rynet Gems left and right. Now Thorgru be arguin' that 'e be the one ta get 'em in that cavern right 'fore Stantul took lead so twas sheer luck..." Hort continued on about the politics of Lochlann for another hour until Davion realized he was avoiding talking about one thing.

"And Glondora?" Davion interrupted, "How is she?"

Hort grunted and went quiet. Davion was starting to think he wasn't going to answer him, but after several minutes he finally sighed again and said, "Ahhh, ye know laidens; never satisfied." He grunted and grumbled some more, and Davion realized he wasn't going to get his talkative uncle to talk so easily.

"What about the wedding?" Davion asked, pushing the subject, "Has that changed?"

"Hmmm... Well..." Hort dragged out. "I 'ave not exactly asked 'er yet, not tickinically. I dunno, me boy, she's tellin' me that if I dunna' give up the road patrols and get me a job in the mines, then she'll find 'er someone who will." He sighed loudly again. "She snores louder than me anyway...and 'er blockendarf tastes more like blocken*barf*. No good dwarfen wife ever made such terrible blockendarf. Ye ask anyone! I'm tellin' ye; she's jus' a terrible cook. So, I'm prolly better off without the likes of 'er anyway."

Davion shook his head. He had had her blockendarf, and Hort wasn't wrong, but he knew that had nothing to do with his uncle's gripe. Hort was simply looking for reasons to make it her fault that things weren't working out. "Uncle Hort," he began, "I'm sorry. Perhaps once we get back, you should stay for a bit and see how things go."

"Hmmm..." the dwarf grumbled and clenched his lips in anger. Davion knew that Hort lived for the battles, and perhaps that was enough for him. His inquisition accomplished one thing though—Hort had stopped talking. They rode on in silence until the wagon master brought everyone to a halt so they could break for lunch. The day had grown warmer, and Hort was starting to sweat under his armor. Davion was still fairly comfortable in his robe, but both of them were ready for the break.

Everyone dismounted, except for the guards, and stretched out their limbs, breathing in the warm summer breeze. Hort and

Davion each grabbed some dried meat and a piece of bread then sat on some nearby rocks while they ate. Davion watched as the head guards ripped bits of meat off with their teeth, never breaking their gaze to the hills surrounding them. They seemed entranced by the horizon, and Davion was reassured that they were ready for anything. That is until he noticed the guards at the flank and rear, paying no attention to the surroundings.

The two guards at the back were flirting with a young girl who was sitting in the back of a wagon, and she didn't look at all like she was enjoying the attention. Two other guards were together, drinking from their flasks and laughing loudly about something. Davion watched the two with the girl, hoping that they didn't take it too far. It was suicide to confront one of the king's guards, but Davion was not someone who could just sit back and watch an innocent get hurt.

"Let it go, me boy," Davion heard his uncle's cautionary voice say lowly.

Without breaking his gaze, he nodded to his uncle.

One of the guards reached to the girl and tugged at the bottom of her skirts. She pulled away, tucking her legs under her, and moved further up the wagon. Davion instinctively stood up and took several steps toward the wagon but stopped when he saw another man approaching. He couldn't hear them, but he recognized the man as being her father. Her father said something to the guards then motioned for the girl to come out of the wagon, which she did. Putting his arms around her, he led her away from them, and Davion was relieved when the guards departed in the opposite direction.

He saw that Hort had stood as well and was right beside him. They nodded to each other, wordlessly agreeing that they would be keeping an eye on the guards as much as on the hills, and then headed back to Helna and Orbek. Everyone returned to their places in the line, and the wagon master motioned them on to resume the journey.

Later that night, when the sun was beginning to set, they found an open spot to set up camp, and everyone positioned themselves in a large cluster. Campfires were lit, and packs were removed from the horses and wagons to set up places to sleep. Those with tents had them pitched, and those without found a spot near the fires that would do for the night. Hort and Davion found an area close to the guards that were harassing the young girl at lunch and munched on their mutton and bread.

After Davion had finished his meal, he began playing with the flames of the fire, practicing some of his incantations. "*Ominous Verte*," he whispered to the fire causing it to flame up larger before settling back down. He continued to do it a few more times, each one growing stronger and larger.

"Neat trick," Hort nodded before taking a swig of wine from his flask. "Glondora got a new place over by the mines. I usually stay there when I'm 'ome now, but I still 'ave our place and will stay there with ye." He continued to eat his bread, talking in between bites. "Maybe when we get back, we can get ye some real armor instead of them flimsy robes 'fore we leave."

Pausing his magic practices, Davion looked to his uncle, confused. "Where is it we're going?" he asked Hort. "I thought I was going to be working in the foundries when we got back, making my contribution to the mines."

"The mines? The MINES?! Don't be daft, me boy!" Hort tossed his flask to Davion, who caught it and took a sip. "The mines be no place fer someone with yer skills. Jus' a bunch of meatheads workin' those mines, aside from me mum, Goddess Mother rest her soul, but they're not meant fer the battlefield like ye and meself. We've got bigger things in store for us, we do."

"Uncle," Davion sighed, "I was hoping to stay in Lochlann and wait to hear about the apprenticeship positions I applied for. If we leave, they won't know where to find me. I'm really not finished with my training yet if I'm ever going to be truly great."

Hort looked silently into the fire and shook his head. "Hmmm... First Glondora..." He sighed but never finished his sentence. He didn't need to. Davion knew that he was disappointed with his plans, but they had a lot of time to discuss it further before they would get back to Lochlann, so he decided to let it rest for the night. He looked around at the other parties, particularly where those guards were hanging out, and was happy to see everyone was settling in well after the long day, keeping to themselves. Two of the guards had already passed out, clearly from too much drink, but the other four seemed well and alert. Davion and Hort decided to call it a night.

The next few days went fairly smoothly. Davion and Hort continued to keep an eye both on the guards and the girl, but luckily all had been relatively quiet. On the fourth day of riding, they were nearing the stop at the Silex Valley Outpost when they heard a commotion coming from ahead. The guards kicked their horses, rearing them before darting off ahead of the party, leaving only two guards behind with the caravan.

"What is it, Uncle?" Davion asked quietly to Hort while coming up alongside him on Helna.

Hort shook his head. "Whatever it is, it doesna' sound good," he replied.

"Stay back!" one of the remaining guards called, holding up his hand to the party.

Everyone brought their horses and oxen to a halt. The wagons rocked backward, and horses nervously stomped the ground with ears tucked back, neighing and snorting wildly. All the people were whispering amongst themselves panic-stricken, wondering what was going on.

Hort and Davion looked ahead to where the guards had disappeared over the hills in the distance, but then Davion heard a low growl coming from the hills to his left. He looked over his shoulder just in time to see two large beasts sneaking up between the rocks, ready to pounce.

"UNCLE!" Davion yelled and pulled his horse's reins, turning Helna to face them. He unstrapped the pouch on his waist full of spell ingredients.

"ROCK FIENDS!" Hort screamed at the group as he grabbed his axe from off his back.

Women and children started screaming as the fiends ran towards the caravan, and the remaining two guards rode their horses forward, swords drawn, prepared to attack the beasts. They were the same muddy color as the dried land around them and had razor-sharp claws and teeth. Pouncing forward on all fours, they swung long tails with spiked clubs at the tips and flexed a razor mane that cascaded down firm backs. The fiends' glassy-yellow eyes chose their targets; one darted towards Davion and another towards the family wagon.

Davion fumbled through his pouch, trying to find his red sand to inflame the beast, but it was charging faster than he could have imagined. Helna bucked, propelling him off her back, and he landed hard on the ground below. Ignoring Helna, the rock fiend continued to head straight for Davion and opened its large jaws about to bite into him. He closed his eyes while raising his hand and shaking like a leaf, convinced he was about to die. But then he heard the fiend yelp. Opening his eyes again, he saw Hort standing near him with his axe held out tightly in front of him. The rock fiend's shoulder had a gash from the axe, and it redirected its attention to the dwarf. Hort raised his weapon to swing again as the beast lunged forward. Letting out a strong battle cry, he swung his weapon down and hit the fiend in its front leg. The vicious creature continued to come at him, and he brought his shield around, blocking its fangs from his throat just before it reached him.

"Get up, boy!" Hort yelled at Davion as he pushed against the shield, trying to hold the fiend back, struggling against the beast while it forced him to the ground.

Davion remained shaking on the ground, unable to move, as one of the guards rode up beside the fiend and stabbed it through the chest with his sword, slaying it instantly. Hort pushed the head of the beast back away from him with his shield, stood up, and walked over to Davion, stretching out his hand. "Are ye alright?" he asked. "They're dead now, me boy."

Davion blushed in shame and embarrassment as he took his uncle's hand and stood back up. He dusted the dirt from his robes and picked up some of the ingredients that had leaked from his pouch.

"Yes, Uncle," Davion muttered, mostly to himself.

He couldn't believe it was the first chance he had to prove himself as a real fighter-mage, and he completely froze. There was only one other time in his life, long ago, that he had felt so useless. He was so ashamed that he couldn't even look Hort in the eye as he headed off to reclaim his horse that had run to the other side of the group. Thankfully, someone stopped her and grabbed the reins before she fled. Hort put his axe and shield on his back and mounted Orbek, who had never left him.

While everyone recomposed themselves, they heard a horn being sounded from ahead.

"Let's go!" called one of the guards. "Everyone, move!"

The party kicked and whipped their horses, galloping after the guards, wagons rattling in protest of the speed. As they came over a hill, they could see the Silex Valley Outpost about a half-mile ahead with more rock fiends attacking it. The outpost had one tall watchtower near the gates, a wooden wall surrounding a few buildings, and an open area intended just for passersby to rest. There were already four dead fiends at the gates, but another five were attacking the guards outside.

The watchtower guard blew the horn again, and arrows flew from the barracks at the fiends. Most ricocheted off their thick, leathery hides, but a few took root, wounding them, causing them to falter. Davion, Hort, and the remaining two guards kicked their mounts and rode as fast as they could toward the battle.

Davion had his second chance! He would prove he was not useless and help save the day! His adrenaline was kicking in, and he could feel his heart beating through his chest and pounding in his ears. *I can't fail again,* he swore to himself. *I can do this!* Leaning forward in his saddle as he rode toward one of the fiends, he quickly and effortlessly grabbed his fire sand from his pouch and held it high, ready to release.

"*Omine Ekia!*" Davion yelled at the top of his lungs as he threw the sand forward.

When the sand left his fingers, it darted unnaturally fast through the air toward the fiend and scattered on the beast's hide.

"*Illioso!*" he shouted, and the sand went up in flames, covering the fiend in fire. The beast kicked and screeched an unholy sound and then ran at Davion, engulfed in flames, like a demon from hell. Davion stopped Helna in her tracks, his eyes wide in fear, completely caught off guard, and having no idea what to do next. Hort raised his axe and threw it toward the fiend, nailing it securely in the skull. The rock fiend fell hard on its chest and skidded forward, stopping only a few feet from Davion.

"*Dimisna,*" Davion said, holding his hand out and rolling his fingers into a fist, causing the flames on the fiend to extinguish.

Hort rode over to him, jumped off Orbek, and then put his foot on the scorched head, yanking out his axe. "Be careful, boy," he said before running after another rock fiend.

Davion's heart sank. For a brief moment, he had felt so proud by making that spell land, but all it did was anger the beast. Everything was slow and straightforward back at the academy, leaving him feeling completely over his head out here. *Had it all been a waste?* he wondered to himself. He looked to the other fiends, watching as the guards slashed and sliced at them, killing them all. Only one guard appeared to be seriously injured. Davion strode Helna over to the rest of the guards and tried hard not to show how worthless he was feeling in this moment.

"Mage!" one of the guards called to Davion. "Can you heal him?" And just when Davion thought he couldn't feel any more useless, he was proven wrong.

Davion lowered his head and shook it mournfully, closing his eyes. "No," he replied, "I am not a healer." He half expected someone to tell him that he wasn't much of a fighter either, but no one did. He may have graduated from the prestigious Silex Valley Magi Academy, but he was realizing just how much more he had to learn.

CHAPTER 3

CHAPTER FOUR

APPARITION

A couple of hours had passed since Lupé Pavula had fallen into a stupor in the dead grass. Sitting up groggily and rubbing her eyes awake, she looked south toward the river, hearing its hypnotically flowing water.

"I'd like to take a walk to clear my head," Pavula said aloud to Lupé Caelis, who hadn't left her side. She had been laying a few feet away from her with front paws crossed and tail resting at her side. "If that's okay?" she added, approaching her mother.

Lupé Caelis nodded and kissed Pavula's cheek with her tongue. *'Alright, my dear. Take your time. Just be careful; it's getting late.'*

Before leaving, Pavula wrapped her arms around her mother's neck and gave her a quick embrace, rubbing her face against the softness of her mane lovingly and comfortingly.

Walking in a daze through the forest toward the river, Pavula hummed a lullaby that repeated in her head occasionally. She ran her hand across nearby twigs while she roamed and could feel their life-spirit tickle her fingertips. The river was her favorite place to be no matter what her mood, feeling the water's spirit as it continuously trickled across the rocks and flowed through the land. Through Lupé Caelis' teachings, Pavula had now connected with three of the spirits; water, air, and earth. It was both overwhelming and comforting all at the same time, but she was getting better at finding the balance within herself.

When Pavula reached the river, it was nearly dusk, and she felt Jayenne, the goddess and moon deity of love, life, and wisdom, rising in the north. Jayenne was a bright blue circle in a darkening sky. Still very light-headed, she felt as though her body was being animated by some other force with her as the observer. She could sense that the earth spirit was still connected with her, circling around inside.

Closing her eyes, she opened her mind to everything around her, becoming one with the earth, air, and water, and even touched lightly on the spirit world. The spirit world was not something that she had learned how to access from her mother. In fact, Pavula never told her mother about the spirit world connection, knowing how strictly Lupé Caelis desired her adherence to the teachings and feared how she would respond.

A soft breeze blew across Pavula's face as she connected with the world around her, but instead of it relaxing her, it sent a cold chill up her spine with a new sensation that startled her. Opening her eyes abruptly, she realized there was an unusual aura in the air this evening, a foreign touch that brushed against her thoughts. It wasn't just the usual quiet whispers she was used to from her connections to the spirit world, but more of a presence.

Pavula looked around nervously while maintaining the connection. It was coming from across the river to the south in the meadow beyond, but she could see nothing there. *What is that?* She concentrated harder on the area where she sensed the presence and could vaguely spot a shimmer amongst the tall blades of grass. By wincing her eyes, the shimmer took on the form of a ghostly figure, staring up at the northern sky. A plague of mist surrounded it, and there was no substantial evidence in the encompassing grass that it

CHAPTER 4

was actually there. She realized that she could not see shins nor feet at all. *It must be a ghost!* Her jaw fell as she studied the apparition for a moment. It was covered in a long cloth garment with pouches strapped at the waist and had short hair with ears and eyes both small and round. Pavula thought it looked rather strange, but she didn't have much experience in the matter of what another person would look like, having assumed they would look a lot like her.

The ghostly figure turned its attention from the sky and looked toward Pavula. She froze in her place as the ghost's eyes met with hers, afraid to move a muscle. It seemed intrigued by her and was studying her just as she had studied it. This moment was the first time Pavula had seen another two-legged, and although she was convinced it was of the dead, she felt no fear. The face was soft and gentle, and it made no threatening movements.

Pavula startled slightly as she heard a wolf howling softly in the wind. She shook her head slowly, choosing to ignore the howl, and continued to watch the ghost as though compelled to do so. As its lips parted, presumably about to speak, her body leaned forward on the balls of her feet, waiting intensely to discover what the ghost had to say. However, before any sound could part its lips, there was a bright glimmer, and, with a passing gust of wind, the figure quickly vaporized, disappearing as though it never was.

No, no, no! Pavula tried to hold onto the spirit world a little longer, searching the meadow across the river, but there was nothing there to be found. Giving up in her search, she could still feel her heart racing from the experience.

'*Mother!*' Pavula called out, running back to the den as fast as her slender feet could carry her. '*Mother! I saw something!*'

Darting through the tall grass, she leaped and bounded over stumps and rocks, not stopping until she found Lupé Caelis sitting by the den entrance. She panted, trying to catch her breath, unable to focus enough to use her mind-speak. "Mother, I saw a ghost!"

she exclaimed excitedly. "Across the river. It was just standing there staring at me! I couldn't believe my eyes!"

Lupé Caelis flicked her tail and stood up, taking a step toward Pavula while looking deep into her eyes. Pavula continued to tell her all about the encounter with the ghost, sending a mental image of it, right up until it disappeared. The Great Wolf remained silent, letting her tell the tale.

"Isn't that incredible?" Pavula prompted Lupé Caelis when she didn't say anything.

Finally, after much thought, she realized Pavula wasn't going to let it go. *'You were very drained after your last lesson,'* Lupé Caelis began, attempting to deflect, *'perhaps your mind is playing tricks on you. I am sure you have yet to fully recover.'*

Pavula's heart sank, confused by her lack of excitement, but she believed that there was more to it than that, that it wasn't just a hallucination. "I can't explain it, Mother, but it felt so real. Like I could have reached out and touched it."

Lupé Caelis strode past Pavula into the brush toward the river, *'Perhaps you should get some more rest. We can discuss this later.'*

Pavula watched as she disappeared into the thick forest and then crossed her arms over her chest in frustration. With the evening being as late as it was, she decided her mother was right, that perhaps some more sleep wouldn't be such a bad idea. However, she would not stop thinking about her encounter that night, not now, nor for one moment of the following days to come.

* * *

The following evening, Pavula was working with the earth spirit to further her training with Lupé Caelis by willing vines to grow and bend to her will. It was all coming so easy to her, becoming almost like a dance as she swirled the vines around her and then retreated them back up into the trees.

'*That is enough for today,*' Lupé Caelis mind-spoke. Pavula smiled, proud of herself and how quickly she had controlled another magic spirit. Then, she sat down and ate a bundle of red berries that one of her kin had lovingly brought for her. She still couldn't get the ghost's face out of her mind, and Lupé Caelis had sensed it in her thoughts all day; her keen desire to understand her connection with the apparition and what it all meant. The last rays of sun were disappearing through the trees as twilight came quickly upon them. '*You did very well with your earth magic lesson today, my child. I am proud of you,*' Lupé Caelis said earnestly.

Pavula smiled at her mother and mind-sent, '*It helps to have such a great teacher. It was really hard at first, but once I found the earth spirit, everything seemed to come much easier.*'

'*I am glad to hear it,*' Lupé Caelis said. '*I am actually not sure water is your main source of magic, as I originally believed. The earth spirit is very strong in you too.*' However, the wolf's happiness was fleeting and faded all too quickly as Lupé Caelis recalled a debate she had held with herself earlier that day. '*Lupé Pavula, there is...something I want to talk to you about.*' Lupé Caelis sat majestically in front of Pavula, commanding her attention. '*I have been thinking a lot about the image you saw at the river yesterday,*' she continued. '*I do not believe it was a ghost that you saw, Lupé Pavula. I believe it was a vision.*'

'*A vision?*' Intrigued, Pavula looked up at her mother, berry juice running down her chin. '*What do you mean?*'

'*I am not really sure what the vision was trying to tell you. You need to search within yourself for that answer. But, this human must have some sort of significance. I doubt that he was a spy. No humans know where we are.*'

"He?" Pavula said aloud, captivated.

'*Yes. You saw a human male.*' Lupé Caelis looked down sternly at the small elf cub. '*Lupé Pavula, how long have you been connecting with the phantom realm?*'

Pavula blushed and looked away. Unconsciously, she remembered her first experience when she was a young child and felt the presence of unusual spirits, unlike those from the elements. Lupé Caelis read the thoughts inside her mind and looked to the ground as she let out a sigh.

'*I see,*' she mind-sent simply. Standing up slowly, she flicked her tail back and forth, trying not to get upset. Instead, she decided it best to move past it.

Thankful—and surprised—that she wasn't being lectured about the phantom realm, Pavula looked at her mother nervously and asked, '*Do you think that I'll ever get to see him again?*'

Letting out a long sigh, Lupé Caelis sat back down, looking upon her while she arranged her thoughts. '*I know you wonder about the world apart from our sanctuary. It is only natural to wonder, but I fear for you, my child. I fear that you will leave me too soon before you are ready. You still have much more training, and I have neglected to tell you about the world beyond our quiet place in the forest. It's...not a happy place.*' She paused briefly before continuing, '*I should have told you more about how things are. You have much power but lack the knowledge you will need out there.*'

Pavula looked uneasily away at the ground, not liking the direction the conversation had taken.

'*I don't say this to be mean,*' Lupé Caelis continued. '*It really is all my fault. I have been teaching you magic, but I have not been teaching you how to take care of yourself, nor have I told you about the wars that go on outside of our protected realm. I will not always be there to guard you, and the world is not friendly. There are evil creatures that lurk about, killing innocent people for no other reason than to kill. There are people that lie and cheat and steal from others, including their friends and family.*'

CHAPTER 4

But, they are not always easy to spot by appearances; some are hidden in the form of elves or man, and their evil is the struggle for power or pride. There is no one out there that you can trust completely, as you can with me. They will not always understand, and their ignorance will cause fear. Everyone has a hidden agenda, Pavula, and man is easily corruptible. I do not know who the human is that you saw, but I do not like it. If he were to come here, our home would no longer be safe. I only hope that he does not know what he saw or come looking for you.'

Pavula looked at the grass by her feet, trying to understand. "Surely, not all can be bad. What about the dragons? Aren't they the keepers of the land?"

'Dragons are wise, but with their wisdom and strength comes pride and power.' Lupé Caelis sensed Pavula's tension and wished she knew better how to explain the world to such an innocent as her Wolf Child. 'Dragon clans face their own battles every day, massacring two-leggeds by the dozens and, long ago, by the hundreds. Sometimes their attacks are provoked, but sometimes...they are not. They have become ruthless killers over time, heartless in their war—especially against the elves."

"But what about the human male?" Pavula pushed. "Wouldn't I have a way to know if he meant me harm?"

"As for the man in your vision...' She paused and took a long breath, letting out a passive growl in the back of her throat, 'I know you want to believe he was a good being, but no, there really is no way for you to know for sure. Even if you can enter their mind as I can, their thoughts are still unclear, even to them. Only their actions will reveal their true nature and agenda, and by then, it is usually too late.'

Pavula felt her dreams for the outside world being squashed with her mother's horrible words. "Why are you telling me this now, Mother?" she asked apprehensively.

Lupé Caelis looked up at the sky as though searching the stars for answers. Raising wolf pups was so much easier than a magical elf cub. There were no questions; there was no need to explain why they must stay close to her. Gazing back upon the young cub, she finally replied, *'I sense you looking to the outside more and more; that your curiosities are growing for what's out there. You are not ready, Lupé Pavula, not even close. I fear you will leave before your training is complete, and all will be lost.'*

Pavula quickly grew angry at the implication and stood up abruptly. "You mean, I will be lost...to you. You plan to keep me here forever, don't you?" She looked to Lupé Caelis but continued before she could answer, "I feel the barrier that you put around me, the barrier that you put around this whole place!" Her voice became screechy and whiny as she raised her voice, startling the forest around them.

Letting out a low growl, Lupé Caelis firmly replied, *'The barrier is for your protection! For all of our protection! I know you must leave one day, but not until you are ready! Now, keep your voice down!'*

"Why?! There's nobody here!!" Pavula shouted even louder. "And when will I be ready enough for you? I'm growing stronger every day, and you know it!" she retorted. "I have always done everything you have ever asked of me for as long as I can remember. But, I don't want to be held here like a rabbit caught in a snare!"

Exasperated by Pavula's words, Lupé Caelis growled and snapped her jaw at her warningly.

Her mother's warning snap only aggravated Pavula further as she continued to lash out. "One day, I will break the barrier and leave this place, and that scares you, doesn't it, Mother? The land beyond this calls to me. I feel it within me—pulling at me." A tear rolled down her cheek. Pavula wasn't a disobedient child, but she knew that her heart's desire to see the world was never going to stop. "I must see what's out there! You tell me lies of horrible things just to get me to stay, but I don't believe any of it! You just don't understand!"

CHAPTER 4

Pavula turned and started to tramp away into the forest's darkness, her emotions overcoming her as her eyes filled with tears. Lupé Caelis felt her heart break a little for the young elf. Of course she understood; she just wanted her to be ready. She called out after her sympathetically, '*I love you, Lupé Pavula, and I would not lie to you.*'

'*Wouldn't you?*' Pavula retaliated, stopping in her tracks momentarily while keeping her back to Lupé Caelis. '*But you do withhold truths from me! I am not a wolf*, Mother,' she said bitterly like a stab at the Great Wolf, '*but you say I don't belong with the elves. So, where do I belong then, and who was my real mother? Where is the family I was born to? I must have a real mother and father out there somewhere!*'

'I did not know your parents,' Lupé Caelis half-lied. '*You belong right where you are, with me.*' Of which she did believe to be the truth.

'*And what about all the lessons?*' Pavula pressed, '*Why do you push me to know so much about magic? What's in it for you?*' she fumed, '*You're always telling me that I will understand in time, that I must wait and be patient. I'm tired of being patient. If you won't tell me the truth about who I am and where I came from, then one of these days, I will have to go find it out for myself!*'

As Pavula started heading back into the dark night, Lupé Caelis felt her words like a dagger in her heart. '*Pavula!*' she called after her, hoping that she would stop. '*Pavula! I am sorr...*' And with that, Pavula blocked Lupé Caelis from her mind, throwing up an impenetrable barrier around her thoughts.

Embracing the darkness around her, Pavula became part of the shadows as she headed deep into the forest night.

CHAPTER FIVE

MIRA

he air was stagnant, and the ground was covered in a thick, foggy haze as Davion found himself in what appeared to be a large meadow. He felt rather strange, almost as though something was weighing him down, and he was unable to move his feet or legs. Unfamiliar with his surroundings, he looked up toward the northern sky to determine the time of day, but he could see no sun, only more fog. It was completely covering the land, no light, no shadow, no dark, just fog.

He looked down and saw a parting appear in the mist, revealing a river with water unmoving. However, something beyond the river is what caught his eye. On the other side, there stood a girl in nothing but a loincloth with wild hair down to her waist, staring at him. She was the most beautiful creature he had ever seen, her hair curving around her petite frame as she looked at him with piercing eyes. Unable to make out the color of her hair or anything else, he realized then that everything was in black and white. Even looking as disheveled as she did, to him, she was the vision of an angel. For a moment, he wondered if he had died, and this beautiful creature had come to welcome him into the afterlife. He opened his mouth to say 'Hello,' but instead found himself feeling as though he were falling, and the girl began to vanish from his sight.

Landing with a loud and painful *THUD* on the ground, Davion heard laughter surrounding him while he tried to gather his bearings. As he felt Helna's snout tickle his face while she let out a snort, tousling his hair, he realized he must have dozed off and fallen from his horse.

"Ye forget how to ride, me boy?" Hort chuckled as he rode Orbek up beside him and reached down to offer him a hand.

Embarrassed, Davion grabbed hold of Hort's forearm and pulled himself up. His head was aching as he realized he must have hit it in the fall and, rubbing the back, felt an emerging lump. Unable to resist, he let out a large yawn while tiredly staggering back to Helna.

It had been four long hot days of traveling since Davion and Hort left the Silex Valley Outpost. They were all exhausted and overheated. As the evening drew near, a welcomed summer breeze began blowing over the lands, providing some relief to the scorching sun. While Davion remounted, Helna shook her mane as the breeze hit them, attempting to cool off.

Hort and Davion had exchanged few words since the attack from the rock fiends. Davion kept waiting for Hort to say something about the incident, about his disappointment in him—which he could feel every time he looked in his eyes—but Hort said nothing on the matter, making for an even longer trip. He was thankful it would soon be over.

The road had also been rather quiet since they had left the outpost, and Davion was grateful for that too. Everyone was on high alert since the rock fiend encounter, and the guards were quick to chase off emerging threats with their arrows before anything decided to charge at them. During the nights, they kept the fires lit and torches ready. Davion kept eyes peeled to the hills, praying to the god Kyrash that there would be no more attacks. Several of the party had veered south from the Silex Valley

Outpost, heading toward the humble town of Amillia, where Davion resided as a child. Among them were the two guards that Davion had been worried about. However, the young girl and her family were still with Davion's group, thankfully.

"Mira sits just over them 'ills," Hort said, breaking the silence while gesturing with his chin toward some rolling hills in the distance. "It be a good thing too," he added, "we've exhausted our food supply."

"We?" Davion sneered at Hort.

"Aw, shut yer pie hole!" scoffed Hort, "I canna' 'elp it that we dwarves are so brawn and need more grub to survive than ye scrawny fighter-mage do."

Davion smirked, shaking his head toward the ground while they rode. "Your brawn, is it?" he said, cocking his eye at Hort's gut. Hort gaped down at his paunch and grumbled incoherently. "You're too easy, Uncle," snickered Davion.

"And ye should respect yer elders, boy. Have I taught ye nothin'?" Hort retorted, annoyed.

It seemed everyone in the group was aware of how close they finally were to Mira because they all began picking up the pace, eager to get to the great city. Hort and Davion gave their mounts a gentle kick, heading to the front of the group.

As they scaled the hills, the wagons struggled and creaked up the path. They could see the tall parapets at the corners of the city limits and the tops of the stone walls. Ascending over the hill, the rest of the city came into view. It was perched next to the alluring and glistening Miran Lake that expanded as far north as you could see. The band of wagons and carts approached the eastern gates, still open for the day, and guards in the same navy and gray armor stood watch in the towers above and in the gateway below. They eyeballed the group as they grew closer, looking for

CHAPTER 5

anything off base, but, being satisfied, waved them on by under the raised iron gates.

Hues of orange and yellow from the early setting sun beamed off the lake, reflecting against the stone walls throughout the city. The tips of tall boat masts from ships that paraded up the lake to the Trader's Post and back could be seen over the far embankment, and seabirds hovered overhead looking for their evening meal. Once everyone was through the gates, they all dispersed in different directions with their own agendas, and the accompanying guards remained behind.

Davion watched as Hort said his goodbyes and pleasantries to those he had befriended throughout the journey. Davion gave a shy smile and nod as they looked at him, returning goodbyes and encouraging words for their trip ahead. He looked around at the stores and admired how clean the city was. It was built in a similar style to the capital, Roco, but it was clear that the occupants took much more pride in maintaining its appearance. There was neither trash in the streets nor beggars. There were some performers, but not as many. It was mainly just shops from what he could see, with a tavern up the way.

Riding Helna beside Hort and Orbek through the streets, Davion could feel his stomach growling painfully and realized it was getting late, and they still had not eaten. After turning down a few streets, they arrived at the Miran Lake Inn and took their mounts to the adjacent stables to house for the night. There was a musty smell in the stables due to the humidity from the lake, but the stable boy was very nice and assured them that they would be well cared for. Hort gave the boy a coin as a deposit to cover the hay, then they went back to the inn, entering through the creaky, white-wooden, swinging doors.

Davion took a seat at one of the tables while Hort went to secure them a room for the night. His rump was sore and blistered from the saddle, and he was looking forward to a cool bath after dinner, but there was something else he wanted to do even more now that he had the first decent light since the outpost.

Taking the sack from his back, Davion rested it on the floor by his feet and withdrew a large leather-bound book, placing it on the table. The sack fell loosely to the floor, having nothing else left in it since he had finished his rations earlier that day. He caressed the embossed wording with his fingertips that spelled "Pyromancy Grimoire" and took a deep breath as he opened the cover. Inside the book were dozens of spells, incantations, recipes, and drawings of all the fire magic he had been studying. Hand gestures, combined with words in the elven tongue and pictures of different herbs and sands filled its pages, among other more unpleasant ingredients.

At the academy, he had barely begun his journey through the book, learning only the most basic form of its magic. He didn't even know what a lot of the spells were as he flipped through them, page after page. Everything was written in the elven language, and he knew he would need to find a great firemaster to help him decipher the rest of it. He searched aimlessly for the spells he had already learned so he could study and practice, hoping to be more prepared for the next attack. Not entirely sure what he was after, he thumbed through the pages, looking for anything that appeared powerful enough to take down a great beast or even an orc.

Hort came over to the table and watched Davion for a moment as he took his seat. Then abruptly yelled, "Barmaid!" startling Davion's concentration.

"Evening," said the barmaid as she approached the table. She was a middle-aged human with a friendly enough demeanor and dark-brown hair tied in a loose braid. "What can I get for you boys?"

Hort ordered a mead for himself, wine for Davion, and a couple of beef stews for them both.

"Sure thing, love," the barmaid replied before heading to the kitchen.

"What ye got there?" Hort asked Davion, lifting the edge of the book and letting it fall with a dull *thud* on the table.

It couldn't be avoided anymore; Davion realized he had to bring up the rock fiend attack. He was even finally ready to accept any feedback his uncle might have for him, understanding that he has a lot more experience in battles, even if he didn't know much about magic.

"I'm trying to find some spells that might actually be useful in a fight," he told Hort. When Hort didn't say anything, Davion continued, "I don't know what would kill something like a fiend, or trolls, or orcs. I don't see anything that would pierce their skin like a sword would. Not yet, anyway."

"Hmmm..." Hort played with his beard in thought. "So..." He looked intensely and cautiously at Davion, "What *did* ye learn at the academy? If it wasna ta fight, then what was it fer?"

Sighing, Davion slumped backward and looked down at his book. That was the question he had feared and had been going over in his mind on how to answer. Hort had put forth a lot of money to send him to the academy, and he knew he wouldn't understand that it was just the basics in magic and that it was a lifelong journey to become a true master.

"The academy taught me to access fire magic," he began, "teaching me the basics in hand gesturing and why we do it; the different herbs, sands, and other ingredients used to ignite and amplify spells. We studied the elven language, which is the base of all magic, and we learned the building blocks of spells and incantations." He paused, realizing he was merely reciting what they told him he would learn during his first day at the academy. It wasn't enough, he realized now. It didn't make him a fighter-mage. He felt his capabilities as a fighter-mage were more akin to the performers he had watched doing basic tricks in the streets.

"We practiced some spells against each other with protective wards up, but I never had to kill anything before." Davion was always told to run or hide before his time at the academy—Hort always at the forefront, protecting everyone. Davion, like most, was kept in the confines of their city unless absolutely necessary.

The barmaid dropped off their drinks and disappeared again. Hort took a long sip of his ale then put it down loudly on the table. "So, they didna teach ye ta use a weapon? No sword nor axe nor even a mace?"

Davion shook his head, "I just have the dagger that you gave me before I left. We would sometimes use a powered staff for spells, but not for fighting."

"Hmmm... I see," Hort said, rubbing his beard again. "I've seen a mage use a staff in battle. Perhaps that's what we should be gettin' ye. Also, he used giant balls of fire to hurl at his foes. Ye got any of them firey balls in that there book o' yers?"

Davion smiled, realizing he knew a spell for that. "Yes, Uncle! I do! I'll have to practice it some more before we leave again."

Nodding to Davion, Hort said, "I may not know magic, but I've fought alongside plenty of folks of all different skills. I'm sure ye'll figure it out, me boy."

"Here you go, boys," the barmaid said, setting their stews and some fresh bread down in front of them.

They ate their meals in silence eagerly until every last bite was gone, the smell of the fresh bread and stew intoxicating after having dried and stale rations for the past several days. As he put

CHAPTER 5

down his spoon, Hort rumbled a loud burp, beating his fist over his chest to help it escape.

"Well, me boy, I better go get us some supplies. See ye back 'ere when I'm through." Hort dropped some coins on the table to cover the meal. Davion nodded "goodbye" to his uncle before returning his attention to his book of spells, searching for anything else that might help him in battle.

* * *

"Davion. Wake up, me boy." Hort's voice rang in his ears.

Davion lifted his head, pulling a stuck page from his spellbook off of his cheek as he looked around, orienting himself to his surroundings. His head ached and the glow from the candle on the table burned in his eyes as he tried to focus in the dim lighting. He realized that it must be rather late with most of the customers having departed and only a few seated at the bar, enjoying their drinks. Davion pressed his hand against his temple to get the pain to stop. He felt as though he had drunk too much wine but knew that wasn't the case. As his fingers grazed over his head, he felt a sore lump on the back of his skull from when he fell off his horse and recalled his dream from before.

Davion's thoughts became haunted with visions of the beautiful girl that he had seen in the dream. It had felt so real, not like a dream at all. And there was something about her that he just couldn't shake from his mind. He could still see her whenever he closed his eyes, still feel her eyes peering at him, just as curious about him as he was of her. Although he knew they had never crossed paths before, and it was a transient encounter, he somehow felt a connection to her, knowing it had been more than just a typical dream about a pretty girl.

"I have a surprise fer ye," Hort said, bursting at the seams, clearly excited. "Now, I know it isna' yer birthday fer another few weeks, but me thought it best ta give ye an early birthday gift."

Davion looked at Hort, who was holding something behind his back, and he slowly stood to his feet, using the table for leverage. He smirked at his uncle, feeling pretty confident about what he was hiding, especially since he could see a large part of it jetting up past his shoulder.

Hort brought his gift in front of him and held it out for Davion to observe. Davion looked it over and smiled. It was an oaken quarterstaff of fairly good quality, and he handled it admiringly, feeling its weight and strength. There were some designs etched into the wood for elegance, and the shaft was long and straight. The bottom had a metal tip, not sharp, but slightly pointed. The top of the staff distinguished it as a mage staff from an ordinary one, with two branches twirling around, forming a teardrop shape, designed for holding a large gem that could amplify a mage's magic. This staff did not yet have a gem, but it was more than ideal for beginners nonetheless. Davion waved it around, getting a feel for it in his hands. It was a little heavy but not too cumbersome.

"Thank you, Uncle. I love it!" Davion said to Hort. "Will you show me how to use it?"

Hort laughed and shook his head. "That be one weapon I canna' be teachin' ye." He slapped Davion on the back. "We best be retirin'. Ye have a long day ahead."

Davion grabbed his spellbook and sack along with the staff and started heading for the stairs to the rooms. "Yes, another long, hot journey to the next town," he said gloomily.

"Not yet," Hort interjected. "That be the second part of yer gift. We'll have ta leave the day after tomorra'. Because tomorra', me boy..." Hort paused for dramatic effect before saying with oomph, "ye become a fighter-mage!"

CHAPTER SIX

GODS

Considering the heat of this scorching summer day in Onis, Pavula was waiting rather patiently for her mother outside the den to be further educated on magic, wafting air across her face with a large leaf. It had been a few days since their disagreement, and neither of them had spoken about it since the evening Pavula had walked away from Lupé Caelis.

Pavula certainly loved her wolf mother, but the questions that plagued her mind remained unanswered. She knew that Lupé Caelis would not impart her knowledge graciously so, she decided to find the answers elsewhere. However, how and where to pursue those answers remained another mystery.

Lupé Caelis expelled a fist-size stone from her muzzle several paces from where Pavula perched peacefully with legs crossed and arms now resting upon her knees. Stepping to the side, Lupé Caelis took her post midway between the stone and Pavula. *'Are you prepared for your next lesson?'*

Pavula nodded, concentrating on the stone, and charged to summon the earth spirit.

Sensing her thoughts, Lupé Caelis interjected, *'No, my child, this is not an earth magic lesson.'* Bewildered, Pavula cocked an eyebrow at the Great Wolf. *'Close your eyes and do not summon any of the magics of the land, but picture the stone in your mind.'*

As always, Pavula did as instructed, although quite disconcerted. The grass and dirt encompassing the stone were black and amorphous within her mind, but the stone was vivid and detailed with every curve, crevice, and impression.

'Summon the stone to lift in the air, but gently to keep it from flying away. Just raise it a few feet from the ground.'

Pavula still lacked comprehension. How could she move the stone if she didn't call on the earth spirit? *Summon? Summon what? The stone? But it's just a rock!* She became frustrated in her ignorance and questioned her mother on the practicality of what she was asking of her.

'I am teaching you to use your mind-summoning abilities, the ability of telekinesis. Much different from calling on the spirits, it is similar to your mind-speech, but instead, it uses a different part of your mind to move the stone.' Lupé Caelis wasn't entirely sure this was going to work. It was a power no elf had ever possessed, and only a few ancient creatures had the ability. She knew it was a stretch to ask this of her but needed to try.

Mind-speech had always come naturally to Pavula since she could remember. She could use telepathy with pictures and feelings before even learning to talk, never having to *try* in order to use it. Closing her eyes again, Pavula calmed her thoughts and pictured the stone again. She could see it as purely as if her eyes were open and blanked out everything else. *'Will the stone to rise off the ground. Ask it with your thoughts.'*

Pavula was speechlessly questioning the old wolf's sanity. *You can't talk to a rock without spirit!* Still, she concentrated, weaving tendrils in her mind around the stone with the ends hovering in the air above it. Pulling on the tendrils, a great resistance met her. The rock remained stationary, refusing to leave the ground. The more she exerted on the strings, the more resistance she encountered.

'*I don't understand, Mother. What am I doing wrong?*' she questioned after much frustration. '*All this is doing is making me exhausted.*' Dropping the image of the rock and tendrils like a hot coal, she opened her miserable eyes and pleaded to Lupé Caelis for help, pouting impatiently.

Although Lupé Caelis hated this adolescent behavior, Pavula no longer cared and was ragged from the boundless lessons lately. She selfishly longed for the freedom to do whatever she pleased whenever she pleased and didn't see the necessity for all these "magic tricks" that she would never have the chance to use.

Considering training and hunting were the only responsibilities Lupé Caelis ever insisted on, she often worried she had not been stern enough in Lupé Pavula's upbringing. That in giving her too much freedom, Pavula had become spoiled by the sedentary lifestyle of the wolves.

Lupé Caelis glared down on her briefly, considering how to phrase something that was beyond the abilities of any mere mortal. '*You cannot force nature; it has rules and boundaries. You can only ask that it bend those rules for you for a brief moment of time. The stone is a solid part of nature—just as any non-magically entity is, so you must obey its rules. When you summon the spirits, you are using them to shift nature, to do what no man can: to give life and take it away, to change what is and create what is not. The spirits do the work for you as you command them. Without the spirits, you must ask the rock to bend the rules for you and do as you will. No creature of magic is as strong as the spirits, and you will not be able to change the rock as they can, but you can move it.*'

Pavula considered her mother's words carefully, trying to grasp their meaning. '*Okay, but why wouldn't I just ask the earth spirit to move the rock?*'

CHAPTER 6

Smiling at her insightful question, Lupé Caelis explained, 'When you use the spirits, it uses your energy and wears you out quickly. It is the price you pay to the spirits to use their magic. However, when you mind-speak, you are using a different power. You can speak all day and never become tired, right?' Pavula nodded. 'Although not quite the same, it is similar when you mind-summon. You are using a different part of your natural potential. This means that were you ever in a position where you needed to do many different things, such as in a battle, you would last longer than your opponents by using both your mind-summoning and your magic. Just remember that your mind-summon will only move objects, but the spirits can mold them.'

It was starting to make more sense to Pavula. She understood the need to use both forms, but she still lacked clarity on how to accomplish mind-summoning. *I must ask the rock.* 'Mr. Rock, will you please lift off the ground for me?' Pavula sent into the emptiness of the rock. She giggled to herself, realizing how silly that was. She knew that Lupé Caelis couldn't have meant that so literally, but it never hurts to try.

Concentrating harder, she reached to the rock with her mind, creating more golden-hued tendrils over it, this time shaped like a hand, while holding her own hand out to guide it. Touching the rock delicately with mind-fingers, it shook briefly. There was a magnetic force between her mind-fingers and the rock that was pulling down on her hand. Startled, Pavula jerked her hand up away from the force, and the rock jumped off the ground after it, slapping against the palm of her invisible mind-hand where it stopped. She curled the fingers around the rock and opened her eyes. A few paces from her floated the rock in midair as though it were resting on an invisible board.

Pavula smiled in excitement, finally understanding. Jumping up eagerly, she opened her fingers and reached out her hand toward the stone, her eyes animated with vivacity. The stone only wavered slightly at first, then darted through the air, planting itself into her outreached palm.

"Mother! Mother! Did you see that?!?" Pavula exclaimed, holding up the rock for her mother to see.

Lupé Caelis smiled at the elf and nodded her approval. *'You did wonderfully, my child.'*

Once again, Lupé Caelis was astonished at the seemingly limitless power that the young elf possessed. She had always known of the path that she would someday take but had not been prepared for how powerful Pavula would be so early in her young life. It was clear that her time with Lupé Caelis was coming to an end much faster than she had planned—or wanted.

Pavula practiced moving the rock several more times and tried moving slightly larger rocks skillfully with little resistance. Lupé Caelis decided that it was time for a break, and they went to the river where the rest of the pack was lapping up its cool waters.

Stretching out in the grass, Lupé Caelis focused her sight on the wolves. Pavula sat and ate some nuts she had gathered nearby, enjoying the break. Squinting her eyes from the sun's rays, Lupé Caelis wet her nose with her tongue and watched Pavula for a moment. She took a deep breath, readying herself and her thoughts for the story she would share with her.

'Lupé Pavula,' Lupé Caelis began, commanding her attention, *'I would like to tell you a story. You want to know more about the other races of our land and don't understand how they can be so cruel to one another. So, I will take you to the beginning, the start of it all.'*

Pavula smiled gleefully and scooted up close to her mother, eagerly anticipating the story.

Lupé Caelis crossed her front paws, stared off into the distance, deep in thought, and began:

CHAPTER 6

In the beginning, there were three gods: Kyrash, the son; Jayenne, the daughter; and Caelis, the mother. Kyrash was always pestering Jayenne, constantly goading her to battle with him, but Jayenne did not want to fight. Jayenne was a beautiful being who only wanted peace, tranquility, and something she called 'love.' Kyrash did not know what this 'love' was, and if she would try to explain it, he would tell her that she was childish, thinking such foolish thoughts. Mother was tired of their fighting and so created a land in which she could escape. Mother made a picturesque land with flowing streams, lakes, and oceans and a grand waterfall over 200 feet high in the mountains to the north. She covered the ground with lush, swaying, charming trees to offer her shade from the burning sun. The only part of the main continent without any trees was a long strip down the center that was a large beautiful meadow of flowers and tall grass. Mother loved to roll around in the grass and smell the flowers, but she was lonely in this new land, this one land, Onis. Mother decided to make some creatures for her paradise. They would be instinctive and innocent. There would be those that ate plant and those that ate meat to maintain balance, and they would vary in sizes and abilities.

And so animals came to be, and Mother was no longer lonely, and all was well. Mother's favorite creations were the wolves: so majestic and intuitive, and they loved her dearly.

Kyrash and Jayenne then became lonely without their mother and looked for something to entertain them as it was quite boring, as you can imagine, floating around in a lot of nothingness. They began watching Mother on Onis and decided to try creating other, more superior lives for the land. Kyrash was the first to make a new life form. He made them in his own image; tall and lanky with a broad upper torso and blood-red skin. He gave them intelligence to create weapons from tree branches, and they wore animal skins to protect their flesh.

And so trolls came to be, and Kyrash was very proud of himself and his creation.

Jayenne laughed at Kyrash's trolls. She thought they were dim-witted and ugly and were no better than the swine that Mother had created as food for her and her wolf family. Jayenne *knew* she could do better. *They will be beautiful*, she thought, *in my image with long flowing hair, bright, clear eyes—like the gleaming gems from the mountains—tall and slender with exaggerated features and swift reflexes like Mother's great cats. They will be highly intelligent, much smarter than Kyrash's dim-witted trolls. As a matter of fact,* she exclaimed enthusiastically in her head, *they will be brilliant, and I will give them power over the land and watch how they use it!*

And so elves came to be, and they were everything that Jayenne desired.

The elves kept Jayenne much entertained, and they worshiped and loved her. However, Kyrash was jealous of her creation. He told the trolls to attack the elves and clear the land of them so they could rule, but their efforts were fruitless, and the trolls were dwindling in number. Realizing that they could never defeat the powerful elves, the trolls retreated into the far woods, disobeying their god. Kyrash admitted he failed and then, with shame, turned some of the trolls green, camouflaging them into the brush until he would have use for them again, and the others he turned the color of rock and dirt and sent them to the hills. They became larger and meaner than their cousins, adapting to the harsh environment of heavy rock and mounds that became home.

And so orcs came to be, and they were much larger and more robust than their troll cousins, but twice as dim.

Kyrash then decided he would make his own elves, but not these silly elves of beauty and grace who loved everything and sang and danced around gleefully. No, his elves would be just as smart, but with great ambition. Boiling all of his hatred for his sister's success together, he created his elves. But, in his hatred, they came out dark and burnt in color, embodying tones of navy, ash, and black like the midnight sky. However, this only pleased him more, for now, in their darkened state, they would have stealth in the night as well. He bestowed them with powers over the land as his sister had but, they twisted that power using it differently than the elves, creating Dark Magic—feeding on the life of the land around them instead of sharing and celebrating it.

And so drow came to be, also called dark elves by many, and they were dark, cruel, and cunning. They had a never-ending thirst for everything they believed to be attainable.

As expected, the drow and the elves fought for thousands of years, but being both equally intelligent and powerful, neither side ever won the war. Both were also endowed with very long lives, giving them longer to hold onto their hatreds and resentments, passing it on to each future generation. And so their fighting went on and on and on...

In an attempt to give her elves an advantage, Jayenne thought that if the elves could form more advanced weaponry than their bows, arrows, and spears, they could defeat the drow, and there would be peace throughout the land. However, there was a predicament with her idea; the metals and minerals needed for the weapons were in the mountains far away from her elves. She realized that even if she sent them there, they were not built for the laborious task of mining the minerals needed. So, she decided she would need to make another race; a race strong, hardy, and small enough to tunnel easily through the mountains. Because she didn't want them to pose a threat to the elves, she gave them only enough intelligence to perform the task she needed of them.

And so dwarves came to be, and they were tough and determined.

Unfortunately, the dwarves turned out to be more than Jayenne had anticipated. They were hardy like she had desired, but they were also very stubborn. They did not like her elves and did not want to make the weapons for them. They ended up trading a few swords, daggers, and some minerals to both sides in exchange for elegant gifts and a truce between the feuding elves, but mostly they mined the mountains and made weapons for themselves. Their mountains were in the northern part of the land, out of the way of the feuding elves, and they wanted nothing to do with their problems. So, they worked hard at fortifying the mountains and building weapons for their defense. They quickly learned to make strong mead to pass the time and acquired rosy cheeks and hairy chests, including the women, but they were happy minding their own business and ignoring the gods and the elves.

Several hundred years went by, and the battles continued on, the gods weary in their boredom.

One day while watching her beautiful elves fighting the cunning drow, Jayenne had another idea. She confronted Kyrash saying, "I will admit that my elves lack the cunning way of your drow, but your drow lack the grace and dignity of my elves." Kyrash just stared at her, vaguely interested. "What if we combine our ideas to make another race, a neutral race?"

"Neutral?" Kyrash blared overdramatically, "How BORING! Your dwarves are already neutral. Look at them! They just SIT there getting drunk and passing gas!" He crossed his arms and watched his sister think.

Jayenne tapped her bottom lip with two fingers deep in thought. "You're right," she said finally. "Okay, how about this: We give them the capability of being good OR evil and free will to choose?"

This intrigued Kyrash. He looked down toward the battles again on Onis between the elves and the drow and then at the drunken dwarves and sniveling trolls and orcs in their corners. Considering how this could play in his favor, he quickly devised his plan. He looked back to Jayenne and nodded.

"Okay," he confirmed, "but none of the fairy-folk look."

"Fine," Jayenne replied, "With good and evil in their hearts, they should be plainly unadorned so that they are not influenced or associated with either side just by their physical appearance alone. Fair?"

He nodded, and they shook hands.

And so humans came to be, and some were good, and some were not, and some remained neutral.

Meanwhile, Mother had been silently watching as her children tried to destroy the other's creations. She became annoyed over the years as they began to populate her once-quiet land with the quibbling she attempted to escape so long ago. *I have had enough*, she decided one day to herself. She resolved to make her own race, a mediator between all the feuding, a great and powerful race. *They will be massive and strong, highly intelligent, and magical. They will be feared and maintain balance over good and* evil. They will rule over earth, air, fire, and water, and I will call them Dragons!

And so dragons came to be, and they were feared throughout the land, and they were all-powerful, with four clans each controlling one of the four elements. Then something happened—the fighting stopped. Not completely, of course, for the hatred still remained. But, fear of the mighty dragons created balance throughout Onis, halting the non-stop battles.

Lupé Caelis looked back to Pavula, who had been listening intently, captivated by the story. *'A lot has happened since then,'* Lupé Caelis continued, *'The dragons are no longer the great protectors they once were. They have tragically become part of the never-ending feuding. You see, Pavula,'* she paused, *'there are thousands of years full of hatred, anger, and a quest for power between the races. This once beautiful world has grown hard and barren through it. The once lush trees of the drow have all shriveled and snarled with death. The lavish meadow with its wildflowers and patch of tall purple Hydrillia blooms has become a cracked dessert of hard and molten rock. Only the eastern forests remain flourishing and stable due to the magics of the elves and myself, but it isn't enough to sustain the whole of Onis.'*

Pavula was staring at Lupé Caelis strangely, and the Great Wolf acknowledged her, *'I am sure you have many questions. What plagues your mind, my child?'* she inquired.

The young elf opened her mouth to speak but hesitated. Lupé Caelis nodded for her to go on. "Are you..." she paused briefly, "Are you Caelis? I mean, THE mother?" Her eyes were wide with anticipation.

Laughing softly, Lupé Caelis shook her head slowly. *'No, my child. I am not. But this is her clan, and I am her descendant. I have not* seen her in many millennia, but I have felt her spirit from time to time. She still watches over all of us and has a hand in much of what goes on in her land.'

Pavula played with a stick in the grass, dumb-struck at how old her mother must be. She was fascinated with the story, but it only created more questions in her mind about herself. Also, it was no surprise to her that Lupé Caelis was old, but she had no idea that she was ancient, probably as old as the oldest of dragons, or more!

"What about elves?" Pavula asked curiously, "Wolves only live to be about twenty, and I know I'm not a wolf, but I'm not a God like you or the dragons, so how long will I live, Mother?"

Lupé Caelis cocked her head at Pavula wondering if she knew anything about elves, realizing she hadn't told her much before now. 'There is no telling for sure. Elven lives are tricky, based on outside factors usually, but elves will usually live several hundred years at least. There was one I know of who lived to be nearly 2,000 years old before meeting his demise.' She shook her head, tilting it side to side as a bug buzzed by her ear. 'And to be clear, my child, dragons are not gods. They are just as mortal as elves, which depending on your point of view, is as close to being immortal as one could hope to be.'

Still so young and innocent, Pavula dreamed of how wonderful life would be as an immortal. "And you? Will you die?"

Lupé Caelis smiled at her, 'Not by time.'

"I wish I could never die." Pavula dreamed as her eyes stared off across the river into nothingness.

'No, my child, you know not of what you speak.'

Swinging back to reality, Pavula felt cantankerous once again by the oh-so-old and oh-so-wise. "Sure I do!" she contorted.

'It is one thing to never die...' the Great Wolf continued, 'it is another to live forever.'

CHAPTER 6

Cocking an eyebrow at her, Pavula saw no difference and figured she was playing mind games with her. "Fair enough," Pavula nodded and smiled, "then I will live forever, and you shall never die."

Lupé Caelis gleamed at the young elf delightedly. *'Perhaps. Now, no more talk of death.'*

Still, Pavula continued to wonder to herself what it all meant and what role she was to play in it. There was obviously a reason for all of her training, but her mother still had not told her what it was. Was she just getting her ready to return to the world outside, or did she have another agenda? Pavula crossed her arms in front of her as she tried to figure it all out, already knowing her mother wouldn't be so forthcoming as she had asked her many times before. She decided she would not press the issue any more tonight and hoped that Lupé Caelis would tell her in time.

'It is getting late,' Lupé Caelis said. *'Get some rest, my child. You will be going hunting tomorrow with your brothers and sisters to practice your new skills.'*

Pavula nodded and stood up. "Thank you for the story, Mother," she said, nuzzling into her thick mane before she turned and headed back to the den.

CHAPTER SEVEN

FIREMASTER

The morning rays from the hot sun beamed through the city streets bringing in the day as the shopkeepers dusted off stands and laid out their wares. Mira glistened brightly in the early morning, and most of the residents were in their usual cheery mood. They were generally safe within the stone walls from most creatures of this land and in overall better spirits than the other villages, which were victim to regular attacks and plundering. As the sun rose higher, filling the sky with its full rays, the city came to a full bustle, and everyone was engaged with their morning routines.

Davion was feeling exhilarated with the morning good cheer and clamor as he and Hort made their way through the town, admiring its beauty on the way to the second part of Hort's early-birthday surprise. His new mage staff proudly strapped to his back, he was ecstatic at the chance to further his abilities. During his time at the academy, they taught him how to hold and cast spells with a mage staff, but he still lacked the knowledge he needed for actual combat.

Most mages who graduated from the academy would have been recruited into the army, where they would not be expected to do any melee combat. Fire mages would stand in the back, casting spells from afar to either fortify the troops with protections and wards or to cast against the enemy. Seldom would they have need for physical close-combat skills. However, this would not work for Davion since he had no intention of joining the king's army. It was already clear that to fight alongside his uncle, he would need to be better prepared.

Hort turned down a narrow pathway to a back alley where the sun was not yet touching. It smelled musty from the morning condensation, and Davion could see a crooked wooden door at the far end. They walked towards the door, their feet echoing on the stone path with each step. The alley was so gloomy compared to the rest of the city, making Davion pause his excitement, wary of his surroundings.

"Where are we, Uncle?" Davion asked, feeling a bit nervous. There were no signs or welcoming decorations of any sort, just the ugly door and dewy cobwebs filling the corners. Davion watched as a rat skittered from a small pile of trash down along the wall towards the city streets. Hort looked back at Davion and gave him a smile, then touched the side of his nose with a wink.

When they reached the door, Hort knocked three times, paused, then knocked two more. The door creaked open slightly, and a shape draped in darkness peeked at them through the crack.

"For Onis. For Freedom," Hort spoke quietly into the gloomy darkness of the opening, causing the door to creak noisily open all the way. A man stood there clothed in a maroon-colored robe with a large hood concealing his shadowed face.

"Follow me," came the deep voice from the robed figure as he turned and walked further into the darkness within. Davion and Hort stepped through the doorway toward the blackness, but when they passed over the threshold, they didn't find themselves in a dark place at all. Davion's jaw dropped open as he suddenly found himself in a lush-green open field surrounded by arches and stone walls. The clearing was at least five times the size of the training grounds at the academy, and he imagined he could fit all the citizens of Roco in here. There were a couple dozen more robed figures walking and talking on the grounds. Some wore the maroon color of their host, while others wore robes of either navy blue, ash white, or hunter green.

"Keep up," the shrouded figure said to Davion, who had started to fall behind while studying his surroundings.

"Uncle, what is this place?" Davion whispered, still looking around.

Hort kept looking straight ahead at their host, whispering through tight lips, "An underground mage emporium. Tis a great honor that they've let us in."

Before Davion could ask any more, they approached another figure dressed in the same maroon robes. Seeing them approach, the figure pulled back his hood, revealing an old human with a medium-length gray beard, bushy eyebrows, and dark-brown eyes. He twitched his large rosy nose while he inspected Davion after they came to a stop in front of him.

"I hear we have another fire sorcerer in the making," the man said, smiling under his whiskers, which were curled over his lips. "I am Firemaster Thornton." He held out his frail hand to Davion, who took it, shaking it proudly.

"Yes, sir," Davion replied. "I'm Davion Collins. A new graduate of Silex Valley Magi Academy."

Thornton rubbed his chin, looking Davion over again, "I see," he finally said.

"A little wet behind the ears, but a bright kid," Hort interjected.

"Well, let us not waste any more time, New Grad," Thornton said, "we have much work to do and very little time to do it." He motioned for them to follow and took them over to a part of the clearing, several paces from a large mound of rocks piled about seven feet high. Gesturing to the rocks, he said, "Let me see what you can do."

Davion looked between the firemaster and the rocks. He wasn't exactly sure what he was supposed to do. In fact, he had no idea. "I...don't understand."

Sighing, Thornton grabbed the staff from Davion's back and thrust it into his hands, then pointed back to the rocks.

"Blow 'em up, me boy!" Hort said enthusiastically.

Thornton raised his hand to Hort and said, "Please step back, Hort Strongarm of Lochlann," and Hort apologized, withdrawing several paces.

Davion's heart raced with nervous energy, eager to impress the firemaster. Holding the staff upright, he waved it in a figure-eight pattern and said an incantation he remembered from school when using a staff, "*Solas Luminas!*" A small, white orb of light emerged from the top of the staff and moved over to the rocks, hovering above them. Davion flushed with embarrassment. He was so nervous he had mixed up his spells. "I'm sorry," he said to the firemaster. "I wasn't ready." The light orb fizzled and faded.

Thornton grabbed his own staff from his back, a staff made of hard metal, though it looked light as a feather in his hands. There was a large garnet stone embedded in the top, which had five fine-metallic tendrils weaving like hands around the gem. "We'll start with some basic spells," he told Davion, "Then once you get the hang of those, we can move on to melee combat. You already have the orb light down in case you're ever stuck in a dark place, so we'll skip that one." He winked at Davion. "You should already know firebolt?" he queried, and Davion nodded.

"But not with a staff," he admitted.

"Watch closely." Thornton raised his staff and waved it elegantly in a back and forth motion twice, then wove it round wide, and finally thrust the tip forward toward the rocks, "*Ominus Lacarté!*" he shouted. A large bolt of fire flew forward from the tip of his staff, sped across the field within a second, and exploded over the rocks, sending flames up into the sky. The once-gray rocks now had a substantial ring of black soot.

"Well, color me green. That went faster than a dwarf's first pint! Excellent, sir, just excellent!" Hort said, impressed, applauding the performance. "Alright, me boy. Show 'im what ye got!"

Davion stepped forward, grasping his staff tightly, and mimicked the motions. "*Ominus Lacarté!*" he shouted as he pointed the staff at the rocks. A small flame spat out of the tip and fell to the ground a few feet away. He ground his teeth in frustration and embarrassment, then looked to his instructor, trying to conceal his dismay.

Hort threw his arms up in the air. "Aw, come on, me boy! I can whiz further than that!"

Thornton raised his hand to Hort, silencing him, and Hort stepped back to his place, crossing his arms over his chest, slightly disgruntled.

"It will take practice," Thornton told Davion, "Fire magic is one of the hardest magics to master. It comes from a different place than the others, and you will need to pull from the darkness deep within yourself. Fire can also be unpredictable. Every movement has to be precise. When using a staff, there is not as much leeway as there is with hand casting, but when you get it right, the staff will amplify your spells. Thus, your fireballs will be larger and stronger, and more deadly. This is the first spell you need to master for combat, both with a staff and without. Every spell you learn, you should know how to do it both with and without the staff in case the need arises. Now, go again, but this time raise your hand higher at the end during the rounding press."

Nodding in acknowledgment, Davion wrung his hands over his staff in preparation. He held it out, waving it back and forth as before, then around, repeating the steps again, and he failed again...and again. However, each time, he seemed to get a slightly greater response from the staff, and he was determined to get it right.

By the eighth time, Davion had become increasingly frustrated and felt his heart racing and anger boiling up inside him, feeling like a failure. As Davion thrust the tip toward the rocks this time, a fist-sized ball of orange and red fire emerged from the staff and shot to the rocks, splatting against them, then fizzled away. It wasn't a glorious sight, but it was most definitely progress.

"Alright!" Hort cheered. "Now we're talkin'!"

"Much better," said Thornton. "AGAIN!"

Davion repeated the spell over and over, feeling the heat boiling up inside him as he forced each bolt across the field. The firebolts only got slightly larger but did get faster and stronger until finally blasting against the rocks in a rapid stream, exploding against the hard stone surface, leaving behind a black scorch mark next to Thornton's.

Hort startled Davion by slapping him proudly on the back. "Thatta boy!" he boasted proudly.

"Very good," Thornton added. "I could sense you finding that darkness that I had mentioned. You will need to learn how to pull from it without the emotional attachment to be truly great. But, for now, let's continue."

Davion took a deep breath looking back to the rocks. He was already feeling the magic draining him. Although not as much as he had anticipated. It felt as though, even as he stood here, his magic was somehow being replenished. He could feel himself being reinvigorated and believed it was coming from this mystical place.

Thornton showed Davion how to use the staff for different types of fire attacks. He didn't get to master all of them but felt like he was getting a good basis for practicing. Many of them he already knew the mechanics of from school, so Thornton focused on introducing him to a few new ones, such as a spread shot that would shoot fire out in five different directions or more—depending on the version—and a rapid-fire shot that would keep shooting fireballs at the assailant with just a repeated word. These proved to be much more challenging for Davion, and he wasn't able to get them quite right before they had to move on. He was becoming overwhelmed with all of the spells and the staff and hand motions, trying to absorb it all. If only he had more time with Thornton, he could be so much greater.

It was reaching late afternoon, and Davion's stomach was aching. He had been oblivious to time, captivated by his training, but realized it was now well past lunchtime. As if reading his mind, Thornton put away his staff on his back and announced that they would break for a snack.

All three of them made their way over to the arches along the perimeter. Behind one of the arches sat a stone table with four stone stools, and Davion eagerly took to one of them and began eating the fruit that someone had placed in the center. He saw Thornton looking discontentedly at him and put the fruit down on the table.

"We do not partake in Onis' bounty until we have properly thanked the Goddess Jayenne for her good favor and the spirits for providing us with this nourishment," Thornton said.

Davion lowered his head. "My apologies."

He observed Thornton press his hands together in prayer and bow his head, and did the same. Waiting for him to begin a prayer, he listened intently but heard nothing, so he peeked cautiously at him and Hort and saw them both holding the prayer stance in silence. He closed his eyes and continued to bow.

"Now you may eat," said the firemaster after many moments, startling Davion, but Thornton did not take one of the seats. "Is there anything else you would like to know before we continue to your last lessons?"

Davion's leg shook up and down as he internally questioned whether it was appropriate for him to ask what he had wanted to all day. Hort sensed his turmoil and prompted, "Out with it, me boy."

"Well, I was just wondering...that is..." Davion stammered nervously, "It's just that this is all very helpful and amazing, but there is so much more, and I wondered if you would consider taking me on as an apprentice." He tried hard to maintain eye contact with Thornton, wanting so much to look away, afraid of his response.

"Apprentice?" Thornton said, somewhat surprised. "Well, I've taught many young sorcerers, but I have never taken one on as an apprentice. I'm afraid that it wouldn't do you much good." Seeing the disappointment overcome Davion's face, he explained, "I am old, son. I have done my battling and rarely step outside these walls." He motioned to the surrounding walls with an outstretched hand. "You do have much potential and have picked up your training faster than any other I have assisted. Perhaps that is due to your training at the academy. It is a great starting point for your skills. But, I'm afraid I'm not the one that will bring you to greatness. I can only offer you today."

Davion tried to hide his disappointment while nodding his understanding to Thornton, praying one of the others he had applied to for apprenticeship would respond. It was apparent how much more he could learn from a true firemaster. Hort and Davion finished their fruit quickly so that Davion could continue his lessons, and then Thornton took them back to the field to begin the second half of his instruction: Staff melee combat.

Rubbing his hands together enthusiastically, Hort said, "Finally! Time fer some action! Yer magics pretty and all, but me still thinks this is where tis all at. Right in the face of yer opponent, looking 'im dead in the eye as ye gut 'em!" Hort made a jabbing motion with an invisible sword. Davion smirked at his uncle and rolled his eyes.

Thornton instructed and demonstrated the proper way to hold the staff, allowing him to be able to cast a quick spell if needed between attacks, and showed him how to protect himself. At first, Davion was rather clumsy with his staff, dropping it nearly every time Thornton hit it with his own. But, through his guidance, he became better at holding his stance and taking the blows. Thornton moved in slow motion, giving Davion a chance to block each swipe and jut, then slowly sped up until Davion could no longer block them.

"You're doing well," Thornton said encouragingly. "You take to the staff rather naturally. Now, let's have you attack me." They continued their dance of attacking and defending around each other as their staffs clacked together repeatedly. When Thornton felt that he had the basics underfoot, he stepped back and held up his hand to Davion. "Now, let's see how you do against a different weapon." He looked over to Hort. "If you will, Mr. Strongarm?"

Hort gleamed at Davion and drew his axe from his back, then held it in front of him with both hands in a ready position. "If a stick stands a chance against me axe, then I be a hobbit's uncle!"

"Uncle, you and I both know halflings are a myth," Davion chuckled while approaching him nervously.

"Me point exacitally," Hort said with a smile. "A quarterstaff against me axe hardly seems fair, methinks. I'll just end up slaughtering the poor boy without even tryin'!"

Remaining stern, Thornton continued with his instruction, "Davion, your staff cannot withstand a direct blow from an axe; it will most definitely break. The trick is to use the staff to push the axe away from you and, if possible, to disarm your attacker. Use the sideswipe."

Hort came at Davion with the axe and halfheartedly swung down at the boy, afraid of hurting him. Davion, holding the staff firmly with both hands, quickly swung the staff, hitting the axe's shaft, forcing it sideways away from him, and then in one fluid motion, used the other end of the staff to jab Hort's hand, causing him to drop the axe. Hort cursed, rubbing his fist, and then bent down to retrieve his weapon, glaring up at Davion with surprise.

"Now wait one minute, I wasna' tryin'!" Hort exclaimed, picking his weapon back up from the soft grass. "Let's go again!"

Hort came at Davion again, letting out a battle cry, axe held high, and brought it down towards him. Davion quickly sidestepped, swung the staff outward, and knocked the axe away from Hort, causing him to falter, then spun around and thwacked Hort in the back with his staff. Hort fell forward to his knees, and his oversized helmet flopped down over his eyes. Letting out a bunch of curses, Hort gained his bearings and got back to his feet.

Both Hort and Davion looked to Thornton, who was clapping, pleased with his pupil. "You certainly are a natural with a staff!" he complimented Davion, who blushed with pride.

"Aw, he caught me off guard!" Hort huffed. "But alright, ye did good, me boy," he added, humbly patting Davion on the back.

The three of them continued training and practicing until it grew dark, and once again, Davion's stomach got the best of him. He felt so alive and invigorated out on this field. There was an energy here unlike any he'd ever felt, and he wished he could stay and continue to train.

When they wrapped up the lessons, Davion looked around one last time at the hooded figures and wondered who they all were and why they were here. He also realized that with a force like this here to protect Mira, it was no wonder it was the least attacked city in Silex Valley and that everyone felt safe here. He wondered how many people knew about this place.

Thornton led Davion and Hort back to the door where they came in, and Hort gave him several coins from his satchel. "Ye kept good on yer word, and I keep good on mine, old friend," he said to the firemaster. "Perhaps there's hope fer the boy yet, no?" Hort nudged Thornton mirthfully, looking at Davion.

Smiling, Thornton nodded, "He shows much promise," and pulled a small bag from his pocket. "There's one last thing I have for you. Consider this my birthday gift to you." He tossed the bag over to Davion, who caught it and held it up to see. "Your uncle told me of the rock fiends and of your new horse running off. Inside that pouch, you'll find a spell along with ingredients needed to bind her to you. I wish you both safe journeys ahead. May Jayenne and Kyrash both be in your favor." Thornton bowed to them, and they returned the gesture.

Davion thanked Thornton for everything and looked up at the blue and red moons now floating high in the sky, and smiled. This had been one of the best days of his life, getting to study one-on-one under such a great master. He felt he finally had the ability to make his uncle proud. Even though he knew there was much more to learn, Davion believed he was off to a great start. He was both nervous and eager to continue practicing what he had learned and to try out his new skills in a real battle.

As they stepped out through the door returning to the alley, Davion looked back for one last glimpse of the magical place, but all he saw was the empty blackness as the door closed noiselessly behind them.

CHAPTER EIGHT

HUNT

he darkness was overwhelming. Not a single star shone in the sky, and Pavula had to use all her senses to make her way through the forest. She felt the tips of leaves and twigs from bushes graze against her fingers, grass blades against her toes, and heard a crackling sound in the distance. It was calling to her, pulling her forward through the forest, through the dark. A burning smell filled the air, and she had an eerie feeling as though she were being watched.

When Pavula turned around a large oak, she stopped in her tracks. There before her, through the darkness, she saw and marveled at an enormous creature standing at least thirty feet high. There was a fire in its eyes that burned so brightly she could discern its monstrous silhouette and knew instantly that she was gazing upon a dragon.

As the dragon looked over the young elf inquisitively, the forest came alight with tall flames burning all around, but Pavula felt no heat emanating from the inferno. With the dragon illuminated, she could see it was covered in blood-red scales with quills spread thick like fur down its spine to the tip of its tail. Smoke drifted up from great nostrils as it lowered its head down toward her.

Pavula wasn't sure why, but she was not afraid of this beast. Instead, she stood perfectly still while the dragon cast its eye over her, examining her curiously. After several moments, it pulled back its head, and Pavula heard a rumbling within its chest. Suddenly, the dragon opened its great jaws, and she realized that it was preparing to breathe fire. Every part of her body told her to run, but she couldn't move. She stood there, frozen in place, staring the colossal beast in its fiery eyes, and then she saw it. The fire came forth from the dragon right toward Pavula, engulfing her in flames. Screaming an unholy shrill, she raised her hand to block the fire, expecting to die right then and there.

Panicked, Pavula jetted upright and looked around her. Realizing that she was safely in her den, she relaxed somewhat. She felt the soft fur of her mother and nuzzled into her warmth. Pavula wondered if the dream meant anything. She had never seen a dragon up close before.

'Big hunt day,' Lupé Caelis mind-spoke softly to Pavula.

Pavula stretched out then started heading to the den entrance. 'Yes, Mother,' she replied before progressing toward the river for a drink. Going about her morning ritual, the wolves joined her by the river, lapping up water and splashing around in it. Her sister pup nipped at her feet once again while she walked. She picked her up, scratching under her chin, only to have her hand grabbed by its tiny paws and attacked with tiny playful teeth.

From the forest wall, a great howl filled the air, majestic and strong, and all the wolves ran immediately to Lupé Caelis. Pavula strapped her stone dagger to her loincloth and grabbed a spear she had fashioned from a rock and strong branch, then headed to Lupé Caelis as well.

The Great Wolf howled again, and five of the wolves took off into the forest. She looked sternly at Pavula and nodded. 'You know what to do.'

Pavula nodded and then ran into the woods after the wolves with incredible speed.

Running west through the tall trees, Pavula hardly made a sound as she gracefully flew through the forest, her feet barely touching the ground, and she caught up to the rest of the wolves. She dashed around trees, knowing the forest like the back of her hand the way one knows where the furniture lay in their room even after the light has been extinguished. They ran for nearly an hour, looking this way and that for signs of prey, but it had become rather scarce as of late.

Pavula stopped, and the wolves stopped with her. She looked up through the tops of the trees for the sun. Its rays gleamed down through the swaying leaves, and Pavula sensed her heading through the star-shaped opening above her. Turning north, Pavula began the hunt again, the wolves trailing at her feet as she continued darting amongst the trees, around bushes, and over fallen logs.

They continued running that way, searching for any signs of life but were starting to tire. Pavula sensed the wolves slowing down, and she felt the need to do the same. She also knew they were getting close to the protective border that her mother had put up and would have to turn back in the other direction soon. If only her mother would loosen her hold on them a little so they could find new hunting grounds, then they might have better luck. It was as though their prey had figured out their territory and knew not to come within the boundaries.

Pavula stopped and squatted down to catch her breath and assess. The wolves hovered quietly, looking outward while she did. *Time to use my skills,* Pavula thought to herself. She set her spear down beside her and dug her hands into the ground, then concentrated on summoning the earth spirit.

Sending her thoughts into the dirt, she searched outward for sounds of galloping hooves, or the thumping feet of rabbits, or any sign of other animals, but she couldn't sense any animal life

CHAPTER 8

nearby. Expanding outward, she hit some resistance and had to concentrate harder to push through it. She continued pushing out until she hit another wall, but this time she could see in her mind's eye that it was a large body of water. *A Lake, she realized.* Miran Lake, to be precise.

In the distance to the north, she could sense many vibrations coming through the earth. *Perhaps a herd,* she hoped, ready to resume her hunt. Stretching further outward, north along the lake, Pavula could make out the rumbling noises through the earth, but it wasn't hooves at all. It was laughing and beautiful sounds of music. There were also many muffled voices talking and yelling in a strange language. Astonished by what she found, Pavula opened her eyes, and the connection was severed instantly. *What WAS that?* she wondered. She had never felt or heard anything like it.

Abruptly, there was a wet feeling on her face as one of the wolves licked her cheek. She looked around at them all waiting for her cue and remembered what she was there to do. Peering outward in the direction of her strange discovery, Pavula made a mental note of her location so that she could return the next chance she had.

It was already mid-day, and Pavula still hadn't found anything to hunt. She was running out of ground within the barrier and headed back east, the wolves running at her side. After another few hours of running and tracking, one of the wolves started growling, and the others joined its lead, heading slowly in attack pose toward a large thicket. Pavula saw the brush rustle and sensed something massive on the other side.

The wolves stopped advancing and continued growling at the brush when suddenly a giant boar-beast emerged from its cover and snorted at the wolves. It was at least twice the height of Lupé Caelis, standing a good ten to twelve feet at its shoulder, with a thick leathery hide and patches of fur dangling from its body. Its orange eyes were tiny for its massive head, and it had sharply pointed tusks the length of Pavula's arm. Long, mangy fur hung around its face and chin like a beard.

Pavula could see its sharp teeth as it curled its lips in a snarl before darting swiftly for the first wolf, ramming it with its tusks before tossing it aside. The wolf yelped as it flew into a nearby tree and fell limply to the ground. Pavula raised her spear and threw it as hard as she could at the hog before it could charge again, but it merely grazed its thick hide, angering it further. The hog turned its small orange eyes to Pavula and pawed at the ground, kicking dirt behind it while it snorted and lowered its head aggressively. Pavula grabbed her dagger quickly from her waist and posed, ready for the hog's attack. This was definitely the largest, most dangerous foe she had ever faced. She had never even seen a giant boar in these woods before.

The boar thundered forward in attack toward Pavula, but she waited until the last moment and then jumped high, grabbing its tusk. She swung herself around, catapulting herself over its shoulder, and landed on its back. Grabbing on with one hand as the boar kicked and thrashed, she took her dagger with the other and stabbed the boar hard in the side behind the shoulder blade. The boar squealed in pain, then bucked hard, causing Pavula to lose her grip and fly from the boar's back. Dagger hilt still in hand, it snapped in half, leaving the stone blade embedded in the boar's side as she departed the beast. Pavula, graceful as a cat, landed on her feet and braced herself with her left hand, still grasping the hilt with her right.

The remaining four wolves leaped at the slightly weakened boar, grabbing onto its hide with their teeth and bearing down as hard as they could, trying hard not to let go as the beast thrashed and kicked to free itself. One by one, it was managing to dislodge the wolves from its hide, and Pavula had to think fast before it came at her again. Her weapons were useless, but she had ignored her greatest weapon—herself.

Looking to the trees, Pavula saw vines hanging down from some nearby branches and reached out to them with her mind, raising her hand toward them in command. The vines quickly grew and reached out for the boar, entangling it and tightening around its limbs and body. *I'm doing it!* Pavula smiled excitedly as she willed the vines to pull tighter. The three wolves that still had some fight in them jumped back on the boar, biting and clawing at the great beast, snarling and barking as they attacked. The boar let out a massive moan in pain, unable to buck them again. It tried stepping forward, pulling against the vines. To her dismay, they began to snap one after the other, and the boar was becoming free once again. Unshackled from the ensnaring vines, it stomped angrily at the ground, fury in its eyes, and then stampeded en route for Pavula.

Pavula's heart was in her throat as she feared for her young life. She would never get to explore the world outside her forest and would die before ever getting to experience life. Just as the boar was nearing her, ready to jab its long tusks into her gut, Pavula raised her hands and let out a loud holler. A great energy flared from Pavula's outstretched hands, and the boar lifted off the ground, then flew backward twenty paces before landing hard in the dirt, a dust cloud surrounding it.

Gaping at her hands, Pavula realized what she had just done. Then, without waiting another moment, she reached for the vines again, but this time they came from everywhere. Vines shot forth from the dirt and trees and brush nearby, binding the boar to the ground before it could get back up. Pavula looked at her spear lying in the dirt far away and called to it with her mind, asking it to join her. The spear lifted from the ground and, within the blink of an eye, shot across the clearing, landing firmly in her palm.

Pavula ran to the beast while the wolves pounced upon it, making small punctures with their teeth anywhere they could, trying to hold on. Raising the spear high over her head, Pavula thrust the tip down hard, directly into the boar's exposed chest and through its heart. The boar groaned and squealed, and then its head fell hard against the ground, dead. The adrenaline coursing through her veins, Pavula pulled out her spear and stabbed the lifeless beast again, then fell back onto her bottom in the dirt and took a deep breath. Three wolves came trotting over to her and licked her proudly, trampling her, causing her to fall backward and laugh. The other two wolves limped their way over and rested beside her.

"Not bad, my brothers and sisters, not bad at all," Pavula said while mentally sending them warm and delighted thoughts. The eldest wolf of the pack raised his head to the sky and howled, the rest joining in proudly. Pavula stood up, looked up to the sky, fists balled tight, head held high, and triumphantly belted out with her kin, "Ahh-wooooooo!"

CHAPTER 8

CHAPTER NINE

ORBEK

lop...Clop...Clop... The horse and okullo's hooves pitter-pattered on the dusty trail. Davion was extremely grateful for the spell that Firemaster Thornton had given him for Helna, along with a handful of elven commands that he could use in conjunction with the binding. He could already feel the bond between them strengthening, and she would follow him even without having to hold her reins.

The sun was burning in the sky again, and Davion had shielded himself with his hood. Mira lay a day and a half behind them as Hort and Davion headed north along the east side of Miran Lake. The trials awaiting them, the obstacles they would face, they could not predict. Thus, Hort was fully clad in his armor, prepared for anything, his shield and axe strapped to his back. Davion, in his unflatteringly-brown mage robe, had his pouches tied securely at his waist and his new staff across his back. He also still kept his dagger strapped at his side just in case, but he really believed the staff was going to help him move up a level in his mage skills.

They, like most others, had chosen to travel along the eastern side that lined the Sacred Forest, maintaining the advantage of foraging for food, including the occasional rabbit or other small prey. It would also cut half a day off their journey. However, it was debatable which way was safer.

The east side of Miran Lake contained plenty of wildlife that was to be feared as well, and of course, there were also orcs and trolls roaming the woods, watching the trails for vulnerable travelers. However, on the west side of Miran Lake, the land was nearly desolate. It was an exposed plain with a scarce arrangement of vegetation alongside the bank. Were they to travel west past the plains, they would find themselves roaming the scorching cracked earth of the Syraho Desert. Few men would ever willingly proceed into the Syraho Desert, predicting the unholy death that would await them. Too few tales had been brought back to comprehend what honestly lurked in the Syraho, with the exception of one certainty; it was the domain of the Red Dragon Clan.

Red dragons, or "Reds" or "fire dragons," were the most fierce and deadly of the dragons, breathing fire at their foes, giving them their nickname. They were also the largest of the dragons, nearly twice that of the smaller Silver dragons, and twice as deadly. No humanoid had ever willfully encountered one, and the unwilling never lived to tell the tale. They prevailed as the only dragon clan whose head would not be found mounted on any castle wall. Therefore, the desert remained abandoned from all humanoids, giving the Reds plenty of territory to rule.

Davion spotted the clear waters of the Miran River up ahead and could hear the flowing currents. Approaching, Hort slowed his steed, looking around apprehensively, and grabbed his axe one-handed from his back.

"What is it, Uncle?" Davion asked, following his gaze.

There was a large wooden bridge before them crossing over the fast-flowing river. It was a little worn with age but still sturdy enough for carts and wagons. Definitely strong enough for the two of them.

Riding Orbek slowly up to the bridge, Hort stopped just before it and continued glaring into the trees on both sides of the river.

"Uncle?" Davion prodded nervously.

"Quickly now," Hort told him and gave Orbek a mighty kick, sending him into a gallop across the bridge.

Davion thrashed Helna's reins and shouted, "Iret!" from the binding spell, causing her to lunge forward into a full gallop, overtaking Hort and Orbek.

They quickly made their way over the bridge, and as they neared the other side, Davion heard Hort give out a great battle cry while waving his axe around in the air threateningly. That's when Davion saw them; ORCS! Two monstrously large, ugly, rock-colored mounds of muscle breaching out of the forest and heading straight for the bridge. Davion thrashed the reins harder, trying to keep watch on Hort but was unsure which way he was meant to go.

"Keep going, boy! JUST RUN!" Hort screamed ahead at him as though reading his thoughts.

As an orc ran toward Davion, he veered Helna left and kept thrashing and kicking, pushing her to top speed. The orc swung a large mace around, just barely missing Davion, and he kept galloping as quick as he could, his heart pounding in his ears.

Hort managed to graze the other orc heading at him with the tip of his axe, but he had no intention of engaging in battle. Instead, he used the opportunity to keep Orbek running, but the orc was hot on his heels.

When he was safely ahead of the orc pursuing him, Davion shouted, "*Ominus Lacarté!*" combined with hand gestures, and a ball of fire formed above his palms. He hurled it in the direction of the orc chasing Hort, and the fireball flew through the air, slamming into the beast. The orc waved its hands around in annoyance, making grunts and squeals as the flames quickly sizzled away. Although the fireball didn't do any real damage to the orc, it, fortunately, did give Hort just enough time to create some distance between them and catch up to Davion.

Hort and Davion drove on at full speed up the path, back into the woods, afraid to look back. A large rock the size of Davion's head went flying by his shoulder from a mighty throw of an orc, and it crashed to the ground in front of him. Without faltering, Helna swerved around it and kept going. When they could no longer hear the orcs' grunts and grumbles from behind them, Hort began to pull back on Orbek and slowed down. He looked back and came to a near stop when he saw that the road was clear. Davion did the same and trotted Helna over to him.

"What a rush! Ye alright, me boy?" Hort bellowed.

His adrenaline still burning off, Davion looked himself over, not entirely certain. "Looks like it, Uncle," he said after his self-examination. *Only five more days to the next town...* he thought sardonically to himself as he gave Helna a gentle nudge to resume their journey.

* * *

Two more long days of traveling had passed, and they had been lucky to avoid any more altercations with orcs or other dangers. It was early afternoon as they made their way along the dirt path formed by the many travelers before them. With the sun still overhead, the trees weren't offering much protection from the heat, so they carried on at a slow-but-steady pace, Davion with his hood drawn, covering his face, and Hort had removed some of his armor, including his helmet, trying not to overheat.

CHAPTER 9

Bringing the horse to a halt, Davion suddenly had a strange notion that they were being followed.

"What we waitin' fer?" Hort complained as Orbek stopped beside Helna.

Davion pulled his hood back to get a better look, letting it fall over his shoulders, then glared deep into the forest. As he did, he swore he heard a twig snap from the direction he was looking. "Over there." He bobbed his head slightly toward the brush. "I heard...something." Davion peered through the trees, searching for some sign that he was not losing his mind.

Squinting through the sun's rays, Hort tried to follow his gaze but saw and heard nothing. "Okullo dung!" he exclaimed, "Prolly jus' a squirrel. Would make good eatin', but we need ta cross the next river before nightfall. Now move on."

Davion figured that Hort was probably right, and, with a flick of the reins, they continued on their course.

After a few more hours, the sun moved over the trees between them and the lake, allowing some relief as the shade loomed over the trail. Through the foliage a few leagues ahead, Davion spotted the bank curve to the right, where it joined with the Norn River. He could hear its running waters, and even the smell in the air had changed and dampened.

Remembering the last river they had crossed, Davion grew anxious as he stuck close to Hort's side. Ready to put the dark and murky waters of the Norn River behind them, Davion gave a squeeze to the mare with his heels, eager to cross. Helna lifted her head, accelerating to a light trot, with Hort following closely behind on Orbek.

As they approached the river, Davion and Hort held back when they came upon a disheartening sight. The bridge to cross the river had been destroyed, and not just from time, but clearly sabotaged. Some wood planks and poles at each side of the river were all that remained. Marks from weapons nicked the wood where the bridge had once been attached, and the water flowed rapidly in between. Davion brought his horse to a halt and looked over to Hort, advancing up beside him.

"Dragon pong!" Hort cursed.

"What now?" Davion asked his uncle.

Sighing, Hort looked up the river and pulled at his beard. "Hmmm... We'll need ta find a shallow crossin' further down." He veered Orbek to the right and proceeded steadily. Davion joined him in pursuit.

The water darkened as they traveled east, and after nearly an hour along the riverbank, the Norn River began to narrow and become more shallow as the water broke and crashed over the rocks jutting out of its stream. Hort motioned to a possible spot where they could cross over, and they advanced to the river's edge. Helna began to waver when Davion nudged her to go forward into the water, but he steadied her with a gentle hand and the command, "Essa," to calm her.

Hort maneuvered Orbek past Davion. "Let me lead, me boy," he said to Davion, "Orbek has no fear." Orbek took a few steps into the murky river water and then stopped, rearing his head. "Come on, boy! Move it!" Hort gave him a swift kick, and Orbek began to walk forward again. Helna pulled in behind him and followed cautiously. They pushed through the flowing, dark water at a slow pace, their mounts faltering every few feet on slippery and uneven rocks underfoot but managing to regain their balance.

Halfway across the river, the water had reached halfway up Orbek's side, just touching Helna's underbelly. Orbek began to growl and stomp.

"What is it?" Hort asked him as though he could answer. The okullo then reared his front legs suddenly, causing Hort to fall

CHAPTER 9

back into the water with a loud splash. Orbek continued to buck and rear, yelping in fear as it clopped at the water. Something slithered near Hort, parting the water, and he saw its scaly hide. His eyes popped in alarm. "Basalures!" he shouted as he drew his axe. "MOVE!"

Panic-stricken, Davion kicked at Helna, "Iret!" and she stumbled, trying to get the rest of the way across the river over the slippery rocks. A basalure brushed across her legs, causing her to buck, but Davion held on tight. When Helna settled, Davion rolled his hands together and shouted, "*Ominus Lacarté!*" A fireball formed in his hands, and he threw it towards where a basalure was. The fireball whirred through the air, speeding toward the basalure, but just sizzled as it hit the water and went up in smoke.

"Jus' go!" Hort yelled to him while awkwardly swinging his axe at the waters. A screech emitted from the water, and bubbling, yellow blood surrounded the dwarf.

Pushing Helna to the other side, Davion looked back and saw more basalures approaching. He was feeling so helpless until he remembered a spell he had practiced in school. *Here goes nothing*, he thought. He swiftly grabbed a yellow powder from his pouch, made a series of hand gestures, then held out his palm outward to Hort, who was slashing away at the waters, and yelled, "*Veriness!*" The powder flew out, and a shimmering, translucent orb surrounded Hort and Orbek, causing the basalures to slam angrily against it, unable to pass.

"Come on!" he yelled to his uncle.

Grabbing Orbek's reins, Hort pulled his steed with all his might to get him through the waters. After only a few feet, Davion's protection spell weakened by the water against his fire magic. It shimmered around them, falling away as it quickly lost power. As soon as the protection fell away, a basalure whirled through the water, heading straight for Hort. Orbek leaped forward between

Hort and the basalure, burrowing its horns deep in the water, and thrust them into the basalure, piercing its skin and sending it writhing back into the black waters. Soon they were being joined by another basalure and another. The okullo bucked and reared and charged at their assailants, and Hort thrashed frantically at the water with his axe.

Davion tried to cast another protection spell, but it was even weaker than the last, only surrounding Hort. Suddenly, Orbek screamed an unholy sound and kicked at another basalure, striking it in the head. The basalure swam away, and the two of them made it out of the water onto the other side. An overly ambitious basalure followed them and began to crawl out of the water with its two front scaly, short legs, dragging the rest of its body behind. As the creature's gray beady eyes fixed on the okullo, it licked its slimy lips with its serpentine tongue and got ready to lunge.

Hort quickly grabbed his axe with both hands and swung it down. The axe went right through into the dirt, chopping off the basalure's head, and its body went limp. Looking back to the river, they could see the other basalures swimming near the shore before veering back downstream, swimming away into the darkness of the water.

Smiling, Hort looked at the dead basalure by his feet, then over to Davion and said, "Dinner?"

Davion took a deep breath and nodded, "I'll start a fire." He winked, relieved that it was over, and they all survived.

Hort grabbed Orbek's rein and started to walk him further from the water when he realized that Orbek was limping unbearably, and the okullo let out a squeal. He looked him over and saw a large bite in the okullo's hind leg, flesh torn and bleeding. His heart sank at the sight as he examined the wound closer. Davion jumped down off Helna to join him, fearing the worst.

CHAPTER 9

"No!" Hort gasped. "I'll be the son of an elf before I let them basalures be yer downfall!" he said to Orbek, stroking his back. "This okullo has saved me life more than a dozen times. Is there nothin' ta be done? Any magics ye may have up that slack sleeve o' yers? Please dunna' let me friend become wolf fodder!" Hort pleaded to Davion.

Davion sighed apprehensively. "I'm sorry, Uncle. I don't know that kind of magic," he replied. "I might have something we could try, but I'm not a healer," he reminded his uncle.

Hort nodded at him, comprehending, "Let's see what ye got," he said. "I might be able ta make a salve until we can get 'im ta the Trader's Post."

Davion grabbed a small package wrapped in a suede cloth from his saddlebag along with a flask of water. Bringing it back over to Orbek, he unraveled the package, revealing some thin green leaves inside. "Mindletwine," he said to Hort, who took the leaves from him. "It might help."

Hort took his flask and poured some water over the wound. He then took some of the leaves, crushed them in his hand between his fingers, and added some of the water to the leaves.

"Let me see what else ye got," he told Davion, who handed over the pouch from his waist. After a few minutes of working the water into the leaves, he reached into the mage's pouch and pulled out a strange-looking bean, then ground that into the leaf mixture as well, turning it into a paste. Hort spread the paste over Orbek's wound while Davion held him steady. The okullo snorted and stomped his foot, agitated and sore as Hort pressed the paste into the crevices of the open wound. Then he ran into the Sacred Forest and grabbed a couple of sizeable green and red leaves from a ten-foot plant with vibrant blue flowers shooting upward. They wrapped nicely around Orbek's leg, and Hort secured them with some straps of leather.

"I'm not sure how much this will help," he said dishearteningly, "but I'm hopin' twill be enough ta get us ta the Trader's Post. There should be a healer there." Hort brushed his hand over Orbek lovingly while stifling back tears. "Ye'll be alright, old friend."

"You'll have to ride with me," Davion told him. "He won't be able to support your weight."

Hort nodded and pet Orbek gently along his neck. "If it'll help me Orbek, I'll ride a blastit horse." He gave his friend a firm pat on his hide then headed back toward the dead basalure. "Now," Hort said, rubbing his hands together eagerly, trying to stay positive, "time fer dinner!"

* * *

Sitting high on Helna behind Davion was Hort, arms crossed and head bobbing with his chin tucked against his chest as he attempted an afternoon nap. They were on the final day of their journey, the attack from the Norn River well behind them, and were finally getting close to the Trader's Post.

The brown mare hung her head low, exhausted from the sweltering heat. Her long mane tangled and matted with perspiration. Flicking her tail back and forth at the bugs attacking her flank, she whacked Hort against his leg. The sleeping dwarf muttered something, shifted in the saddle, and then nodded back off.

After a few more hours, Davion could see in the distance the lake narrowing where it ended and ran into the Emerald River. From there, past the Trader's Post, the river would take them all the way to the Gorén Mountains where their home, Lochlann, lay. Eager for their current journey to be over, a warm meal, and a bath, Davion kicked Helna into a fast trot.

"Whoa!" Hort shouted as he was jolted awake. He grabbed onto Davion's waist to keep his balance. "Ye could warn me 'fore doing that, ye know?"

Davion chuckled, "Sorry, Uncle. The Emerald River is up ahead."

Hort peeked around Davion's shoulder, holding on tightly, afraid of falling off. The horse's movements were so unnatural to him, and he already had bruises and a sore rump to show for it. Davion had made promises of it getting better as he got more used to the horse's movements, but Hort didn't ever want to get used to riding a horse. His okullo moved very differently, and he prayed to Jayenne that Orbek would recover. He praised every moment they stopped for a break, and he could climb off the beast.

Hort looked back to see how Orbek was doing. Trailing behind, tied to Helna's saddle with a long rope, the okullo wasn't looking too swift and was struggling greatly with the trot. Flies were swarming its wound, and its rancid smell was noticeable even to them. It was most certainly infected at this point, and Hort was losing hope that Orbek was going to survive if they couldn't find a healer soon.

"Look," Hort pointed past Davion, "there's the bridge." Quickly he clung back on to Davion as he felt his balance falter. "Stupid horse," Davion heard him mutter.

The mare was panting hard to keep in the trot and wavered her head to the side, pleading for Davion to let her stop. "Easy there, girl." Davion comforted her with a soft pat on the neck. "Just a little further." She maintained her trot with visions of the cool river water up ahead. Orbek, hardly using his rear leg now, hobbled clumsily towards the river as well, eager for a break.

Hort and Davion remained mounted while Orbek and Helna took a quick drink to refresh themselves, then they led them over the wooden bridge across the Emerald River. On the other side were several small hills with a worn path leading over them to the town. The vegetation quickly became more sparse as they went until it was nothing but dirt and rock. After climbing over another hill, they could finally see the Trader's Post on the other side in a large open plain with the shores of Miran Lake only a short walk to the south. It didn't have great stone buildings or walls, no parapets and towers, but was simple with its wooden fences and gates and a few buildings inside.

Everything in the town was new due to being rebuilt over and over between attacks from orcs, trolls, and occasionally even dragons. Most of the traders were lined up selling wares out of the backs of their wagons, and several locals had rudimentary stands. Being a human-run village, the guards wore the blue and gray armor of the king's army, but many races were walking through its dirt streets. It was a neutral town for all races, although everyone always remained on edge, never knowing who to trust. It was the one place where everyone could come together and benefit from the skills and goods of the other races with zero tolerance of violence between them. However, even though they weren't forbidden, the drow would scarcely appear in the town, knowing how unwelcomed they would be.

Entering through the wooden gates, Davion nodded to the guards eyeballing them as they walked past. They ignored his nod and turned their attention back to the trees. Once again, they had no intention of staying any longer than necessary and planned to leave again as soon as they found a healer for Orbek and got a good night's rest. However, they found that there were no healers in the Trader's Post that day, and Orbek's infection was only intensifying. Hort cleaned the wound the best he could but was preparing himself for the worst. He knew Orbek wouldn't last more than a few more days without help.

CHAPTER 9

"Hang in there, fella," Hort said, giving Orbek's neck a tight squeeze. He sniffled and stood, wiping a tear from his cheek. "Bloody dust in here gettin' ta me," Hort lied when he saw Davion watching him. Then, with a heavy heart, Hort left Orbek in the stalls and went with Davion to the Traveler's Inn to get settled for the night. He prayed silently to Jayenne that Orbek would still be there in the morning.

CHAPTER TEN

DESTINY

*T*wilight was approaching as Pavula returned to the den with her brethren, each proudly carrying large pieces of boar back to display for Lupé Caelis, who came out to greet their return. Pavula dragged most of the boar pieces behind her on a travois she had formed with vines and branches.

When near enough to the den, she called out, "Mother, look! You won't believe what happened!" She dropped the travois and kept walking toward Lupé Caelis. "The wolves and I were running out of places to search, unable to find any prey for hours and hours, but then, there in the bushes..."

'*What have you done?!*' interrupted Lupé Caelis angrily.

Stopping in her tracks, Pavula looked in confusion at her mother, for the first time recognizing the anger on her face, and didn't understand. She looked back to the scattered remnants of the boar and back to her mother, bewildered why she wasn't proud of her. All the wolves tore and dragged pieces of flesh from the travois, clearly not unhappy about their kill as their mother seemed to be.

'*That boar should not have been able to come through the barrier,*' the Great Wolf clarified. '*So, I ask you again, what have you done?*'

"I thought you would be pleased!" retorted Pavula. "I used the skills you taught me, and we will be well fed. I don't understand what's wrong."

Taking a deep breath, Lupé Caelis continued to stare into Pavula's eyes. *'I sensed a break in the barrier,'* she explained. *'The break has allowed this beast and others to cross into our lands. Did you break through the barrier?'*

Pavula looked past Lupé Caelis, trying to think what she meant. "I never crossed the barrier," she replied, "but..." She remembered the resistance she felt when searching for prey through the ground. "Oh, no!" Pavula gasped, realizing it was her that did indeed cause a tear in her mother's barrier. "I didn't mean to, Mother! I was just looking for food with earth magic. Is the barrier gone?"

The Great Wolf shook her head. *'Not gone,'* she replied, *'but broken. I will need to seal it again, but it is not safe in our woods anymore.'*

"I'm sorry, Mother. I didn't mean to," Pavula said earnestly. "There was something else too," she said, remembering her search past the barrier. "When I was looking for food, I could hear many voices in the distance near a lake. Some were singing, others talking and yelling. It was a strange place, and none of them were making any sense."

'You heard a village, I assume,' Lupé Caelis said. *'They were most likely speaking another language.'* She walked past Pavula grabbing a boar leg with her jaws, and then headed towards the river. *'Come now. Let's eat before it's too late for you to light a fire,'* she added, attempting to change the subject.

Pavula joined her mother, gathering twigs and broken branches on the way to the river, thankful she would not have to eat raw meat tonight. The wolves hungrily tore at the boar flesh, snapping at each other over the choice meats, and Lupé Caelis kept the leg for herself, swallowing large chunks at a time.

Pavula filled a pit surrounding a large flat stone with the twigs and branches along with some dried leaves and then placed a chunk of the boar meat in the center on the stone.

'It is time for you to find the final spirit; the fire spirit,' Lupé Caelis said while ripping off another piece of flesh. 'Open yourself up to your surroundings and seek out the heat nearby; from the air, from the ground and rocks, from everything.'

As always, Pavula did as she was instructed. Sitting with her legs crossed in front of the firepit she had built, she closed her eyes and began to feel for the heat, like Lupé Caelis had described. Once she could sense all the sources of heat around her, she nodded to her mother. This was not her first attempt, but she had not yet been able to make the connection.

'Good. Now, pull it together, into the leaves and twigs, focus all of it into one spot.'

Pavula did. She could feel the air around her chill as she pushed the heat towards the firepit. Smoke began to rise from the twigs and leaves where she aimed it—progress from the last lesson. Several minutes passed, and she was starting to have trouble maintaining the stream of heat, but there was still no fire.

'PUSH!' came Lupé Caelis' voice in her head.

Pavula summoned all her willpower and heaved a heatwave toward the twigs in one big motion. She opened her eyes, looking to the fire but saw only smoke. "I can't." She said, throwing a stone at the pit with her mind. "I don't know why fire is so hard. I just can't do it," she pouted.

Sensing the energy Pavula had exerted, Lupé Caelis decided not to push her any further today. She tipped her ebony nose down to the leaves and breathed softly over them. A small flame emerged from the leaves and then spread quickly to the twigs and branches until the fire was roaring.

'You will,' Lupé Caelis replied encouragingly.

While Pavula's meat cooked in the fire, her mind kept churning over the events of the day, the voices repeating in her mind, calling to her. She could not shake the feeling, the *need* to see the source of the sounds she had heard. It was consuming her.

"I want to see the village," Pavula stated after a long silence, poking at the meat with a stick. She waited for her mother to say something, but nothing came. Finally, she looked up to the Great Wolf, who was staring down, watching her silently. "I want to see the people," she urged.

Lupé Caelis slowly glanced overtop of Pavula into the forest beyond and then tilted her head to the sky at the setting sun. *'It is time to put out the fire.'*

"The village!" Pavula pressed, frustrated.

Glaring back down at her elf cub, Lupé Caelis simply said, 'No,' then began licking her paws and grooming her face from her meal. *'You are not ready,'* she added after she finished grooming her paws.

Pavula fumed inside but didn't say anything else. She didn't care what her mother said; she believed she was ready and she was going to see that village. Nothing had pulled at her heart more than now. She couldn't explain it but felt it deep in her soul that she had to find this village and soon.

* * *

The following morning Pavula bided her time, repairing her dagger and playing coy with her mother as they went about their daily routine. She went through the motions of the morning, watching impatiently as the sun rose high into the sky. Words of no importance came blubbering out of her mouth in nervous nonsensical jabber as she tried to keep her thoughts to herself and away from her mother's prying mind. Even though she knew how much she was rambling, Pavula couldn't seem to stop herself and hoped her mother didn't find it suspicious.

Waiting out the sun for the Great Wolf's afternoon nap, Pavula grew nervous as she knew the time was quickly approaching. Never having betrayed her mother before, she was overwhelmed with both guilt and excitement—not knowing what her consequences would be. She didn't want to betray her, but she had to know more; she had to connect with the village again and learn all she could.

The sun had passed its peak when Pavula watched as Lupé Caelis' eyes grew heavy, and the Great Wolf stretched out her limbs before strolling back towards the den. Pavula's leg started to shake nervously as she watched her leave and waited until she was completely out of sight. She looked around at the other wolves, who were all lying in the grass, basking in the sun, letting themselves also be lulled to sleep.

This is it! Pavula thought nervously. She stood slowly, trying hard to act natural while casually grabbing her dagger and spear that were conveniently planted against a nearby tree and made her way awkwardly northwest toward the trees. Once concealed within the brush, she began to walk faster and faster until she broke out into a jog. Adrenaline was coursing through her as she continued to increase her pace.

Pavula had been running a couple of hours when a strange sense suddenly overwhelmed her. There was a force pulling at her, tearing her away from her current path. Looking around, she could see no one and heard nothing, but the feeling was still there—and strong. This time, it was coming through the forest from the west, close to where she had sensed the village, but not as far north. Her mind told her to keep heading for the village connection, but her heart was being yanked in the other direction. *I have to know...*

Deviating westward, Pavula stayed close along the riverbank but trailed through the trees and shrubs to remain concealed. Her momentum increased as she felt the sensation get stronger and closer. She continued west, jumping over stumps and through the trees and bushes. Her heart was racing fast in her chest, pounding in tune with her feet pattering against the forest floor. She had been running now for a few hours, exhausted, but too driven to rest, and had stopped recognizing the forest from her usual hunting grounds some time ago. But she didn't care. She continued to run, lured towards the unknown energy she felt tugging at her chest.

Suddenly, Pavula slammed hard against an invisible wall and fell backward to the ground. She detected something forcing her back. *The barrier*, she realized, *I'm at the edge of our territory.* Standing back up, she strained against the force, pushing her hands out in front of her, waving them back and forth over the wall, when she suddenly sensed something in the distance.

Stretching tall, straining to see through the foliage, she could see a worn pathway several yards away, covered in an eerie fog. On it was a brown horse with a beautiful white mane and another foreign beast she didn't recognize, each carrying a passenger. The passenger in front was tall and held the reins tightly, wearing some sort of brown garment that covered his head and flowed down to his feet in the stirrups. Behind him, on the other steed, was a much smaller but more robust figure. The afternoon sun reflected off the short one's metal armor as she strained to get a better look.

Suddenly, the first driver stopped the horse, causing the man behind to stop as well and say something that Pavula couldn't make out. The tall man reached his arms up slowly and drew back his hood, letting it fall across his shoulders, and then glared directly toward where Pavula was hidden, his eyes peering to see through the shadowed forest.

Pavula's heart stopped as she dropped briskly to the ground, a twig snapping under her. She shivered in fear, trying not to move. The figure bobbed his head in her direction and said something to his companion. The short man also turned to look in Pavula's direction but did not focus his eyes near her position. He mumbled something to the other rider, then they both turned and, with a flick of the reins, continued on their course.

Pavula realized she had stopped breathing and exhaled an immense breath as her heart throbbed fiercely in her chest. *He looked right at me! That man! That... That...* She peered at them as they trotted off, and the familiarity of the rider electrified her, everything manifesting before her. Even through the fog and foliage, she could see and sense the same unmistakable feeling that led her to him—she knew. *That was the ghost... No, the vision! Did he see me?*

'No.' Lupé Caelis' mind-voice hit her loud and clear, causing her to whirl around, swallowing a scream. Lupé Caelis loomed over her, looking very upset. 'No, he did not,' the Great Wolf repeated sternly, answering her self-asked query. 'What are you doing, my child?' Her voice boomed in Pavula's mind.

"Mother, I saw him. The vision!" Pavula pointed in the direction of the riders, looking to her mother expectantly.

Lupé Caelis lifted her head and stared off in the direction of the riders, but she could not see anyone there, only what had been in Pavula's mind. She growled a soft sigh. 'They are not really there,' she told Pavula. 'You were looking through the phantom realm again. It is hard to know how far they are from here or if they are even there at all.'

Looking back through the foliage, Pavula's heart sank when she couldn't see a road anymore. All that was there were more trees

CHAPTER 10

and bushes. Pavula pouted at her mother, looking up to her with sad cub eyes, dropping to her knees.

"Mother, please! I must find him! I have to know who he is!" She clasped her hands out before her, pleading from her heart that Lupé Caelis would understand.

Setting her flank down in the grass, Lupé Caelis glared at Pavula, her heart aching with the knowledge that she wanted to leave her. Nevertheless, she knew this day would come. She prepared for it since the elven baby was bestowed upon her those many years ago. *Was it time? Was she ready?* She searched the elf's eyes deeply, desiring to find the answers, but knew it wasn't that simple. Swallowing the emotional lump building in her throat, she looked to the west then back to the pleading child. *No. She is no longer a child. She can't be if she is to do this alone.* She licked a tear away that had traced down Pavula's cheek.

'Lupé Pavula,' she began formally, aspiring to suppress her emotions, *'you are not, nor have ever been a prisoner here. I knew the day would come when your fate would be shown to you.'*

Pavula stood up in disbelief.

'Not so fast,' Lupé Caelis continued. *'I still believe you are not ready. You have not even discovered all of the spirits yet, and there is still much more training that should be done. However...'* she paused, suppressing her affections. *'You have a destiny, Lupé Pavula. We may not know what it involves yet, but I won't keep you from discovering it. So, if you truly believe this is it, that finding this boy is where you must be—and only you can know this for certain—then I support your decision to leave.'*

As Lupé Caelis finished her words, Pavula saw out of the corner of her eye something glowing behind her. She turned around, facing a shimmering transparent hole in the barrier, just tall and wide enough for her to pass. Pavula turned back to Lupé Caelis and flung her arms around her neck, holding her tight.

"Thank you, Mother!" Tears ran from her eyes into the Great Wolf's mane. "I will come home soon! I love you so much! Thank you... Thank you!"

Bowing her great head over Pavula's shoulder, she nuzzled the elf against her and clamped her eyes shut, knowing this was the last time she would ever hold her.

'*Please be careful, Lupé Pavula. Remember always what I taught you.*' Lupé Caelis hesitantly lifted her head, and Pavula stood back.

"Don't worry, Mother. I will never forget. And I will be back soon with stories to share with you!" Stepping through the hole in the barrier, she conveyed silently with her mind, '*I'll see you soon!*' Then, the hole shut quickly behind her, and, looking back, she could no longer see her mother on the other side.

No, you won't, Lupé Caelis sighed to herself. *I only hope I did enough by you, Great Spirit.* She watched Pavula squint in an attempt at seeing her mother one last time, but she would not see her again, even though only three feet away.

Pavula touched her lips with the tips of her fingers, then raised them to the sky, waving in the direction she sensed her mother still watching from. Realizing she was now in the open and no longer protected, she crouched behind a bush and then cautiously leapt north behind the trees and shrubs, letting her senses guide her.

Lupé Caelis watched as Pavula disappeared into the forest beyond. *Goodbye, my child. May Jayenne guide you and Kyrash keep you safe.* She hung her head low and then somberly returned to her pack.

CHAPTER ELEVEN

TROLLS

*T*aking a long sip of his ale, Davion observed the minstrel's performance in the corner of the tavern, whose selection of music was of a dispirited tale unfamiliar to Davion. The melody was slow and forlorn, earning the minstrel some foes in his audience. He was a young human boy of maybe thirteen or fourteen, dressed in bright colors with a sack full of instruments by his side. A glass smashed against the wall next to him by the fireplace mantle, and drunken curses were hollered from the crowd. It was only lunchtime, but that didn't seem to matter much at the Trader's Post as many were already overindulging in their drinks.

"Oiy now, boys! We'll 'ave nun of that now in 'ere!" shouted the tavern's barmaid, a dwarf named Esla, over the commotion. "Come lad, givus a 'appy tune!"

Nearly falling off his short stool, the young minstrel fumbled with his lute after being startled by the glass. Then, he sighed as he recomposed himself. Commencing with a few humdrum notes, he managed to strum his fingers up to speed and achieved an upbeat melody about an old drunken king. The crowd cheered and raised their steins above their heads, clanking them with fellow friends.

Davion shook his head at the audience's performance and turned back to his meal. He looked at the mixture of mush that slightly resembled a stew, Today's Special, and toyed at it with the tip of his spoon, trying to make out what type of meat was boiled into it.

Hort was convinced that a healer would arrive at any moment, that there were always healers coming through here—except when you actually needed one, it seemed. So, he was out harassing the locals to inquire when one would arrive while he gathered some more provisions for their next long trek.

A small candle resting on Davion's round, wooden table flickered in the dim tavern. Davion wasn't sure if the horrid smell was coming from his food or his dingy surroundings but decided it was probably both. Closing his eyes and attempting not to inhale, he took a large spoonful of the slop and swallowed it quickly, chewing only when necessary.

"'Ow's about more ale, lad?" asked the barmaid hovering next to Davion. He looked up at her and, shaking his head, held up his hand to prevent her from pouring. The ale was inexpensive even for a poor man, but it wasn't much for the taste buds either, and Davion could not stomach another swig.

"This will do just fine, madam," he replied after swallowing his mouthful of stew.

"Madam?" she laughed. "I ain't 'erd that in a long time. Jus' call me Esla, lad." She then turned and left him in peace.

As hungry as Davion was, he couldn't stomach the stew either and pushed it out of the way. He straightened his cape and robe, then stood and sought the barmaid. Esla caught his eye and headed back over to him. Flicking a coin in the air to her, she grabbed it effortlessly and smiled her blackened crooked teeth at him. Her hair was tousled loosely on her head with strands shagging everywhere in one big mess, and her bright red lipstick

CHAPTER 11

was smeared outside the lines of her thin lips. Even in the dimness of the tavern, Davion could see the gray entangled in her brown thatch. She slipped the coin into the front pocket of her tattered garb then pushed one of the rebellious locks out of her face. "Thanky, lad."

Davion leaned in toward her so she would hear him over the commotion of the intoxicated crowd and asked, "Are there any rooms available here?"

Esla thought for a moment, then looked in his eyes with her cheery soul. "Aye," she replied, "buh nigh if yer lookin' fer anythin' nice. There jus' be the one lef', but tis yers." She leaned in slyly, closer to Davion. "Dat 'andsome dwarf I seen ye wit' earlier, he be stayin' too?" Davion nodded, and Esla grinned widely. "Not that I's one ta' gossip now, but we don't always get many fine dwarfs like 'im in 'ere. I seen 'im in 'ere a few times now. Der be some other dwarves 'ere days back causin' all sortsa trouble. 'Ad em too much o' dat fine ale, as dey do, ye knows. So jus' ye keep dat one o' yers in check, or he'll have me ta answer to." She smiled and friskily straightened her skirts with the last statement.

Davion grinned uncomfortably at Esla and replied, "I will."

As Davion finished his words, the door to the tavern flung open, and a gust of wind flew in, extinguishing the candles that rested on the nearby tables as Hort fumbled over the threshold. Everyone gawked as the dwarf looked up with blood running down his cheekbone from somewhere under his oversized dented helmet, caking into his thick beard. The dingy feathers of an arrow sticking out of his back could be seen over his stout shoulder, and he clutched the door frame for support. The whole tavern glared at the dwarf, squinting their eyes against the brilliant light streaming through the entrance.

Davion ran to Hort's side, assisting him to stand upright, but Hort jerked his elbow proudly from the boy's grasp and gruffly spoke a single word, "Trolls," then the alarm bells of the Trader's Post were heard.

All the men in the pub sprang to their feet, grabbing weapons where they had rested them, and headed for the door, nearly trampling over the beaten dwarf. Davion held the arrow and tore it out of his uncle's back with a quick yank.

"Baccat!" he cursed in pain.

Davion hastily went back to the table to grab his belongings, securing his dagger to his belt strap and snatching his staff.

"Davion, me boy! Come join the fight!" Hort turned and headed limply back out the tavern door. "I'll watch yer back!"

"And I yours, Uncle!" Davion declared as he darted up to Hort and patted him on the shoulder. The dwarf cursed the stars as the friendly pat knocked his helm down over his eyes and stung his wound. "Maybe I'll get to try a new spell!" Davion added nervously excited as they both made their way out toward the commotion.

"Eh?" Hort adjusted his helm and wobbled to keep up. "New spell? I still say what's wrong with usin' a good ol' axe or sword?" he teased Davion, like old times. "That's where the real blows come from. But no, ye gotta make it all fancy with yer swirlin' lights and flashy tricks..." Hort's blabbering was snuffed out by the sounds of swords clashing, shouting of man and beast, and several screams from women and children up ahead.

Davion rushed up the path, over the hill towards the northern entrance, passing several small shops along the way where the shopkeepers were gathering up their exposed goods frantically. As he reached the top of the hill, he saw the trolls and several of the tavern men, among others, battling below. One man already lay lifeless, tossed to the side of the path with blood staining the dirt.

"Uncle Hort, come on!" he bellowed back to the dwarf fumbling up the hill.

On the battlefield were three troll warriors, an oracle, and their chieftain, all at least seven feet tall. The trolls' bald greenish skins were beading with sweat, and their tattered animal skin pelts bulged with monstrous muscles. Some men were running toward the woods, ready to attack hidden trolls that were shooting arrows at them. Meanwhile, four men were battling the chieftain, who held them off with two large swords nearly the length of a man's height and at least an inch thick.

Three guards had surrounded one of the warriors and were taking turns slashing at the monstrous beast. One lucky man jabbed the troll warrior from behind, causing it to howl in agony as it fell to its knees, and then another man hurriedly lopped off its head with one fierce hack. The body of the troll dropped in slow motion, its head already rolling on the ground. As the corpse hit the earth, the impact stirred the dirt, surrounding it in a cloud of dust. The men cheered and then hastily ran to aid their comrades.

The oracle raised his crooked staff, garnished with large ornate bird feathers and beads, and began waving it around in the air. Magical green and yellow swirls trailed behind it, and Davion scrambled down the path to get closer. The clouds above crackled with thunder, and Davion realized the oracle was preparing to cast a fatal lightning spell on the town's defenders.

Panicked and determined to stop the spell, Davion began waving his hands in a circular motion in front of him and murmured, "*Ominous lacarté.*" A ball of red and orange fire formed between his palms, and pulling energy from within, he shot the fireball toward the oracle, disrupting its cast. However, the attack was blocked by a forcefield that surrounded the troll.

"Blastit!" he cursed as the oracle looked up at him with annoyance flaming in its large red eyes. Davion quickly tried to remember the words to bring down the shield while he dodged a red firebolt from the oracle. *Annas? No, that's not it. Baccat!*

Not yet feeling confident in his staff melee skills, he instead grabbed instinctively for his dagger. He rolled to the ground as he dodged another bolt, then jumped to his feet and darted towards the troll with his dagger held high, roaring in attack. Reaching out his free hand when he got within two paces of the monster, he shouted, "*Annalsa!*" and the field around the oracle shimmered and died.

The troll bulwarked Davion's melee attack, blocking it with his staff, and then pushed Davion backward with it. The young fighter-mage attacked again, striking at the troll with his dagger, unsuccessfully, while dodging a series of assaults from the troll's staff until one landed, bashing callously into his side before he could evade. The blow knocked Davion several feet, causing him to lose hold of the dagger. His frail body plummeted to the earth, hitting his head on the cobblestones, distorting him momentarily. Faintly, he heard Hort cursing, followed by a war cry.

The sound of Hort's axe being deflected off the wooden staff bucked in Davion's mind as he dazedly looked back towards the commotion. Hort kept swinging and chipping at the magical staff, unable to get by the oracle's blocks. Davion then heard unholy words being chanted by the troll.

No! he tried to call out but did not produce a sound. Suddenly, he saw Hort flying backward through the air, a red beam of light glowing from his torso. Hort's body smashed against a towering boulder, then he crashed several feet to the ground and lay motionless, toppled face down in the dirt.

Davion jumped to his feet, anger swelling up inside of him as he grabbed the staff from his back. He waved the staff back and forth with all the power he could muster, and his eyes began to glow red while he chanted, "*Ominus unasceiry... Ominus unasceiry... Ominus unasceiry...*" A blue ball covered in large flames grew stronger and larger at the tip of his staff. With a final, "*OMINUS*

UNASCEIRY!" he thrust the staff's tip forward, and the fireball bolted toward the oracle.

The green hulk raised its staff and fist to block but failed as the burning flame tore into its flesh. The oracle let out an unnerving scream as its flesh burned away, turning it black and flaky, continuing to burn down through to the bones. The oracle's inflamed and rapidly deteriorating body fell to its knees, then forward on its hands as its scream died out, and all that was left of it were ashes.

Davion stumbled forward, looking at Hort's motionless body before he, himself, collapsed to the ground. Darkness was narrowing and blurring his sight as it rapidly overtook him.

* * *

Drip... Drip...Drip... Davion raised his hand slowly to his forehead, resting his palm above his brow while lying with his eyelids sealed in blackness. *Drip... Drip... Drip...* He moaned softly before letting his elbow fall back onto the mattress and placed his hand over his chest. A frightful pain drilled into his right side, throbbing with every movement and breath he made, and he feared his ribs had been broken.

Thunder crashed in the distance, and Davion slowly opened his eyes as the smell of stale bread reached his nostrils. He stared at the wooden planks of the ceiling and pushed himself up onto his elbows, wincing in agony while clutching at his bandaged ribs. While his sight adjusted to the dim room, he tried to figure out where he was. The last thing he remembered was seeing a strange woman with long wild hair. *No, that was a dream,* he realized. *The trolls... I was in a battle.*

Inside the room against each wall sat two musty cots, one with Davion, the other empty. They contained dirty sheets covering thin hay mattresses with old, scratchy gray quilts, one draped over Davion and the other at the foot of the adjacent bed. Strands of straw from a worn pillow pierced through into Davion's scalp. On the far wall sat a wobbly, three-legged table with a burning candle and a copper basin of dirty water. There was no rug on the dull floorboards or any sort of decor to make one feel at home. He also spotted a pot in the middle of the floor that held water from a leaky roof of a storm not-quite-passed, the source of the dripping that was pounding in his head.

Davion sat up and put his bare feet on the floorboards. The blanket fell down off his chest, and he lightly touched the bandages that wrapped around his entire torso with his fingertips. The bandages were clean and white; no blood seemed to be showing through, which gave Davion some relief. Other than the dressings, Davion realized he had been stripped down to his undergarment and bathed. As he maneuvered to stand up, his foot hit a metal plate on the floor.

Bread and cheese were sitting on the plate with a flask of wine next to it, and Davion suddenly realized how famished he was. He reached down and grabbed the plate while searing with pain from the movement, but it seemed to be lessening as he tore at the bread hungrily with his teeth. Although it was hard and chewy, it felt good in his stomach. The cheese also tasted a little old, but it too was edible. The wine tasted refreshing and fulfilling as he gulped it down thirstily, feeling a little strength return. *I'm back at the inn*, he realized finally as his thoughts began to clear. *We must have won against the trolls. I hope Uncle Hort is okay.* He glanced at the empty bed across the room, worried.

Davion put the plate back down on the floor, and it thudded softly against the wood. Looking around, he found his robe hanging on a nail by the table at the far end, and his few belongings of his pouches and dagger were resting against one of

CHAPTER II

the table legs, his staff against the wall. He tested his strength and pushed himself up off the bed and onto his feet, wavering over to his things. After dressing, he turned around as the door opened and smiled when he saw his uncle entering.

"Welcome back, me boy!" Hort said excitedly, seeing him up and dressed.

Davion finished fastening his belt and attaching his pouches, then walked back to his bed to fasten his boots. "How long was I out?"

Hort stroked his beard and replied, "About two days, I'm afraid. Was startin' ta think ye'd never wake." He frowned as he saw Davion clutch his side. "The doctor laiden said ye nearly broke them ribs but was lucky. Jus' some bad bruises, says she. Does ye feel like gettin' outta this room? There be a storm outside, but we can get Esla and Finlay to whip ye up somethin'."

Davion flushed, suddenly remembering Orbek. "So a healer arrived?" he asked hesitantly.

"Nay a healer. Jus' a physician." Hort replied.

A healer, being of the magics, heals and binds wounds at an advanced rate. Whereas a physician holds no magical powers, requiring medicines and procedures with long healing times—if the required medicines could even be acquired at all.

"In time?"

"Aye," Hort nodded. "Orbek's infection should be goin' away, but he still be in a bad way."

"That's great news, Uncle," Davion said, smiling at him. "I'm sure he'll be better soon. And thanks for helping me with that oracle. He may have killed me had you not."

"Dragon pong!" Hort exclaimed, waving his hand in dismissal of the theory, "It was ye who got 'im. I didna' do a thing!" He patted Davion gently on the shoulder. "Ye ready? Sounds like the rain's lettin' up." Hort headed out the door, leaving it ajar behind him.

Davion ran his hands through his short brown hair in an attempt to look halfway presentable, then followed Hort down the hall and steps to the tavern below.

It was quiet in the tavern, somewhere between lunch and dinner, and there was an old man hunched over the bar counter, drinking peacefully. The only other folks in the place were Esla, the tavern wench, Finlay, the cook who was preparing the kitchen for the dinner crowd, and a young girl, no older than eight, mopping the floor by the fireplace. The girl looked up at Davion with the large gloomy eyes of a child lost and caught in a war she doesn't understand. Davion nodded politely to her, and then she resumed her mopping. He sighed, watching her.

Unfortunately, most of the children shared a similar sorrow as the innocent girl. In small towns, such as the Trader's Post, and desolate areas like the one Davion grew up in, there was little protection from the attacks of the trolls and orcs. The streets at the post usually stayed empty except for the travelers and the merchants trying to earn a living. Women wore the darkest cloth draped over their heads in mourning of loved ones lost to the battles. He knew that the king of Roco, King Lyson, sent out as many troops as he could spare to these small outposts and surrounding human towns, but it was never enough. They were usually sent unprepared and too young to have the experience to handle what would cross their paths.

"Ah, Davion da great sorcerer!" called Esla, raising her hands in the air toward him. "Good ta' see ye up 'n about! Der anythin' I can git fer ye?"

Davion let her give him a friendly embrace, trying not to show his pain, and patted her nicely on the back before replying full of sincerity, "I thank you, madam, for the bread and wine. I appreciate the offer."

"Dunna' mention it, lad. But, ye must be starvin' after havin' slept so long. Why, look at ye! Skin 'n bones, ye are!" Esla pinched Davion playfully in the arm. "Tell ye what. I might 'av a lil' somethin' I can spare ye, and I won't take no fer an answer!"

Smiling kindly to his hostess, Davion nodded in agreement, "Thank you very much."

Esla gave Hort a flirtatious wink before disappearing to the kitchen, and Davion and Hort took a couple of seats at a nearby table and settled in. Davion found it odd that Esla was paying him so much kindness.

"Where are all the other warriors?" Davion inquired to Hort.

Hort looked down, frowning genuinely. "Many didna' make it. And I'm afraid there's more trouble. Those weren't the only trolls in the area, and they've gone off ta find the rest. A lot of men have been dyin' since ye've been snoozin', most of them guards." He looked off into the distance, staring blankly at the far wall.

Davion could sense that Hort was holding something back. "What is it, Uncle?" He asked. "Do you want to go join the hunt?"

Looking back to Davion, Hort shrugged under his armor. "Tis not that. Rumor tis they're not just killin' them elves and humans no more. We got word that a band of orcs attacked Lochlann." He paused for a moment. "Our people won, of course," he said proudly. "I bet they saw 'em comin' and slaughtered 'em like a bunch of hogs before an autumn feast. Why I bet they didna' know what hit 'em. Blastit orcs!"

After several moments of silence, Davion asked cautiously, "Do you know if anyone was hurt in the battle?"

With a loud sigh, Hort replied, "Alas, no."

The Traveler's Inn was moderately filling up with guests of all sorts as dinner time drew near, and the same minstrel was in the corner beside the fireplace, tuning his lute. A couple of dwarves walked by, nodding to Hort as they passed. Davion even noticed a small group had taken to a back corner. Their leather hoods were drawn over their faces, but there was no doubt in Davion's mind that they were elves from their attire and stature.

"There ye go, loves," Esla said, setting down two steins of ale. "It'll jus' be a few now. Finlay's got somethin' special for ye." She gave Davion a friendly wink before heading off to tend to the other guests.

"I sure am hungry!" Hort exclaimed while tapping his round belly.

After Esla was out of earshot, Davion said, "Esla is being very kind. I feel somewhat bad taking her up on her hospitality with nothing to offer in return."

Hort stared at Davion, who was watching the minstrel set up his stool in the corner. "She said somethin' ta me while ye was restin'. She thinks ye're goin' ta be some kind of hero. Said she has a sense for these things. I didna' pay much mind ta it, but methinks she believes ye'll gossip up a right word of her, which, comin' from a hero, would bring in many a purse. That'd be me guess anyway."

Davion laughed, "Yeah, right! Me, a hero. That'll be the day. I can't even cast a decent spell without going into a coma for two days." He paused while turning back to Hort. "You know, I'm surprised to see a bard playing in small towns like this, even if he is inexperienced."

"Bard? That boy?" Hort huffed. "That's Gett. He jus' be a minstrel in fancy garb. If there's magic in that boy, then I'm the son of an elf!" He smirked, then clanked mugs with Davion. "To our journey home! May we find all ta be well and be greeted with more ale!" Hort took a long swig from his stein, and Davion took a quick sip before placing it down.

Commotion stirred as Gett began playing an upbeat tune that nearly everyone knew, and several of the crowd even joined in, singing with their husky, off-tune voices. It was a popular song that wayward travelers and warriors would sing around campfires called Distant Lover. To Davion's surprise, even Hort joined in, waving his mug in the air.

(To hear this song online, go to https://youtu.be/KO1_5yfNQ4c)

Been on the road for several months, and I can't wait to see
My lover, who is back at home, still waiting up for me.
Her hair, like silk, flows down her back and curves around her frame.
She'll look at me with starlit eyes and whisper out my name.

It's a long way home. It's a long way home,
But I know someone's waiting, waiting there for me.
It's a long way home. It's a long way home.
My distant lover and all her worry will finally be free.

Her face will light as I approach and take her in my arms.
I'll bring her to our marriage bed and woo her with my charms.
She knows just how to make me feel like I'm the very best.
It's been too long since I have felt her soft and supple...hair.

It's a long way home. It's a long way home,
But I know someone's waiting, waiting there for me.
It's a long way home. It's a long way home.
My distant lover and all her worry will finally be free.

I'll tell her I will be back soon and kiss her worried frown.
I'll hear her crying mournful tears but journey out of town.
She'll know that I'll be gone longer than I can rightly say,
But knowing that she waits for me will bring me back someday.

It's a long way home. It's a long way home,
But I know someone's waiting, waiting there for me.
It's a long way home. It's a long way home.
My distant lover and all her worry will finally be free.

By the time Gett reached the end of the song, the crowd had grown rowdy, clanking steins and roaring loudly. It seemed to have helped lighten everyone's spirits.

Esla came and laid down two plates with roast pheasant, mixed vegetables, and a baked potato with chives and butter. Davion and Hort had several jealous looks as the aroma made its way to the surrounding tables, but they ignored them while they thanked Esla wholeheartedly.

Looking over his plate while the aroma pleased his senses, Hort exclaimed, "If we're goin' ta be livin' off bread and cheese again, I'm goin' ta take me time and enjoy this meal!" Hort hadn't been blessed to have a meal this tasty in a long time, and he enjoyed every bite.

No sooner had they cleared their plates when the distinct sound of the southern alarm bells rang gloomily throughout the village.

"That'd be fer us," Hort said, grabbing his stein and chugging down the rest of his ale. Davion quickly grabbed his things as Hort slammed his empty stein down on the table, wiping

CHAPTER 11

his dripping mustache with the back of his hand. "Let's go, me boy! Time ta kill us s'more trolls!"

CHAPTER TWELVE

LOST

ay one.

A soft breeze blew through the trees as the sun began to set over the horizon. Pavula closed her eyes, feeling the wind's gentle kiss across her face, and inhaled deeply, smelling the sweet flowers' and leaves' aroma in the air. Convinced that everything on this side of the forest was sweeter, more vibrant, and enchanting, Pavula spread her arms out, twirling in the last of the sun's rays of the day. She felt so alive and free, like she could do anything.

Skipping along down her invisible path, she frolicked happily, off to find her destiny. A hop, skip, and a jump away, and then she would return home in a few days to tell her mother all about her wild adventure. *Maybe a week,* she nodded decidedly to herself.

Darkness was slowly taking over the forest, and a chill came over Pavula. The bugs were chirping in the bushes, loud croaking sounds were all around her, and strange cooing sounds came from up in the trees. She slowed down, looking warily around her for the source of all the new sounds. *Why does it sound so different here?* she wondered. She listened for her brethren's twilight howls but found nothing except the strange noises around her.

Hearing loud cracking branches in the distance from some unknown presence, Pavula suddenly remembered her mother's warnings about beasts that lived in the forest outside their boundary. She thought back to the boar and began to feel nervous. For the first time since leaving her protected land, the smile disappeared from her face as she hid behind a tree, looking around cautiously. The sound of a large beast was growing nearer, and she could feel her heart pounding against her chest.

With all the grace of a cat, she grabbed a low branch on the tree and scaled her way up, higher and higher into its foliage, not stopping until she was nearly one hundred feet up. Peering down through the boughs, she searched for the beast. A tree shook nearby, and thunderous vibrations came through the ground, shaking her branches with each step of the monster. A loud crack echoed through the air, and she watched as a smaller tree nearby snapped and fell to the ground, plummeting with a loud crash. She swallowed hard, eyes wide and alert, combing for what lurked in the darkness, and then she saw it.

It came at a slow pace out from around the trees and headed towards her own, stomping thunderously with each step. The beast was even larger than the boar she had killed, but this one looked like it had armor plates for a hide and was a smoky-gray color from what she could make out in the dim light of the nearly-set sun. It walked on all fours, its muscles flexing and moving with its stride. Two horns protruded tandemly out of its snout, and three extended from its large, monstrous head, clearly a force to be reckoned with.

As the beast passed below Pavula, it stopped and snorted at the base of her tree. The monstrous head swayed back and forth, searching for the source of her unfamiliar scent, then it continued stomping away, forming a path by clearing everything in its way.

She watched as it flicked its short, hairless tail side to side and disappeared into the brush beyond.

Pavula took a deep breath and chuckled quietly to herself. *That wasn't so bad*, she lied as her heart continued to race in her chest. Nevertheless, she decided it best to stay up in the tree for the night and get some rest. The sun's final rays had left her alone in darkness with only the dim glow from the two moons above, and there was no telling what else was lurking in the forest below.

Nestled in her tree, she rested her spear and dagger against the trunk at the base of her branch, stretched out over the bough, and closed her eyes. The soothing sounds of the forest chirping and cooing eventually helped her to doze off peacefully.

Falling into a deep sleep, her body exhausted from all the running, Pavula dreamt of her family.

She frolicked joyfully with her brothers and sisters and splashed water at them from the river. Her mother was watching over them, shaking her head at their foolishness, but smiling ever so slightly. She ran over to her mother to embrace her but, instead, found her mother looming over her angrily, staring down at her. It seemed as though her mother had grown, but then she realized it was herself that was shrinking while the Great Wolf continued to stare down at her, shaking her great mane disapprovingly. 'You are not ready,' Lupé Caelis' voice echoed in her mind. Suddenly, all of her brethren snarled and barked as they all jumped on top of her, crushing her. She found herself unable to breathe and grabbed at her chest, kicking and thrashing at the wolves to stop, trying to catch her breath as her mother just continued to stare with eyes cold as steel.

Day two.

Pavula was jerked out of her sleep to find herself in the clutches of a giant snake. Its body, covered in green and bright blue stripes, was as thick around as the bough she was on, and it had coiled itself around her body, squeezing tighter and tighter, crushing her lungs. She clawed at the snake, but it didn't flinch, and her head started pulsating with the lack of oxygen. *So this is it. This is how I'm going to die,* she told herself.

The snake curved its way around to where Pavula could see its menacing yellow eyes watching hers as it squeezed the life from her petite elven frame, but instead of being scared, Pavula found herself becoming irate. She didn't leave her family just to die on her first day of freedom. This couldn't be the end of her fate, to be killed by a meager snake. *Mother will NOT be right! I AM ready! I have to go back and show her that she was wrong!*

Pavula spotted her spear and dagger still lying against the tree, and she reached her hand out for the dagger. Falling about four feet too short, she strained to grab its hilt but wasn't getting any closer. She fought with all she had through her body's weakening state. *PLEASE!* she pleaded. To Pavula's delight, the dagger vibrated and then lifted into the air and flew over to her, landing perfectly in her outreached palm. Without hesitation, Pavula took the stone blade and stabbed it hard into the snake's flesh. She heard it screeching as she repeatedly stabbed it over and over, and it started to loosen its grip on her. After a final jab, the snake reluctantly let go and dropped her into a freefall.

Gasping for breath, Pavula reached out, grabbing frantically at the branches whizzing by her as she tumbled towards the ground. Running out of branches, she finally managed to snag onto one only twenty feet from the hard forest floor. The branch bent and bowed with her weight as she dangled, clinging with her left hand, dagger still held tight in her right. She took the blade and bit onto it, securing it with her teeth, then threw her hand over the branch and tried to pull herself up. The branch bowed again, cracking at its base, and Pavula realized it wasn't going to support her. It was then she remembered the spirits and closed her eyes, reaching through the branch, searching for the earth spirit. It only took her a moment to grasp onto its golden light, and the branch began to strengthen and grow, its cracks healing and binding, until it had become strong enough to support her.

Pavula reopened her eyes and pulled herself up onto the branch but then immediately heard wood cracking above her head. Looking up, she saw the giant snake, a jumbled mess of cold-blooded predator, descending quickly towards her. She could see it glaring at her with its mouth agape, ready for round two.

Knowing the dagger wasn't going to be enough to save her this time, Pavula pulled and summoned all the air from around her. She forced it into a strong gale, thrusting it at the snake just before it reached her. All the trees whipped rapidly as the wind tore through them and headed for Pavula and the snake. As the gale slammed against her foe, she kept pushing it, watching it lift the snake back away from her and up through the trees, far into the sky. It snapped its jaws wildly with no idea what was happening to it. Using the force of the wind, Pavula hurled the serpent into the thick woods somewhere far from her, hearing the breaking branches echo in the distance with its crash.

Collapsing onto her limb, Pavula suddenly realized how sore she was from the snake's embrace and felt nearly drained of all energy. This wasn't exactly how she thought her journey would begin, but she refused to let this stop her. Her mother's symbolic voice rang irritatingly in her mind; *It's not too late to turn back,* she imagined her saying. *You'd like that, wouldn't you, Mother?* she snidely retorted to herself.

With her mind aflame, Pavula reached for her spear a ways up the tree, still resting on the branch, and it flew down to her without hesitation. She snatched it proudly from the air as it reached her and strapped it to her back. Then, she jumped down from the tree the remaining twenty feet, using the wind spirit to soften her landing. Her magic was coming more naturally to her, and she did not have to concentrate as hard to access the spirits. It seemed they were just there now, as though waiting for her.

The forest was waking up around her, stirred by the winds she had created, and kissed awake with the sun's morning light. Pavula looked around to gather her senses and listened to the forest, searching for her direction, but there was nothing. She could no longer feel the pulling for her toward the boy in her vision. There was only silence, and she suddenly felt truly alone. Shaking it off, she would not let this stop her either. *I'll head to the village,* she decided.

Closing her eyes, she connected to the earth spirit again: flowing her thoughts through the ground, seeking the familiar sounds of the village, until she finally found it. It was quieter than before, and she thought she heard many people moaning and crying, but she was certain that was the place. Pavula took off running in the direction of the village at full speed, unknowingly pulling energy from the ground as she ran, healing her tender ribs and chest.

The forest was whooshing by her as Pavula ran through its tall, old trees looming overhead; its spotted and blotchy shadows with sunrays peering through its branches, its thick bushes, its leaf-covered bed, and the minutes quickly turned into hours. Her thoughts began to travel back to her family. Back to her *Mother...*

Suddenly those thoughts turned to darkness and anger again. *How could she think I wasn't ready? She treats me like I'm still a cub, but I'm not! How horrible of her to tell me that I'm free to go even though she doesn't believe I will succeed. That I still have too much to learn!* Pavula stopped seeing the trees, the shadows, the bushes, the ground. Her feet carried her forward, but everything was a blur as she stewed in her thoughts. *She'll see that I'm ready! Or maybe she won't. Maybe I just won't go back!* Pavula's anger fueled her as she pushed herself forward on her quest.

Day three.

Resuming shortly after sunrise, Pavula was starting to wonder if she would ever reach her destination. Everything seemed so close when looking through the spirits, the land seemed so small, but her little legs could only carry her so fast.

Deep down, Pavula had been telling herself she would return home soon, that this was just a quick adventure that she had to take. Hours had passed since she genuinely believed that. Yet, she continued to try and convince herself that maybe it would just be a little longer than she had anticipated; that she would go and see more of the world past the village first and then come home with all sorts of stories to tell her mother and kin. They would gather by the river and listen in awe of her journey and laugh together about the crazy things that might happen along the way. Best of all, her mother would be so proud of her, seeing that she was ready after all. She smiled and nodded to herself. *Yes, that's it. I'll just go for a little while, a few weeks at least, to do some great things and come back and tell mother all about them.*

Hopeful of her new compromise, she prayed to Jayenne to guide and watch over her. She promised her that if the goddess could simply help her get to the village and let her have her adventure, she would return home to her mother and never leave again.

Day four.

Heart pounding in her chest and rain pouring all around her, Pavula forced her legs to move with each step, growing weaker and weaker. She refused to give in to her fatigue, to every muscle in her body aching in sheer agony. No, she would not succumb to such insignificant things but pressed herself on, being pulled by a force she didn't understand.

She felt the pulling for her return sometime after midday and had been running at full speed ever since. It was coming from the village now, and Pavula was ecstatic, knowing she had been going the right way all along. The young elf had questioned herself many times if she was even still in the Sacred Forest. Everything appeared the same everywhere she looked. It was like running on a loop in a dream that she couldn't wake up from.

Only stopping to rest a few times, Pavula couldn't remember the last time she had eaten anything. Her thoughts filled with visions of the juicy boar meat, of fresh fruit and berries from her trees, and succulent fish from her river. She missed her trees. She missed her brothers and sisters. She missed...her mother.

Tears started streaking down Pavula's cheeks, lost in the rain, as her thoughts succumbed to uncertainty. *What am I doing?* she began doubting herself. *What if I'm not ready? What if I'm lost and never find the human?*

Suddenly, just as thunder cracked through the sky, she felt herself falling face-first into a muddy puddle, scraping her arm on a rock as she tried to catch herself. Her foot was trapped, her ankle in pain. She looked to find her bare foot had lodged into a burrower's hole. Pulling it out gently, she tucked her legs against her chest, burying her head into her knees, and wept.

Exhaustion and hunger were overtaking her; she couldn't think anymore. Her heart ached with regret and with missing her mother. She didn't even care about staying hidden anymore, letting out all of her tears and whimpering as she mourned the loss of her home, of her life as she knew it. Never before had she ever felt so alone, lost, and confused. *I'm not ready!* she finally admitted to herself. *Why did I have to leave?!*

Pavula sat there, on the soggy forest floor, feeling sorry for herself as she wept. *I can't do this!* she whined. She was feeling so hollow and worn and wanted nothing more than to collapse on the ground and let the forest take her.

'*GET UP!*' came a strong voice in Pavula's mind, startling her back to reality.

She looked up and around, searching the forest, praying that perhaps her mother had come for her. But, there was no one there. What was most startling was that she realized it wasn't her mother's voice at all, but a voice she had never sensed before. Apprehensively, she stood up, still searching the woods around her. The rain began to lessen, and she listened intently for any discernible sounds.

"Who's there?" Pavula called into the damp forest.

There was no response.

Great. Now I'm losing my mind, Pavula thought to herself as the only sound was the pitter-pattering of the rain around her.

The pain in her ankle started throbbing, distracting her for a moment, and she sniffled, wiping the tears and rain from her face while looking down at it. Taking a step forward, Pavula's ankle gave out under her, and she stumbled back to the ground from the shooting pain. Pavula whimpered and grabbed at her ankle, wondering how she could go on now. She looked around again, this time trying to remember which way she had been heading. Her body had become too weak, and the pain too strong for her to sense the pulling feeling that showed her the way. She was lost.

The sky cracked and rumbled as she sat on the forest floor, feeling sorry for herself, and it shook her to her core. She needed to come up with a plan and pull herself together. Pressing her fingers into the mud at her sides, Pavula passed her thoughts into the ground again, seeking out the village. It didn't take her long at all. She sensed she was much closer than she had imagined, and a glimmer of hope lit up inside her. As she pulled her thoughts back from the earth, she felt a rush of energy coming back with it, flowing up through her arms and down into her body. She felt as it invigorated her, replenishing her all the way down into her feet. The sensation stopped, and she withdrew her fingers from the ground.

Looking down at her ankle again, she tried to move it. To her delight, she found it moved freely. She pushed herself up to stand and carefully bore some weight onto her bad ankle. It seemed to support her. Taking a step, she realized it was still quite sore but much better than before, as though days had passed in its healing. Unexpectedly, and for the first time, she perceptively realized that she could pull energy from the earth spirit to help her heal.

With a new sense of optimism, she turned toward the direction of the village and limped quickly along, back on track to her calling. A few steps in, with her body recovering, she started to feel the pull once again, lightening her steps, speeding her stride, and filling her with renewed purpose.

Shortly back into her run, she was distracted by new sounds up ahead.

In the distance, Pavula could hear people shouting and screaming and loud clanking of metal on metal. She could also hear something else, some sort of beasts, perhaps, that sounded like swine trying to talk in their gruff guttural voices. Pavula took off in a jog towards the sounds, as fast as her sore ankle would allow, and stopped just before breaking out through the forest wall. She found herself staring out into a clearing where a bridge crossed over a rapid-flowing river, and a battle raged on the other side.

Pavula watched in amazement as she saw so many strange-looking people, all wearing different garb and wielding several unusual weapons. She marveled at the trolls' grand statures and rough-green skin with tattered animal skins covering their bodies.

Looking past the green monsters, she saw several paler-skinned, much smaller individuals attacking and defending against the trolls. She spotted two that were slightly taller and seemed to move with a feline grace in their attacks. They wore garments more muted in appearance than the blue and gray shining metal armor of the other men.

One of the graceful figures was pulling arrows from a quiver on his back and shooting them at the green monsters, most of them being deflected by swords and shields. He had blond hair cascading past his shoulders, decorated with beads that tied two thin ponytails back behind his long pointed ears and bright orange eyes. *An elf!* Pavula suddenly realized. He was strikingly handsome and wore dull green and brown armor that was etched with vines and roses on the chest-piece. Stepping up beside him, approached another elf with long beautiful dark-brown hair and bright-purple eyes. She wore a busty reddish-brown garment that flowed to the ground with slits all the way up to the tops of her outer thighs, allowing her to move freely. Her large fine-tipped ears were frosted with elegant gems and metals, and she wore a chain around her neck with what looked like claws clasping a dewdrop gem. In her hand, she grasped a large sacred oak branch, twisted at the end, and adorned with feathers and etchings on the shaft.

Pavula couldn't believe that she was staring at elves, but something else stole her attention away from them. Rising from beyond a hill in the distance, Pavula saw a horse's head cresting over the top, a horse she recognized, a horse she couldn't forget. Her heart stopped as she held her breath while the horse with the beautiful white mane cleared the horizon, and then she saw him—the boy from her vision!

CHAPTER THIRTEEN

FOUND

*D*avion raced out of the tavern, searching the village for the disturbance. He saw several armor-clad soldiers heading out through the south gates and over the hills in the distance. Then Davion heard a familiar sound—the sound of battle. He sprinted to the stables, grabbing Helna from her stall, and mounted her bareback.

"Uncle Hort, come on!" he shouted as the dwarf slowly emerged from the tavern, scratching himself through his leather britches. Ignoring Davion's insistence, he wobbled his way over to him. "Come on, Uncle!" Davion persisted, "They need your help!"

Hort scarcely looked up the path but heard the combat loud and clear and fumbled with haste to get to Davion. With a strained pull, Davion swung Hort up onto the horse's back behind him. "Hold tight!" He called as he gave Helna a swift hard kick, and they bolted towards the commotion, Hort holding on for dear life.

"Hmmm... I should've jus' ran," Davion heard Hort mutter over the sound of Helna's hooves splashing on the puddled path as she galloped toward the hills.

The battle wasn't far off at all. Just as they flew over the second hill, it all came into view. They came upon a band of trolls, no chieftain or oracle this time, but a group of what appeared to be five warriors. The troll warriors were attacking two elves along with several of the guards from the Trader's Post who had come to the town's defense.

Davion yanked back on Helna's mane, and she slipped and skidded to a halt. Then Hort leapt off her back, instantly forgetting his fear of heights, and yanked his axe from its sheath across his back while running toward the battlefield.

"Uncle, NO!" Davion called too late. *Reckless!* he cursed inwardly as he grabbed for his herbs. Crushing the herbs hastily in his hand, he made a series of gestures before throwing them in Hort's direction and yelled, "*Excassida lorrenette!*" casting a protection spell on Hort to increase his strength. The dwarf could feel the increased power flowing through him, and he let out a war cry, bringing his axe overhead with both hands as he charged for the trolls.

Filled with courage upon the success of his strength spell, Davion quickly decided on another. "*Ominus Lacarté!*" Davion said, casting his favorite spell and threw a bolt of fire at a troll. Helna stammered but held her ground, the horse-binding spell from Firemaster Thornton clearly working. The firebolt fell a few feet short of the troll nearest the female elf, extinguishing with a sizzle as it hit the saturated ground. Davion realized that he was too far away and would need his staff.

The female elf, undoubtedly a type of sorceress, raised a crooked wooden staff adorned with large colorful feathers and swirled it over her head. Clouds formed above her, growing dark with thunder and lightning crackling in their mass. A bolt of lightning shot down from her clouds and struck the troll off guard, knocking it off its feet. The earth shook as the troll hit the ground with a thud. Before it had a chance to get up, a second bolt of lightning shot out of the clouds hitting the troll, burning a hole into its chest—killing it.

Davion looked back to the elves to see if they were okay. The male elf, presumably a ranger by his appearance, had a quiver full of arrows strapped to his back that he was shooting rapidly at an approaching troll. When the troll became too close, the elf strapped his bow to his back with great agility and grabbed two short swords from their sheaths at his sides. The elf's blades were the most flawless and beautifully crafted that Davion had ever seen, and they almost looked as though they were made of glass. He realized they must be from the icen ore that the dwarves mined back home. The elf met the troll's charge in sword-to-sword combat while the female whispered and spun her staff. She was casting protection spells on her partner.

Grabbing hold of his own staff from his back, Davion rode Helna over to assist Hort and the other soldiers, several of them already fallen; wounded, or killed by the trolls. As he neared the battlefield, he heard a bellow from the male elf and looked over again quickly to see what was wrong. The troll that was attacking the elf was stumbling backward. He watched as the male elf took a peculiar stance with his arms out before him, bent at the elbows in a ninety-degree angle, fists up to the sky. As he lowered to the ground on one knee while the troll gathered its footing, Davion watched as six-inch thorns sprouted out of the elf's skin, covering his body down to his knees. Without any caster trolls nearby, he realized that it wasn't an attack on the elf but was another protection that the elf had cast on himself. He gazed in awe as he watched while the troll would swing and continually be pierced by the sturdy thorns, raging with every gash.

Falling prey to his curiosity, Davion failed to see one of the warriors charging at him until it was too late to block his bash, causing Davion to fly from Helna through the air and land on his backside. *Blastit, that's getting old!* Helna galloped away from the troll to safety but stayed close for Davion. Spitting to the side, he concentrated on the troll who was already charging again. He fumbled to get to his feet fast enough, but something had stopped the troll in its tracks. Roots were sprouting from the ground beneath, grabbing the troll's feet, holding him anchored, enraging him further.

Davion looked to the elves, but they were engrossed in their own conflict, and then, he saw her. His jaw dropped, and once again, he forgot about the troll in all of his gawking. There she stood, arms out before her, aimed at the troll, one foot braced ahead of the other in a sprinter's stance. Her long golden hair was waving down around her shoulders to her waist, covering everything a tunic would have. Her petite pointed ears peeked out through her luxurious locks, and her eyes were bluer than the skies. Her tanned skin glistened in the sun, and—mesmerized—he was convinced again that he was gazing upon an angel.

The angelic elf saw him too, their eyes locked, both entranced, and silence fell all around them. Not real silence, of course, only to them was the world still, for the battle played on around them, and in that battle, the troll's roots were being neglected, and it easily slashed itself free. Then the troll chose a new target—the petite, elven beauty. The silence was broken as reality stepped back into play, and the angel shoved her arms out, causing the troll to fumble backward momentarily. It laughed at her attempt and charged again.

As though the trolls weren't enough for them to contend with, the most dreaded word in any language was screamed from the dwarf in his hoarse dominating voice: "DRAGON!!!"

Everyone froze instantly; troll, elf, dwarf, and man all gawking up to the sky—all but one troll, one troll too engrossed in his rage to care for anything else than vengeance. The angel parried the troll's sword attack but was caught by the back of his forearm as he thwarted her, knocking her several paces directly into a tree, and she fell to the ground, unconscious.

A great Silver dragon dove down from the sky, its massive body descending rapidly, creating panic in all below. The sun reflected off of its silver and white scales, creating a blinding light to those below. The great dragon came crashing down onto two trolls simultaneously with its talons, crushing and killing them instantly. Veering its long neck, it snatched up a third troll in its powerful jaws—the one that Davion and his angel had been fighting—splitting it in half, the remains dropping over ten feet to the ground. Screams and squeals had filled the air but were drowned out by the ear-piercing roar of the dragon as it glared its pitch-black eyes around for its next target.

Davion felt Hort's presence and grabbed his arm. "Slowly," Hort whispered, "it'll charge us if we run." They back-walked quietly and slowly as the great beast lunged to the troll that had been attacking the elven couple, ripping its head from its body, partial spine dangling from its mouth, and the large green decapitated hulk fell lifeless to the ground.

Good, the other elves got away, Davion noticed as he saw them heading for the trees.

With all the trolls dead, the dragon brought Davion's attention back to his angel, lying helplessly under the tree. To his horror, the dragon had also noticed her there and was slowly advancing toward her. Stretching out its long silver neck, the dragon sniffed at the motionless body of the elf.

It's gonna kill her! Davion gasped, "NO!!!" he shouted at the beast.

Doing the quickest thing that came to mind, he tossed a stone at it. The stone feebly pinged off of the dragon's hind leg, and it turned its head slightly, glancing back his way dispassionately, before turning its attention back to the girl. Davion waved his staff back and forth, building up his next attack, "*OMINUS LACARTÉ!!!*" and a fire-bolt flew through the air, striking the monster in the wing.

The dragon was not dispassionate to the bolt. It screeched in pain and aggravation as it glared back to Davion with wrath this time and a bloodcurdling roar.

"Oh Goddess Mother, Jayenne and Kyrash, we're gonna die," Hort sniveled beside him.

Davion hesitated, terror-stricken, unsure of whether to run or to fight.

Astonishingly, the Silver did not attack them, but instead, it spread its wings, plunging them forcefully as the beast lifted into the air, pulling all of the wind from around them as it gained altitude, one great stroke of its monstrous wings at a time. They all watched it curve north, and its massive form became slighter. Then as quickly as it had appeared, the dragon disappeared back into the clouds.

Everyone raised their hands to the air and cheered wildly. Davion was overwhelmed with pride.

"And don't ye come back!" Hort proclaimed, shaking his fist in the air after the beast was completely out of sight. Looking up to the now-empty skies, he said in amazement, "Hmmm... First an oracle, and now a dragon! We should've brought a bard with us ta record all yer feats!"

Davion assumed the Silvers must be afraid of fire and made a mental note to make their firepits extra-large on the coming nights with plenty of torches handy.

The Girl! he remembered suddenly and ran to her aid—he was her hero after all. Rushing to her side, Davion knelt near the elven angel and wedged his hand under her head. It was moist and sticky. He gulped as he pulled his crimson-soaked hand back. *Blood!*

CHAPTER 13

"Are there any more wounded?" Davion heard the tall, muscular elf man call out in the common tongue, Onish, with his gallant elven accent. The elf man stood up from beside one of the soldiers lying on the ground. Davion was surprised to see that the elves had returned, knowing their fear of the dragons.

"The girl!" Davion cried out. Hort and the elves followed promptly. "Her head, it's bleeding!" He gaped at the elf for guidance. *Elves are magic; he must heal her!*

"What is her name?" demanded the elf as he knelt on the opposing side and rested his hand on her chest.

Davion confusedly looked at the elf. "I thought she was with you."

The elf shook his head, "No, but she does look strangely familiar." Davion cocked an eyebrow, waiting for him to go on. "Perhaps displaced in this cursed war. Our kind will stop at nothing to destroy every last one of those dragon monsters, ancient or not."

Anyone could see the anger festering in the elf's eyes, and the female sorceress rested a gentle palm on his shoulder.

"The girl, can you help her?" Davion probed.

The elf examined the back of her head, which was caked and matted with blood, tarnishing her perfect golden locks. He shook his head, distressed, "She is badly wounded, and I can only perform minor healing. I can close the wound. However, she will need a lot of rest to recover. We will take her back to Má Lyndor."

"How far is that?" Davion interjected. He did not like the idea of these strangers taking his angel away from him when he had just found her. He instantly felt the deep sickness of guilt, knowing that they needed to do whatever they could to help her.

Sighing, the elf lay the girl back down and stood up, arms crossed over his chest, but continued to study her. "A week's journey north. It is where Shakiera and I are headed."

"A week?" Hort jumped in. "Okullo dung!" *Good old Hort.* Davion thought. "She can rest at the Trader's Post!"

"He's right!" Davion contributed to the debate. "We'll take her to the Trader's Post until she's better."

The elf conferred with his lovely Shakiera in their elven tongue, of which Davion did not know enough to follow the conversation. Both elves glanced at the girl a few times and more at Hort and Davion, and Hort quickly became annoyed. "We 'ave-na' got all day! The poor lass is bleedin' ta death! Outta' me way! I'll carry 'er meself!" Hort pushed past Davion to get to the girl.

"Wait," countered the male elf, "my wife and I agree that it would not be appropriate for her to go with you. We shall take her to Má Lyndor."

"Appropriate? Why? Because she's an elf an' we're nobodies? Bah! If yer customs would allow this lass to die jus' so long as she doesna' go with us, then the lotta ye can kiss me arse!"

Davion, still kneeling on the ground, peered up at the male to see his reaction, which was shock.

"*Infidel,*" Shakiera muttered in elvish. That word Davion understood, but the male elf raised his hand to silence her.

"At least let me heal her wound, Mister...?" He signaled Hort, letting him know that was his cue.

"Hort. Me name's Hort *Strong*arm," he said, emphasizing "Strong" while puffing out his chest. "Hmmm..." He stroked his beard in thought. "Alright then, get on with it so's we can get 'er to a proper bed ta lie 'er head on, Mister...?" he said patronizingly, then took a step back out of the way from the girl.

"Alright," replied the elf as he knelt back down beside her, "I am Salyaman Dula'Sintos."

A noble! Davion gasped. He knew that an elf with "Dula" in their title meant they were either a noble or royalty. He flushed with embarrassment at Hort's behavior. *Please don't let him say anything else!*

Salyaman Dula'Sintos placed his hand on the bloody mass at the back of her head and closed his eyes. They watched as he whispered something inaudible, and the back of her head began to emit a faint-blue light from his palm. After several moments, the light faded away, and he slowly removed his hand.

"That will have to suffice for now." Salyaman Dula'Sintos nodded as he stood back up, wiping his hand clean on his trousers. "At least until we get her to the Trader's Post." He smirked at Hort and then unbuckled the cape from his back, draping it over the elf's nearly-naked form. "We shall accompany you, of course."

"Yes, of course," Davion interjected before Hort could respond.

Salyaman added, "We will wait until tomorrow for her to rest. Then," he paused, making sure he had both of their attention, "we will take her with us to Má Lyndor."

Hort opened his mouth to protest, but Davion quickly cut him off, fearing the worst. "That would be fine. Thank you, Salyaman *Dula*'Sintos," he said, accentuating "Dula" for Hort to note.

Salyaman nodded to Davion before taking Shakiera's hand and leading her toward another fallen soldier needing attention.

With Hort's assistance, Davion hoisted the girl onto Helna and strapped her down, then the two of them escorted her west over the hills, back to the southern entrance of the Trader's Post.

Davion lost Hort to the crowd on his way to the stables, telling the tale of The Great Sorcerer Davion who took on a dragon and scared the beast away. After leaving Helna with the stablehand, Davion carried the girl, wrapped in Salyaman's cape, dangling in his arms into the Traveler's Inn. He pushed past all the inquisitive onlookers wondering who she was, asking what happened with the trolls and, mostly, the dragon. He ignored most of his audience, making his way to the room with the girl, where he laid her gently on his cot, still fast asleep.

Pulling up the three-legged stool, Davion sat next to the bed, staring at her exquisite face. He brushed away some hair from her eyes. As she lay motionless, he found himself being overcome with fervency for the girl before him, his heart aching in his angst. Davion thought back to his dream in Silex Valley.

"You can't leave me," he whispered softly, "I just found you." Bowing his head dolefully, he clasped his hands together and prayed to Jayenne that she would recover.

Hort came stumbling in several minutes later with a stein of ale in his hand and raised it high. "Yer a blastit hero, me boy!" he exclaimed before fumbling over to his cot on the other side of the small room. "Hmmm... 'Ow's 'er 'ead?" he asked, followed by a garish belch.

Lifting her ever-so-gently, Davion inspected the back of the elven girl's head. Though it was still stained with blood, he could not see any wound at all.

"Perfect," Davion replied. "The wound is no more."

Hort rushed over to see for himself in amazement, and then Davion laid her back down, trying not to stir her.

"Well, I'll be the son of an elf!" Hort exclaimed. Just then came a light knock at the door, and Hort bound over, swinging it open. "Speakin' o' which," he added as Salyaman and Shakiera gracefully entered the room, moving as though floating on air. "Oiy, Mister Sal. I got me an okullo in need o' yer fancy healin' Joo Joo if ye could take a look."

Salyaman looked to the dwarf, then over to the cot where the girl lay. "I am only here for the girl," he said, nodding in her direction.

CHAPTER 13

"Please!" Hort pressed, trying to stay on his best behavior. "I'll pay anythin' if ye could just save him. At least 'ave a look!" He stepped forward, seeing no compassion in the elf's eyes. "This isna' jus' an okullo! He's saved me life more than I can say. He's a blastit hero and a half!"

The elf peered down at him and then looked back to the girl. "I suppose I could take a look," he said nonchalantly, "but keep your coin."

Hort pressed his hands together, bowing slightly to Salyaman. "Thank ye!" he said earnestly.

Coming around from behind Salyaman, Shakiera held out a bundle of white clothing. "I purchased this for her," she said as she placed it delicately at the foot of the bed. "It will have to do until we can get her home and get proper attire. This village is full of faux elven wear, nothing of the fine quality that we will find back in Má Lyndor." Shakiera held her head high as she walked back to Salyaman's side, taking his hand.

Davion looked at the neatly folded clothing and thanked them both. They all turned to look as the elven angel groaned softly and stirred in the bed. Davion held his breath, hoping to see her open her eyes, but she settled back down and continued to slumber.

Sighing, Salyaman turned for the door, "Well, let us go see this okullo, Mr. Strongarm."

"I will stay with the girl," Shakiera added.

As much as it pained Davion to leave her side, he really wanted to see how Orbek was doing and decided to go with them.

It was a quick walk over to the stables, and Hort sped ahead with his short legs, leading them to Orbek's stall. They approached but didn't see the okullo until they opened the five-foot door. Lying on the ground, head resting in the dirt, lay Orbek, wheezing with every shallow breath, sweat pouring off of him and the smell of infection heavy in the air. Davion covered his nose with the back of his sleeve. It reeked like death.

Salyaman walked quickly into the stall and shook his head, inspecting the okullo. He removed the bandaging from his hind leg, and it peeled away with pieces of flesh and green pus. Underneath, the leg was already being eaten by maggots.

"This poor creature should have been put out of its misery days ago," Salyaman told them. "It should not have been left to suffer this way."

Hort didn't want to hear it. "The laiden doctor said 'is infection was better. I didna' realize. Can ye help 'im or not, elf?" he pressed.

Taking a deep breath, Salyaman ordered Hort to get some water so he could clean the wound and had him start wiping down the okullo.

A half-hour had passed before the wound was cleaned out enough for Salyaman to begin, and Orbek was on his last breaths. He held both hands over the wound and began to concentrate, chanting something quietly. The same blue light they had seen in the battlefield emitted from underneath his hands, but this time it shone twice as bright. He continued this way for nearly an hour, and his brow beaded with perspiration, his face clenched with strain. Davion saw tears begin to stream down his face until, finally, he opened his eyes. The glowing light faded away, and Salyaman lifted his hands.

Running to Orbek, Hort pushed the elf aside to see. However, his heart sank when he saw that the wound still remained. It didn't look anywhere near as bad as it had before, but it was still open.

"What happened?" he questioned Salyaman.

Pressing a salve over the open flesh, Salyaman dressed the wound and stood to face Hort. "I have removed the infection and

CHAPTER 13

dead tissue. I was not able to rebuild all of the flesh, but I will be able to try again in the morning before I leave for Má Lyndor." He began to leave the stall. "That is the best I can do. This animal would have been dead in another hour, but it will live. It will take time to fully recover with my limited healing abilities."

Hort and Davion followed him out, taking a last look at Orbek, who had fallen asleep. He was breathing easier and more regular, no longer looking so distressed. They were both extremely relieved of the improvement. Although the okullo was still very weak, Hort finally had some real hope for his friend.

Returning to the inn, Davion rushed down the hallway when he heard a crash from within his room. Upon entering, he was happy to see that his angel was awake, but she did not seem as happy as he. Shakiera was backed into a corner on the other side of the room, a ceramic pot in pieces around her feet. She was talking elvish soothingly at the girl, her hands outstretched toward her, trying to calm her down, but the elf girl was panic-stricken and shouting at her in a language Davion didn't understand nor recognize. Hort and Salyaman, catching up, remained in the back, blocking the doorway.

"Hello there," Davion said softly, his hand held out openly. The girl whipped around, her attention now to Davion, and her panic lessened slightly. "Don't be afraid," Davion said. "Friend."

The girl stared at him, looking him over, but still poised, ready to either flee or attack; Davion wasn't sure which. "Aimiadal," he repeated in elvish. Her eyes bore into his, and he began to feel a little dizzy, as a strange feeling came shooting through his head, but then it was gone again just as quickly. He continued to stare at the girl, the dizziness subsiding, and her tension relaxed as she stood upright.

The beautiful elf's supple pink lips parted as she spoke to Davion with her sweet angelic voice, "Friend."

CHAPTER FOURTEEN

COGNIZANT

*N*othing but blackness. No sound but the beating of her own heart throbbing in her ears. Pavula found herself surrounded by nothingness, her senses all useless. *What's happening to me?* she managed a thought. Slowly, she became aware of her breathing: her slow, shallow breaths and her chest rising up and down, but she still couldn't bring herself to move nor open her eyes.

Pavula concentrated, focusing her thoughts to her body, trying to regain control. Gradually she began to feel the pain throbbing in her head as it spun in the darkness, giving her a feeling of vertigo. She tried to reach out and grab hold of something, but she could not move her hands or arms. Outside of her spinning head, she started to hear voices. Although quite muffled and distant sounding, she believed they were actually much closer. Too close. She began to panic, afraid of what was going on around her. *Why can't I move?!* she questioned her body. Trying to open her mouth, she managed to let out a moan but then was quickly overcome with exhaustion and drifted back into nothingness.

Pavula found herself lost in the dark, traveling towards a light in the distance. As she approached, she realized the light was fire. The fire flared up around her, leaving a black-stone path for her to follow. At the end of the path between the fiery walls, she came across two eyes glowing red in the darkness, watching her intently.

"I know you," Pavula said confidently to the eyes. "Why am I here?"

The eyes continued to glare into her. Then, they came closer. The great dragon stepped forward into the light, where she could see its blood-red scales reflecting the flames of fire around them. Its wings were tucked tightly at its sides.

"Are you the fire spirit?" Pavula asked the great dragon, wondering if this was the last spirit she had been unable to tame. She waited anxiously for an answer, but none came.

The dragon then turned from Pavula, whipping its long spiked tail around, and began to walk away into the fire beyond. Its massive body sent shock waves throughout the ground with each of its thundering steps. Just before it disappeared into the flames, it turned its great head, looking back to her with its burning eyes, and waited for a moment, as though expecting her to follow. Then the dragon disappeared into the wall of fire, and flames shot up around Pavula at least fifty feet high.

The light was blinding as she blinked her eyes, trying to adjust to the glare, and Pavula found herself staring at a strange wood wall. She blinked again, her vision adjusting, and she realized she could move her hand as she brought it up to her temple to press against the throbbing pain.

"Salvath," Pavula heard someone say behind her. She turned her head over on the pillow and saw a strange woman with long dark-brown hair and bright-purple eyes staring down at her.

Kicking at the sheets violently, Pavula fought to sit up and get herself out of the bed to defend herself against the stranger. She looked at her, noticing her pointed ears and breasts pushed up by her long frock, and realized that she was looking at another female elf. Her mother's warning about not trusting the elves shot into her mind, so she tried desperately to get up.

"Get away from me!" Pavula yelled at the elf. The elf looked at her confused as though she didn't understand and raised her hands up toward Pavula, who mistook it as an assault.

Pavula looked frantically around for her weapons but didn't see them. So, she quickly grabbed a strange-looking bowl from beside her on a wooden table and threw it at the elf. The ceramic pot shattered against the wall and the elf backed away, yammering something nonsensical at her. Pavula sprang up to her feet, prepared to fight.

"Where am I?!" Pavula yelled at the elf. "Why am I here?!" She shook with fear and confusion.

Just then, Pavula realized that others had entered the room as she heard another much deeper voice behind her say something else she didn't understand. She turned to the intruder and saw it was the boy from her vision. The memories began flooding back to her about the battle and the trolls and how she had run in to help him. She looked at his outstretched hand and back to his non-threatening face as he said something else.

Pavula stared into his eyes, looking past them into his mind. She went gently, trying not to alert him, and searched for what he was trying to say. The strangers' words were all so unfamiliar, and she needed to know what was going on. Searching through his recent thoughts, she grabbed onto what he had said and the meaning. *'Hello there... Don't be afraid... Friend... Friend.'*

Pavula understood. She released her hold on his mind and stood upright, relaxing her stance. Remembering the words from his mind, she opened her mouth and replied timidly, "Friend."

CHAPTER 14

The boy smiled widely at her, causing her to blush to see his pleasure. "Hello," he repeated, chuckling. "So you *do* speak Onish!"

Pavula once again didn't understand his new words and began feeling frustrated. The boy looked to the elves, and she followed his gaze.

"Vall lingaithio elfah?" Shakiera asked her if she spoke elvish, but it all sounded like gibberish to Pavula. She needed to find a way to communicate with them.

"I don't understand," Pavula said to them. "Please help me to understand."

Startled, she turned to a tall male elf who had entered the room from behind the boy. She recognized him from the battlefield. "You speak the language of the ancients," he said to her clearly. Then, he took her two hands in his own and held them in front of him, feeling a strange connection to her as he did. She nervously shook in his grasp while she looked into his serious orange eyes. "What is your name?" he asked in her language.

Pavula was so grateful that one of them understood. "Lupé Pavula," she responded.

"Lupé?" the elf repeated and looked to the others and then started talking at them in the strange language again. Frustrated, she bore into the elf's mind to find out what was going on, finding it more receptive and familiar than the human's mind had been.

"Wolf," Salyaman said to the others. "She says that her name is Wolf Child, or Lupé Pavula, and she is speaking the language of the ancients." He looked back to her at her disheveled hair and loincloth. "I do not know what this girl has been through or who taught her the language of the ancients, but all the more reason that we need to get her back to Má Lyndor."

The girl yanked her hands from Salyaman and ran behind Davion, grasping onto his shoulder as she angrily stared back at the elf.

"I dunna' think she wants ta be goin' with ye, Sal," Hort chuckled.

Salyaman grew cross, "I am afraid it is irrelevant. She will accompany us back to Má Lyndor first thing tomorrow."

"Anna!" the girl yelled at Salyaman. Everyone looked at him, and he shook his head, *no.*

Salyaman tried explaining calmly to her in the ancient tongue that he believed the elders in his city might know her identity, that it would be safe for her there, and they would take care of her. She seemed to comprehend, but she was still not convinced.

"Anna!" the girl shouted again sharply. "Elo anna reliensa!"

Taking a deep breath, Salyaman studied the girl, contemplating how he could change her mind. "She says she will not go," he sighed, confused why she seemed to trust a human over her own kind.

"Elo anna únethera ess," Pavula added.

"She does not know me," Salyaman translated to the others. "I am Salyaman Dula'Sintos," he said calmly to her in Onish, realizing she was somehow understanding it even though she didn't seem to be able to speak it, "son of Rath Beldroth Dula'Sintos, Ruler of Má Lyndor. A great elven city. Where you belong," he added.

Hort's eyes grew wide, and he looked away uncomfortably, biting his tongue, realizing he was with royalty.

Davion turned, taking her hand, and looked into Pavula's eyes. She stared back into his light-brown eyes unstintingly. "What if we come with you?" he said to Salyaman without taking his eyes off of Pavula. "We are headed to Lochlann anyway, and she seems to trust me." The girl looked back to Salyaman keenly, seeming to comprehend.

"Out of the question!" Salyaman stormed, and Pavula growled at him. "She is our kind, and we will take her ourselves back to our homeland. This is not up for debate."

"So ye be takin' 'er 'gainst 'er will then?" Hort confronted Salyaman, "I'll not 'ave that. We're all goin' the same direction. We can fight 'bout it on the way." He pointed to Pavula and Davion. "The laiden's clearly made 'er choice. So either we come with, or ye leave 'er with us."

Salyaman snarled, noticeably irate, clenching his teeth, and Shakiera lovingly grabbed his arm. He stroked her fingers for a moment, then finally said with disdain, "I suppose it would not hurt to have some company along the way."

Pavula shook Davion's arm in excitement.

Smiling contentedly at her, he said, "I'm Davion."

"Davion," she repeated softly. Then curiously looked around to the others.

"Hort, lass," Hort said gruffly when she looked at him.

"Hortlass," she repeated.

"No, no, no. Me name's Hort." Pavula looked at him, confused. "Hort!" he repeated, flustered.

She smiled and nodded, "Hort."

"Aye," he said, relieved with a sigh.

Pavula then looked to the female elf.

"Shakiera Nesu. Or, Kiera."

"Kiera." Pavula nodded.

"She will need more rest," Salyaman added sternly. "We all will. Kiera, get her some food and water. We will sleep tonight, and then I suppose we shall *all* leave for Má Lyndor in the morning. Gather any supplies you may need for the trip. I will not wait for you once the sun has touched the sky."

Shakiera and Hort immediately headed for the door. Then, and without warning, Davion watched as Pavula's eyes rolled to the back of her head, and her feet gave out from under her, succumbing to her exhaustion and injury. Davion quickly reached out and caught her as she fell, lifting her up in his arms. She had passed out, cold. He carefully carried Pavula back over to his cot and laid her down gently, pausing for a moment before letting go.

"Is she alright?" he asked Salyaman.

Examining Pavula briefly, Salyaman nodded, "She will be fine. Let us leave her to get some sleep."

But Davion couldn't leave her. He sat by her side while the others left and watched her as she breathed in and out lightly, resisting the urge to kiss her peaceful face.

CHAPTER 14

CHAPTER FIFTEEN

PROVOCATION

*G*leaming on the horizon toward the desert, the sun was beginning to set, painting the skies with beautiful swirls of yellow, orange, red, and hues of violet, reflecting in the wispy cirrus clouds.

Davion walked alongside Helna as she followed him obediently along the trail north toward Ashwood Forest, west of the Emerald River, and he checked every so often on the elf girl that was sleeping upon the horse's back. *Lupé Pavula*. He'd never heard such a strange name before, even for an elf. Salyaman and Shakiera walked on ahead of them, talking quietly amongst themselves but mostly staying silent while attentively watching the surrounding trees.

The silence was broken as Hort cursed several paces behind him from underneath his oversized helm that was dipping over his eyes after stumbling on an unearthed root in the path. Orbek limped alongside him, his wound now closed, courtesy of Salyaman from the morning they left on their journey. However, the okullo was still not healed enough for riders, so Hort was forced to walk instead.

They were an unlikely band of traveling companions, which made for a rather quiet journey, each keeping to their own. Riding, the journey to Má Lyndor would take at least seven days, but by foot, it would take much longer, and only one nightfall had passed since they left the Trader's Post. Davion secretly hoped that they would continue to walk just so he would have more time with his angel, even though it was taking its toll on Hort.

For the first time in two days, Davion heard Pavula begin to stir in the saddle as she slowly regained consciousness. Davion whistled up the path to the elves. They stopped and looked back before coming to join Davion and the others while Davion stood by Pavula, unstrapping her from the saddle.

"We stoppin'?" Hort called out. "I got blisters on me blisters!"

Pavula, remembering what had happened, willingly allowed Davion to gently hoist her down off of the horse, wrapping her arms around him for stability as she descended. Setting her feet on the ground, she tested her strength and seemed capable of standing, only faltering slightly. They grasped each other's forearms until she gained her balance and looked up at him gratefully. Davion smiled softly back at her.

The white dress that Shakiera had bought for her was very favorable on her petite elven frame. It had small tuft sleeves on the tips of her shoulders, lace accents around the bodice and bosom, which was tight and flattering, and then streamed down to the ground around her ankles. The dress flowed over her frame like waves and swayed in the gentle breeze. On her previously-bare feet now lay leather sandals that were tied up around her calves. Although beautiful, he sensed Pavula wasn't quite as thrilled about her new attire while he observed her pawing at the material uncomfortably.

"Do you feel alright?" Davion asked, praying she understood.

Pavula nodded.

CHAPTER 15

With the day turning into night, Salyaman called out to the group, "Let us leave the road." He then asked Pavula if she could walk, and he took her hand, leading her gently to see. Pavula looked at him, feeling strange with his touch. She was feeling a connection to him as well, but not in the same way as Davion, and wasn't quite sure what to make of it. Salyaman was irritated by her attachment to Davion and wished for her to come to her senses and choose to stay near him.

The travelers headed off of the path into the woods, trailing Helna and Orbek behind them, until they found a small clearing where they could set up for the night. Davion spread out his blanket on the ground and led Pavula over to it, helping her sit down while Hort sat on a large boulder, taking off his thick-hide boots and rubbing his blistered swollen feet. Salyaman and Shakiera disappeared into the rapidly darkening woods without a word.

"Hmmm... Not much fer chit-chat, those two," Hort grumbled after them.

"Nice to see you finally awake," Davion said coyly to Pavula. He waited for a response, but she just sat there studying him. "We're headed to Má Lyndor, one of the elven cities." She continued gazing at him, and he wasn't confident that she was following any of what he said. "...Of your people," he added, searching for some sign of understanding. Sighing, Davion gave up and started to form a pit for a fire before continuing, "Anyway, it's been two days since we left, but we still have many more until we get there. I hope that you're up for the journey."

"Yes." Pavula said simply, startling Davion.

"You understand me?" he asked.

"Yes." Pavula said again.

Davion began to get excited. "So, you *do* speak common tongue... Onish?"

"No." she replied.

Confused, Davion looked away.

"Dunna' look ta me, lad," Hort said, scratching his nether regions through his britches. "That lass is a right odd sort. Even fer an elf."

Huffing, Davion went back to preparing the firepit just as Salyaman and Shakiera appeared carrying bundles of wood in their arms and then placed them in the hole he had created.

Pavula smiled uncomfortably at Salyaman when he looked her way, then watched as Davion waved his hands over the pile of wood in a strange motion and pressed his hands out toward it. "*Ominus illioso!*" he said forcefully, and the twigs and limbs ignited in a roaring fire before dying back down to a gentle burn.

She couldn't believe her eyes and jumped up. Rushing over to Davion, she grabbed his sleeve excitedly. "Fire! You fire méa!" she shouted as she pointed to his flames.

Davion looked at her bewildered—albeit flattered. It was nice to see someone get excited about his skills, especially her. "Yes, fire," he replied. "I don't understand; 'méa'?"

Pavula looked at him, having trouble finding the word, then over to Salyaman for aid.

"Spirit." He took out a piece of elven bread, then added, "I believe she is inferring that you have fire magic." He tore off a bite with his teeth while he thought. When he finished swallowing the bread, Salyaman added, "Considering how long she has survived on her own, I would not be surprised if she also has one of the elemental magics. Perhaps fire as well." After a slight pause, he added cynically, "It would explain her connection to you."

Davion looked down at her. "You fire méa?" he asked.

Pavula frowned, shaking her head, and then looked away. She inwardly questioned how much she could trust these strange beings but desperately wanted to know how to access the last spirit.

Davion was relieved that Salyaman had been wrong, that fire magic wasn't the cause of her link to him, but that there was, perhaps, some greater reason behind it.

Before long, the crackling fire was the only lighting in the surrounding forest, aside from the dim light of the moons dancing behind the clouds. Davion offered Pavula some of his dried meat and bread along with a flask of water.

"Elves do not partake in the ingestion of flesh," Salyaman said smugly, waiting for her to refuse him.

She grabbed the meat eagerly, tearing it wildly with her teeth.

"Hmmm... Methinks nobody told the lass that," Hort laughed, and Salyaman and Shakiera watched her, disgusted.

Pavula didn't realize how hungry she was until she started eating. She vaguely remembered being fed some water and some of the bread—a new experience for her—while she was in and out of consciousness, but it was few and far between, leaving her stomach aching with emptiness. Taking a bite of the bread, she fell instantly in love with its taste and yeasty fragrance, the tough-brown outer crust hiding a soft and spongy center, with a hint of sweetness from honey.

"Mmmmmm," she moaned as she took another huge bite of the bread, believing it to be the best thing she had ever tasted.

Hort and Davion chuckled at her reaction while the elves looked on studiously.

"Shoulda' brought ye some cakes," Hort chuckled. "Ye ain't tasted nothin' till ye've had a barden cake from Lochlann. Got us some o' the best bakers in the land there. Me Glondora's isna' so bad, I s'pose." He drifted off in melancholy thought of his love back home, then sighed and pulled out a large, smoked drumstick from his sack and began ripping at it messily. "Hmmm... So, lass.

Seein' as ye be understandin' us now, how's bout ye tell us who ye be?"

"Uncle!" Davion hissed, embarrassed. "I'm sorry, Lupé Pavula," he apologized.

"What?" Hort spat.

But, Pavula didn't understand. She told them her name; what was he asking her? Even though she tried to search his mind, she wasn't convinced he knew what he was asking either. She found his mind much more akin to an animal than to Davion or the other elves. Pavula furrowed her brow in distress, not sure how to respond.

Sitting against a tree, Salyaman held Shakiera in the comfort of its strong base and looked to the group. He then spoke to Pavula in the ancient tongue, "How did you come to be at the Trader's Post—the place where we met you? And how is it you suddenly seem to know the common tongue?"

The fire crackled as Davion threw on another log. Pavula opened her mouth to answer Salyaman but stopped herself. '*Can you not hear my thoughts?*' she directed toward him, wondering if that was the connection she felt with him. Salyaman remained poised with no response, and Pavula realized that they might not be able to communicate as she did with her mother. Perhaps only certain elves had the ability. She decided she would continue to study them further before revealing too much about herself.

"I not know," Pavula answered Salyaman in Onish. She had been learning their language while secretly studying it from their minds.

"I find that very difficult to believe," Salyaman said in Onish also. "Where did you come from?" he pressed.

Davion didn't like feeling as though they were interrogating her and sensed her uneasiness. "Perhaps she'd like to ask us something?" he attempted to mediate.

CHAPTER 15

Pavula nodded gratefully. "Yes," she responded hastily, "Dragons. Why hate? Why war?"

The group was taken aback, expecting questions about them, not dragons. However, Pavula knew more about them than they could possibly be aware of from peeking into their minds, and she had always been fascinated by the dragons. Her mother had avoided talking about them with her, aside from the brief history lesson she recently received. Whenever she did, it was simply that they, along with everyone else, were not to be trusted. It all left her very confused. Was she really not supposed to trust *anyone*?

Amongst these elves, she had hoped to finally find out why they were at war. After all, how untrustworthy could this group be that has taken care of her since they met? If they meant to do her harm, they had ample opportunity. However, that didn't mean that she was going to tell them her whole life story either. She still respected the teachings of her mother and the sanctity of her clan's location and safety.

"Hmmm... Well now, there be a big question," Hort huffed. "Perhaps the elf should tell ye since they be the ones that started the war."

Salyaman scowled at Hort, clearly not pleased with the accusation. "The elves were not the ones."

"Okay," Hort responded sardonically, "then why's they think ye are?"

Scooting Shakiera to the side, Salyaman sat upright, leaning toward them with his arms over his knees, and decided to entertain his cohorts. Before continuing, he asked Pavula if she could follow along in Onish, and she nodded in agreement.

A chill blew through the summer-night air, and Davion laid a green cloth cape over Pavula's shoulders to keep her warm. She felt strange not having a blanket of fur to nuzzle up to but decided this wasn't such a terrible alternative, and she pulled it tight around her.

Salyaman, in his strong, stern voice, focused their attention as he began to tell the tale of the dragon war from the elves' point of view, "Although it is rumored that the dragons are the eldest living race in Onis, the elves have a different record of how they came to be. Dragons are referred to as the ancient ones, and perhaps they are the oldest, but our books are written that it was the elves and other races that had come to Onis before them. The elves believe that the dragons abandoned their homeland from the east in Ardet and decided to settle in Onis for reasons knownst only to them.

"Before they came, the land was in turmoil with constant battles and wars breaking out in struggles for power. When the dragons appeared in our land, the great and powerful monsters that they are, they instilled a fear among all the races, and through that fear had managed to create an illusion of peace between them, which lasted for several millennia. They had appointed themselves as the almighty council between the races, and we each stayed in our corners of Onis, afraid of the wrath we would face if we crossed out of our territories.

"The factions all kept to themselves until one day the mother dragon; the One Dragon, Onis Caelis, ruler of all dragons and all the land, was found slain in her den. It had appeared as though the high elves of the forest had committed this treason, our weapons being found in the heart of the beast, and so the dragons declared war against the elves out of revenge. We still do not know why our weapons had been found there. There is no record of any plan to kill the mother dragon, and it is unlikely it was done out of self-defense. Elves are a peace-seeking people and would not have committed this act.

"The dragon, Onis Caelis, was all-powerful, the most powerful of any dragon. Without a full-scale attack of hundreds of thousands of men, she could only have been slain while she slumbered. We suspected that orcs or trolls had done so with stolen weapons. However, we were unable to find the perpetrators that committed this treason, were unable to bring them to justice, and, therefore, were unable to clear the high elves' name of this act. So, instead, the war lingered on between the dragons and the elves, never finding any peace or resolution.

"We elves became adept at defending ourselves from the dragons in our greatly-fortified cities, but we are still vulnerable outside of the walls. The Silvers—dragons of the air—hovered in the skies, watching and waiting for us to step beyond our protective walls, tearing us apart when we did, pecking us down little by little, and our numbers were dwindling. The Blues—serpent dragons of the seas—would hunt the Emerald Canal to the east and the North Sea, eating all of our fish and destroying every vessel, including any new ones that we would try to build. Our once-prominent port city, Ballat Sueda, was left completely in ruins.

"After much time, the full wrath of the dragons began to lessen, and they gradually became more negligent at keeping us confined within our walls. However, the Silvers still continue to commit random attacks against our kind, reminding us of whom are in power and of whom we must always fear. The Blues have since ceased their attacks on us so long as we keep clear of the waters. The Golds—dragons of the earth—have remained in mourning over Onis Caelis, keeping to themselves. No one has seen Reds—dragons of fire—and lived to tell the tale. They seem to stay within their desert and kill every race equally without prejudice.

"As the war raged on, the dragons, in their hate, became less particular about which race did them wrong. Instead of being the protectors and mediators of the land, they became its tormentors."

Taking a long sip from his flask, Salyaman looked around at the others for their reactions, but mostly to the strange elven girl.

"So, elves killed Caelis dragon," Pavula said in Onish.

"As it would appear," replied Salyaman, disheartened by what she took from that. "But appearances can be deceiving," he added.

Looking to the fire deep in thought, Pavula didn't understand why anyone would have done such a thing. "But dragons protectors. Dragons...good?"

"No," Davion interjected, "dragons are cold-blooded killers."

Pavula looked at Davion as though he had just said something foolish. It was all very confusing, and she was still trying to interpret Salyaman's story. To her, it sounded like the elves were at fault.

"They'll rip ye ta shreds given the chance, lass," Hort added. "Davion saved ye from one after ye knocked yer noggin'!"

Davion blushed as Pavula looked at him in wonder. "You *killed* dragon?!" she gasped.

"No, no, no..." Davion chuckled at the thought.

"He scared the beast off right 'fore it ate ye up!" Hort declared enthusiastically, waving his large drum-bone in the air.

Pavula looked back into the fire again, in shock that she had nearly been killed by a dragon. Davion had saved her life. She owed him a great debt. Already feeling connected to him, she knew he was definitely what was pulling at her. She was meant to be here, with him, now. Looking back into his eyes, she smiled at him and said, "Thank you, Davion."

The sound of his name on her lips sent a chill up his spine. He had never felt this way about anyone before. He'd had plenty of attention from pretty girls, but none that sent his heart racing every time he looked upon their face. Every muscle in his body yearned for her, to grab her, to kiss her, and to feel her skin against his. He couldn't help but envision it, what her skin would feel like, smell like... He knew he would do anything for this elf—as crazy as that thought seemed to him—that he would travel to the ends of Onis just to walk beside her. A gentle touch of her hand on his woke him back up from his fantasizing, and he blushed, replying, "You're most welcome, Lupé Pavula."

Not liking the chemistry that was growing between Davion and Pavula, Salyaman gruffly interrupted their moment. "It is time to get some rest. We have another long day ahead of us tomorrow."

They all nodded in agreement, and Davion went to Helna to put up his flask. Hort came up behind him, nudging him in his side. "Hmmm... Had ta be an elf," he said dolefully, "of all the laidens in Onis, it just *had* ta be an elf."

Blushing, Davion smirked at him, not falling prey to his goading by responding, but instead continued to prepare for the night ahead.

CHAPTER SIXTEEN

FOLLOWED

*A*s the group headed further north, Pavula noticed the trees begin to change color from the bright emerald-green which she had known her whole life, to bright orange and red leaves, with trunks speckled-white instead of brown. It all looked unnatural and strange to her but very striking. It seemed like something from a dream. Several bushes looked like red, fluffy clouds, while others were yellow or orange. Even the birds looked strange. She watched as one bird flew overhead, covered with many bright colors and a very long orange beak. As the sun shone through the leaves, the morning dewdrops blanketing the forest sparkled as though all the foliage were covered with glitter or gems.

"Where are we?" she asked Davion, in wonder of her surroundings.

"Ashwood Forest," he replied.

"It's beautiful," she said quietly in awe.

"It's the only surviving forest west of the river," Davion pointed out.

Another morning had crested over the horizon to the east through the great trees, the third since they had left the Trader's Post, and the unlikely band of cohorts was well on its way, having begun their trek well before dawn. The roads had thankfully been relatively clear since they defeated the several bands of trolls that had attacked the Trader's Post. As before, Salyaman and Shakiera led the expedition, walking up ahead.

Pavula refused to ride the horse, being so unfamiliar with them, so Davion chose to walk alongside her, Helna trailing closely behind. Hort was up to his cursing early this morning over the pain in his feet, but poor Orbek, still limping along, just wasn't up to the task of hosting any riders yet.

Davion had inquired why the elves didn't have horses of their own, and Salyaman explained that it was easier to get around by foot and that time held little importance to them. They were also much swifter on foot than humans or dwarves and possessed much greater stamina. Davion supposed that if he lived as long as elves did, that time would mean very little to him as well. The thought made him selfishly aware of the long life Pavula had ahead of her, daunting him that his life would be so short compared to the object of his affection.

Trying not to dwell on it, he playfully flirted with Pavula along the road, smiling, jesting, and complimenting her, taking every opportunity to brush his hand against hers or touch her arm. He even picked some strange—but beautiful—flowers for her as they passed them along the way.

As the morning sun gleamed on Pavula's lustrous golden locks, Davion tried not to stare at her beauty, blushing and looking away instead. He felt so silly when he was near her, like a giddy child, no matter how hard he tried to contain himself. Davion found himself regretting most of what he said to her, fearing it was all coming out wrong, making him appear awkward and dim.

The group continued on this way throughout yet another morning, Pavula getting better with her Onish the more she practiced, picking it up surprisingly fast in the opinion of the others. However, just as mid-day grew near, Pavula began to act strangely and distant from Davion, and he couldn't quite understand why. He thought perhaps he had pushed the flirting too far and had made her uncomfortable. Falling silent, he contemplated what he had done wrong.

Pavula, the excellent tracker that she is, knew there was something in the woods, but she wasn't sure yet if it was something good or something bad. She was listening to the trees for nearly an hour, listening to the lurker following them along the forest floor, completely hidden from view. Glancing over her shoulder a few times, she tried to sense what was out there without giving it away to the group in case it was one of her pack keeping an eye on her. Unfortunately, she was unable to covertly sense what the creature was.

After a while, the elves ahead stopped and declared that it was time to break for lunch. They gathered at the side of the road and grabbed some rations from their packs. Davion gave Pavula another piece of honeyed bread and some dried meat.

Spotting berries on the other side of some brush past a few trees, Pavula pranced off into the woods, keeping her eyes alert for their follower.

"Be careful!" Davion called out after her, wondering where she was going.

When she reached the berries, Pavula looked back at the group and saw that no one was paying attention to her. So, she took the opportunity to go further into the woods, sensing herself being watched by whatever had been following them. When out of sight from the group, she laid half of her bread and meat on a tree stump, then glanced around cautiously. Whatever it was, it was not going to make itself known, so she headed back to camp, grabbing a branch full of purple sweetberries on the way.

CHAPTER 16

After a quick lunch, the party began to pack up their belongings, and Davion attempted to make small talk with Salyaman. "So what is Má Lyndor like? I can't wait to see it."

Salyaman looked at the silly human and creased his brow. "We will only be taking Lupé Pavula. Neither you nor the dwarf need come along once we reach the Elven Outpost."

Davion took those words like a punch in the gut. He had no intention of letting Pavula go off with them alone—never to see or hear from her again. How could he know that she would be safe? Happy?

"I disagree," Davion huffed. "We do need to come along. She trusts me, and I won't let her down by abandoning her. When I know she's safe and is ready for me to leave, then I shall leave, but not before." He swallowed the pit in his throat from standing up to a royal elf. It wasn't like him at all.

Salyaman said something angrily in elvish that Davion didn't understand but knew it probably wasn't good. "You arrogant little human," he added in Onish for Davion to comprehend, then said, "I will keep her safe. She is *my* responsibility, and she will stay with me. Besides," he paused, composing himself, "only elves are welcome beyond our gates. Invited guests of other races are very rare and usually only due to special occasion."

"Sounds like ye be needin' ta make a special occasion then," Hort scowled.

"Please, stop," Pavula interjected. They all turned and looked at her quizzically, apparently forgetting that she understood what was going on. "I stay with Davion."

Davion triumphantly smiled as he looked back to Salyaman, who was not at all happy.

"Why do you choose this *human* over your own kind?" Salyaman questioned her.

Pavula knew she couldn't explain it, but she knew she was called to Davion, even though she didn't know why yet. However, she'd been feeling a new pulling to Salyaman as well that she couldn't explain either, ever since he took her hand when she woke on the trail. It was different from her connection to Davion, though, making her uncomfortable around him, especially knowing Salyaman's bound to Shakiera. So, she tried desperately to push him from her thoughts.

"He saved my life," she said, trying to satisfy his curiosity.

"As did I," added the elf resentfully. "I healed your wound."

Shakiera looked at her husband curiously and took his hand, calming him.

"Do you have any idea who your family is?" he inquired, slightly more poised.

Shaking her head, Pavula replied, "No. I not."

"And how is it that you learned the common tongue so quickly?" pressed Salyaman.

Suddenly, Davion stepped forward in front of Pavula, blocking her from the royal elf. "Leave her alone!" he shouted to him. "Perhaps she chooses a *human* because I'm the only one that seems to trust her and doesn't put her on trial!"

"I go to your Má Lyndor," Pavula said, gently pushing Davion to the side, "but Davion come, and his Hort."

Davion smiled at Pavula and thanked her, assuring her that he was there for her and wouldn't let any harm come to her. Hort scoffed at being called 'his Hort' like he was a pet or steed and muttered to himself.

Pavula's attention was distracted back to the bushes behind them as she sensed their lurker nearby. Realizing Davion had still been talking to her, Pavula looked over to him and attempted to listen. Trying to get her mind off of the trees, she opened her mouth to respond to him when, suddenly, Salyaman whipped

CHAPTER 16

around, drawing his bow, and, within the blink of an eye, shot an arrow into the woods behind them. They all turned to look toward the woods when a male voice screamed in agony as he was struck with the arrow.

"Show yourself!" commanded Salyaman to the prowler.

The bushes and limbs rustled, and Salyaman loaded another arrow into his bow, keeping it aimed at the trees. Fumbling out of the forest came forth a man shrouded in dark clothing, clutching at his stomach around where the arrow was embedded. The figure groaned with every movement and cursed at Salyaman with its masculine voice in another language that Pavula hadn't heard thus far. Clad in all dark attire, the man wore a black tunic and trousers, a black cloth cape, black leather boots, and maroon leather-embossed bracers and shoulder pads. There were daggers sheathed at the side of each leg, their hilts shining in the afternoon sun, and the handle of a sword peeked over his shoulder from a strap on his back. The figure was cloaked with his hood hanging low, concealing his face, and his dark gloves revealed nothing to Pavula about what was hidden underneath.

"Baccat!" Hort cursed, hastily drawing his axe, seeming to have a very good idea of what he was looking at. "Don't ye dare move!"

Pavula watched as Davion and Shakiera swiftly grabbed their staffs, ready for battle. *What's going on?* she gaped nervously.

The figure stopped and raised his hands to the air, the arrow still lodged in his gut, and he fell slowly to his knees. "Please," came a soft masculine voice from the shrouded figure, pleading in Onish, "don't kill me."

"Who are you?" Salyaman questioned, still aiming his bow at the man.

Slowly, the man grasped his hood with both hands, pulled it back, and let it fall to his shoulders behind him. Pavula gasped as she saw the strange being underneath. His skin was dark like ash, and his eyes were red as blood. Long white wispy hair flowed down over his shoulders, and his dark-ash ears poked out through his hair into long points. He was not hideous or malformed as she suspected an evil monster would look based on the others' reaction to him but was actually quite beautiful. Even though his hair was white as snow, his face did not appear to be aged. His skin was tight and smooth, no stubble to be seen, and he had two scars streaming down like tears from his right eye to his cheek. The mysterious stranger looked up at them with pained eyes.

"Who are you?!" Salyaman demanded again, pulling back on his bowstring, threatening to release.

Taking a deep breath and releasing it with a loud sigh, the stranger spoke, his voice much gentler-sounding than his appearance, "I am Nikolean Den Faolin, Son of Nikososo Den Faolin of Duep Nordor."

"Why are you so far from home, drow?" Salyaman spat, not impressed by his title. To the dark elves, 'Den' implied that he was from a high-ranking or honored drow family. By naming his father, he was identifying who had attained the family's honor.

"I... I..." The dark stranger's eyes began to roll, and he fell in slow motion sideways to the ground, unconscious.

Salyaman hesitantly lowered his bow. "Let's go," he said to the group and turned to leave, Shakiera at his side.

"Sounds good ta me," Hort added, joining them.

Davion had fortunately never encountered a drow before now and couldn't help but stare. He noticed Pavula watching with the same curiosity. Looking to the others, he realized they were already departing, so he quickly looked back to Pavula.

"Come on," he said gently to her, "let's go."

"No," Pavula surprisingly responded. "I no leave him to death." She looked up the path to Salyaman. "You heal him!" she

CHAPTER 16

called after him. "You healed me; you heal him!"

Salyaman stopped and turned, marching halfway back toward her, and firmly replied, "I will do no such thing! Drow are the vermin of Onis and are all that is unholy and evil. One less drow is one more gain for Onis. I would put another arrow to his chest, but it would be a waste of my arrow. He can stay and suffer until his time is passed."

"No!" Pavula shouted. "You heal him!"

Glaring at Pavula, Salyaman mimicked her, shouting, "No!" and she stepped back, shocked by his anger and behavior toward her. "Let the forest have him! I will NOT heal a drow!" He pulled down on the ends of his tunic, then pivoted and began to walk away haughtily.

Pavula felt anger growing within her; she didn't understand how she could feel any connection at all to such a heartless being, fuming herself into a trance as she glared at Salyaman walking away from her. *How can he be so cruel?* she seethed.

The wind began to whip wildly through the trees around them, stirring all the branches and the dirt from the path. It blew in from the north fiercely and strongly flung loose debris everywhere. Within moments, the bright summer sky had darkened; the sun blocked behind storm clouds that rumbled with thunder, and lightning touched down in the distance. Helna and Orbek pranced back and forth in the gale, confused, and everyone quickly grabbed onto their things to keep them from flying away.

"Looks like there be a storm brewin'!" Hort called out through the howling winds picking up speed. He held his helm tight to his head with one hand, his axe still drawn in the other. "We best be findin' some shelter!"

Shakiera, recognizing the storm's isolation and sudden fierceness, knew something was off and glared wittingly at Pavula.

"Lupé Pavula!" Davion called, shaking her out of her

trance. "Let's go! There's a bad storm coming!" He took her hand and tried to pull her forward, but she held her ground, shaking her head at him. Davion watched Pavula as she closed her eyes, taking a deep breath, then blew out softly through puckered lips. Just as quickly as the storm had picked up, it began to die back down until the skies were once again clear.

Salyaman and Hort were looking around, disoriented, until they saw Davion holding Pavula's hand, staring at her in amazement.

"She's an arcanist!" Shakiera called out, and they walked swiftly back to her. "But not even I can create such a large storm, nor quell it."

"What was that?" Salyaman demanded. "You did that?"

Pavula looked at him sternly and repeated, "You heal him."

His shock quickly returned to anger. Staring back at her equally sternly, Salyaman said, "No," again. "His fate is set. Let us leave now." He held out his hand toward Pavula, who had no intention of taking it.

Suddenly, from behind her, Pavula heard Nikolean coughing and turned to see him spit out blood onto the ground. *He's dying,* she realized and ran to him. Looking over him, she had no idea what to do and began to panic. If Salyaman wasn't going to heal him, then she would have to try to help him herself.

Pavula grabbed the arrow and yanked it as hard as she could until it came out with a gush. Blood began pouring from the wound, and Nikolean went limp. Overwhelmed and over her head, Pavula tried to press her hands over the wound to stop the bleeding, but it didn't seem to be doing anything.

"Please!" she yelled, desperately looking up to Salyaman, hovering over her. "Help!"

Salyaman crossed his arms over his chest, smirking down at the dying drow as he replied, "No."

CHAPTER 16

CHAPTER SEVENTEEN

INTERROGATION

*P*ressing down on the bleeding wound in the drow's gut, Pavula closed her eyes, trying not to cry from all the pressure she was feeling and the aggravation that no one would help her. She strove to concentrate on what to do and barely noticed Davion's hand on her shoulder, nor him telling her to, "Leave him."

A gentle breeze blew through the trees around them. Pavula could hear the leaves rustling and the birds chirping from their branches. A calming feeling began to sweep over her as she connected with the earth spirit, and it warmed and soothed her thoughts. Everything disappeared from her mind except for the sounds, smells, and feel of nature and the dying drow under her palms.

Nikolean's breathing had become shallow and weak. Pavula could feel the bleeding slowing down, but not by anything she had done, and she knew that he was dying. She tried to reach into him the way she reached into the earth, sending her thoughts through her fingertips and flowing out through them into the dark elf beneath. It was a strange feeling, entering her thoughts to his flesh, and she wasn't sure what she hoped to accomplish by doing this. However, images of him filled her cerebrum; all the parts within him, including the wound that was causing his life to drift quietly into nothingness. Through him, she felt his heart beating faintly and the energy slowly leaving his body. Then, like a tidal wave, it hit her. *Energy! Spirit energy!*

Without hesitation, Pavula pulled the energy from the earth surrounding her, up through her legs, up through her torso, down through her arms, hands, and fingers, out into the drow. The energy flowed rapidly through her, causing his heart to beat hard and fast and his lungs to gasp for air. Pavula had forced life back into him, but she also felt his now strongly-beating heart causing more blood to pulse through his open wound.

Directing her thoughts only to the wound under her fingers, Pavula focused on the torn flesh and the hole tearing through him. She also became aware of the further damage she had caused by yanking the arrow out. His flesh was shredded, and the hole was piercing through into his stomach, which had been filling with blood. She concentrated with all of her strength on the wound and envisioned tiny tendrils pulling the broken flesh back together. The torn tissue began to become restored slowly; realigning, and sealing itself. Her hands began burning hot as she continued to push energy into the drow, but she realized that it was working! She couldn't stop now!

Nikolean convulsed and threw up the blood from his stomach, but Pavula didn't let go. She kept pouring her thoughts and energy at the wounds, pulling them closed one by one until she could find no more to mend. Then, when she believed there was nothing left to be done, the energy stopped flowing out into the dark elf. She let him go and fell backward, flat onto the ground. While she lay there, and without thinking, energy continued to seep into her through the dirt, restoring her life force, giving her back just enough to sit herself up.

CHAPTER 17

Davion, kneeling beside her, helped Pavula sit up while the others looked on in astonishment. "Are you okay?" he asked her.

Gathering her bearings, Pavula looked over to the drow, who was still slumped on his side—awake—watching her with heavy eyes. He was very lethargic and wanted to thank her but couldn't bring himself to speak. Pavula sensed his appreciation and smiled before looking around at the trees. She noticed that all of their leaves had withered and died. The grass, flowers, and bushes; all dead within a twenty-foot radius surrounding them. But...Nikolean survived.

"What in Ignisar's lair was that?" Hort scoffed.

"My thoughts as well," Salyaman added. "No arcanist also has the magic to heal." He strode cautiously over to her. "No more lies. Who are you, Lupé Pavula? How do you have both arcane *and* healing magic?"

"I not understand," Pavula replied honestly. She didn't know what arcane magic was. She only knew of the spirits and the energy that they all possessed. "I heal like you."

"No!" Salyaman responded. "Not like me. Why are all of the trees dead?! What did you do?!"

Pavula was exhausted and didn't feel like answering any more questions. She shook her head and looked back to Nikolean again, wondering why he wasn't doing better. "What wrong?" she asked.

Salyaman followed her gaze. "Likely, he has lost too much blood," he told her, looking at the drow grudgingly. "You closed the wound, but it will take time for him to regain what he has lost."

"He be okay?" Pavula asked.

Sighing, Salyaman replied, "Unfortunately, yes."

They all watched as the drow drifted out of consciousness again.

"Now that you know he will be okay, can we resume our traveling?" Salyaman asked her.

"No." Her response didn't surprise any of them. "Come with us until better."

Davion didn't believe he could ever be mad at his beautiful elf, but in this moment, he was not very happy at all. He couldn't see why she refused to believe that he was evil, that all drows were evil. How could even she want to save such a wicked creature?

"We can't just sit here and wait for him to heal," Davion pointed out. "We need to keep moving."

Pavula looked at him disappointedly and pointed to Helna.

"Oh, no!" Davion said with contempt. "Not on Helna!"

"Then, I stay. You all go," Pavula said, knowing they would not leave her.

"Maybe we should," Salyaman said disdainfully. "You are not what you seem. How do we know you are to be trusted when you clearly possess abilities beyond our understanding?" He said the words, but he didn't believe them himself. Salyaman did not like the tug he felt at his heart towards this strange girl and how the thought of leaving her behind made him sick to his stomach.

"What are you saying?" Davion asked.

Pavula realized she was going to have to tell them *something* to satisfy their curiosity. She stood up, uneasily, to stop Davion and Salyaman from fighting again. "Air spirit bring storm. I tell it, 'let go.' Earth spirit give me life for Nikolean elf. I no do. Spirits make magic. I ask them to do."

Trying to wrap his head around her words, Salyaman paced back and forth. "Most elves are a part of magic," he told her, "but we pull from different branches of magic based on our abilities, given to us through birth. I am a ranger, and my magic comes from the earth, which also gives me minor healing abilities."

"I am an arcanist." Shakiera stepped forward. "My power stems from air magic and allows me to control the electricity around us, including manipulation of the storms and the lightning."

"Davion is a pyromancer, using fire magic," Salyaman continued. "And there are several other classes, but each has its own limits. I do not understand what class you are." He looked to her for answers, but she had none. She knew nothing of classes, nor these strange names that they were given.

Pavula said the only thing that made sense to her, "I spirit class then. I talk to all spirits."

"An elementalist, perhaps?" Shakiera chimed in. "There has not been one since...beyond our years. However, they could not heal either."

"My father will know what she is." Salyaman gave up, frustrated. "We just need to get back to Má Lyndor, and he will know. Although, we will never get there if we are to wait for this...thing...to get better," he snarled disdainfully, pointing at Nikolean.

Pavula pointed up to the sun for Salyaman to see that it had become late in the day. None of them believed how much time had passed. "Stay with Nikolean elf tonight. Tomorrow go Má Lyndor."

Weighing the chance of getting her to leave the drow, Salyaman knew he was fighting a losing battle and agreed to her terms. "Fine," he said. "But tie him up in case he wakes. He is likely to slit our throats while we sleep."

Curling her lip at Salyaman, Pavula agreed to his terms.

As they all looked at the dark ashen elf in silence, a loud rumbling was heard, startling Pavula and the others.

"Hmmm... Must be time fer me dinner," Hort said, patting his rumbling belly.

* * *

After they had all eaten their dried food provisions and washed them down with wine and water, Shakiera led Salyaman away from the group. Something had been bothering her greatly. He joined her willingly, all the while keeping a close eye on the dark elf, as well as the others. They had brought the drow along, further into the woods off the path, binding his hands around his back to a tree. He had remained unconscious since Pavula had healed him, and the group was starting to get settled for the night.

"I am worried for you, husband," Shakiera said softly in elvish, taking his hand. "You have been acting not yourself since we met the young girl."

Salyaman looked lovingly at his wife and smiled. "You should not worry, my love. All will be better once we get her back to Má Lyndor and away from the others."

"Forgive me," Shakiera added hesitantly, "but what is the girl to you? Why do her affections for the human seem to distress you so?"

The smile left Salyaman's face as he realized her true concern. "Oh, Kiera," he said, trying to find the words, "I do not understand why I feel drawn to Lupé Pavula, but I can assure you that it is not what you are thinking. There is some force beyond my understanding that makes me feel responsible for her well-being; that makes me feel like I need to keep her safe, that I must protect her. That is all, I promise you." And he meant every word.

"If that is what it is," Shakiera replied, "then I shall assist you in protecting her. In protecting all of us." She took his hand, placing it gently over her abdomen, waiting a moment for him to understand, and then wrapped her arms around his neck.

He smiled at her, knowingly, and embraced her most tenderly.

CHAPTER 17

Pavula was feeling very much alone, and witnessing the loving exchange between the elves wasn't helping. Even Davion wasn't talking to her, and she didn't know what she should do. She missed her mother more than anything right now and wished she could ask for her guidance. There was no lesson on any of this; no lesson on the drow and why they were hated so severely; no lesson on how to stop the hatred. He had been following them for some time and never once tried to harm them, not even when she was alone in the woods with him close by. *How could they know his intentions or hate him so much when they were the ones that have done the harm to him?*

Pavula heard a wolf howl far in the distance and looked up at the glowing moons, nearly side-by-side rising up high in the sky; the sun still not quite set. Many nights she had stared at those moons, Jayenne and Kyrash, had marveled at them beside her kin and mother, howling at them herself along with her family. The wolf that she heard wasn't of her pack; she knew that. It was unfamiliar, and that made her feel even more separated from her home. *Mother...*

A single tear rolled down her cheek, and Pavula wiped it quickly away with the back of her arm before looking over at the drow. She was startled to find him looking back at her, having assumed that he was still unconscious. *How long has he been awake?* she pondered. A quick, subtle glance around at the others assured her that she was the only one that knew. *'Can you hear me?'* she thought toward him, wondering if any of these creatures were capable of mind-speech. There was no response. She would have to find another way.

Nikolean bore into Pavula with his burning-red eyes, his face without expression. It irked her not to know what he was thinking, and she wished more than anything to be able to talk to him before the others knew he was awake, to find out more about him without their hatred getting in the way.

"Well, look who's up!" Hort barked, bringing everyone's attention to the drow. Nikolean sneered at the dwarf. Pavula, startled, realized she wouldn't get her chance.

"I Lupé Pavula," she introduced herself. Nikolean looked back at her, softening his gaze as she continued, "I heal..."

"Enough with the introductions," Salyaman cut her off. "Why were you following us, drow?" he demanded.

Turning his gaze to Salyaman, Nikolean glared at him without answering.

"What is your purpose here, so far from your territory? What ploy are you up to?"

Nikolean spat at the ground without turning his eyes from Salyaman. The high elf haughtily drew one of his swords, ready to get some answers out of him—one way or another.

Pavula interceded, "He need food."

Davion sighed heavily. "We're not sharing our food with this monster, Lupé Pavula. He's received more than enough kindness from us simply by not being dead."

"I get." Pavula grabbed her dagger from where she had tucked it in her belt and, without another word, disappeared into the darkening forest.

"Lupé Pavula!" Davion called out after her. "I should go with her," he added, turning to the others.

"No," Salyaman replied. "Something tells me she knows what she is doing."

"Daft laiden," Hort said. "I'd go, but I'd be damned ta help a dark elf. She be on 'er own." He began sharpening his axe with a stone, attempting to intimidate their hostage.

Davion was getting frustrated with Pavula, not knowing how to get through to her about how evil and sinister the drow of

Onis are, with the darkness of their skin penetrating through to the depths of their hearts. The stories Davion had heard growing up of the drow's lust for power, and their delight in the torture, pain, and suffering of others, was a thing of nightmares to scare children into behaving. Otherwise, the drow would come for them and drag them away in the night to their underground fortresses of torture.

"If you expect to get anything to eat, you better start giving us some answers," Salyaman said to Nikolean.

"I will tell Lupé Pavula when she returns," he responded assertively in his soft, but firm, masculine voice.

Hort stood up, waving his axe toward the drow, and ranted, "This is utter nonsense. Why dunna' we kill 'em now while we can, 'fore she returns."

"I'm pretty sure she'll figure out who did it, Uncle," Davion said sarcastically. "Do you know her?" he asked Nikolean—no answer.

Before they could ask him anything else, Pavula emerged from the bushes holding up a large, dead mole-rat creature by the tail, a smile across her face. "Need fire," she said to Davion.

"Well, I'll be a hobbit's uncle," Hort said, admiring Pavula. "Why the baccat 'ave we been eatin' dried meat and stale bread? Fire up the pit, boy!"

Unpleased that he was assisting in feeding the drow, Davion half-heartedly started preparing a firepit. "We needed a fire anyway," he snarked.

"Let's hear it, drow," Hort said to Nikolean. "The laiden be back now, so spit it out."

Pavula looked between the two of them, confused.

"I am Nikolean Den Faolin..."

"Yeah, we 'erd that part. Answer the questions!" Hort demanded.

"I am Nikolean Den Faolin," he repeated to Pavula, "son of Nikososo Den Faolin of Duep Nordor. I, like many before me, have rebelled against the elders and their ways and left my homeland." He took a deep breath, clearly struggling to talk so much so soon, and Pavula handed the rodent to Salyaman, who took it hesitantly before passing it to Davion. Pavula sat down near Nikolean. "We believe they have upset the natural balance, and our land has been suffering from their actions. It was no longer about which race is more superior but became so dark that the land had forsaken us. Our trees are all dead, we can grow nothing without magic, and the desert's heat has crept into our lands, causing cracks in the terrain with hot lava coursing through its veins. The Drakka—drow rebels—have uncovered secrets about the elders, discovering what has caused all of this turmoil and death. Some have stayed to fight, and others have left, wandering the lands aimlessly, searching for a solution."

Davion had started the fire while Nikolean talked, trying hard to bite his tongue. Hort wasn't as reserved. "What a load o' okullo dung!" Hort exclaimed. "I s'pose ye be tellin' us yer a *good* drow?" He leaned his head back in laughter. "That be the dumbest thing I had tickle me ears."

"Why have we never heard of the Drakka?" Salyaman asked skeptically.

"We don't exactly go around announcing our betrayal to our own kind. It has only been a few years since we discovered the truth."

"And what is this truth?" said Salyaman.

"I cannot tell you," Nikolean replied.

"Of course not," Hort said.

"Perhaps you will tell the tip of my sword," Salyaman added, eager for an excuse to slit the drow's throat. He pointed the tip of his flawless elven-blade to the drow's face, who remained steadfast.

"No!" Pavula yelled at Salyaman, standing before his blade.

"Lass, ye better get outta the way!" Hort growled, stepping up beside Salyaman.

Salyaman lowered his sword. "It is okay, Mr. Strongarm." He looked at Pavula, waiting for her to back down, and calmly continued, "But I do still have questions."

Pavula turned and looked at Nikolean, who nodded to her that it was okay. This angered Davion greatly. Pavula stepped to the side but remained close, ready to retaliate if needed.

"It is a fascinating tale, drow," Salyaman said, "but it still does not explain why you were following us."

Looking to Pavula, Nikolean said simply, "Her. Not you."

Pavula looked back at him bewildered. *This was all my fault? Him getting hurt?* she wondered, feeling pangs of guilt.

Everyone turned their gaze to Pavula, all wondering the same thing: *Why her? Who is she?* Salyaman feared it was the same reason he could not leave her, as tempted as he had been a few times—his fear was correct. Nikolean felt that same pull toward Pavula as Davion and Salyaman did from the moment he spotted them in the forest. Beyond his control, he had to find out who she was, what was so intriguing about her.

Pavula didn't know what to say; she didn't understand any of this. Davion, on the other hand, had a lot that he wanted to say but was trying to choose his words wisely and not speak purely out of anger.

"So, what are we going to do with him now?" Davion asked Salyaman quietly, pulling him aside and struggling to remain calm.

"I do not know," he responded. "We cannot exactly leave him. He has recovered at an alarming rate for having lost so much blood. He would likely just continue to follow us and kill us given a chance."

"And Lupé Pavula will not let us kill him," Davion pointed out, agitated.

"I fear," Salyaman said, hesitating before finishing his thought, "we will have to take him with us to Má Lyndor. They will bring him to trial and decide what is to be done with him. Perhaps he will be more forthcoming with them about the Drow Rebellion."

Davion saw the way Nikolean was staring at Pavula, who was smiling at him uncomfortably, so he cut away from Salyaman. He took Pavula's arm and led her further away. "You can't trust him," he told her. "I don't know what I'd do if he hurt you."

Pavula still wasn't sure what to think of Nikolean—or any of this. She simply nodded and stood back.

Shakiera strode over to her husband, wrapping her arm in his. "What have you decided, my love?" she inquired.

"Lupé Pavula," Salyaman began, "you have left us with no other alternative than to take him with us."

"Baccat!" Hort cursed and threw his axe, impaling it into the ground.

"He will be our prisoner until we arrive in Má Lyndor, where he will then be tried, and his fate will be determined." Seeing the confusion in her eyes, Salyaman clarified, "He will remain tied up for the journey, and the elves will choose what will become of him."

Taking a moment to consider his decision, Pavula nodded and said, "Okay."

"Great," Davion griped sarcastically under his breath.

The drow seemed uninterested in Salyaman's announcement and continued staring at Pavula hauntingly. She fidgeted with the cords from her dress uneasily under his gaze.

"Now that we've got that settled, let's see ta this 'ere meat," Hort said, grabbing the large rodent and hacking it apart.

Davion led Pavula over to sit beside the fire, resting his hand on the small of her back, and glanced over at the drow, who was staring at them eerily. He laid out his blanket for her to sit on, as before, and sat beside her, his arm presumptuously around her. Pavula, accustomed to the closeness of her kin, enjoyed the warmth and comfort.

"I'll take the first watch tonight," Davion volunteered, devising a plan to get rid of the drow. He figured he could stage an escape, giving him just cause to kill him. Perhaps he would let Hort know his plan so he could assist. Davion really didn't have any experience planning assassinations.

"I will join you," Salyaman said firmly. "We shall keep watch in groups of two now that we have more than the forest predators to keep an eye on."

Nikolean snarled at Salyaman but didn't respond, and Davion ground his teeth; his plan thwarted. *Maybe not tonight, but there's still more nights, drow.* Davion schemed, scowling at Nikolean.

CHAPTER EIGHTEEN

PURPOSE

Relieved to finally be back in Helna's saddle, Davion smiled at the feeling of Pavula holding him tightly around the waist from behind. Having given into the invitation from Davion two days prior, Pavula was very sore and uncomfortable on the horse's back; however, she was not used to walking so far every day and had become weary. With her new healing knowledge, Pavula was able to completely restore Orbek's health, leaving a very grateful dwarf, also happy to be back in his saddle. Three nightfalls had passed since then and since the encounter with the drow, but even with the aid of the mounts, everyone was exhausted from the long journey.

With their speed and stamina, the elves insisted that they didn't need a horse and kept up with Helna and Orbek's slow trot, managing to pick up some of their lost time from the encounter with the drow. Said drow was now being pulled by tied hands behind Orbek, with Hort holding Nikolean's lead, purposely tugging on the rope from time to time, making him stumble and fall.

Pavula hated how they were treating Nikolean, but he had recovered speedily, his blood replenishing at an alarming rate given the energy she had pumped into him. So, she tried to take comfort in knowing he was at least well, even if her cohorts insisted on treating him like a rabid animal.

All six travelers were grateful that there was only one more night ahead of them before they would reach Má Lyndor. Since Pavula had made it clear that they would *all* be going on to Má Lyndor, to save time, Salyaman agreed to bypass the Elven Outpost, where he originally planned to leave the others. Overall, they had to agree that it was a relatively easy trip and were surprised that the only real trouble they had encountered was the drow.

Nikolean, being hauled along, kept to himself, not conversing with any of them. However, he maintained his creepy gazing toward Pavula. Davion wanted to pummel him every time the drow looked at her, but he managed to maintain his cool—for the most part.

Up ahead, Salyaman had stopped and whistled at them, signaling to move into the forest. Davion led Helna off into the shrubbery after the elves, and Hort followed with Orbek, dragging Nikolean behind them. A rumbling came from the path ahead, and they quickly took cover in the woods, dismounting from their steeds.

"What is it?" Davion whispered to Salyaman while ducking behind a bush and trying to spy on the road.

"Orcs," he replied quietly. "We're getting closer to their home ground."

Davion nodded, understanding, and signaled an 'O' with his hand to Hort; the universal warning sign for 'orcs.' Hort nodded and quickly pulled Nikolean to cover. Davion raised Pavula's hood, covering her head, then ducked with her behind a bush. He kept his hand on the small of her back protectively, ready to guide her if needed.

The group peered through the brush and watched the path nervously as a band of three large orcs made their way noisily down the road, grunting in their guttural language to each other. They were large monstrous creatures standing over eight feet tall, bulging with a combination of fat and muscle. Their rounded heads, with their beady yellow eyes, were too small for their bodies, and tusks jutted out from their muzzles. The third orc's tusks were broken off short, while the others were long and sharply pointed. Their skin was a muddy grayish-brown, and they wore tattered animal-skin loincloths. Each of them was carrying a large wooden mallet, the size of a human leg, covered in metal spikes. The one with the broken tusks had a dead deer-like animal flung over its shoulder.

As the orcs made their way down the path, the others all held their breath, trying not to move. Salyaman fidgeted anxiously with his bow, debating whether or not they should attack, but Shakiera touched his hand to calm him and shook her head. He knew she was right, but it didn't change how much he wanted to wipe the earth of the orcs. He hated them almost as much as the dragons, and they had been moving further in on the elves' territory. Davion also hated holding back but still lacked enough confidence to warrant anything reckless.

Once the orcs were gone from view and all appeared to be safe, the group began to relax and move about.

"We will set up here for the night," Salyaman said to the group, gesturing at the small span around them. The others agreed and began to prepare for their final night before reaching Má Lyndor.

It seemed as though they had been on the road forever, and Davion was already dreading the three-day trek from Má Lyndor to Lochlann—especially without his angel, Pavula. The only bright side was that they would be able to move faster without having to pace themselves for the elves and drow. *Ah yes, the drow.* He'd be rid of that scum too. *I suppose that would be a plus,* Davion smirked to

CHAPTER 18

himself, although it wasn't enough to compensate for being without Pavula. He quickly grew forlorn again.

Hort busied himself with tying Nikolean to a nearby tree and purposely kicked dirt at him before he left, smiling smugly to himself.

"I'll be glad ta not be draggin' that lout around after tomorra'," Hort said, elbowing Davion.

"Me too, Uncle," he replied, trying not to show his sorrow. Davion glanced over at Pavula, who was helping to gather stones for a firepit. He watched her as she worked while he relieved Helna of her saddle.

After making a decent pit, Pavula said bluntly to the group, "I go get food," then headed into the woods, dagger in hand.

"I'll take one of them rabbits if ye please, or another mole-rat be jus' fine too!" Hort called out before she disappeared, his mouth salivating as he recalled the fresh meat from the last few nights. "Or perhaps a nice fat hog, or miliak..." he continued muttering, mostly to himself.

Davion grabbed some nearby twigs and dried leaves, tossing them in the pit before sitting down next to Hort on a stump. The elves dispersed to gather some logs. Hort, as every night, was sharpening his axe attentively.

"What do you think they'll do with him?" Davion asked Hort, looking over at Nikolean.

The drow sat in silence watching them, no one ever knowing what was going on in that wretched drow-mind of his.

"So long as I dunna' have ta look at 'is face after tomorra', I dun care if they make dragon fodder of 'im," Hort replied, then spat on his sharpening stone.

"But what if they let him go?" Davion proceeded. "I was thinking...what if you and I take first watch? This is our last night before it's out of our control."

Hort looked over at Davion, surprised. "Boy, I knows what yer thinkin', and tis one thing ta kill a man in self-defense, but there be no comin' back from what yer talkin'." He took a deep breath, sighing loudly. "As much as I dun like trustin' the elves fer anythin', I dun think we have much choice in the matter."

"What if he breaks loose?" Davion said. "You know he'd kill us if given the chance. So, wouldn't it be self-defense to make sure he doesn't get that chance?"

Looking at Davion with disappointment, Hort shook his head. "Let it go, me boy. He be gone tomorra', and the two of us can be on our way."

Hort feared the boy's hatred toward Nikolean had more to do with jealousy than anything else. Pavula had continued to show nothing but kindness to the ill-deserved drow, and the way Nikolean would stare at her even made Hort's skin crawl. He had grown rather fond of Pavula, despite her being an elf, perhaps because of how happy she made Davion, he had concluded. He'd miss the spirited young elf and worried how Davion was going to manage after leaving her with the elves.

Pavula found herself deep in the strange wood, searching for something to hunt; a bent limb, a set of fresh prints in the soil, the rustling of nearby brush. But, to her dismay, she could find nothing. She looked around at the strange leaves and bushes and felt so out of place, and...lost, she realized. Sighing, she decided she would have to connect with the earth spirit again, both to find nearby animals and to figure out where she was.

Closing her eyes, she bent one knee to the ground, and, just as she was about to place her fingers into the earth, she heard, 'Lupé Pavula...'

Startled, Pavula jumped to her feet, looking around rapidly to find the source of the mind-touch. "Who's there?" she called out. The voice seemed familiar to her, yet strange.

'*Lupé Pavula...*' the voice came again. '*I am here.*'

"Who are you?" she called again. '*Where are you?*' Pavula sent out aimlessly in mind-speech, unsure of where exactly it was coming from.

'*Walk forward through the trees, and you shall see me. Do not be afraid, Lupé Pavula, I will not harm you.*'

Pavula tightened her grip on her dagger and walked slowly forward, shaking in her sandals, heart pounding in her chest. For a moment, she considered running in the other direction to go and find the others, but she *had* to know the source of the voice. She walked cautiously through bushes and over fallen tree trunks and unearthed roots, pushing her way little by little through the thick forest, glancing nervously around each limb. After shoving aside a large branch full of red leaves and flowers, Pavula's jaw dropped when she came into a clearing on the other side. There, sitting in the grass in the middle of the clearing, was the most magnificent being Pavula had ever beheld—*a dragon!*

The dragon's massive form nearly filled the entire clearing, making Pavula feel about the size of a mouse as she stood before it. Standing only a mere distance away, she admired the beautiful creature towering over her. The dragon's exquisite silver scales ran like metal armor along its frame, glistening in the evening sun, and its wings were tucked firmly against its sides. The dragon's head, less than twenty feet from her, was full of quills jutting out the back and down its long graceful neck, all the way to the tip of its tail. The front of its neck had scales of luminescent white cascading to its underbelly, which was mostly hidden by the ground. It looked at Pavula with its jaw shut, teeth protruding tightly over its lips in a non-threatening manner, and its solid-black eyes gazing down at her gently.

Pavula's dagger clattered against stone as she dropped it beside her in shock and awe. She couldn't believe what she was looking at, fearing she must be dreaming again, but it didn't feel like her other dreams. She could feel its breath on her face as it exhaled, could hear the rumbling in its chest. *'Who...?'* she began to send to the dragon.

'I am Turathyl of the Silvers, a dragon clan to the north,' the dragon's mind-voice bore into her, booming through her thoughts like thunder. It had been so quiet in her mind without her mother around, and she had to put up a slight wall to dampen the dragon's strong force. *'I have come on behalf of Lupé Caelis.'*

'You know my mother?' Pavula asked her, bewildered.

The dragon hesitated for a moment then replied, *'I do,'* when she realized Pavula was referring to the wolf god. *'She has sent me to watch over you on your journey.'*

Pavula was momentarily stunned and slightly hurt. Even after all of this, she was reminded that her mother didn't think that she could do this on her own. Yet, standing here in the presence of this great being, she could not bring herself to be angry.

'You were with me when I was lost in the Sacred Forest,' Pavula said to her, realizing why the voice had seemed familiar.

'Young one,' Turathyl responded, *'I have been with you since the first day you left your home, watching you from a distance. I was glad to come when Lupé Caelis called on me. I saved you from the trolls outside of that village.'*

Considering the dragon's words, Pavula thought back to the battle and what Hort had told her. *'You were the dragon Davion scared off?'*

CHAPTER 18

Turathyl rumbled in laughter, slowly waving her head from side to side. 'Scared off?' she chortled. *'I knew he was protecting you as well. So, I took my leave.'*

'Why are you here now? I mean, why are you letting me see you now?' she asked, trying to comprehend. Turathyl crossed her paws before her, and Pavula took the cue, kneeling to sit before the great dragon, and they both took ease.

'Much has been kept from you, young one. I have no intention of keeping anything more from you. So, if you are ready, I will share with you a little about why I am here.' Pavula nodded for Turathyl to continue. *'The war between we dragons—the ancient ones of this land—and the elves has been raging for far too long, each of us playing our parts. The ancients have reigned over Onis for many millennia. However, there was a time when it wasn't all mayhem and massacres; a time when there was peace in the great Onis. Alas, no more.'* Turathyl paused, lowering her head, recalling the countless years of war and loss. *'Long ago, there was rumor of a prophecy that would end this war. It was said that one day an elf would be born that would face the dragons and unite the races, not just bringing peace between the dragons and the elves, but between all the evolved races.'*

'Evolved races?' Pavula asked.

'Unfortunately, the trolls and orcs know only two truths: blood and hate. They are little more than savage animals that eat the meat of others, and of each other. There is nothing in them that can be tamed. However, the dragons, the elves, the humans, the dwarves, and even the drow, are said to someday become united due to a prophesied elf, the Omi Méa, or Great Spirit. Not everyone believes in this prophecy or that it will be an elf. Most dragons chaffed at the notion that an elf would dare come before us and live and would definitely not convince them to stop the war against them. Over the years, the prophecy has been nearly forgotten. Even I had forgotten of it long ago until Lupé Caelis reminded me when she called

upon me. I have grown tired of this war, tired of the fighting and killing with no end in sight.' The dragon sighed a loud rumbling breath.

'Lupé Caelis believes you to be the prophesied elf,' she continued earnestly, 'I cannot confirm if she is right, but if there is a chance that you are the one that can put an end to this war, well, then I offer my life to serve your cause. I will follow and protect you wherever your path may lead.'

Pavula shook her head, overwhelmed by what she was saying and still very confused. 'Is that what Mother was training me for? This prophecy?'

The great dragon nodded her head grandly. 'It is,' she replied.

'Why did she never tell me any of this?'

'I am afraid only she can answer that. But know that she believed in you wholeheartedly; believed that you were the Omi Méa, and that is good enough for me to believe it as well.'

'Mother said that dragons were ruthless killers, especially to the elves. I don't understand why you would offer to help me,' she said to the dragon. 'Don't you hate me? I am an elf, after all.'

Turathyl frowned down at the little elven child and, hiding the emotion from her speech, replied, 'Lupé Caelis is very wise. She is a god and knows knowledge far beyond any of us, but I never killed without cause.' She swallowed, feeling guilt over Pavula's true mother. 'I do not hate you, young one. I do not hate any elves, not really. I hate this war.' Turathyl said the last part bitterly.

'If I am this elf, what am I supposed to do? How am I supposed to end a war that has gone on for so long? I don't understand!' Pavula was feeling frustrated hearing the expectations being put before her. How could she possibly be this great elf that they think she is?

'Only you can answer that, Lupé Pavula. However, I have come before you tonight because you will be among the elves tomorrow. I suggest you start there. Perhaps get them on your side in ending this feud.' Raising her long neck to the sky, Turathyl sniffed the air and scanned towards the setting sun. The sky was golden with hues of pinks and oranges kissing the horizon. The air had begun to chill, letting a soft cool breeze sweep over the land, rustling the trees ever so slightly.

'You should head back to your friends before they come looking for you,' Turathyl said. *'I must leave for now, but call for me if you need me. I will not be far away.'*

Turathyl stood slowly to her feet, bones cracking and muscles aching after the long repose, and stretched herself out the best she could in the limited space of the clearing. The great dragon scratched her scaly neck with her hind leg, impacting the ground encircling her, and a radiant silver scale broke free and descended to the ground. Then, summoning the air around her, Turathyl spread her wings.

Pavula guarded her face as dust flew across her with Turathyl's liftoff into the air. After a great gust of wind and several wing-flaps, she wafted the dust from around her face and squinted to the sky. She watched as the silhouette of the dragon slowly disappeared into the nearly-dark sky, blending into the clouds above. Staring up for a long while, she tried to grasp what had just transpired, all the words repeating in her mind like stinging thorns.

Why do they think I'm the prophecy? How am I supposed to unite all of the races?! Her head was spinning with questions and doubts. *She said she never killed without cause, so mother was wrong. Dragons aren't as horrible as she said. And why would she have sent a dragon if she believed them to be so horrible?* Pavula, unsure of what all this meant for her or what she was supposed to do next, wished that the dragon could have stayed longer or at least given her more direction. So many questions were plaguing her mind that she couldn't think straight.

Suddenly, she was distracted from her thoughts when she heard her name being called frantically through the trees.

"Lupé Pavula!!!" Davion called out. "Where are you?!"

Picking up her dagger, Pavula ran into the clearing, grabbed the fallen palm-sized silver scale, and then darted back out, back into the forest toward Davion's voice.

"I here!" she called out to him.

Both of them running and calling out, they suddenly found themselves colliding into each other. Davion grabbed her arms to keep her from falling and then embraced her tightly.

"I was so worried!" he exclaimed. "We saw the dragon! Are you okay? Are you hurt?" He pulled her away, looking her over for any injuries. "What happened?!"

Pavula looked up at him warmly. All of the dragon's words floating around in her head were beginning to settle in fragments of clarity. "We go back to others. There much to say."

CHAPTER 18

CHAPTER NINETEEN

ALLEGIANCE

*G*athered around the lit fire, the group was eager to hear what happened in the forest. They had, of course, come up with their own theories in their heads after seeing a dragon take flight so close by. Mostly, they believed Pavula had hidden from it, but one amongst them remained suspicious, as always. Salyaman stood, arms crossed over his chest, waiting for her tales of the dragon.

"So, did the dragon see you?" Davion asked impatiently.

Pavula nodded slowly. "Yes," she replied. "Dragon call me and tell me something very big. Tell me...umm...story?" she looked at Salyaman, "fetian?"

"Prophecy," Salyaman translated for her. "And what do you mean, told you something? Dragons cannot speak to elves."

Pavula wasn't sure how or if she should explain it. So, she simply said, "Dragon speak to *me*."

They all looked at each other confused and alarmed, pondering whether to believe it or not.

Ignoring their reactions, Pavula nodded to Salyaman and continued, "Dragon tell prophecy of elf that make happy again." Getting frustrated to find the right words, she relied back to her own language, and Salyaman translated to the group.

While telling her story, she made sure to leave out any mention of Lupé Caelis. Instead, she told them all about the great dragon that she encountered, showing off her souvenir scale, and they admired it with awe. She told them about the prophecy and how the dragon believed her to be the prophesied elf. She explained that she was to unite the races, bringing an end to the war. Lastly, she told them of the dragon's vow to protect her.

As Salyaman finished translating to the group, they all looked at her like she was crazy—all but one. Nikolean, arms bound to the tree behind him, wiggled his way up to stand and cleared his throat. "I, like your great dragon, also pledge my life to your cause, Lupé Pavula. Since you saved my life, I owe you a life-debt, and I see no better way to repay it than to join you on your mission."

"Ta Ignisar's lair with that!" Hort yelled at him, raising his axe threateningly, but Pavula raised her hand to him and approached Nikolean calmly.

"I also wish to see an end to this war," Nikolean continued. "And, perhaps, it is what I've been searching for."

"Figured there 'ad to be some sorta personal gain fer 'im," Hort said to Davion under his breath.

"I accept," Pavula said firmly to Nikolean. The others sighed and mumbled displeasures under their breath.

Salyaman stepped forward to Pavula. "This seems like a far-fetched tale of fantasy," he said to her. "However," he sighed, "I saw the dragon with my own eyes, and I have seen things in you that I cannot explain. If there is any truth to what you say, and you *really* can put an end to this war," he paused, searching her eyes for reassurance that she was not insane, "then there is no one that would rather see that day come than the elves, myself included. I will join you."

Looking at Nikolean, Salyaman added, "As for the drow, he still must await trial in Má Lyndor. If they agree to let him honor

CHAPTER 19

his life-debt to you, then it is your choice whether or not he comes with us—wherever this endeavor may lead."

"I will join you as well!" Davion chimed in eagerly. He took her hands in his, looking into her beautiful eyes earnestly. "You have my word; I will let no harm come to you." He didn't know if he believed anything about the prophecy and was nervous about what he had just agreed to, but he was excited that tomorrow would not be his last day with Pavula. He only hoped that he could keep his word to her.

Pavula smiled back at him warmly. Her heart was filling with love as each of them supported her in her mission, even though she still had no idea what exactly it was. She had expected to be telling them all goodbye tomorrow but now was relieved that she would not be losing her new friends so soon and would not be alone in whatever was next to come.

"Hmmm... Well, if the boy be goin' with ye, then 'spose I best as well. Someone's gotta watch out fer 'im," Hort said, elbowing Davion, who smiled back at him.

Nodding her acceptance to Hort and the others, Pavula turned to Shakiera expectantly.

Shakiera said softly to Salyaman, "Husband, are you sure about this? This all seems..."

"I know, my love," he responded.

"And the baby..." she added, placing her hand caressingly over her stomach.

"Yes, I know." He kissed her forehead and held her close.

"Baby?" Hort interrupted. "Why ye not say nothin'?"

Davion held his hand out to Salyaman, unsure of the proper etiquette for an expectant elf-couple. "Congratulations!" he exclaimed.

Salyaman shook Davion's hand briefly, indulging him, then turned back to Pavula. "I will go on this quest with you, Lupé

Pavula, but Kiera will need to stay in Má Lyndor." He turned back to Shakiera, taking her hands and holding them to his chest. "I will be back to you as soon as I am able. You know this could mean a much brighter future for our son, my love."

"Or daughter," Shakiera said, smiling at Salyaman as they touched their foreheads together lovingly. "But, I could also be helpful if I came along."

"I could not risk our child," Salyaman objected. "I will be back to you both as soon as it is over. You have my word."

Shakiera nodded in acceptance, although she would never admit to him how nervous she was to agree to this; nervous he would never return; nervous of his unusual connection to Pavula. However, despite her nervousness, Shakiera knew that Salyaman would never sit idly by when there was a chance to bring an end to the war.

"It's settled then!" Hort exclaimed. "So, what'll be next?"

Everyone looked to Pavula for the plan, but she didn't have one. She only had the suggestion from Turathyl and replied, "We go Má Lyndor and speak with elves."

"Yes," Salyaman added. "The elders of the council may have some insight to this prophecy and will hopefully be able to offer their assistance. I will request reinforcements, and they will also need to determine the drow's fate."

Pavula still had doubts about her role in the prophecy. Her mother always told her she was destined for greatness, but she had no idea of the responsibility that would land on her shoulders—and so soon. Everyone would be looking to her to accomplish something that no one was able to in a millennium, and yet, here she was, still very much a child, with the weight of all civilizations on her shoulders. She had absolutely no idea what she was going to do—what any of them could do. However, she knew one thing for sure; she would not be going home any time soon.

CHAPTER 19

Sighing softly, she thought of her mother and how much she missed her: her beautiful snow-white fur, her warm embrace, her loving guidance. *Goodbye, Mother,* she thought sadly to herself, *I hope we will see each other again one day.* She wiped a tear from her cheek as she accepted that it was time to let go of her hopes of seeing her again erelong. Pavula now had a destiny to fulfill, and there would be no looking back after tonight.

Hort raised his flask, excited about the unknown journey: the new places he would get to see, the unknown creatures he would face, the stories he would have for back home. "Ta endin' the war!" he toasted.

Davion, Salyaman, and Shakiera each grabbed a flask—of various beverages—and held them high. "To ending the war!" they echoed.

Pavula smiled at their positive attitude, then looked over to Nikolean, who was staring intently at her with a weird smirk upon his lips. Looking away uneasily, she wished she could believe in herself the way they all seemed to.

Gazing up into the starry sky, Pavula closed her eyes after finding the blue moon, Jayenne, and prayed to her for a safe journey and guidance. After finishing her pleasantries with the goddess, she turned her eyes to the red moon, Kyrash. *I'm going to need you the most, Kyrash. Please protect us from the evils we will most certainly face, guide us to victory, and, if necessary, tear down all who try to stop us.* Pavula looked back to the group enjoying their drinks and telling stories and wondered what she had just got herself into.

* * *

Making their way through the forest, the path had vanished below them several hours prior, and Davion had been wondering if they were still going the right way. Salyaman trekked on without hesitation, and Helna and Orbek had to be guided by Davion and Hort on foot through the thick brush.

Shielded by the trees from the afternoon sun, Davion swatted at a bug on his neck. The bugs had become much worse—and bigger—since leaving the path, and he was eager to get to the elven city and out of this misery. He tugged Helna along behind him, bitterly watching as Pavula walked with Nikolean up ahead. The drow's hands were still bound before him, but he was no longer being dragged by Hort, attributable to Pavula's insistence. It was all very vexing to Davion, and he prayed to Kyrash that the elves would kill him at Má Lyndor, or, at the very least, imprison him.

Davion scowled as he watched Pavula draw nearer to Nikolean while they walked. Clenching his teeth, he tried hard not to intervene per Pavula's request after the last three times he had. It sickened him how protective and trusting she was of the drow.

"There is something I want to tell you before we reach the city," Nikolean said quietly to Pavula. She moved closer to him to hear. "I know the truth about what started the war; it is why I left Duep Nordor and the drows to join the Drakka."

Pavula gaped at him as he glanced around to make sure everyone was out of earshot before continuing. She leaned toward him attentively. "The secret the drow elders keep, the reason that our lands are desolate, and why the Drakka exist:" He paused, enjoying Pavula's intrigue, "the elves did not kill Onis Caelis, the mother dragon—it was the drow elders."

Nikolean looked again to make sure no one else had heard. Pavula pondered his words for a moment, staring straight ahead. Having not been part of the ongoing war, she really had no idea the gravity of what he was telling her but listened, trying to put the pieces together.

"It will probably all come to light in Má Lyndor, but I wanted you to know first." There was a slight smugness in his voice as he flicked his long-white hair from his eyes before continuing, "The Drakka believe it to be an affront on the balance and the reason why the drow have been suffering ever since." He leaned in closer. "I was drawn to you, Lupé Pavula, and now I believe I know why. It is my destiny to help you put an end to this war. I believe in you, and I will stay with you through to the end."

Pavula looked at Nikolean as they continued walking. *He doesn't even know me. How can he believe in me?* He was looking deeply into her eyes, captivating her with his blood-red stare. She believed she saw something in those eyes, much more than his words were saying. Blushing, she looked back to the path before them. *It's probably all in my head*, she thought to herself but wasn't convinced. Peeking over at him, she was disappointed to find him now looking away and pulling his hood over his face. The space between them had grown and was continuing to grow.

"We're not alone," Nikolean said quietly to Pavula before increasing his distance even further.

Pavula glanced around at the trees but saw and heard nothing. *Orcs?* she wondered, feeling anxious.

Suddenly, out from the encompassing trees came half a dozen elves, surrounding them with swords drawn, forcing them all into a tight circle. Pavula followed everyone's lead by huddling close to the others. She felt Davion grab her hand and pull her to him. The elves were tall like Salyaman and Shakiera; their clothes very prominent but camouflaged red and yellow like the trees around them. Their long swords were pristine with intricate markings adorning them, and they sparkled brilliantly from the sun's rays poking through the canopy above. The swords resembled Salyaman's fine blades in style, but his were of a different glass-like metal and even more beautiful than the others.

Ahead of them, another elf emerged from the brush, walking to them with a cocky stride. He was ensconced in exquisite, white plate armor, but it appeared much thinner and lighter than what Davion had seen from either the dwarves or humans. Yet, knowing what little he did about elves, he assumed it was probably twice as strong. The elf's swords remained sheathed at his sides as he approached them. He wore no helmet, and his long golden hair was tied back in a ponytail with two tidy braids hanging at the sides of his face. He looked at the group with his bright-violet eyes and smiled, opening his arms.

"Salyaman Dula'Sintos, my lord!" the armored elf exclaimed in elvish. "I did not recognize you with this..." Glancing to the rest of the group, his smile turned to a look of disgust. "Well, I did not recognize you." He looked back to Salyaman, smiling again, grasping his shoulders at arms' length.

Salyaman bowed his head sternly to the newcomer, then grabbed his plated forearm from his shoulder, shaking it firmly. "Lieutenant Neremyn," Salyaman said in a formal greeting before continuing in Onish. "How fare thee?"

"Well!" he replied, still in elvish. With a wave of his hands to the other elves, the lieutenant relieved the scouts. In unison, like a ballet, the elves withdrew their swords, held them straight up, and, in one fluid motion, sheathed them in their scabbards. They then took a step back, keeping the circle around the group, arms straight at their sides, and stared forward beyond them.

Startling everyone, one of the elves broke formation when he spotted ashen fingers poking out beyond the edges of Nikolean's sleeves.

"DROW!" he called out to the lieutenant while he grabbed his sword, wielding it at Nikolean with both hands. The other elves quickly followed suit, all drawing their weapons and holding them

CHAPTER 19

pointed at Nikolean. One of them inched forward and grabbed the drow's hood from behind, pulling it back to reveal his face.

"What is the meaning of this?" Neremyn questioned Salyaman.

Salyaman walked calmly to Nikolean, grabbed his wrist, and raised his hands for them to see that he was bound. "This is Nikolean Den Faolin, our prisoner," he declared for them all to hear. "I am bringing him before the council."

Neremyn looked back and forth between Nikolean and Salayman hesitantly. "I am afraid, my lord, that I will be taking him from here," he said firmly in Onish, giving Salyaman a respectful bow before turning to his men. "Take the prisoner! We have ourselves a drow roasting to perform!" Pavula's skin crawled as all the elves laughed eerily at Nikolean, and she wondered how literal they were being.

The scouts grabbed Nikolean roughly and quickly replaced his twine bindings with chains clamped at both his wrists and ankles. They then proceeded to gag and blindfold him.

Pavula watched in horror as Nikolean was pushed about and jabbed with the hilts of their swords, more than one of them spitting on him. She began to question internally which of the elven races the "evil" ones were. Davion held her back, afraid she might do something stupid, and Hort stayed close to both of them, at the ready.

When they were through with the drow, the scouts began to approach Davion and Hort, blindfolds in their hands.

"Is that really necessary?" Salyaman asked Neremyn.

"You know the law, my lord," he replied, and Salyaman stepped back, nodding.

"Hey! Wait a baccat minute!" Hort shouted, raising his hands to block them.

"It is okay, Mr. Strongarm," Salyaman said assertively. "It is just until we get to Má Lyndor. No outsider is to know its exact location."

Hort grumbled while he let them put a blindfold around his eyes, and Davion ground his teeth, remaining quiet as they did the same to him. Thankfully, that was all they did to them.

"Who is the girl?" Neremyn asked Salyaman in elvish, looking at Pavula's strange human clothes and darkly tanned skin. "She looks woodland." (The wood elves, or "woodland elves," being of a shorter stature and more tanned appearance than that of the high elves.)

"I suspect she is," Salyaman replied in elvish before switching back to common. "Her name is Lupé Pavula. She does not speak elvish."

Neremyn gawked at Salyaman, confused. "That is not an elven name either, of either faction," he said quietly, still in elvish. "Is she a stray?"

Salyaman nodded, unsure how much to reveal. "A victim of the war," he replied.

A look of understanding washed over Neremyn's face as he nodded slowly. "Ahh," he said empathetically. "Greetings, Lupé Pavula," he added in Onish, smiling creepily at her. She smiled back uncomfortably.

Neremyn gestured to two of the elves. "Grab the mounts!" he called to them. Then, he placed two fingers in his mouth and whistled toward the trees. Immediately, out of the brush where Neremyn had emerged earlier, came galloping a beautiful hoofed creature known as an elkah. It was slightly taller than Helna, with long slender legs, and was silky-white with brown speckles like the tree trunks around them. It had long, thick red antlers protruding up high from its strong but dainty head. The elkah had big dough-brown eyes, brown nose and lips, and a red-leather bridle over its face. It slowed down as it neared Neremyn, its head bobbing gently with each step before stopping in front of him.

With one quick motion, Neremyn leaped off the ground, flew gracefully onto the bare back of the elkah, and then grabbed its reins. "To Má Lyndor!" he commanded before giving the elkah a gentle kick.

CHAPTER TWENTY

MÁ LYNDOR

They had been traveling for nearly an hour with Neremyn talking incessantly at Salyaman about all of the goings-on since he was last in Má Lyndor. Not much of it was news to him as he had been getting regular updates from his friend, the captain of the guards.

Salyaman had left Má Lyndor two years prior, directly after marrying his love, Shakiera Nesu, who was neither a royal nor a lady of the court. His father had shamed him in front of everyone on what was supposed to be the most joyous day of his life, declaring that he, the rightful heir to the throne of Má Lyndor, would never be king after marrying a commoner.

One thing that he hadn't heard, and was quite perturbed about, was that his younger ill-suited brother, Saelethil, had been named crowned prince of Má Lyndor in his stead. Salyaman wasn't surprised since it was quite clear that he had brought shame upon the Sintos name, but it was still hard for him to accept. He gritted his teeth, trying not to say anything as Neremyn continued on, oblivious to the possibility of his news being upsetting in any way.

Meanwhile, Pavula sat atop Helna while Davion and Hort were forced to walk—no one riding the okullo, which was tied to Helna's saddle. One of the scouts guided Helna's reins ahead of

Pavula while the girl looked longingly into the trees, daydreaming. She couldn't get the image of Turathyl out of her mind. Wondering where the great dragon was now, she hoped that she could see her again soon.

Without understanding why, she was feeling rather lonely, as though she were missing a part of herself since Turathyl departed. She barely knew the dragon, yet she found herself missing her nearly as much as she missed her mother. Pavula looked up past the trees to the skies, searching hopelessly for any sign of a dragon in its clouds. The sky was rather clear that day and, other than a few fluffy cumulus clouds, she could see nothing except a small bird fly by above.

More than once, she sent thoughts out for the dragon, asking where she was, but there was never an answer. The image of walking into the clearing, finding a great Silver dragon replayed over and over in her head; the dragon's black eyes gazing on her; its gigantic, muscular form; its large, beautiful wings; its luminescent silver scales. While keeping it hidden and safe, she thumbed the silver scale that was palmed in her hand, feeling its smoothness, its coolness against her warmth.

Letting out a deep sigh, Pavula looked again to the road before her, wondering how much further it was to this grand elven city that Neremyn wouldn't stop talking about. It did sound like there were a lot of elves there from all of his gossiping, dozens perhaps. She wondered how they would take to her: Would they reject her as her mother anticipated? Would they have any answers for her? Would they be cruel to her? Kind? Would they think her crazy? Pavula had felt rather crazy herself since hearing of the prophecy. She even questioned if it was real or just another one of her visions, possibly even a dream.

Up ahead, she noticed a slight shimmering through the trees where everything looked a little out of focus. She was familiar with such a shimmer as she had lived inside of one her whole life.

Neremyn flicked the reins of his elkah and darted toward the shimmer but then stopped and turned to face the group right before reaching it. "Welcome," he said in common, "Miss Lupé Pavula, to Má Lyndor!" The elkah reared, Neremyn holding on tight, then he led it through the shimmer, disappearing beyond.

Pavula looked to Davion and Hort, who were still blindfolded and clearly oblivious to what was happening. Nikolean was also still bound, gagged, and blindfolded. All of them were led to the shimmer and guided through one at a time. As she approached, she realized it wasn't a forcefield like the one that surrounded her home—something impenetrable without the use of magic—but was simply an illusion.

She reached out her hand first as the horse's head disappeared before her and watched as her fingers and then hand became blurry before they disappeared also. Closing her eyes, she felt nothing as she passed through the field to the other side. When she opened her eyes again, she saw the most amazing sight she had ever beheld, even beyond that of her dragon and far beyond that of any dreams or fabrications of what she might discover one day.

On the other side of the veil, a large, beautiful city of white slowly came into focus. A wall of white stone stretched beyond their field of vision with tall battlements every hundred feet, each sporting large ballistas pointing up toward the skies. The pearly walls and parapets were etched to mimic the trees of Ashwood Forest, but they shone and glistened exquisitely. Above the city walls, Pavula could see towering, rounded buildings of the same white stone winding up into extended points with arched windows carved into them. Pavula was amazed at how many buildings she could already see before even reaching the gates and how massive the city appeared to be. There had to be hundreds of the tall stone buildings, which didn't even include the smaller dwellings they would discover hidden from view behind the walls.

Davion and Horts' blindfolds were removed, but Nikolean's remained, and the scouts dragged the drow past all of them toward the gates. Davion's eyes grew wide as he looked in marvel upon the tall city walls that expanded across the horizon. Hort tried his utmost to hide his admiration but was unsuccessful as he gaped at the city before him.

Several ornately uniformed elves greeted them as they approached the city's gateway, their white-plate armor camouflaging them against the stone. As they walked through the gates, Pavula looked up at the guards staring down austerely at them from the watchtowers atop the gatehouse. Up close, she could see that the stone was smooth and flawless, with only natural gray and brown veins decorating the creamy-white surface. It was as though the city had grown out from the ground itself like the trees of the surrounding forest. She looked up nervously as she walked beneath the sharply pointed bars of the portcullis half drawn in the arched gateway. It was forged from the same glass-like metal as Salyaman's swords.

On the other side of the walls, the city was brimming with elves, more than Pavula had imagined in existence, all going about their daily lives, dressed in luxuriously crafted clothing and armor. They were tall and beautiful, with slender forms, long-pointed ears, and most of them dressed as though ready for battle at any moment. Pavula could tell, even from her limited experience, those that were robed as sorcerers versus those armed for melee in their thin plate and mail.

Past the intricately designed and crafted buildings, at the far side of the city, a cliff loomed high above the tallest buildings, run with aqueducts that transported water from the river, sending it spilling over the ledge as three glorious waterfalls into artificial ponds below. The ponds had carved fountains resembling large white birds spraying water to each other. Green flowery vines festooned the ledges around the ponds, which were carved for seating. It all seemed like something from a dream to the newcomers.

Once they were clear of the gate, two guards came forward and grabbed Nikolean from the scouts. Neremyn said something to them in elvish that Pavula didn't catch, and then they began to drag him away. She stiffened in her saddle as she watched them drag him off, wanting to scream for them to stop, but instead watched in horror, trusting Salyaman that he would not be harmed before the trial. They took him into a building nearby, which was lower and much less luxurious than the buildings surrounding it: Má Lyndor's dungeon.

Near the dungeon lay several large roosts with strange creatures lying lazily about. They were four-legged beasts about twice the size of the horses. From the front half, they appeared to be large birds, feathered with the head, legs, claws, and wings of a bird of prey, such as an owl or eagle, none quite the same as the other. However, the back half was more like that of a great cat, including a long fur-covered tail, tufted at the tip. Smiling at Pavula's intrigue, Salyaman told her they were griffins, once used in the wars, but now grounded due to the dragons' relentless attacks whenever they would take flight. She nodded, understanding and feeling sorry for the poor—yet beautiful—creatures.

In the center of the city lay the tallest and most robust building. It looked as though it were carved from a giant stone tree. The steps at its base appeared as overlapping roots, and it reached up into the sky with stone branches curved around it, creating balconies perched randomly over its trunk. However, instead of fanning out at the top, as a tree would, it weaved itself back into a point like the others. It was to this building that the remainder of the group was being led.

Pavula had quietly been studying Neremyn's mind while he babbled on in elvish the whole trip and had picked up some of Salyaman's and Shakiera's conversations as well. She was learning elvish, hoping to address the council in their tongue but wasn't feeling very confident with her knowledge yet.

As they headed toward the center building, they passed many elves along the way, most of which looked on at them in curiosity, but a few stared too hard at Pavula, making her uncomfortable. She looked away, trying to ignore their disturbing stares, and sought to distract herself by thinking about what she would say before the council. When they reached the front of the building, they stood before a large opening where she was lifted off Helna's back by Salyaman. Neremyn also dismounted, and a petite tanned elf came and took the reins of the three mounts, then led them away. Pavula looked on after him, noticing how much more like her he appeared than the other elves she'd seen so far.

"Why he different?" Pavula whispered to Salyaman.

Following her gaze, he glanced at the stable boy and then back to her. "He is a wood elf, like you," he replied, "from Othsuda Theora. Má Lyndor is home to high elves, but a few wood elves have joined our city over time. Some came here seeking refuge from the war."

Pavula continued to watch after the boy until he rounded a corner and was out of sight. She then walked up the root-like steps to the building's entrance. The opening stretched over twenty feet high, and she gazed above her at the arch as she walked through it, admiring its grandness.

Once inside, they were led to a large room. The walls were decorated with swords and murals of battles between dragons and elves, and they were huddled into the center by the scouts, still standing guard over them.

"Please tell my father we must speak with the council as soon as possible," Salyaman said firmly to Neremyn. Looking at him for a moment, intrigued, he then disappeared through another high-arched doorway, his heels clicking against the stone floor, echoing through the hall as he left.

Pavula felt a chill and shuddered. Davion quickly responded by putting his hands on her shoulders, then rubbed her arms, warming her. It was much cooler in here than outside.

"It's all the stone," Davion said quietly as though reading her thoughts. "It must be keeping the city cool."

Salyaman nodded at them, confirming his theory.

After several long minutes, Neremyn returned without a word, and then loud footsteps echoed through the hallways beyond. A burly old elf, wearing a white faux-fur cloak and a metal crown of golden vines and thorns, then appeared in the doorway.

"Sal," he said gruffly.

"Father," Salyaman coldly replied.

"Rath Beldroth Dula'Sintos," the old king corrected him spitefully. Salyaman refused to respond, so Beldroth continued, "What is the meaning of this? You do not call council meetings any longer."

"I have news of great importance that I believe you will want to hear and that the council will want to hear."

The old elf-king looked around at the group, eyeballing each of them long and hard—all except for Shakiera, whom he refused to gaze upon. "Does this have to do with the drow you were traveling with?" he finally asked Salyaman.

Shaking his head, Salyaman responded, "Please, let us meet with the council. I believe we have...something...that will bring an end to the war." He unconsciously glanced quickly at Pavula.

Not being hard-of-sight, Beldroth followed his son's glance and stared at Pavula for a long moment. She became nervous as he strutted slowly over to her, looking her over more closely.

"Mall...sithio vall," *I...know you,* he said to her finally, his eyes looking into hers inquisitively.

"She does not know our tongue, father," Salyaman stated in Onish.

"Mallva Lupé Pavula," she responded in elvish, her voice cracking slightly as she sought courage within her. "Mall ekia lat onsilith." *I seek the council.*

Shocked, yet not completely surprised considering what they knew of her, Salyaman and the others gaped at Pavula.

"VALL ekia lat onsilith?" *YOU seek the council?* Beldroth blurted. "And who are you to seek the council of Má Lyndor?" he questioned, continuing in elvish.

"She is the one who will end this war," Salyaman responded for her.

Beldroth looked at his son with pity. "Well, if that is all, let us call a council meeting then," he said mockingly.

Pavula's heart was racing, and she quivered nervously. This all felt like too much for her. How was she going to speak to the council, let alone stop an entire war, when she felt so intimidated just speaking to the king?

"Please, father..."

"RATH BELDROTH DULA'SINTOS!" he yelled at Salyaman angrily, fuming through his nostrils. "You have shamed me enough and have lost the right to call me father! Now you bring this lunacy before me and look to shame me further?! Have you gone mad?" he hissed, stomping over to him, glaring him right in the eye.

Salyaman bowed his head. "Rath Beldroth Dula'Sintos," he said humbly, "believe me when I tell you that I understand your hesitation. Had I not seen certain things for myself, I would join you in your skepticism. However, I assure you that it will be worth your time—and the council's time—to hear what Lupé Pavula has to say. If the prophecy holds any truth, and we can bring an end to this war, then I believe we all owe it to her to hear her out."

"Prophecy? What prophecy?" Beldroth sneered.

Salyaman continued, "I believe that she is the elf born to bring an end to the war with the dragons, and I intend to aid her in her journey through to the end."

Beldroth looked keenly at his son and over to Pavula, then back again. It seemed a lifetime had passed while Beldroth mulled Salyaman's words over in his mind. Without looking away from his disowned son, he commanded, "Lieutenant Neremyn, take our guests to the hall and ensure that they are fed. It seems I have a council meeting to prepare."

CHAPTER TWENTY-ONE

COUNCIL

*W*hile Hort and Davion admired the grandeur of the great hall they had been taken to for dining, Pavula was captivated by an elf in the corner strumming a tranquilizing melody on a harp-like instrument that stood twice the height of the tall high elves. However, she thought the room and the ridiculously-large table seemed rather unnecessary for only five people. They ate unattended, and their conversations echoed against the walls, causing them to speak quietly to one another, except for Hort, who seemed to enjoy the echo of his own voice.

After their vegetarian feast, five servants came and removed their empty plates in unison, and Pavula was left feeling unsatisfied, disappointed that there had been no meat. It only occurred to her then that she had never witnessed Salyaman or Shakiera eat meat either but was too embarrassed to ask them why after having eaten like a wolf in their presence.

An oddly dressed young elf entered the room and announced that the council was ready to see them now, then waited for them to follow. He was wearing a flamboyant uniform of bright blue and purple, a contrast to most of the muted tones of the elves in the city. Aside from the scouts' attire, camouflaging them against the red and yellow foliage, Pavula hadn't seen any other elves wearing such gaudy clothing thus far.

The group gathered the few belongings they were allowed to keep with them and walked over to the pageboy.

"Only Lord Salyaman and Lupé Pavula beyond this point," he instructed.

Davion and Hort were then escorted gently by the arm by two female elves who led them in the opposite direction, Shakiera following closely behind. Pavula and Salyaman went with the pageboy down a long corridor towards another room. At the end of the corridor loomed two colossal wooden doors etched intricately with majestic trees, indicating the great importance of the room. As they approached, the doors were pulled open by guards, one on each door, allowing them to enter a very grand, round legislative chamber. After passing into the room, the doors boomed loudly as they closed behind them, startling Pavula.

There was ample seating wrapped around the sides holding thirty elves, not including the king, mostly elders with wrinkles and white-streaked hair. They sat facing the far wall where the king was awaiting them beside a podium. Pavula walked nervously with Salyaman down the center of the room, and he guided her up to the podium with his hand gently on her back, all sixty-one eyes glaring at her.

Standing behind the podium, Pavula looked out over the crowd, all gazing up at her unimpressed. The room felt even colder than the stone city with their stares and whispers. She looked over to Salyaman, who nodded for her to begin.

"I will translate for you," he said quietly.

She smiled, knowing she wasn't quite ready to address them in all elvish yet.

"Well, let us hear it, child," Rath Beldroth said to Pavula.

Before she could speak, the doors to the room drummed open again, commanding everyone's attention. The council all stood respectfully, unlike when Pavula and Salyaman had entered, as an extravagantly adorned elf entered the room, walking heavily, his heels clacking loudly with each step. His face was stern as he made his way toward the front of the room, and his plate clanked together along the way. Unlike the subdued tones and white plate of the others, he was brightly decorated and embellished with gems and gold trim. He wore a heavy long blue cape that dragged along the ground and shoulder pads that jutted out and up into a point at least a foot past his actual shoulders. The elf had long ash-blond hair and a thin-vine crown resting over his brow. Pavula thought the man looked rather silly in his ostentatiously impractical attire but remained silent.

Stopping before the podium, he looked over Pavula judgingly, his head held high, looking down upon her. He hmphed at her before taking his place beside Rath Beldroth.

"Rathca Saelethil," Beldroth addressed him, "nice of you to join us."

The crown prince ignored his father while the council took their seats once more, and Salyaman nodded again to Pavula.

Looking back to the crowd, she tried her best to stand tall and remain strong. "Thank you all for allowing me to address you," she began in the ancient language, Salyaman translating as she spoke. "My name is Lupé Pavula. I was not raised among elves, and I do not know the struggles you have all faced with the dragons. However, I have spoken with a dragon who told me of your prophecy and who believes me to be the elf that will bring an end to your war. I have come before you to ask for your aid in my journey."

Uproar swept through the crowd, everyone speaking at once, no one being heard. Rath Beldroth raised his hands, commanding silence.

"What do you mean...you *spoke* with a dragon?" the king asked her, echoing everyone's thoughts.

The crowd bellowed out again, irate, "Yes, what do you mean?!"

"Elves cannot speak to dragons, silly child," Beldroth declared, chuckling at her sardonically, the council members cackling along with him. "Perhaps if we could talk to the dragons, we could get through to them the absurdity that this war has even come about!"

"That is my thought as well," Salyaman interceded, "and why she just might be the one to help us put an end to it!" He paused, having grabbed their interest, and turned grandly to the council. "I saw the dragon she speaks of; a great Silver from the mountains." He grabbed the silver scale from her pocket and held it up high for the council to see. Their interest grew.

"Her name is Turathyl," Pavula said more confidently, "and she has promised to protect me and help me in my quest." The council members whispered and gasped to each other in disbelief but also engrossed.

Down in the front row, an old female elf stood awkwardly. She leaned on a cane and held her hand up, hushing the audience instantly, all of them looking at her curiously and with great respect. Pavula watched attentively as the old elf hobbled over to her and looked up into her face. She noticed that, although her skin was gray and shriveled, and her hair white as the city's stones, she was shorter than Pavula and her ears were petite like hers. The old elf looked deep into Pavula's eyes and lifted a strand of her hair, inspecting it.

CHAPTER 21

"I know you," the elf finally said softly in the ancient tongue for her and her alone.

"Annallee," Rath Beldroth said, "Seer, what is it?"

"I remember your mother," Annallee said to Pavula.

A chill ran down her spine as those words hit her, and tears welled in Pavula's eyes as she gaped at the old elf, knowing she couldn't possibly mean Lupé Caelis. She stood there, staring at the old lady, her mouth agape, wanting to speak, but only a strange croaking noise escaped. So many questions suddenly flooded her mind, yet she found herself speechless.

Annallee turned and addressed the rest of the council, "I remember the prophecy of which she speaks," she told them. "There will be born of an elf a Great Spirit. That spirit will face the ancients of the land of Onis and will know no boundaries between them. The Great Spirit will bring forth peace among all of the evolved races, and replenish life over the land." She looked back to Pavula and added, "I suspect that elf would need to be able to communicate with *all* of the races." Annallee paused, collecting her thoughts. "She speaks the language of the ancients, only taught to royals anymore as a way to honor traditions of old. However, she was not taught by elves. I sense something in this child, this child who was lost to us sixteen years ago when a flock of great Silvers descended from the skies. They slaughtered a caravan of wood elves on their way back to Othsuda Theora. They were transporting a lady of the royal wood elf court, Lady Leonallan Dula'Quoy, cousin to the ruler of Othsuda Theora, Rath Almon, and her baby, Lailalanthelus."

The room grew boisterous with questions from the astonished members of the council, and Annallee raised her hand again, instilling instant silence throughout the chamber. "This *is* that baby." She turned to Pavula. "You are not a wolf child, Lupé Pavula. You *are* Lailalanthelus Dula'Quoy, royal daughter of the greatly respected and beautiful Lady Leona." Annallee opened her arms to her, "Welcome home, Lady Laila. We had thought you lost to the gods." Pavula, or Laila, stood there confused, not sure how to respond, so Annallee stepped forward and embraced her, causing tears to stream down the young elf's face as she shook in the seer's arms.

A royal. My mother was a royal... She returned the old elf's hug as she tried to understand it all, then pulled away from Annallee and wiped the tears from her eyes, smiling at her.

Then Rath Beldroth exclaimed, "Ah, yes! I thought she looked familiar! I knew your mother as well, Laila. She had been to our court many times before her horrible demise." Rath Beldroth stepped to Pavula taking her hand. "Forgive me, child. I did not realize you were a royal." He then kissed the back of her hand, smiling eerily at her. She nodded politely to him, accepting his apology, although not comprehending why it made a difference.

The king stepped back and whispered something quickly to Saelethil, who seemed disgruntled by his words.

Looking back at Annallee, her message suddenly sank in as Pavula realized her birth mother was dead. It then hit her; a Silver had killed her mother—her real mother. She was overcome with shock, not knowing how to feel about this new information or what to do with it.

"And my father?" she asked hesitantly, fearing the answer.

Annallee frowned sadly at the young elf, confirming her fears. "Lord Dalton." She sighed. "Killed by the dragons while seeking revenge, I am afraid. It was very tragic the loss he felt when he believed he had lost you both; all he loved and cared for in this world." She paused and then asked, "Where have you been, Laila? How have you survived all of these years?"

The young elf, still in a state of shock, didn't respond.

CHAPTER 21

"And how can you speak to dragons but not to your own kind?" Rath Beldroth questioned.

Pavula looked to the king and responded to him in elvish, "I am learning. I listened to you and learned, just as I learned the common speak since I met Salyaman and others."

The king looked at her oddly again, "You expect me to believe you learned how to speak elvish in such a short time? Is this some sort of trick?"

"No trick," Pavula responded. "I learn."

"No boundaries between them." Annallee smiled.

"So, what now?" Beldroth asked. "What is it that you expect from us? Where is your dragon now?"

Pavula looked around the room at all the curious, whispering elves, those last words repeating in her mind: *Where is your dragon now?* "I no know," she replied, shaking her head honestly. "I look for help to go dragons. Speak of war. Ask to stop."

The king scoffed and said in a condescending tone, "Forgive me, but you are just going to waltz into a dragon's lair and say what? Excuse me, can you please stop killing us?" He let out a roar of laughter, with the council members joining in. "And you expect us to go with you before the dragons? They kill us without hesitation, without pause, and without remorse. Why would it be any different with you?"

"They no kill me," she retorted. "Turathyl be with me." *'Turathyl, where are you?'* she sent out desperately beyond the walls of the city, searching for her dragon, but there was only silence. She felt very alone at this moment before all of these strange elves and their questions and doubts. Pavula only hoped that she wasn't making them empty promises. "I go to dragons with or without elves, but I want you know that I go and I end war. I end hate."

Salyaman came and took her hand, everyone looking on in bewilderment. She felt the warmth of his hand in hers, feeling a little less alone. "And I will join her!" he said firmly. "I have pledged my life to bring an end to this war, and I have seen her do great things already. I believe she is the one that will make the difference."

Saelethil peered keenly at his older brother, deep in thought, finding it curious that Salyaman would stand behind such absurdity.

Rath Beldroth, annoyed with his son, looked to Annallee. "What do you think, Seer?"

Annallee closed her eyes while taking Pavula's free hand, then slowly shook her head after a long moment. "I am unsure," she replied. "There is much uncertainty. I see her dragon come to her. I see her before a Silver, a Gold, a Blue, and even a Red. But, I also see great fear. I see skies full of dragons. I see war, much worse, many dead." Opening her eyes, she frowned at Pavula, her lower jaw quivering slightly. "No," she said finally, releasing her hand, "I do not think the elf, Lailalanthelus Dula'Quoy, will be the one to end the war." Turning to the king, she added, "I have seen too much hatred between the dragons and our kind and believe it is too great for any elf to stop."

The chamber grew abuzz with commotion, everyone speaking over each other again.

"She is not just any elf!" Salyaman objected. "I do not know what the seer has foreseen, but no future is certain, and I stand by my word!"

Rath Beldroth raised a hand for Salyaman to halt, then nodded in acknowledgment to Annallee. Turning back to the council, he raised both palms for their attention, ready to announce his decision.

"While I am glad to know that Lady Leona's daughter has survived the dragons' devastating attack, we will need to discuss further what Má Lyndor's responsibility will be toward her

CHAPTER 21

endeavor. I do not wish to risk any more lives to these monsters, and I have yet to be convinced that this is not a fool's errand.

"Now, Salyaman has decided that he will go with her on this quest, and I will not stop him or any free man that chooses to risk their own lives to join her."

Turning back to the young elf, he continued, "Laila," her skin tingling at the sound of that name, "I will, however, ensure that you are equipped with the proper armor and supplies along with our prayers, but this may be a journey you will be making without the elves. I truly hope that Salyaman is right and that you do find a way to put an end to this war, one way or another, but I will need more time to further consider Má Lyndor's involvement."

Looking back to the council members, he added. "In three days' time, we shall reconvene for my final decision. At that time, we will also decide the fate of the drow that you have captured and brought here. Is there anyone who would like to speak to the girl's request?"

Waiting several moments, the council remained silent and still.

"Then it is decided!" Rath Beldroth declared. "Of course, the human and dwarf are welcome to stay until your departure but until then, please, enjoy our great city, take care of your affairs, and we shall meet back here in three days."

Pavula looked at him strangely. "Affairs?" she asked, confused.

"You are the long-lost daughter of Lady Leona. I insist that you visit our city, get to know the elven people. Also, I will have my finest craftsman make you some armor and weapons for your journey. This will take a few days at least."

"And Nikolean?" she inquired.

Rath Beldroth looked at Salyaman quizzically.

"The drow," Salyaman told him.

"Ah, yes." The king cleared his throat. "He will remain in our dungeons until the trial. Now let us all take leave, and I will have arrangements made for you to stay in the palace."

Pavula smiled gratefully. She wished Nikolean could join them, but she was also excited to see more of the city.

"The council is dismissed," Rath Beldroth announced, and all the members slowly began making their way out of the chamber.

The king grabbed Saelethil's arm before he could depart, holding him back for a moment.

"You and I have some important matters to discuss," he whispered to the crown prince, glaring contemplatively at the young royal elf as she was escorted out through the immaculate doors by Annallee and Salyaman.

CHAPTER TWENTY-TWO

BENEVOLENCE

*S*tretching out her limbs against the extremely soft linens of her bed, Laila slowly opened her eyes, not quite ready to start her day. Since the council meeting, everyone had been calling her Laila, and it was growing on her. Her last two days in Má Lyndor had been like a dream.

On the first day following her arrival, she was pampered and prepared by five handmaidens as an elven princess upon rising. They gave her a warm bath with soothing oils, dressed her handsomely, and styled her hair. Then, Laila was shown around the castle and royal gardens. After her tour, she insisted that her hosts take her by the dungeon to check on Nikolean and ensure that he was fairly treated, as she would also do the following day. Although she hated seeing him caged, she was relieved to find no physical harm had been done to him.

On the second day, yesterday, Laila was taken into town by the crown prince himself, Rathca Saelethil Dula'Sintos, who had been very hospitable as he showed off *his* kingdom. Davion, who had not been permitted to see the palace with her the day prior, accompanied them to the market where Laila saw some of the finest garments and jewelry, among many other things she didn't recognize. Saelethil purchased a tiara and jeweled clasps with aqua gems for her hair. Davion used what little coin he had to purchase—at a very deep discount—a thin silver chain, which Laila prized and attached her precious Silver scale to, wearing it proudly around her neck. Davion tried staying close to her throughout the day, but Rathca Saelethil would take her hand, leading her this way and that every time the human drew too near. This aggravated him greatly, but he bit his tongue and bided his time, knowing he would be leaving with her soon.

After the market, Laila was shown the villages within the walls and met many more people, some of whom knew her mother that shared stories of how beautiful and kind she was. While there, she spoke with Annallee again, who explained her mother had been a diplomat between the elven factions, traveling from city to city. She also told Laila that her mother, although not very skilled in her art, was a druid—a magic class that uses earth magic as its source. Laila assumed this was why the earth spirit took to her so well and further fantasized other possible ways in how she and her mother may have been alike.

Unfortunately, all of her excitement had come to a drastic halt last evening when she was faced with a dilemma that had since been plaguing her mind and had kept her up most of the night.

After having dined with the king and crown prince as their special guest, Rathca Saelethil led her to the beautiful palace gardens and took a stroll with her, bragging about his city's many splendors, as though she weren't already overly impressed with everything she had seen. As they stopped under a large tree full of pink flowers emitting a blissful aroma, the prince turned to her and took her hand.

"Lady Laila, there is something I need to discuss with you before you leave Má Lyndor." Laila looked up at the prince, curious, and waited for him to continue. "As a fellow royal and the elf believed to end the Dragon War, my father has sanctioned for us to become married. As I am

sure that you are aware, you would become the next Rathelle of Má Lyndor, and no greater offer could be received. I would like for the union to take place before you depart. Our alliance would give people hope; to have the prophesied elf as their next queen," he said, "and all of the elven kingdoms would rejoice in our union."

Laila stared confusedly at him. The only thing she knew of marriage was from watching Salyaman and Shakiera.

Seeing her look of confusion, Rathca Saelethil added, "You are probably wondering how this union would benefit you since you would be leaving for your quest. Aside from becoming Rathelle, Rath Beldroth has agreed to give you one hundred of our finest men to aid you in your quest against the dragons to help ensure your success."

Although Laila did not know much about marriage, she was very drawn to the idea of having additional support to increase her and her new friends' chances of survival and success. Thankfully, he had given her until the next council meeting, which was today, to make her decision. She was flattered to receive such a proposal but, not truly understanding what it was she would be committing to, she was anxious to speak with Salyaman about what she should do.

As she hesitantly swung her legs over the side of her bed, Laila looked around admiring the beautiful room that she was given: its sheer curtains leading out to a large balcony, its luxuriously woven rugs to keep her bare feet warm against the cold stone, its walls decorated with painted vines and flowers that looked real enough to pluck, and its tall bedposts of naturally twisting wood.

The moment that her feet touched the soft rug, the door swung open to her room following a soft rattle, and in came the five handmaidens to repeat the same routine as the prior two mornings, always starting the moment her feet touch the floor.

After she was bathed and dressed, they placed golden-vine bands around her arms and ankles, and one of the ladies brushed Laila's hair, weaving a few intricate braids while leaving the rest to flow and shine beautifully. She then attached the hair clasps and tiara gifted to her by the prince.

"Rathca Saelethil awaits you in the dining hall for your breakfast, my lady," said the elf.

All five of them then grabbed their effects and wheeled the wooden tub out through the door, closing it quietly behind them.

Laila was excited about what today might bring but was also dreading having to decide on Saelethil's proposal, praying he wasn't expecting her decision during breakfast.

Upon entering the dining hall, Laila was led to where Rath Beldroth and Rathca Saelethil were already seated along with Salyaman's mother, Rathelle Saelihn Dula'Sintos. Rathca Saelethil stood, greeting her, and motioned for her to sit beside him—as he did each morning.

Salyaman and Shakiera had been fairly absent since the council meeting, trying to spend as much time together as they could before Salyaman would have to leave her behind for their adventure. So, she had not been surprised by his absence at the meals, not realizing he wouldn't have been welcome anyway.

"Good day to you, Lady Laila. I trust that you slept well?" Saelethil said in elvish.

"I did, Rathca Saelethil. Thank you," she fibbed in elvish as she took her seat next to the prince.

As with onish, she picked up elvish extremely quickly by searching the minds of those she conversed with over the past couple of days, being careful not to alert them of her presence.

"So, what is the plan for today?" Rathelle Saelihn inquired to Laila.

CHAPTER 22

Laila looked up into her orange eyes while chewing on a piece of bread, caught off guard. The queen seldom spoke directly to her, usually remaining very poised at all of their encounters. She appeared almost ghostly with her pale white skin, her white-blond hair, and her white flowing dress and robes. Innocent Laila, unfortunately, failed to see the contempt that was in her eyes or condescending demeanor toward her, believing the queen just to be quiet and reserved. The queen, however, was displeased with her husband's plan and anxious for the newcomer to be on her way.

Before Laila had a chance to respond, Saelethil answered for her, "Today, we shall visit the armory. I am told that your armor and weapons are completed and ready for your journey."

Laila could see the excitement in the prince's eyes as he smiled at her, but that news suddenly made her very sad. In all of the excitement, she had not been thinking as much about the prophecy or the journey ahead. She had been enjoying learning about the elven people and relishing in all of their hospitality and benevolence, wishing she could stay much longer. She was also not prepared to give the prince her answer yet and needed to find Salyaman.

"Is something the matter?" Saelethil asked suspiciously. "I thought this would make you happy. We are all anxious for you to begin your quest to end the war and be done with the dragon attacks on us once and for all." He looked at her expectantly and added, "And perhaps a celebration of sorts before you depart?"

Laila forced a smile. "Nothing is matter. I look forward to armory." She went back to eating her breakfast, trying to hide her disappointment, and avoided answering his last question while averting her eyes from his gaze.

The dream was starting to fade as she was reminded of her reality. Part of her wished that she hadn't told them about the prophecy, and then maybe she could have stayed here forever or even gone to see the other elven cities first. She especially wished to see the wood elf city and home of her family, Othsuda Theora.

After breakfast, Laila quickly snuck out in search of Salyaman, finding him easily at Shakiera's family home. Sensing her anxiety, he led her to a private room where they could speak freely. She was grateful that he could follow along in the ancient tongue as she told him about the crown prince's proposal the night before and of his promise for a hundred men if she agreed.

Salyaman quickly grew angry with her news. Mulling over the information in his mind, he paced back and forth before her. "I bet my father put him up to this."

"What should I do?" she asked. "All those men would give us a better chance with our quest."

"Do you understand what he has asked of you?" He turned and looked at her.

Sensing her nerves, he realized that she really didn't. He took her hand tenderly and continued while trying to restrain his anger towards his father and brother, "He wants you for your name, both because you are a royal and would give him a hold in Othsuda Theora, and also because you will be renowned as the elf destined to end the war. How great it would look for him and Má Lyndor if the prophesied elf were named the next Rathelle. I gave up my chance at being crown prince so that I could marry for love, and I would not change that decision for all of the elven kingdoms. Once you are bound to him, he will own and control you. Elves do not separate from our unions once made. You will become his puppet that will bring him to fame and fortune. Is that really something that you want?"

Laila hadn't realized the gravity of what her commitment would mean. "He has been so nice to me," she said softly. "Surely, his intentions aren't all bad?"

CHAPTER 22

"Do you love him?" Salyaman asked. "Do you even care for him?"

Even though she wasn't quite sure what love was when it came to mating-type rituals, she knew she felt very little affection toward Saelethil. Sighing gravely, she shook her head, still feeling that she would be giving up a great opportunity. Part of her also wondered what it would be like to be a queen.

Salyaman wrapped his arms around Laila in a friendly embrace. "The decision is yours and yours alone, but know that my brother's and father's intentions are not pure, or the proposal would not have included blackmail. If he truly cared for you and believed it would help, then he would have offered those men, whatever your decision."

Pulling back, Laila looked up at Salyaman, knowing he was right, and nodded. "Thank you, Salyaman. I will think on your words."

* * *

When it was time to meet the prince for her visit to the armory, Laila left Salyaman and Shakiera and wandered back to the palace entrance deep in thought. Upon arriving, like every morning, she found Davion waiting for her there on the steps with a bright smile and a warm hug. Just then, Saelethil descended down the staircase and nodded to Davion sternly but smiled upon seeing Laila returning. She wasn't surprised that Hort was not there again. Not being overly fond of the elves, the dwarf had mostly remained in his quarters with an elven family near the stables, where he and Davion had been placed. He had been happy there as he enjoyed visiting with Orbek each day.

Saelethil led Laila and Davion around the side of the palace to a much smaller and shorter building with several armed guards keeping watch. There were monstrous, ironclad doors requiring two elven guards on each door to pull open. Stepping inside from the bright morning sun, Laila had to squint to make out her surroundings. Once adjusted, she admired all the artistry painted on the walls of the hallway as they passed. There was also what appeared to be relic weaponry displayed on the walls with elvish writing underneath them, presumably detailing why they were significant enough to be hung there.

Entering through a second set of doors, the three of them came to a large room filled with all types of beautiful and exquisitely decorated armor. Although, it seemed as though they were made more for show instead of protection, appearing to be too thin to absorb any type of blow. In addition to the white plate made for the city guards, there were thin elven mail and leather armor draped about the room.

Suddenly, everyone turned as they heard heavy footsteps echoing through the building of someone running down the hallway towards them. Laila smiled as she saw Hort emerge, panting heavily. When he reached them, he bent over, grasping his knees, wheezing, and trying to catch his breath.

"How's about lettin' a fella know yer goin' ta look at the armory beforehand?" Hort panted at the group. "Had ta hear it through the chatterin' of nosy elves." He looked up at the prince. "Hmmm... No disrespect, mind ye."

Rathca Saelethil ignored the dwarf's comment while another elf entered the room, carrying a large case. He had light-orange hair with a very sparse goatee and unusually large muscles for an elf, bulging through his thin shirt. His features were a little strange as well, with smaller ears and slightly rounder eyes, and he was a tad shorter than the other elves but not so short as Laila. The man nodded to the prince, laying the case on the table near them, before stepping back.

Saelethil went and stood before the case then turned to address them. "I have been spreading the news that we are preparing the prophesied elf for the greatest challenge of putting a stop to the Dragon War!" he announced enthusiastically, "So, I charged my blacksmith with making you the finest elven armor and weapon to aid you on your journey. Fine enough for a queen, if I dare say myself. He has been working without pause to get these made for you in time before your departure."

Laila blushed uncomfortably as he turned dramatically, his heavy cape whipping around with him, and unlatched the case. The case itself wasn't anything fancy, just a long wooden box with a handle and latches, but inside, the real treasure glistened and gleamed as he slowly opened the lid. The first thing that he removed was a set of intricate leather and bronze arm bracers with matching armored shoulder pads.

"My brother tells me you are a caster," Rathca Saelethil said. "Therefore, we do not want you to be burdened down with a lot of heavy armor, but these should help protect your arms in battle. They are stronger than they look and can be used as a shield if needed, absorbing much of the blow." He laid them on the table in front of Laila.

She picked them up to examine them and instantly sensed that they had been enchanted with a magical protection embedded into their very fabric. Saelethil then continued taking out more pieces of armor: shin guards, armored corset, and a brown cloak, all with similar—but different—enchantments. The cloak looked rather plain, and Laila pawed at its material, thinking how strange it felt.

"It will camouflage you if needed, but it can also withstand great fire and block piercing weapons," Rathca Saelethil explained. "Or just use it to keep you warm on a cold night." He gave Laila a wink.

"Now, my brother did not seem to know what type of caster you are. I had suggested a staff be made for you, but that did not seem to be the popular opinion for some reason." The prince paused, waiting for her to respond.

"I like my spear and dagger," Laila stated.

"He said that too," Saelethil replied. "I had those made for you as well. I wanted to be prepared with whichever you decided."

Out of the case, he removed a pristine dagger with a blade made of dark metal. The hilt was a lot longer than Laila was used to, but it was surprisingly light, and the grip was comfortable in her small grasp. She looked it over admiringly, appreciating its craftsmanship and the elven etchings on the blade and crossguard. It was truly quite beautiful for a dagger.

"Open it," Saelethil said to her excitedly.

Laila looked up at him, confused.

Saelethil took the blade from her and twisted the middle of the handle. Laila gasped as she hadn't even seen a seam there. From there, he grabbed each side and pulled outward. The dagger hilt grew and grew until it had become a full-sized spear. He handed the spear back to her, and she marveled at it even more. Davion and Hort both watched on in awe. The blacksmith cleared his throat to get Saelethil's attention.

"Ah, yes!" he said, remembering. "Hit the bottom pommel hard on the ground twice."

She did as he instructed, and another blade, the same as the first, popped out from the other side of the spear. The blacksmith stepped forward and took the spear from her to show her more.

"You can use it as a double-edged spear, a dagger, or two daggers. Twist the ends here, and here, to retreat the blades, and you have a staff." He then showed her how to shorten the shaft, how to split it into two to make dual daggers, then how to reattach them into one. Laila couldn't believe what she was seeing and thought it must be magic as well, though she did not sense any emanating from it. She was astonished as she fiddled with the weapon for several minutes, not knowing how she had survived all of these years with her rudimentary dagger and spear carved from branches and stones. Laila practiced using its mechanisms and getting a feel for it in her hands while the others watched on, enjoying her happiness.

Hort leaned close to Laila and said quietly (for a dwarf,) "Ye'll have ta let me get a look at that someday. Would love ta see how it works."

As a dwarf, he was proud of his people's skills with making weapons and armor, but he had never seen anything as clever as this before. It appeared as though it would be flimsy, but it proved to be strong and solid as he watched Laila swinging it around. He also knew that the elves used only the finest quality materials. Trading the mined materials from the mountains with the elves was the dwarves' largest profit center. They had no problem charging the elves an extra premium either, knowing they would pay handsomely.

"These all so wonderful!" Laila finally exclaimed after feeling comfortable with the weapon.

"The weapon's name is Dragonsbane—its blades will pierce any scaly hide," the blacksmith declared, smiling proudly.

Laila cringed at the thought but appreciated the weapon nevertheless.

"You know..." he continued, stroking his goatee, "if we knew your magic, we could add gems to Dragonsbane for your spellcasting as well."

Saelethil turned and looked at Laila, curious as to which power it was that she held.

"Let me guess," said Saelethil, "druid—like your mother?"

Laila smiled. "I not know," she replied honestly, "I not practice magic same as elves. I guess could say, all of them?" she looked at the prince nervously.

Saelethil did not act as shocked as she had anticipated. "Ah. So, elementalist," he said and then turned back to the blacksmith, exchanging nods between them. Laila remembered this term from Salyaman and Shakiera and didn't believe it to be accurate but felt that having all elemental stones might benefit her regardless, so, remained silent.

"Give me an hour," the blacksmith replied. "I will have my wife infuse one of each gem into the shaft."

"The best enchanter in the business!" Saelethil said, patting the blacksmith gently on the shoulder.

"I will have all of these brought to your chambers when completed, Lady Laila." The blacksmith took Dragonsbane back, then retracted it into a dagger, and Laila bowed her head gratefully.

"I have one last gift to give you," Saelethil told Laila. "Please accompany me to the stables." He held out his elbow for her to take, which she did awkwardly while Davion followed behind, suspicious of the prince's intentions.

"I s'pose I could go see me Orbek now," Hort decided, tagging along.

As they walked to the stables, the prince seemed to almost demand attention from those they passed with his exaggerated gestures, waves, and smiles, as though they were in a parade. Laila smiled at all the elves as they walked by, Davion ignored most of them, and Hort grumbled and huffed at all the unwanted attention, looking mostly to the ground.

The stables didn't look like stables at all, but more like just another of their beautifully crafted white-stone buildings. Laila was happy to spot Helna and Orbek right away in the first few stalls, running to Helna to pat her nose, the horse greeting her cheerfully.

Hort went eagerly over to Orbek and opened the stall. "Come now, old friend. Let's get ye some exercise," he told the okullo as they headed out of the stalls together, its hooves clip-clopping on the stone.

Saelethil motioned to a stableman who went briskly to a nearby stall and grabbed a beautiful young elkah, bringing it to Laila. "This is for you," Saelethil stated to her, motioning his arms in a grand gesture.

As it approached, Laila tried to mind-touch the elkah to form a connection but was met with resistance. She studied its face and mind, seeking some form of awareness, but saw nothing except empty, glazed eyes. The animal was quite stunning, but there was just something off about it that made her uncomfortable. However, when she was about to retract her mind-touch, she felt another presence brush the tip of her reach. She closed her eyes and sent out her mind further, seeking out the source. Down near the end of the stables, she sensed a warm and highly intelligent presence. Laila opened her eyes again, smiling, and looked at the prince.

"There is another," she said excitedly. "This is not the one."

Saelethil looked at her, insulted. "This is the most beautiful elkah in the stable, as good as my mother's!" he exclaimed, annoyed. "*And* one of the fastest! What more could you possibly want?"

Without a word, Laila walked past the prince and headed toward the end of the stables, Davion following her. As she walked, she felt herself being pulled toward whatever the creature was.

"Where are you going?" the prince called after her, arms in the air.

Facing the final stall at the far end of the stables, Laila stared at the animal before her and said, "This one."

"You do not want her, Lady Laila," the stableman said, catching up. "We have not been able to tame her and are not even entirely sure *what* she is."

The prince strode quickly to see what animal Laila was staring at. She opened the stall despite the stableman's protesting, and the creature strode calmly out to see her, lowering its muzzle for her to stroke. At first glance, it looked like an albino elkah with its pink eyes and all-white fur, but upon closer inspection, it appeared to be a cross between a horse and an elkah. Instead of the short hair and stubby tail of an elkah, the creature had a long white mane and a flowing, long-white tail. The backs of its legs were also covered in long white tufts of fur. However, its muscular form and facial features, as well as its size, were definitely that of an elkah, including its large and gallant elkan antlers, which were also white in contrast to the red of a normal elkah.

"What is that thing?" Saelethil asked the stableman, disturbed.

"We believe it is a crossbreed between a white horse and an elkah," he replied. "We found her wandering outside the city walls the day before last. She came in willingly but will not let us touch her since."

"This animal has magic," Laila said, mostly to herself, then turned to the prince. "This is the one. Can I have her?"

Saelethil looked back and forth between the animal and Laila. "You say you could not tame her?" he asked the stableman, who shook his head, "no."

As though understanding, the beautiful creature bent its leg down to Laila. She stepped on its leg and swung herself high over the side onto its back. The animal didn't buck or bother at all until the stableman took a step towards it, causing the creature to rear and shriek loudly at him. Laila held onto its mane tightly, and he immediately took a step back.

"I see," said the prince. "Well, it looks as though you have chosen each other."

"What will you name her?" Davion asked.

Merimer. Laila heard in the back of her mind. "Merimer," she repeated out loud, unsure if it was her idea or the creature's. Laila dismounted gracefully, already feeling connected to this animal, and then led it back into the stall. The beautiful creature followed her gestures without complaint. *'I shall see you soon, Merimer,'* Laila mind-sent to her, and Merimer snorted, lowering her head in response, seeming to understand. Giving Merimer a final stroke down her long nose, Laila left the stall and closed it behind her, then followed the prince alongside Davion out of the stables.

Saelethil reminded her that it was nearing the time for the next council meeting and requested that she walk with him back to the palace. So, after giving Davion a friendly farewell hug, who hated to let her go, Laila nervously approached the crown prince. He took her hand and placed it in his arm while they strolled down the stone path.

"I trust you have enjoyed my great city and the gifts bestowed on you?" Saelethil asked rhetorically, not waiting for her to answer, "And I am sure you are aware that the time has come for your decision."

Laila nodded, feeling a hard pit in her stomach. "Yes, Rathca Saelethil." She knew it could no longer be avoided. The time was now, and she needed to decide the price she'd be willing to pay for his reinforcements. She felt herself begin to tremble but couldn't seem to stop, not realizing how much this was going to affect her.

Giving herself to him would give her a greater chance of success before the dragons, having the city backing her, and she would get to become a queen. But...she didn't love him. What was finding love worth to her? Did she even understand what it was? Was she even meant to experience such things when her purpose had clearly been laid out for her?

"So, Lady Laila," Rathca Saelethil interrupted her thoughts without breaking his stride, "what shall be your answer? Will you become the next Rathelle of Má Lyndor?"

CHAPTER 22

CHAPTER TWENTY-THREE

RAMIFICATIONS

"So, Lady Laila, what shall be your answer? Will you become the next Rathelle of Má Lyndor?"

The prince gleamed over the young elf, waiting for her to accept his proposal.

"Rathca Saelethil," Laila said nervously while they walked, her voice breaking. "what if I be Rathelle but stay in Má Lyndor?"

Saelethil stopped for a moment, surprised at first, then quickly agitated.

Taking a deep breath and releasing a sigh, the prince resumed their walking. "Do not be nervous of your destiny, Lady Laila. I am glad you have enjoyed your visit to my great city. However, we are all invested in helping you succeed, and word is traveling throughout the elven kingdoms of the prophesied elf, off to fight the dragons with the support of Má Lyndor behind her."

"Never said I *fight* dragons," Laila said quietly.

The prince raised his hand. "How you kill them, stop them, or whatever is of no importance to me, so long as you at least try. Live or die; you are a hero already. And as Rathelle, Má Lyndor will be required to support you for your increased chance of success." Seeing her getting upset with his answer, Saelethil decided it was time to try a different approach.

"I understand you have been visiting the drow each day in the dungeons."

Laila hesitantly replied, "Yes."

"Well, as the next Rathelle, you would have a say in what is to happen to him, giving him a better chance of not being sentenced to death, as every other drow has been that was brought before the council. I might even be persuaded to support your vote for sparing his life."

Her eyes grew wide in alarm. She was told Nikolean would receive a fair trial. How could no other drow have been released? It dawned on her that the prince was once again using blackmail to convince her to be his bride. Frustrated with the games and deceit, she decided it was time to find out his true intentions for herself. So, she secretly reached into his mind, gently enough not to call attention, and searched for his true desires.

Wrapping around his thoughts of her, she could see that this prince did not care for her at all and had only proposed because he was ordered to by the king. He wants to be the most powerful king Má Lyndor has ever seen and doesn't care what he has to do to achieve his goal. He even secretly wishes for her failure against the dragons so that she will not return but die a hero in her attempt, giving him the sympathy and support of his people. Everything about the mind of this elf disgusted and appalled Laila, and she eagerly withdrew from his thoughts. Although she recalled what her mother said about the minds of man being unclear, it was pretty clear to her that the prince's mind was shallow enough to see what she needed in order to make her decision.

"Rathca Saelithil," Laila began, stopping to face him, "I cannot accept proposal. I go without your men, and I fight for Nikolean drow myself."

"I see," he said, angered and insulted by her decision. Rathca Saelithil clenched his teeth before responding with disdain,

"You have made the wrong decision, Lailalanthelus Dula'Quoy." He pivoted and stormed off hastily, leaving Laila with her heart racing, praying that he was wrong.

Left to herself, Laila was suddenly finding it hard to breathe, and her heart pounded heavily in her chest. *What have I done?* she questioned herself. *What if they kill Nikolean because I refused the prince? What if I get the others killed because I failed to get the one hundred men?*

Laila began to run toward the waterfalls, her favorite place in the city, needing to clear her head. She was suddenly terrified that she had made the wrong choice because it wasn't just her life that was on the line.

On her way to the ponds, she ran past Davion, who chased after her, calling to her. When he caught up, he accompanied her toward the waterfalls. As they walked, he could sense her distress but remained silent, waiting for her to speak. Once they reached the falls, he sat beside her on the pond ledge, but still, they both remained silent.

After several minutes of watching her stare off into the fountains, Davion broke their silence and finally asked, "What's bothering you?"

Laila sighed softly while observing the city. "I not ready," she said sadly. "I no know I up for this. Don't want to go."

Davion placed his hand over Laila's, which was resting on the ledge. "I understand," he told her sympathetically. "I was a little worried about that. I mean, I've been watching you and have seen how happy you are here. Just know I will be here for you no matter what comes next." He picked up her hand and held it between both of his.

Laila looked at him warmly, grateful for his support, and she was able to relax a little, knowing his words were genuine. She wanted to tell him everything about the prince's offer and his blackmail but didn't know what good it would do, and also was afraid of his reaction. Sighing, she thought it best not to but instead began hypothesizing that if she were to never leave for the quest, then the others would never be put in danger by her either. She could just stay in Má Lyndor, or even go to Othsuda Theora, not as a queen but as herself.

'*What are you doing, young one?*' Laila heard the familiar voice of Turathyl penetrate her mind. She jumped to her feet, startled and excited.

"Turathyl!" she exclaimed both out loud and to the dragon through mind-speech. Davion stood beside her, still holding her hand. '*Where have you been?!*'

'*Have you forgotten why you have come here? I have been watching you. Waiting for you. I have sensed your desire to give up before you even begin. Have you forgotten how important this is to all the races of Onis?*'

Laila lowered her head. '*I know, I am sorry,*' she told her dragon, feeling ashamed while also frustrated. '*But what about what I want? Can I really not stay?*'

Turathyl sent her a feeling of warmth and understanding. '*I am sorry, young one, but I fear only you can heal the divide over the land. Perhaps when it is all over, you will have the rest of your days to explore the elven cities and discover your own happiness.*'

Sensing Laila's lingering fear and worry, she added, '*I know you are scared. Your task will not be an easy one, but know that you do not need the elf prince nor his men to succeed.*' Laila blushed with embarrassment, not realizing she had known about Saelethil's proposal. It had been a while since she shared a connection like this, making it hard to hide anything. '*You have my support and, from what I have seen, the support of your friends. Things will happen as they are meant to, and you are meant to stop this war with or without their aid. So... When are you leaving?*'

CHAPTER 23

'*I suppose I could leave tomorrow.*' Laila replied. '*They still have Nikolean imprisoned, but the trial is today.*'

'*Are you sure you want him along?*' Turathyl questioned skeptically.

Laila didn't need to think about it; she knew he was a part of this journey as well. '*Yes. I need him to be,*' she replied.

For several moments there was nothing but silence, and Laila feared that Turathyl had gone again. Finally, the dragon responded, '*Alright. Get your drow, but do not forget your destiny and who you are, Lupé Pavula. It is time.*'

Feeling a little bitter, still wishing she didn't have to leave, the young elf girl sent back a final statement with a new sense of self before closing her mind, '*My name is Lady Lailalanthelus Dula'Quoy, and I will not forget my destiny.*'

* * *

It was late afternoon, and Laila found herself back in the same legislative chamber as before, but this time she was seated in the front row among the council members. She was daydreaming back to her time with Davion at the waterfall and anxious for the trial to be over. As the day wore on, the reality of her situation sank in, and she was anxious to get on with her quest, to put an end to this war that she had nothing to do with.

The young elf thought of her elven mother and wondered if she was watching over her somehow, in some way. It bothered her that, having found her people, she could not just stay and visit with them, but instead had the weight of all the races hanging over her shoulders. Yet, at the same time, she had always known she was special; Lupé Caelis would often remind her of that. She was grateful she finally knew why but wished beyond wishing that it was an easier task she was being faced with. It was easy enough to say she was the elf that was going to put an end to their war, but she had absolutely no idea how she was supposed to do that and was terrified, not just for her own life but for those who pledged their lives to help her.

Laila hoped that Davion could have been with her for the trial, but they refused to let him or "the dwarf" be a part of elven proceedings. Instead, Annallee sat with Laila, offering her kindness and support.

During her stay in Má Lyndor, Laila was mostly thankful to have met Annallee and learn so much about her mother and family, but also about her mother's people, the wood elves. She hoped that she would be able to visit them one day. She learned her father, Darton Dula'Quoy, was a high elf paladin who had fallen in love with her mother during one of her visits to the capital of Thas Duar Moran, where they spent most of their married lives. Laila feared she would never get to know them beyond the few stories she had heard.

Looking around, Laila noticed that Rathca Saelithil was not in the room and wondered if he was planning to make an entrance like he did the last time. However, she prayed that he wouldn't show at all, nervous about her next encounter with him.

As the sound of chains dragging across the stone floors echoed through the hall, Laila turned to the door, along with every other of the council members' glares. Through the doorway came Nikolean being led by two guards, and they brought him towards the front of the room. He looked like a man already sentenced; despair draped over his face. His hair tousled and unkempt, and his black clothes were covered in dirt and dust, appearing brown instead of black. Staring down at the floor just beyond his feet, he held his bound hands before him and didn't even look up to see Laila as he walked past. He was taken up onto the platform, where the guards shackled his hands to a hook on the podium. Laila

CHAPTER 23

fidgeted in her seat, hoping Nikolean would look up to see her but stayed silent amidst the crowd.

Rath Beldroth stood and walked cautiously up onto the platform where Nikolean was while keeping ample distance, as though he expected the drow to go mad and kill everyone at any moment. The drow continued looking down at the ground, hands restrained before him to the podium and ankles clasped in heavy chains. Aside from his spirits, Laila didn't notice any physical harm done to him and was relieved of that.

A few seats over from Laila, Salyaman stood from his chair and went up to the platform as well, standing next to his father. The room was buzzing with chatter and gossip. Rath Beldroth raised both of his hands, creating stillness over the council.

"Let us begin," Beldroth said to everyone. "Before we address the drow, I would like to announce my decision regarding the prophecy's quest. Lailalanthelus Dula'Quoy, please stand."

Laila stood nervously, although already knowing what his decision would be.

"Laila, I hope you have enjoyed visiting our great city and the gifts that we have given to aid you on your journey."

"Yes, Rath Beldroth. Thank you," she replied earnestly.

"However, I have decided that it is not in our best interest to sacrifice any more of my men to these dragons. I can only offer you my prayers for success for all of our sakes. Council members, are there any who would object?"

The room remained silent; most of the council nodding their agreement. Laila's heart sank for a moment as the reality sank in that they would be doing this alone, and she took her seat.

"It is settled then. Now, Salyaman Dula'Sintos, you have brought us this drow, Nikolean Den Faolin, as your prisoner, but you wish for him to have a trial instead of sythca. Is this correct?"

Salyaman turned to Rath Beldroth and bowed his head. "I do."

"Sythca?" Laila quietly questioned Annallee.

"Death without trial–standard elven practice with drow prisoners," she replied.

Laila shifted nervously in her seat.

"So be it," Beldroth continued. "Is there a second who would claim this drow's life worth discussing?" He looked around at the council, feeling confident that they would be wrapping up the trial quickly. Without a second plea, the sythca would take place.

Laila saw Salyaman motion to her and realized she was supposed to say something. Standing quickly, she yelled out, "I do!"

For the first time, Nikolean raised his head and looked at her, a slight smile crossing his lips upon seeing her there speaking out in his defense. Laila was overwhelmed with nerves, and a tingle ran down her spine as he looked at her with those blood-red eyes.

The king looked at her, unsurprised and slightly annoyed, then waved for her to come forth. "Let us hear your plea," he said unenthusiastically.

Realizing she knew nothing about how elven trials went, she wished she had talked with Salyaman more before now, having assumed she was just to be part of the audience. Laila stepped forward and stood beside Nikolean, glancing at him briefly with compassion and then back to the council, trying to think of what she was supposed to say.

"I believe Nikolean to be good." She paused as everyone in the room chortled and snickered at her words, but Laila cleared her throat, trying to find the strength within her, and spoke louder. "We found him in forest to Má Lyndor. He had chance to harm but never hurt any." The council quieted down, somewhat intrigued. "He will help me in quest to stop war."

CHAPTER 23

"And what would a drow care of our war with the dragons?" a man from the council spoke out.

Beldroth raised a hand to the councilman. "I would like to know that as well. The drows benefit from the dragon's hatred towards us. Why would they help us to stop it?"

Laila looked back and forth between Salyaman and Nikolean, unsure of how to respond. Nikolean raised his hand, as much as his binding would allow, and pointed his finger out for attention, saying hoarsely, "I can answer that, if I may."

"And listen to you spout lies and trickery at us?" Beldroth bellowed. "I am sure that is the only reason you are still alive now!"

"Please let him tell you," Laila pleaded, remembering what he told her about revealing the truth in Má Lyndor and prayed he wasn't going to back down, but mostly, that it wasn't a lie. "I think you want know what he tell you."

Both Salyaman and Beldroth looked at her curiously.

"Alright," Beldroth stated. "I will allow it. Let us hear from the drow." He crossed his arms, waiting to be unimpressed.

Clearing his throat, Nikolean looked over his captivated audience. "The drow have long been rivals of the elves. We all know the stories of long ago, the time when dragons kept the peace between the races, up to the day when the mother dragon, Onis Caelis, was slain by an elf."

The room instantly became outraged by his words, all shouting out against him, but Beldroth raised his hands again to quiet them and nodded to Nikolean to continue.

"After the death of Onis Caelis, the dragons declared war against the elves, but the death of the great dragon affected more than just the elves. The ramifications of this tragedy spilled over into the drow lands as they quickly dried up of all streams and vegetation, the land dying and cracking around us. Where our once-lush forest was, there is now nothing but withered black trees.

Even the animals of our land changed into twisted and gnarled creatures of destruction."

"What does this history lesson have to do with your trial?" Beldroth interrupted, growing impatient.

"Several years ago," Nikolean continued, "some of my people discovered the elders' scrolls, revealing the cause of our land's destruction. These scrolls told of the elder leaders' plans to tip the scales of the war against the elves in their favor. They told of a plan to kill a dragon and frame the elves for its death."

Disorder swept over the council members, standing and shouting toward the podium. "Kill the drow! All drow must die!"

"Wait!" Beldroth yelled to the council while raising his hands to halt them. Most settled down to hear their king. "Why are you telling us this? We have believed this as a possibility for nearly a millennium, so why do you come forward now? What have you to gain from this?"

Nikolean continued, "They had spotted the mother dragon, Onis Caelis, and proudly believed the effect of their plot would be much greater than had it been any other dragon. So, they tracked the dragon to her lair on Iyos Island and waited and watched until the beast slumbered. With great stealth, they snuck into her cavern and felled her while she slept, not considering what the ramifications would be to the drow people. Since that day, our lands have perished, requiring magic to keep us alive, and everything for us became much worse than before. This made the leaders hate the elves even more. But, when the truth was revealed about what started the Dragon War and what happened to our lands, many of my people became enraged. Even drows honor and protect magic, and what the elders did to Onis Caelis goes against nature itself, regardless of their intent.

"Several of us turned our backs on our leaders after the truth was revealed because we could not bear what they had done to the powers and magic of this land, and we formed a rebellion. We are known as the Drakka." The room had become quiet as they all stared at Nikolean, engrossed. "Some of the Drakka stayed behind in secret, while others of us have left the drow cities in search of a way to make things right, a search for something greater. I am dedicated to righting the wrong done by my people and bringing balance once again to the land of Onis." He looked over at Laila, who had been watching him intently, and smiled softly. "I believe that this magnificent elf could very well be the one to fix all that has gone so very wrong, and I dedicate my life to serving her on her quest."

Rath Beldroth sighed deeply, considering Nikolean's words while the council waited anxiously, whispering amongst themselves. After a long moment, Beldroth said, "While this is all very revealing, I still do not see why we should let you go."

"I can speak to that," Salyaman interrupted, stepping forward. "One thing that neither of them has mentioned is that when we first encountered this drow, I had shot him with my arrow." Smiles and smirks waved over the council members' faces, and Beldroth glared crossly at them like misbehaving children, commanding silence. "I was ready to leave him to die," Salyaman continued, "but Lady Laila refused to leave him. Instead, she stayed with him, healed him, and insisted that we keep him with us so the wildlife could not take him before he had recovered. I agreed to bring him simply because I did not want to leave her behind. She made it very clear that she would not leave him." Salyaman paused, the council's whispers growing louder.

Beldroth raised his hand again. "Go on," he said to Salyaman, curious where he was going with this.

Salyaman hesitated briefly, wondering why he was helping the drow, but continued anyway, believing it was the right thing to do. "Lady Laila saved Nikolean's life, and, in return, he pledged his life to serve her cause as his life-debt."

Sighing loudly again, Beldroth considered his son's words. "A life-debt, you say," he finally responded. "Well, if you both believe your lives are safe with him on your journey..." He looked at Salyaman and Laila, both nodding in response, "then I suppose we should let him honor his life-debt to Lady Lailalanthelus. I am sure I do not need to remind you to sleep with one eye open," Beldroth added, looking sternly at Salyaman. "However, he will need to remain in the dungeon until you all are ready to leave the city." Turning to the council, he asked, "What say you? If any of the council disagrees with my decision, you are welcome to announce your concerns now."

Unlike the silence of their last inquiry, the members were all clamorously discussing the decision amongst themselves. After several moments, one of the elves a few rows back stood and asked, "How do we know this is not all part of some ploy? How can we trust a drow?"

The other members nodded and voiced their agreement with his concerns.

"I understand," Beldroth replied, "and your concerns are valid. I do not know that there is a way for us to be sure. However, aside from saving his own life, he has nothing to gain from us. He will not be staying here and, thus, would not be any danger to us. He will also be escorted by Salyaman, Lady Laila, and their two other companions, who will ensure that he leaves our forests." Beldroth paused and looked at Salyaman, making sure the last part was clearly understood, then turned back to the council. "They have chosen to risk their lives by bringing him on their quest, and we will have to trust that they are not making their own grave mistake."

CHAPTER 23

Rath Beldroth strode over to Nikolean with more confidence than before. "And IF their quest is successful..." he said, pausing for dramatic effect, "and he has shown to be an honorable drow..." The council's eyes rolled and scowled at the oxymoron. "then I shall personally pardon him and grant him immunity for helping to put an end to the war!"

Laila, without thinking, gave Rath Beldroth a big hug. "Thank you!" she exclaimed and then, embarrassed, released him when she realized what she had done.

"Do not thank me yet, Lady Lailalanthelus," the king replied. "First, you must show us a victory and that he has held his word to help achieve it."

"I understand," Laila said.

"Thank you, Rath Beldroth," Nikolean added. "I promise I will not disappoint you."

Looking at him scornfully, Beldroth said, "My expectations of you are not very high, so let us hope that you do not." Turning back to the council, he declared, "It is decided. Guards return the drow to the dungeon until further notice!"

The same two guards grabbed each of Nikolean's arms and led him off the platform toward the door. The council members watched as he was roughly dragged away, all talking amongst themselves, wondering how long it would be before he betrayed Laila and the others, slitting their throats while they slept or stabbing them in the backs the first chance he got.

Laila didn't care how hard-hearted they were towards Nikolean. She was just relieved that they were giving him a chance to prove what she had felt from the beginning; Nikolean was not their enemy.

"Oh, and one more thing!" Beldroth called after him before he reached the door, "Nikolean Den Faolin, some advice before you go. Be sure to stay clear of our forests in the future, or the next time we find you in our courts, you will be facing some unfortunate ramifications of your own."

CHAPTER 23

CHAPTER TWENTY-FOUR

GUARDIAN

erimer stayed steady under Laila as she gently held her reins and waited to leave. Looking back at the city of Má Lyndor, donned in her new armor with Dragonsbane sheathed at her hip, she knew she was going to miss this place and wondered if she would ever have a chance to return.

Davion was mounted next to her atop Helna, and Hort with Orbek. Salyaman was approaching from the stables on foot, guiding a majestic and embellished male elkah named Friet with Shakiera by his side. Shakiera grabbed his hand as they drew near, sadness in her eyes, and she stopped Salyaman before they reached the gates to give him a long passionate kiss. Too curious about this form of affection, Laila gawked at the couple while everyone else looked away respectfully.

"You return to me as soon as you can," Shakiera told him, her heart breaking inside.

"I will, malléalan," *my love,* Salyaman replied, giving her a soft kiss on her forehead before continuing toward the gates. Shakiera stood back, watching as he prepared to leave, her hand gently cradling her stomach.

"Where is Nikolean?" Laila asked Salyaman eagerly.

Before Salyaman could answer, the group turned to see Nikolean being brought forth through the dungeon doors by two guards, still bound by his hands and feet. Laila was relieved that he would be out of those chains soon enough—Nikolean was even more relieved.

Laila dismounted from Merimer and waited anxiously for them. As they got close, she went and grabbed an old speckled-gray horse that they purchased for Nikolean and brought it over to meet him.

"So, I understand you go by Lady Laila now," the drow said as she approached.

Laila smiled awkwardly and replied, "Yes. They tell me was my name." Before he could respond, she led the old horse forward and exclaimed, overly excited, "Got this for you!"

Looking over the horse while the guards removed his bindings, he replied, "It looks half dead."

The smile faded from Laila's lips in disappointment. "We had to beg them to let us buy for you. I sorry."

Nikolean gently lifted her chin, raising her eyes to meet his, and smiled. "It's quite alright," he told her. "I'm sure it will work out just fine." Laila gave him a half-smile, and he stepped forward, free from his bindings at last.

"Let's get on with it!" Hort yelled impatiently. "Ye can debate the geriatric horse later."

A crowd had gathered around the group, wishing them well and good luck with their journey. Rath Beldroth and Rathca Saelithil had already said their farewells and good fortunes and were waiting patiently to see them off, making sure to make a spectacle of themselves in their support for the elf that would end the war. Laila was not surprised that no others had volunteered to join them on their quest, all having lost so many to the war already, but she was still disappointed.

CHAPTER 24

"Farewell, Má Lyndor!" Salyaman hollered. Then he said to the others, "I agree with Mr. Strongarm. Let us depart." He exchanged a final loving glance with his pregnant wife before heading through the gates to the beautiful forest beyond.

Laila rushed back over to Merimer and mounted her swiftly. Her comfort with Merimer was a strange feeling to her, as though this magical creature had become an extension of herself.

Nikolean mounted the old mare and joined the others. Then, four guards came forward toward the group; all of them mounted on elkahs. Two of the guards approached Nikolean, one of them placing a blindfold on him.

"Hmmm... Not again." Hort mumbled as the other two guards blindfolded him.

"Just until you are beyond our forest," one of them replied.

Davion found it rather insulting that they were part of the group that would free the elves from the dragons' wrath but couldn't be trusted to know the city's location. However, he honored their laws and leaned forward for them while they placed the blindfold over his eyes. The guards hooked a lead to Helna, Orbek, and the old mare and then led them through the gates after Salyaman, who was watching from the other side.

Laila looked back to Má Lyndor one final time, a half-hearted smile on her lips. She had been so eager to see the world, leaving her home and her mother, missing her more than she ever thought possible. Now, she had to leave a new home, one where she felt that she could have belonged, with people who could have loved and accepted her. In the back of her mind, she wondered if she would ever be able to stay in one place again or if this destiny of hers would keep her traveling and risking her life until she was no more.

Trying to let go of her sadness, Laila turned and followed the rest of the group. *Farewell, Má Lyndor,* she sighed softly to herself, and then, without having to issue a command, Merimer trotted through the gates after the others.

It was still rather early in the day, and the group had already gone several miles past the concealing border of Má Lyndor. They had been heading north since they left the city and could hear the river's flowing waters ahead of them. The sky was clear, with a light summer breeze blowing through the red and orange leaves of the Ashwood Forest.

"Gorén River lies ahead!" called one of the guards coming to a halt. "We'll part ways here."

Salyaman trotted over to the guard and grasped his forearm in a farewell shake. The guards then turned and gently kicked their elkahs, disappearing into the woods where they had emerged from. Davion, Hort, and Nikolean all reached up and removed their blindfolds, tossing them off into the bushes, grateful to be rid of them.

"So, what now?" Davion asked Laila.

"I need to speak with Silver dragons in Gorén Mountains," she replied.

"We can stop by me home, Lochlann, on the way. Gather some supplies fer climbin'," Hort suggested.

Laila nodded. She had been reaching out to Turathyl since they left Má Lyndor, but the skies and her mind had been quiet. Her grief about having to leave Má Lyndor so soon had nagged at her since they left the shimmering white-stone city behind them. She was more than glad to go to Lochlann first, unsure of what she was supposed to do once she reached the dragons. She needed more time, and she knew it, even if she wasn't ready to admit it out loud.

"That sounds fine," Salyaman said.

Nikolean watched in silence, keeping his eyes on Laila, studying her eerily. Davion, annoyed with his glares, maneuvered himself and Helna between them, blocking the drow's view. "Sounds like a plan," he added.

Giving his elkah a swift kick, Salyaman began galloping toward the Gorén River, and the rest of the party did the same, following close behind. Davion kept by Laila's side while Hort stayed close to Salyaman. Nikolean was starting to trail behind on his old mare, watching after them.

"Drow!" Hort called back to him. "Up where we can see ye!"

Obliging, Nikolean gave the old mare another kick. Davion scowled at the drow as he galloped past him to ride steadily between the two groups.

"Are you sure about this?" Davion asked quietly to Laila. "Do we really have to have him with us? Couldn't we just let him go or something?"

Watching Nikolean, Laila shook her head. "No," she replied softly. "He supposed to be here." She couldn't explain any of it; she just had a feeling that all of them were supposed to be together in this.

Sighing, Davion continued to scowl ahead, not comprehending her desire to have a drow come along.

When they broke through the trees to the Gorén River at a fast gallop, all the mounts reared and faltered as they stumbled upon a horrific sight—orcs!

Salyaman quickly grabbed his bow and arrows; Hort, his sword and shield; Davion, his staff; Nikolean, his sword; and Laila, Dragonsbane. They were instantly spotted by the orcs, who began to charge at them. There were six orcs total, large and brawny beasts, with white muddy-colored skin and dark orange eyes. Their skin was bald as a baby's bottom, and they had large crooked tusks jutting out from their bottom lips. The orcs were robust, bulging with muscles and fat alike. Most of them were holding spiked or chained clubs, while others carried long spears.

Trembling atop Merimer, Laila gasped as one darted right for her, but Merimer held steady beneath. The hideous creature raised its club ready to strike, and then, as he brought it down, the club slammed against an invisible shield, emitting a bright blinding light. Laila squinted through the light and saw the orc fly backward through the air, shaking the ground as it slammed against some rocks. Her mouth dropped as she looked around to see who had helped her, but everyone was engaged in their own attacks with the orcs. Merimer kicked at the dirt as though preparing to charge the orc, despite Laila trying to hold her steady. Before Merimer could move, there was a loud shriek in the sky, dominating everyone's attention.

Turathyl! Laila realized as she looked up to see the outline of a great dragon descending quickly from the sky, the sun at its back. She watched in awe as the massive Silver dragon dove and crushed the orc under its claws effortlessly, killing it instantly. The orc barely had a chance to let out a cry as its bones shattered against the dirt and rocks. Turathyl picked up and tossed her victim to the side, and the mangled orc's body flopped limply against a boulder.

"Turathyl!" Laila yelled, thrilled to see her.

Both the orcs and others alike all stopped their feuding and turned to see the enormous dragon before them, no one quite knowing what to do. The orcs quickly decided to run, but Turathyl pounced after them; swiping one with her tail, causing it to fly backward; grabbing one in her jaws, crushing it with her teeth; and snatching one with her front claws, squeezing it tightly as its bones cracked and broke in her grasp, and its guttural screams pierced the air. As Turathyl crippled and destroyed the five orcs around her,

Salyaman and Hort chased after a renegade orc who had escaped into the trees.

Davion and Nikolean both rode over to Laila quickly, standing between her and the dragon. "Should we run?" Davion asked her nervously.

"No!" Laila said joyfully as she jumped off the back of Merimer. "It's Turathyl!" She suddenly felt all the sadness she had been feeling fall away from her as her heart filled with warmth upon the sight of the beautiful shining dragon.

All the orcs dead, Turathyl turned to see Laila running toward her. The small elf stopped only feet away, and the dragon lowered her head to greet her. *'Hello, young one.'* Turathyl mind-sent to Laila.

'You came!' Laila sent back.

'Of course, I did. I have been watching you, young one. I was never far away.' Turathyl raised her head and snarled at Davion and Nikolean as they approached behind Laila. They stopped and took a few steps back.

"Are you okay?" Davion called out to her.

Laila turned to him, smiling. "Yes! She been watching us, guarding us."

"She's been around this whole time?" Davion asked.

"Yes!" she replied. "She swore she would protect me," Laila looked back at the dragon, still smiling from ear to ear. "and she did."

Everyone turned to look at the trees as Salyaman and Hort came galloping back into the clearing by the river, coming to a sudden halt, kicking up dust when they saw how close they were to the dragon. Hort had some blood dripping down his arm, and Laila rushed over to see him.

"Let me see that!" she insisted.

"Ah, tis jus' a scratch. Ye got bigger things right now," he said, not taking his eyes off of the dragon.

The ground creaked as Turathyl shifted her weight, rocks crunching underneath her claws. Watching the others intently with piercing eyes, she sat down slowly.

"Soooo, it's staying then?" Davion asked Laila nervously.

"Are we safe here?" Salyaman inquired warily.

Laila looked at all of them, seeing how scared they all were, and sighed. *'They think you're going to eat them!'* she said to Turathyl.

She chortled her dragon laughter and replied, *'Yes, they do.'* Baring her teeth and letting out a low growl at the others, she added, *'I just might!'* Laila looked at the dragon, shocked and terrified. The dragon tilted her head back and laughed. *'I am only jesting, dear child. Dragon humor, I suppose. I will not harm your friends as long as they keep their distance. I do not know if I trust them...yet.'*

Turning back to the group, Laila assured them they would not be harmed but to keep their distance for now.

"So be it," Salyaman replied. "Let us break for lunch, and you two can catch up." The group dismounted and brought their mounts over to the river for a drink while they gathered food from the satchels, looking over their shoulders nervously at the dragon the whole time. Salyaman was most uneasy having the beast nearby, having been at war with them for so long, and having seen so many loved ones killed by their talons. It was hard for him to believe that any of them could be trusted, but he was desperate for a resolution to the endless massacres.

'Where did you get the unicorn?' Turathyl asked Laila while staring toward the river.

Laila followed her glare, confused, and replied. *'Merimer? I don't know what you mean.'*

'I haven't seen one in hundreds of years; thought they were extinct. It's not pure, of course, but it is definitely part unicorn. I can feel its magic

CHAPTER 24

from here. I also sensed its protective shield against that orc. Very impressive."

Laila smiled as she realized it was Merimer that had saved her from the orc's attack. 'I knew it was magical! She called to me from the stable in Má Lyndor!' Laila responded. 'But I did not know what she was, and neither did the elves.'

'Probably because they are believed to be a myth,' Turathyl explained. 'So what else happened in Má Lyndor?'

The events of Má Lyndor flowed forth into Turathyl's mind, both descriptions and visual pictures of her memories. It felt comforting being able to communicate with another being again this way since leaving Lupé Caelis. Laila was excited to share all of the things she had learned about her people, the town, and her...mother. Suddenly, Laila broke the connection with Turathyl and looked away sadly.

'What is it, young one?' Turathyl inquired.

Laila fidgeted with the cloth of her cape, afraid to ask the question weighing on her mind since she heard about her...about Lady Leona's death. Her body trembled as she sent her thoughts back to the dragon. 'I learned that my mother was Lady Leonallan Dula'Quoy, a wood elf diplomat and a druid.' She paused, gathering the courage to look Turathyl in her deep black eyes. Expressionless, the great dragon looked back at her, waiting for her to continue. 'They said she was killed by Silver dragons while traveling home to Othsuda Theora. Everyone had thought I was also killed.' Laila continued to look into Turathyl's eyes, searching for some type of reaction, but there was none. 'I guess I was wondering if you knew who killed my mother.'

Sighing deeply, Turathyl's eyes suddenly saddened as she bowed head slightly. 'Yes, I do.' She had known this question was coming but hadn't anticipated how it would make her feel. Deciding it best to explain why it happened first, Turathyl told her,

'An order was issued by Aeris to attack the diplomatic caravans that traveled between the elven cities to send a message to the elves. Aeris wished to cut off the communication between the elves and instill fear into them to keep them barricaded within their cities and away from us. They became proficient at defending their cities from our attacks after the fall of Ballat Sueda, so the roads had become an open warzone.'

Laila looked down at the dirt and ran her fingers in the sand, fidgeting uneasily while she listened. 'But, do you know which dragon?'

Turathyl paced herself, hoping that the elf would understand. However, knowing that she probably wouldn't, she couldn't bring herself to confess. 'It could have been any dragon that was given an order that day...' She studied Laila, who had gone silent, and decided to leave it at that.

After a moment, Laila finally stood up. 'Okay,' she blurted, breaking the silence as tears welled in the corner of her eyes, not wanting to hear any more. 'I guess I'll never know then. Maybe it's better that way since I'm about to confront the Silvers about the war.'

Turathyl suspected that the elf knew the answer but wasn't ready to hear it, as she felt Laila's mind was becoming increasingly resistant to her touch. The guilt bubbled inside of her, and she wished she could just tell her the truth but wasn't sure how she could help if Laila were to push her away. 'It is a war, Lupé...pardon me, Lailalanthelus, and there have been many casualties on both sides, but I am glad that you got to find out who your mother was.'

'What about my father?' Laila pressed. 'Do you know who killed him? His name was Darton Dula'Quoy.'

Taking a moment to think, Turathyl finally shook her head and answered honestly, 'I do not recall anything about him. I am sorry.' Turathyl stiffened and started growling at something behind Laila. She turned to see Davion approaching, hands high in the air holding some rations and a flask of water.

CHAPTER 24

"I'm just bringing her some food, great dragon," Davion announced humbly, waiting for an indication that he was safe to proceed. Turathyl snorted, wind gusting over Laila, and then nodded ever-so-slightly while watching him closely.

"It's okay," Laila called to him. "Thank you."

Davion brought her the rations and flask, then backed away slowly. Once comfortably far enough away, he turned his back and returned to the group.

'So you have decided to go and speak with my clan?' Turathyl asked Laila, getting back to the conversation, annoyed by the disruption.

Laila nodded, taking a bite out of some elven bread.

'I don't think you are ready,' Turathyl stated bluntly. Looking up from her bread, Laila slowed her chewing, surprised by the dragon. 'You need more training. Or more time. I'm not sure which, but you need to be strong before you go in front of Aeris. You are not ready.'

Her heart pounded in her chest, the words of Lupé Caelis being repeated from Turathyl, and her limbs began to shake as Laila slowly put down her bread. 'What are you saying?' Laila asked, even the voice in her head quivering. 'Should I have married the prince and acquired more men?' She felt self-conscious enough as it was, feeling ill-prepared and ill-suited for this mission, and now Turathyl was not only confirming her fears but bringing back her feelings of inadequacy. She hoped that she had left all that behind in the Sacred Forest with her mother.

'Forget the prince. Do not give him another thought. The Great Aeris will not be so welcoming to you as the elves or as I have been. She will see your powers and presence as a threat instead of a blessing. You need to be ready for anything. We do not know for certain how she will react or what she might do.' Turathyl paused, looking down on the young elf. 'When was the last time you even used your powers?' she asked, rather harshly.

Caught off guard, Laila thought back to when that was and realized that she hadn't used them since she saved Nikolean. Her mother had her training every day, and she had been neglecting her training and practicing. Ashamed, she looked at the ground and replied, *'Since before we met.'*

Turathyl nodded.

'We're going through Lochlann first on our way to see the dwarves and stock up on supplies. Perhaps it will give me enough time to be ready.' Laila looked at Turathyl, hopefully.

'Perhaps,' Turathyl replied unconvinced.

"Lady Laila," Salyaman interrupted while maintaining his distance, "it is time to get moving. We still have two more days before we reach Lochlann."

Standing, Laila brushed the crumbs off her clothes and then nodded to Salyaman.

"Coming," she replied.

Turathyl raised her body and began to spread her wings.

"Must you leave?" Laila asked.

The great dragon cocked her head at the young elf and smiled softly. *'I must,'* she replied. Turathyl saw the disappointment spread over Laila's face and took pity over the elf. *'I will return at nightfall and will not be far away, should you need me.'* She lowered her head down before Laila, and the young elf embraced her muzzle, holding her tightly. The dragon was startled but then remembered the feelings of when she first encountered this elven child all those years ago. She closed her eyes for a moment, enjoying the familiar touch, and then spread her wings to take flight.

Laila let go and stepped back a few paces while Turathyl gathered the wind from around them and lifted off into the air. The dust flew wildly across the two-leggeds' faces as the great powerful dragon flapped her wings and headed further and further into the sky.

CHAPTER 24

Davion rode up next to Laila atop Helna, with Merimer following behind him. "We best get going," he said, stealing her attention away from the slowly-vanishing dragon silhouette in the sky.

"Aye!" Hort called out while riding up beside Davion. "We've got us a celebration to have when we get there!" Davion looked at Hort, embarrassed. "Aw, boy. Ye didna think I'd forgotten, did ye? Me boy's becomin' a man in only four days' time! At least I believe eighteen is when the humans declare it?" He looked to Davion for confirmation.

"Yes, Uncle," Davion replied, flushing, "and no, I knew you wouldn't forget, nor let me forget."

Laila smiled at Davion's embarrassment, although not really understanding what they were talking about, then swung herself onto Merimer's back. The group started heading west along the river, a million thoughts running through Laila's mind of everything she had learned and everything she needed to do before facing Aeris in the mountains.

"Oh!" she exclaimed to the group. "Turathyl told me that Merimer is part unicorn! Isn't that incredible?"

"Incredible," Nikolean said, fascinated.

"That *is* incredible, Laila. It is no wonder she found you," Salyaman added.

"Ah, don't be daft!" Hort exclaimed, "Unicorns ain't real!"

Davion chuckled at his uncle, and they all kicked their mounts, bringing them to a full gallop along the crystal waters of the Gorén River.

CHAPTER TWENTY-FIVE

RANCHETAL

*M*erimer's beautiful white coat gleamed in the late afternoon sun as Laila ran her hands over her lovingly. Laila had tried to communicate with her the way she could with her mother and Turathyl. However, she found the mystical creature to be somewhere between that level of communication and that of her wolfkin, sharing pictures and feelings instead of words, which was still nice.

The burbling brook rushed around the jutting rocks, too loud for Davion's comfort, worried they might not hear something approaching. He gazed at Laila as he unburdened Helna of her saddle and pack, then released the horse to the rolling waters for a drink. Salyaman had disappeared into the forest to gather wood, like always, and Hort was finding rocks to prepare a firepit for the night.

Nikolean dismounted from his old mare, which he had not bothered to name, and gave her a swat on the rear, sending her startled over to the riverbank. He then casually strolled up behind Laila.

"Couldn't get me one of those?" he said playfully, nodding toward Merimer.

Not having heard Nikolean approach, Laila jumped in alarm and turned to face him. "I'm sorry," she replied earnestly, "I tried to get elkah, but elves not even want to give us horse, knowing it for you."

"Relax, my lady," Nikolean said with a smile. "I was only teasing. I am grateful for the horse, truly."

"Thank you, Nikolean," Laila said, half smiling. Even though she wanted to give him the benefit of the doubt and trust him, she still felt nervous around him, especially when he got so close to her. It was mostly a feeling in the pit of her stomach telling her to flee, but, despite the uneasiness and the others' warnings, she wanted desperately to believe he would not harm her.

"Please," he said to her softly, taking her hand gently in his, "call me Niko."

His eyes looking deeply into hers, his mouth curved in a mischievous smile, he stepped in closer to her, increasing her discomfort. Laila felt her face grow flush as her hand tingled in his. It felt cold against hers, causing her to inadvertently withdraw it swiftly. She attempted a smile so as not to insult him, and he continued smiling mischievously at her.

Feeling a sudden hand on her shoulder, Laila jumped again, her nerves on edge, and looked to see Davion standing behind her. She began feeling more relaxed instantly with his touch and took a step backward, bringing herself closer to him.

"Perhaps *Niko* would like to help grab some wood for the fire," Davion said slyly to Nikolean.

Glaring at Davion for a moment, a look of contempt sweeping over his face, Nikolean finally smiled astutely and replied, "Yes, I suppose I would." He briefly looked back at Laila eerily, then bowed his head and said, "My lady," before turning and heading for the forest.

"I don't trust him," Davion said with disdain, turning to Laila concerned. "Are you okay?"

"I'm fine," she replied.

Laila nodded to Merimer, and she trotted off toward the river, keeping some distance from the other mounts.

A strange whooshing sound was barely audible over the loud river but caused Davion and Laila to look around curiously. It wasn't until it was nearly overhead, and their clothes and hair were whipping about in the wind, that they both looked up and gasped at the great Silver dragon descending near them.

"Tury!" Laila called out excitedly. "You came back!"

Davion took several steps back, giving the dragon her requested space, not wanting to anger her. Laila ran over to Turathyl and embraced her muzzle, so Davion took his leave to start a campfire.

'I told you I would, young one,' Turathyl replied, smiling back at the young elf. 'I will stay with you tonight. There are many bands of orcs in this area that I spotted on my way. They seem to be multiplying and are all over the northern territories, including the Gorén Mountains. My clan used to keep them at bay, but our attentions have been elsewhere for some time now.'

Turathyl paused and looked around at the others while they prepared camp. 'Lupé Caelis has told me that you have all four elemental powers.' Looking back at Laila, she continued, 'I would like to see your powers; get a better understanding of what you can do.'

Laila lowered her head. 'All except for fire,' she replied sadly and looked over at Davion. 'I still don't understand why I can't find that one.' She watched Davion forlornly as he easily started the campfire. 'Perhaps having the others will be enough?' Laila looked back at Turathyl, hopefully.

'Give it time,' Turathyl replied, trying to be encouraging. 'I am sure you will far surpass the human.' Settling her mighty figure across the ground, Turathyl tucked her wings tight at her sides and got comfortable. *'Now get yourself something to eat to regain your strength. Afterward, I want to see the powers you have mastered.'*

Blushing, Laila replied, *'I'm not sure about* mastered, *but I will show you what I can do.'*

Laila joined the others and ate her rations while sitting next to Davion. Her companions ate slowly, one hand resting on their weapons while they watched the dragon apprehensively. Turathyl, having just eaten her own dinner, was licking her talons and cleaning her face.

Hort, on the other side of Davion, leaned closer to him and whispered so as not to be heard, "I'm not sure which makes me knickers more twisted, the drow or the dragon."

Turathyl looked up, staring at the dwarf for a moment with a look of annoyance in her eyes, and let out a snort, clearly having heard him. Hort quickly looked back to his food and kept quiet after that, his heart racing nervously.

Eager to show off her skills, Laila hastily finished her food and drink and then dashed back over to Turathyl, ready to get started. *'Which would you like to see first?'* she mind-sent to her as she came running up.

Thinking that the answer would have been obvious, Turathyl snickered, *'Wind, of course!'*

Laila nodded seriously and stretched her arms up to the sky, then closed her eyes and concentrated. Sending out her thoughts, Laila quickly found the wind spirit and grabbed onto its shining white light with her mind. Pulling at the surrounding air and clouds, a gentle breeze began to blow coolly through the campsite. Her long beautiful golden locks swayed in the wind, and its coolness kissed her cheeks.

The others at the camp had grown curious about what she was doing with the dragon. They were enjoying their dinner entertainment while standing around the firepit, munching on their rations.

'*More,*' Turathyl ordered.

With a wave of her arms, Laila pulled harder at the sky. The clouds then gathered closer together, growing darker and darker until they were nearly black. The sky became cold and dark as the sun was blocked behind the storm clouds. A strong gale gusted through the camp, extinguishing the fire that Davion had lit. Hort grabbed onto his helmet to keep it from blowing off but refused to put down his flask of wine, still taking swigs while he watched the commotion. The nearby trees whipped around wildly in the wind.

"Hey, Lass! What ye doin'?!" Hort yelled over the howling winds.

The sky crackled, and lightning shot down in a brilliant light, striking the ground on the other side of the river. A large black scorch mark covered a patch of grass, and the winds continued to increase in speed and power.

"Laila?!" Davion called out. "What's going on?"

Salyaman stepped forward and crossed his arms over his chest, watching her intently. "She is performing a Ranchetal for the dragon, a display of her powers." He took another step forward, enthralled. "I have been waiting for this since I first met her."

'*Is that all?*' Turathyl questioned, causing Laila to falter.

The wind quickly died down, and the storm clouds began to weaken and disperse as though they never were, the sky illuminating once again as the sun rays pierced around the weakened clouds. Laila dropped her arms at her sides and stared confoundedly at the dragon.

'*Could you control where the lightning struck?*' Turathyl asked.

Laila nodded and smiled proudly.

'*Good. Have you used the wind as a weapon?*'

Laila nodded again, '*Yes, against a snake.*'

CHAPTER 25

'*Ah, yes. I remember that. It was resourceful of you.*' Turathyl stood. '*Now watch me.*'

Looking around for a target, she briefly considered their audience but chuckled maliciously to herself and decided she'd better not—for Laila's sake. Instead, she looked to the trees further ahead of them and decided they would have to suffice. Turathyl pulled and summoned the air from around them, bringing her wings back, and then thrust them forward in a strong swooping motion, sending a forceful gale toward the trees. The others found it hard to breathe with the air so thin, watching as the trees trapped in the gale whipped around like they were caught in a hurricane. Some of the weaker trees bent and broke, and a smaller tree was ripped out of the ground and toppled over with the bottom of its roots facing the river. '*With practice, you can be as powerful. That can knock anyone off of a horse or throw them backward away from you.*'

She motioned Laila's attention over to her group that was trying to catch their breath. '*That is another attack—pulling the air away from your foes and suffocating them. Just a side effect in this case, but can kill someone when focused. When you get full control, you can try tornados, although I wouldn't recommend them until you have mastered everything else. They can be quite reckless if not controlled; they do not just disperse when you are finished with them but will need to be brought to a halt by your powers or will continue to wreak havoc.*'

Laila smiled at the thought as she tried to imagine it. She realized she had never thought about her powers in this way. Lupé Caelis had her focusing on her ability to access and manipulate the elements, but not on how to turn them into weapons.

'*Now,*' Turathyl said, '*let me see water.*'

Accessing the blue water spirit as she had with the wind, Laila turned her attention to the river and began doing tricks such as: parting the water, leaving the waterbed dry; stopping the flow of water, making it still and almost glasslike; and having it shoot up into the air, spraying out like a fountain.

Turathyl watched silently as Laila performed for her but was not impressed. To her, it was all child's play, something newborn water dragons could do before their third birthday. With Turathyl's help, Laila learned she could actually turn the water into ice, sending projectile icicles at an enemy. She could also boil water, making a river unpassable, or boil a cup of liquid that she could throw into an enemy's face for a quick diversion. Although unable to perform everything, she was exhilarated to try and know some of the possibilities of what her powers could perhaps one day accomplish. Turathyl also explained that a form of water magic was called blood magic; since most creatures are, in large part, made up of water.

Laila didn't like hearing about blood magic, how she could either boil or freeze someone to death from the inside, or worse. In fact, she didn't like hearing about how she could kill anyone. Laila was not an aggressive person and, while she could see the benefit in using her powers as weapons to defend herself, she wasn't sure how she felt about actually using them to kill anyone. However, she would not miss an opportunity to learn new skills.

Turathyl offered to gather a few specimens for the blood magic attempt, but Laila politely declined. '*I don't think I'm ready for that,*' she told her honestly.

Taking a deep breath, slightly disappointed, Turathyl understood. '*Okay, young one. When you are, then. Now, show me your earth magic.*'

Laila grew excited about the earth magic since it came the easiest to her, and she had already used it in battle on more than one occasion. Feeling herself getting worn from all of the practicing, she thought it best to begin with regaining some of her energy. '*I'm tired from all of the magic,*' Laila told Turathyl.

CHAPTER 25

'*Do you need to stop?*' she asked.

'*No,*' Laila replied as she dug her fingers into the dirt. '*I actually use my earth magic for that.*' The earth spirit seemed to stay with her now, never requiring her to seek it out as she still did with the others. Laila closed her eyes, and Turathyl watched as all of the grass around the elf began to turn black while it withered and died. Although she couldn't see any physical changes happening to Laila, she sensed the magic flowing from the ground into her tiny body. Once the flowing stopped, Laila stood back up, energized, and looked around at the dead grass.

'*Very good,*' Turathyl said, impressed. '*What else can you do?*'

Pulling from the spirit, Laila started with something easy and pleasant by making flowers sprout from the ground all around the dragon. Turathyl, not caring for such things, didn't react, so Laila instead called for roots to grow and grab onto Turathyl's front paw. The dragon tugged on the roots, pleased with the resistance, and smiled before ripping her paw free of them.

'*Okay. What else?*' Turathyl pressed on.

Laila thought for a moment, unsure. So, Turathyl taught her about splitting the earth, a small crack to start, and having large rocks pierce up through the dirt. She could hypothetically turn the soil to quicksand to stop foes from following. Turathyl explained how she could make the trees uproot from the ground and walk where she wanted them or have them twine together to form a wall. Laila was unable to perform all of her tasks but made more progress than with the other spirits, and she reveled in the experience of it all.

Once Laila was done trying out her new skills, she was beginning to get weary again. Having had stolen energy from the earth several times now, she was finding it more ineffective with each attempt, realizing that even this power had its limitations. Laila recognized that she had learned more with Turathyl today than she had learned over several sessions with her mother, but it was all very different from what she was used to. Hours had passed during her lessons, and it was too dark to see anymore except for by the light of the fire that Davion had recast.

Salyaman had been watching Laila fascinated, thinking that if he hadn't been watching the spectacle with his own eyes, he would never have believed it to be true. Her magic was unlike that of the elves, which was usually based on only one of the elements and was conducted through spells and incantations. Instead, hers seemed more natural, like that of the dragons. It didn't make any sense to him.

Davion could see how much the Ranchetal was draining her. He wished to comfort her and convince her to stop for a break. Hort had grown bored a while ago and was sharpening his axe by the fire while Nikolean watched them all silently from against the foot of a tree.

'And you still cannot access fire at all?' Turathyl asked.

Laila shook her head. 'No. I can only make things a little warm.'

'So that's it then?' Turathyl asked as though discontented.

Thinking for a moment, Laila remembered one more thing. 'Well, there's this...' she said as she summoned a rock to fly into her hand from the edge of the river.

'Yes, I saw earth magic,' Turathyl said, uninspired.

'No, not earth magic.' Laila looked around and caught Davion's eyes. She concentrated and shut her eyes, reaching out her hand toward him. Closing her hand into a fist, Davion began to shake and fret as he was lifted about a foot off the ground.

"Laila!" he yelled at her, panicked. His feet kicked around in the air, and he waved his arms frantically while he floated over to her. "Laila! Put me down!"

CHAPTER 25

Answering his request, Laila slowly lowered her hand, and Davion sank with ease to the ground near her. He was relieved to be back on solid ground and unsure of how he felt about what had just happened.

For the first time, Turathyl seemed quite impressed. *'Telekinesis?'* she gasped.

'Yes,' Laila said proudly.

'Very interesting,' Turathyl added. *'A rare gift indeed.'*

"Laila?" Davion said, getting her attention back with his arms crossed over his chest. "It's getting late. We should turn in."

She hadn't even realized how much time had passed and agreed. Davion started to head back to the others and stopped when he realized she wasn't following. He looked back to see her walk over to Turathyl and crawl into the crevice of her elbow, snuggling against the resting dragon. His mouth dropped in disbelief and, when he saw the dragon staring at him, he decidedly skittered back to the campfire.

Being with the dragon felt easy. It was as if she were back home in the den with her mother and kin. She didn't feel uneasy or self-conscious about her words or actions like she did around the others. She wasn't worried about proper etiquette or decorum with the dragon. She was, simply, just herself. Turathyl was in her thoughts, a bond that shattered the barriers of indecisiveness and insecurities. She could never share this with Davion. She could never know what he was truly feeling or his intentions, not with the clearness that she experienced with the wolf god and this dragon. Not having this type of connection with the others left her feeling lost and confused about them and where she belonged. Her comrades feared the dragon's presence and would not get much sleep that night, with one eye open and their hands on their weapons. But, here in the clutch of this giant beast, Laila had never felt more safe.

Keeping watch both around their camp, to the sky, and to the others in the group, Turathyl was warmed by the presence of the elf as she curled against her. Laila drearily asked questions about the dragons, mostly the Silvers—clearly scared of having to face them—and Turathyl did her best to answer without completely frightening her off of her mission. She told Laila stories of the time when dragons lived in harmony—more-or-less—with the other races and how she dreamed of it being that way again. At some point, Turathyl realized that Laila had stopped listening to her stories because she had finally fallen asleep. Smiling down at the slumbering young elf, she then turned her attention back to the world around them, determined to let no harm come to her.

CHAPTER 25

CHAPTER TWENTY-SIX

UNREADY

*urrounded by fire, Laila looked around and around for the dragon she knew she would encounter once again. It was a similar scene as before, fire burning everywhere against blackness, but she felt no heat emanating from it, and she knew with certainty that she was in another dream.

"Hello?" she called out aimlessly into the abyss, searching for the familiar dragon eyes.

No one answered.

After a few minutes of wandering around with the ring of fire following her as she walked, she began to hear heavy breathing and crumbling against the ground due to something very massive moving over it. A loud STOMP rumbled the land beneath her, and Laila shook from the vibrations. Another STOMP and then another. She turned and turned, looking for the dragon. It was as though the stomping was coming from all around her. Her heart began to race as the stomping got closer, and she wondered uneasily why she could not see him as before.

"I know you're there, Fire Spirit! Show yourself!" she called out again, annoyed.

Laila heard loud dragon laughter echoing through the void full of fire. Feeling antagonized, she clenched her hands angrily into fists as she continued to search for the glowing eyes of the dragon.

"Why won't you show yourself?!" she yelled.

Suddenly, the laughter stopped, and everything grew quiet; she couldn't even hear the crackle of the flames anymore. The silence felt deafening as she waited for her answer, and she was about to yell for him again when the dragon's voice gravely boomed through her mind, 'You are not ready.'

The force of it jolted her, causing her to hold the sides of her head in pain. When she looked up, everything was quiet again, and the flames had extinguished around her, leaving her in complete blackness.

Blinking her eyes open slowly, the morning's light shone through Turathyl's protective arms, and Laila rolled over, stretching herself awake, her dream mulling over in her mind.

Turathyl moved her arm and released her embrace as Laila stood up. *'I must go,'* the dragon told her abruptly before spreading her wings. *'I will be near if you need me and return to you tonight.'*

Laila nodded to Turathyl sadly and watched as her dragon lifted off gracefully, wind billowing through the camp, and flew into the sky heading north. Watching gloomily as she flew out of sight, Laila desperately wished she could have stayed. Glancing over at the others starting their day, she decided she was not ready for their company yet. So, instead, Laila headed toward the river to wash her hands and face.

Trying to shake the dream from her mind, Laila stood there for a moment by the water's edge, staring off into the forest on the other side, and took a deep breath. *You are not ready.* Those words breached back into her thoughts, haunting her. She was so tired of hearing them. *Not ready for what? The fire spirit? The prophecy?* As feelings of inadequacy overwhelmed her, a tear rolled down her cheek, and she quickly wiped it away with the back of her arm, fighting to hold back more.

"Are you alright?" Nikolean asked from behind her.

CHAPTER 26

Startled, Laila turned and forced a smile, surprised to see him. She looked over his shoulder but, oddly, didn't see Davion anywhere. Looking back to the drow, she attempted to be polite and replied, "I'm okay."

"You're not." Nikolean said sharply. "What is it? Is it because your dragon left?"

Shaking her head, she replied, "No. No, nothing like that. Was just silly dream." She looked at Nikolean, assuming he'd move on, but realized he seemed to be interested. *Is it possible he actually cares?* "It's just..." she hesitantly decided to continue, "I being told I not ready by those who know more than I. Don't know how supposed to be great elf expected to do impossible. I know they probably right, but if I not ready, why we all here?"

Looking into Nikolean's eyes, she wondered if he had any answers; he was always so quiet and kept to himself, and she realized she honestly had no idea what he thought about any of this.

"What if we wrong and I not the one?" she asked.

Laila felt more tears welling in her eyes, and Nikolean, unexpectedly, stepped forward and embraced her in his arms, pulling her close and tight to him. His rough armor pressed against her chest and his overpowering musk filled her lungs and senses. At first, she resisted, panicked by his gesture, but feeling his warm and—unanticipatedly—gentle embrace, she became more at ease and decided to give in to it, burying her face in his shoulder. Nikolean said nothing while she sobbed softly, letting all of her feelings of insecurity pour out over him. Slowly, she began to relax as she felt his hand running soothingly up and down her back, his cheek pressed softly against the top of her head. As she began to collect herself, she sniffled, embarrassed by her actions, and began to let go of him, pulling gently away.

Nikolean tenderly grabbed her arm before she could pull away too far and lifted her chin with his index finger, forcing her to look deep into his blood-red eyes. Laila stared into them as he glared back at her with a warmth and feeling that she couldn't comprehend. She was consumed with a huge mixture of emotions and feelings, none of which she understood, but she knew she no longer wanted to flee.

Nikolean interrupted the silence and said to her firmly, "We are all here because we all believe in you; because, whatever you are, you are amazing and worth having faith in. I meant it when I swore to protect you with my life. I did not do that lightly."

Her heart warmed, and she relaxed as she smiled up at Nikolean, touched by his words. Laila was quite surprised by him. She felt even more so that the others were wrong about him, thinking him evil simply because he was a drow.

Suddenly, he abruptly stepped back several paces away from her, creating much space between them, but never took his eyes away from hers. She watched him quizzically.

"M'lady," Hort said from behind Nikolean.

Snapping back into reality, Laila looked around the drow's frame at Hort, whom she hadn't even heard approach. She then quickly glanced over to the campsite, hoping that Davion hadn't been watching her, but Davion was still nowhere to be seen.

"I have some bites for ye, and then we have ta go." She nodded as he paused. "And me boy should be back any minute now," Hort added gruffly, glancing at the back of Nikolean's head.

As Hort turned and headed back to the camp, Laila heard him mumbling something to himself, and she felt a pang of guilt even though she didn't believe she had done anything wrong.

"I should go," she said softly to Nikolean. He stepped aside, gesturing respectfully for her to pass. Laila paused for a moment as

CHAPTER 26

she walked past him, not daring to look into those eyes again, and said, "Thank you."

"Of course," he replied.

Composing herself, Laila headed slowly over to the camp, wondering what the day would bring as she tried to swallow the mixture of feelings and doubts she was having about herself. If she was going to do this, she had to stay strong and let go of distractions. She had to focus on her mission and on cultivating her powers so that she could show them with confidence that she *was* ready and that she *was* worth having faith in. It was time for her to take control of herself and the mission and become the Omi Méa.

* * *

Instilled with a new sense of determination, Laila was resolved to focus entirely on the mission at hand as she flung her sack over Merimer's flank then effortlessly swung onto the back of her mount. The others detected a strangeness about her as she kept conversations short and direct, but they gave her space as they prepared their own mounts for the ride to Lochlann.

Starting their journey, Laila stayed in the front this time, leading the way and shouting impatiently for them to move onward. Her companions looked at each other, mostly unsure of whether to say anything.

"Yes, m'lady!" Hort called, liking the new Laila.

Davion didn't feel the same way as Hort and aimed to see what was going on with her. He tried to ride up beside her several times as they traveled, but her mount would speed up every time he would approach until he finally took the hint and let her be, while remaining worried.

As they rode north along the river, Laila practiced her skills with the aid of random things nearby. She would not let herself grow complacent again and neglect to further her skills. If a boulder were in her path, she would simply shoo it away with her mind. She made trees bend and bow to her will, and water from the river leap in spurts alongside her like slender jumping fish. When the water spurts would reach their peaks, she would repeatedly try to freeze them before they could return to the waters beneath. Occasionally, she was even successful, and the icicles would shoot back into the water with a splash, exciting her immensely, although she tried to conceal it. As Laila grew fatigued from working with the spirits, she would stop casting for a while until she felt stronger and then would continue practicing again.

The others all watched in awe as her skills steadily improved with each attempt, except Davion, who couldn't help but feel uneasy about the sudden change. He had never felt so distant from her and in the dark.

When they stopped for lunch, Salyaman approached her and asked to see if she could perform any of the more "elf-type" magics. She didn't understand what he meant.

Knowing she was strong in earth-based magic, he demonstrated the process of making thorns spike out all over his body and guided her through the spell. As much as she tried, she just couldn't seem to do it. Nevertheless, Salyaman was still fascinated by her powers and wondered why she was so different from any elf he had ever met.

Davion tried to sit with Laila as they ate their lunch, but she inhaled her food in record time and then ran over to Merimer to practice more.

"She's going to burn herself out," he told Hort, concerned.

"Hmmm... I think tis good fer 'er," Hort replied, ripping off a chunk of meat from his large smoked drumstick.

CHAPTER 26

"I don't know, Uncle," Davion said, staring morosely at her while she practiced. "Something has changed in her."

"Aye," Hort said. "She be gettin' stronger. Tis a good thing, me boy. Jus' be there fer 'er and support 'er. We need 'er strong if we're ta go 'fore the dragons. She be the only thing that'll stop 'em from crushin' our bones and rippin' our noggins from our shoulders." He tore again messily at his meat, and Davion curled his lip briefly, imagining the dragons tearing at all of them in the same manner.

"I hope you're right," he sighed.

After everyone finished their lunches, they began to gather their belongings. Laila, seeing that they were getting ready, quickly grabbed Merimer and waited impatiently for them to start moving. There were only a few hours more until they would reach Lochlann, and she was more than eager to get there.

"Let's go!" she called out to the others, Merimer prancing in place beneath her, also over-eager due to her telepathic link to Laila's emotions.

Salyaman rode up to her, and she commanded Merimer into a gallop. "Wait!" he called out, trying to catch up. She slowed down to let him talk. "Laila, please let me lead the group. I have more experience with what is around here. The closer we get to Lochlann, the more dangers that await us."

Once again, Laila felt her abilities and competence being questioned and huffed angrily at Salyaman. "I've quite got this," she declared stubbornly and mentally gave Merimer a nudge, the hybrid carrying her further ahead.

The group struggled to keep up as they galloped after her. Salyaman's brow furrowed with anger as he gritted his teeth, trying hard not to curse at her.

Davion watched on in concern. "She's going to get us killed!" he called out to Hort beside him.

"Bah!" Hort replied. "She jus' be eager ta see our home! Canna' blame her fer that! I am too!" He gave Orbek a quick kick trying to speed him up, but the poor okullo was no match for Merimer. However, Hort was too proud to admit it and kept trying to drive him forward.

Nikolean was having a similar problem with the old mare he was stuck with as the poor creature panted and wheezed, its legs galloping clumsily over the rough terrain.

"LAILA!" Salyaman yelled. She had been getting too far ahead even for him. "LAILA! YOU ARE GOING TOO FAST! THE OTHERS CANNOT KEEP UP!"

Tired of being doubted, tired of being treated like a child, Laila thundered on alongside the river. Her frustration refused to let her listen to reason or to anything. *I can do this!* she kept saying to herself.

Focused only on the river's edge with tunnel vision and trapped within her own thoughts, she galloped over a small hill without blinking, and Merimer suddenly reared high into the air, throwing her off. The hybrid made an upsetting noise as it reared again, and Laila was jolted back to reality from the impact of being slammed into the dirt.

"LAILA!" she heard Salyaman call again.

Blinking, she looked up and was horrified to discover that she had blindly led them all right into a large band of orcs. There were at least twenty of them, all staring at her and the others, smiles crossing their wicked faces, as they assessed the easy targets and stepped toward them, weapons drawn.

CHAPTER TWENTY-SEVEN

HEEDLESS

"*Ma* Kyrash!" Davion cursed, calling upon the war god. Kicking Helna hard, he bellowed, "IRET!" and the horse jolted forward at full speed toward Laila. The others, also seeing the imminent danger, did the same, none hesitating to come to her aid.

Watching as the nearest five orcs headed for her, Laila stumbled to get to her feet while Merimer pranced between them, stomping at the dirt and snorting wildly.

'TURY!' Laila mind-sent out to the skies, glancing up briefly for a sign of her. '*TURY, I NEED YOU NOW!*'

Realizing she would have to fend them off until her dragon could arrive to save the day, Laila grabbed Dragonsbane, hastily converting it to spear-form. She held it sturdily before her with both hands but was unsure of what to do next.

The orcs had become close enough for Laila to see the smugness in their eyes, their muscular bodies flexing as they sauntered maliciously toward the group, and one of them was tapping his mace in his hand, his lips curled in a pleased snarl. "This is going to be fun," it said to the others in their guttural speech, and they all broke out in laughter, tusks bouncing up and down.

The group was clearly outnumbered, and Laila trembled anxiously, wondering how soon until Turathyl would appear. She pushed her hand out toward them, summoning the air spirit and a gust of wind whooshed around them, but it was nothing more than a light breeze against their strong, robust bodies.

She pulled from the earth spirit next, causing roots to sprout out of the ground and wrap around their ankles, but they couldn't grab hold fast enough. The orcs ripped through the bindings effortlessly before she could even get them secured. They were closing in, and her heart was pounding in her chest, her arms and legs shaking where she stood.

As the first orcs approached, Merimer charged toward the nearest one but was forcefully struck by its mace, breaking through the mystical creature's shield and bruising her ribs. With great strength, the orc flung Merimer aside, the orc never losing stride as it kept coming for the elf. When it reached her, the beast let out a monstrous battle cry while plunging the mace toward her skull. Laila held her weapon firmly overhead, and Dragonsbane took the brunt of the attack as the mace clanged against the spear's strong shaft. The petite elf let out a cry of her own as her arms buckled under the monster's much greater strength, her knees scraping and digging into the rocks beneath.

"*Ominus Lacarté!*" She heard Davion shout from behind her. A large bolt of orange and red fire flew past her and slammed into the orc looming over her. The bolt exploded across its chest, causing the orc to fly backward, screaming, and sparks ricocheted back at Laila, stinging her arms and cheek.

Riding up beside her, Davion arrived, staff in hand, as he continued to cast, again and again, throwing a series of bolts at the orcs by repeating the word "*lacarté*," the bolts shooting out from the staff like rockets. Unfortunately, it was only a distraction to them; they just kept getting up with their scorched chests and a

CHAPTER 27

look of rage in their eyes as they began charging for both Davion and Laila.

Arrows flew rapidly past them both from Salyaman's bow, landing with a thud into a few orcs, but most were blocked by shields or had struck a shoulder, not even slowing them down. One of the orcs had drawn close enough to Davion and raised a spiked club to take a swing at him. Before Davion could react, an arrow flew past his shoulder and planted right through the monster's eye. The beast froze in its place and then fell in slow motion to the ground, dead.

A dwarven battle cry came next as Hort reached the battlefield and rode with his axe waving high in the air, swinging at the orcs as he went by. More of the beasts began to swarm toward the excitement, realizing it wasn't going to be as quick and easy as they had imagined.

As the dreadful orcs crowded the battlefield, Laila and her comrades became separated from one another; each caught up in their own battles against several orcs. Laila looked frantically at the sky for any sign of her dragon, but there was nothing there. '*Where are you?!*' she called out with her mind. '*HELP!*' But there was no time for distractions; she had to focus on the orc that was about to slice her with its sword, which was as tall as she was.

Still embracing the earth spirit, she grabbed every large boulder around her and flung them, one after the other, at the orc. A boulder slammed the sword from its hand, and the brute scowled at her in a rage, ready to rip her apart with its bare hands while she kept throwing rocks and boulders. The orc managed to grab Laila by the neck, lifting her into the air while she grasped at its monstrous fist and flailed her legs, trying to kick the towering hulk. Then, spotting a fairly large boulder nearby, she hurled it with her mind, striking the beast right in the skull, knocking it unconscious.

Released from its fierce hold, she fell back to the ground and rubbed her sore, bruising neck.

Before she could celebrate, Laila watched as two more came for her at a fast, stomping pace. She took the Dragonsbane spear, aimed it at the closest one, and hurled it with all her might. Heartbroken, she watched as the orc knocked it away with its shield facilely, and a wicked smile curved on its lips while the beast continued stomping toward her. Still relying on the earth spirit, she pulled for roots, harder and faster than before, focusing only on the one orc. She watched as it was brought to a halt, the roots twisting and turning around its feet and legs, tightening increasingly the more the beast resisted.

Quickly, Laila turned to the other orc approaching her and stole harpoons of water from the river at her right, freezing them as they shot through the air and pierced into the orc's side. It howled ferociously in pain, stopping briefly to rip them out, but then tossed them to the ground, the ice shards shattering against the rocks. She had managed to slow the beast down as it oozed and dripped green blood from the wounds, but it still would not stop coming for her.

Looking around desperately for the others, she realized she would have no help as each of them was engrossed in their own perils, struggling greatly to survive. Nikolean moved swiftly and gracefully as he danced around the massive slow beasts, slashing at them with his two daggers before leaping away from their reach, only to strike again without giving them a chance to react. Laila was impressed with his stealth and sensed magic emanating from him as he lept around the towering orcs, swift as the wind and light as a feather. He was using a form of air magic, she realized.

Having grown in his fire magic over their journey, Davion had been managing to keep his group of orcs at bay thus far but was in desperate straits. When one of the orcs got within range, the beast threw a mace at the human, and it whacked into his side. Laila stopped breathing as she watched him keel over, but he quickly poised himself, shouting, "*Ominus unasceiry!*" in combination with his staff casting. The orc became engulfed in blue flames that continued to burn and incinerate it, unholy screams filling the air. Unfortunately, such a potent spell weighed heavily on him and could not be used repeatedly, causing him to resort to his lesser attacks for the others.

Salyaman, wise and skillful in his craft, was covered in his thorns as he dual-wielded his short swords, stabbing and slashing the orcs that had become too close for his arrows. One of the orcs managed to graze him several times with the tip of his long sword, creating several slashes over his skin, but he didn't break from his attacks and swallowed his yelps of pain, refusing to show weakness.

Relieved that they were surviving, Laila focused back on her own attackers. She realized that the one she had trapped was about to break free from its ensnaring roots, and the other was still coming for her, blood dripping from its gaping holes. Spotting Dragonsbane lying at the side of the river's edge, Laila decided she needed to buy herself some time to reach it. The orcs were partially blocking the way, so she knew she couldn't just make a run for it. She glanced around nervously for a distraction, but the bloodied orc was getting dangerously close, and the other had finally broken free from its roots. *I need to stop them*, she realized, and then an idea hit her.

Stretching her hands toward the ground, she pushed past the tiny seedlings, past the loose dirt and rocks, and went deep into the earth until she found what she needed. Pulling with all her might while feeling the resistance beneath, she raised her hands forcibly to the sky. Large stone spears jutted in unison out of the soil, surrounding the orcs nearest her, until they were completely encompassed by a rock wall. Without pausing, Laila stumbled forward, ran as fast as her little feet could carry her over to the river, and grabbed Dragonsbane. The orcs yelled and hollered as they angrily battered at the rocks using both their bodies and weapons, crumbling the wall little by little, demolishing their cage.

Laila converted Dragonsbane into two daggers and prepared herself to face the beasts. As the first one broke free and ran at her, she prepared to attack. Adrenaline coursing through her veins as it approached, she saw that the other one was right behind it. The large orc in front raised its sword high, then brought it down as though in slow motion compared to Laila's elven speed. At the last second, Laila leaped past the assault, scaling and diving over the orc, and landed on the unsuspecting monster behind. She savagely thrust the daggers into either side of the monster's neck and slashed them sideways, decapitating the beast.

The disoriented orc that missed her with its sword was still looking around, trying to figure out where she went, as the headless tower came tumbling down to the ground with a thud behind it, and Laila jumped off of her prey just before it hit the ground. As the other brute started turning to face her, Laila watched as an arrow struck into the side of its head, and it stared blindly at her, its mouth hanging open, before also falling in slow motion with a thud to the ground.

Searching for the source of the arrow, she saw Salyaman heading toward the unconscious orc she had hit with rocks earlier. She watched as he stabbed it through the skull, ensuring it would never wake. The elf ranger was battered and bleeding but overall appeared to be alright.

Observing the battlefield, Laila discovered Davion still caught up with a final orc, and Hort, having just felled one of his own, had got his axe stuck in the beast's skull. Hort's helm was dented, with blood dripping from somewhere underneath, and his leg had been hit with a mallet, causing him to hobble in pain as he approached the dead orc. He pressed his boot on the orc's head and tugged at the handle of his axe, wiggling it in an attempt to get it free. She turned, wondering what happened to Merimer, then spotted her up the river and ran for her.

Davion had managed to kill three orcs with his fire spells, but the final beast was proving resilient, faster than the others, dodging the mage's attacks or blocking them with its shield. In the distance, Davion spotted Hort trying to free his axe from an orc's skull and panicked as he saw another approaching his uncle from behind, the dwarf oblivious.

"Uncle!" he screamed at Hort, his voice barely reaching him.

Hort spun around, panicked, and found an orc hovering above him about to strike with a chained mallet. He let go of the axe's handle, trying to bring up his shield to block the orc's attack, but knowing he would be too late, so he closed his eyes and braced himself for the impact. However, the impact never came. Slowly opening his eyes again, he looked up at the orc who was standing there frozen, mallet still raised in the air. Then, the orc began to fall forward slowly like a tree that had been chopped down at the base. Hort stepped out of the way as the hulking mass came tumbling toward him, then saw one of Nikolean's daggers sticking out the backside of the monster's head. In shock, he looked past the dead orc at Nikolean, observing him still battling his own brute. The dark elf, clearly with his hands full, had stopped to save the dwarf's life. Hort could not believe he had just been saved by a drow. Seeing Nikolean struggling, Hort grabbed his axe handle again and, with a hard yank, was finally able to pull it free, then he rushed over to help Nikolean to repay the favor. He'd be damned if he'd let himself become indebted to a drow.

Distracted by Hort's near death, Davion was unable to completely dodge an attack from his own orc's sword as it struck against his left arm. He howled in pain while the blade sliced through his flesh.

Laila, hearing Davion's screams, gasped and quickly used her telekinesis to throw dust up into the orc's eyes, temporarily blinding him, while she galloped toward them on Merimer. The others, now having slain all their enemies, endeavored to hurry over to Davion's aid as well while the orc continued to swing at him. Davion stumbled backward, trying to dodge the orc's attacks, and tripped over a rock, falling to the ground. Watching as the orc raised its sword high in the air over the human, a wicked smile etched onto its face, Laila screamed in horror, "DAVION!!!" but down came the sword, right through Davion's chest.

Everything slowed down. Laila watched dreadfully as Davion's body jerked while the sword pierced right through his sternum, and then jerked again as the beast quickly withdrew its blade to face the others. She could hear her heartbeat pounding in her head and feel every trickle of sweat beading on her face. The sounds of screaming and war cry all became muffled, and everything seemed to grow dark. The pounding of Merimer's hooves against the dirt echoed and vibrated through her body, each step seeming to last for minutes at a time. The orc's arrogant look infuriated her as it stared, smiling at her.

The others were closing in around the monster when a great gale of wind whipped through the battlefield, so much so that even the orc looked around flabbergasted. The rest of the group looked eagerly up to the skies for Turathyl, anticipating her to come crashing down on the final orc, but they did not see her.

Thunderous clouds rumbled the heavens, blocking out the sun, and just as Laila finally reached near the orc, time began to catch up again. She pulled strongly at Merimer's reins, bringing her to a halt, dust flying up everywhere as the hybrid veered sideways to give her a clear view. Laila cried out at the top of her lungs and

– 309 –   CHAPTER 27

reached her hand out, fingers in a claw-like grasp. A bolt of lightning shot down from the clouds, streaking through the sky with blinding light as it came down and struck the orc directly.

The orc was dead instantly, but before its body could even fall to the ground, another strike of lightning and another came and jerked its lifeless body around, shaking it like a ragdoll. The others ducked and kept back from the fury being poured down onto the orc, scared to get in the crossfire of her rage. The lightning continued until the orc was nothing but crisp and ash in a heap on the ground.

Practically flying off of Merimer, Laila lept over to Davion, kneeling down beside him, examining his body. The boy laid there completely motionless, covered in blood from the large gaping hole in his chest. Blinking several times, she could see no signs of life and felt her heart being torn apart. *This can't be it! He can't be dead!* She flung her arms over him, crying into his chest, becoming covered in his blood. Her body shook from both exhaustion and despair as the air was filled with the sounds of her anguish.

The others all rushed over beside them and stopped when they saw that he was dead. Hort cried out in pain, then bowed his head in grief as he fell to his knees, tears rolling down his rosy cheeks, getting lost in his beard. Nikolean stood back out of respect to give them all their space while Salyaman pushed his way through to see for himself. He knelt beside Davion and Laila, then placed his hand on the boy's chest, closing his eyes to say an elven prayer.

"Laila," he said, opening his eyes to look at her. "It is faint, but his heart still beats within. It is beyond my abilities, but perhaps...you?"

Without stopping to think, Laila jolted upright and dug her right hand deep into the dirt, scratching up her fingers in the process. She then placed her other hand on Davion's chest, immediately pulling energy from the earth, and passing it into his near-lifeless body, while simultaneously sending her thoughts into him to seek out the wounds he had endured.

It was much worse than when she had healed the drow, and although she could feel the energy flowing out of her and into him, she did not notice any improvement. She feared it might be beyond her ability as well. The damage was significant, but she concentrated all of her focus on the torn flesh, knowing she needed to pull it back together. However, her efforts were being resisted, her attempts futile, and she felt critically weakened from the battle, perhaps too weak to save him.

Feeling defeated, Laila felt his heart stop beneath her touch and sobbed hysterically as she continued to push for the energy to restore his life.

"Laila," Salyaman said gently, touching her shoulder. "Laila, he's gone."

"NO!" she cried.

She refused to let him go, refused to let him die. This *could* NOT happen. Not knowing what to do, she reached out and grabbed for every spirit she could; she grabbed the white, the blue, and kept hold of the gold, and another, a shaded form lurking near the body, she grabbed onto it too, anything she could and she pulled for all of them, begging for their help.

Davion's body jolted as he was hit with an electrical shock from her palm, but he continued to lay there dead. She sent it again and again and pushed the spirits and shade into him.

"Laila, stop! Let him go!" Salyaman hollered at her, trying to break her attention from the body while maintaining his distance, but she would not let go.

After the eighth shock, she felt a thump, then another thump, as his heart faintly began to beat again, and she caught a glimmer of hope. She roared through her tears, relieved, and held on, sending more energy into him while searching again for the

CHAPTER 27

severings of his flesh. No holding back, she pulled with her mind, binding each promptly before moving on to the next. As the energy from the earth flowed into him, Davion's heart began to beat stronger, and his lungs began filling up with oxygen once again, though he still lay motionless, blood dripping from the corner of his mouth.

Hort had never been so scared in his whole life as he stood there watching Davion clinging for life under the hands of the young elf. He watched in awe as he witnessed for himself his boy slowly becoming stronger with each passing minute, though still appearing on the brink of death. Everyone was so focused on watching Laila do her magic as she tried desperately to restore Davion's life that only one of them sensed that they were no longer alone.

Looking up past the group, Nikolean watched as Turathyl came strolling into the battlegrounds and quietly laid down beside the riverbed, watching Laila while keeping a great distance from the group. The look on her face was apathetic as she watched Davion on the ground, and Nikolean couldn't help but wonder if she wanted him dead.

Gasping for breath, Davion convulsed, his eyes bulging wide, and he screamed in pain while Laila continued to mend his flesh. Once she finished with his chest, she quickly sealed up the tear on his arm and searched for anything else that could be done, but Davion grabbed her arms, breaking her trance, commanding her attention to him.

"Laila!" She blinked her eyes open, exhausted, scared, and disoriented. "Laila, you saved my life!" He wrapped his arms around her, pulling her into his lap, and winced from the pain that still remained, but he wasn't going to let her go. She laid there in his arms, feeling barely alive herself, not quite sure what just happened. All the spirits releasing from her, the earth spirit continued to flow into her, just enough to keep her conscious before it let go as well.

"My lady," Nikolean interrupted.

Looking dazedly up at Nikolean, Laila saw him staring into the distance past her head, and she followed his glare to find Turathyl sitting nonchalantly by the river, licking her paw.

Anger, rage, wrath, and hatred welled up inside of her while she stomped toward the dragon, hands clenched into fists. Turathyl did not react, knowing she was about to get a mind full.

"WHERE WERE YOU?!" Laila roared at her both mentally and verbally. "We needed you!"

'*I was here, young one,*' Turathyl replied calmly. '*I saw everything.*'

Laila stopped in front of the large dragon, confused and even more furious. '*What do you mean? Why didn't you help us? Davion nearly died! I could have died!*'

The dragon took a deep breath, staring down at the young elf. '*Your friends are not my concern. You are, and making sure that you are ready for what lies ahead. I would not have let you die, little elf, but I have been watching you all day, and you have been completely heedless in all of your actions.*'

'*So, you would have just let them all die?!*' Laila barked, pointing back at the group. Turathyl looked at her blankly, Laila already realizing the answer. '*They are a part of this too! I need them to fulfill this prophecy, and you nearly got them killed! We needed you!*'

Turathyl shifted her weight and began to stand, the earth protesting beneath her colossal mass. Her monumental form was intimidating as she towered over Laila, finally starting to show some emotion herself. '*What you need is more training, more time, more patience. You should never have put your group in that situation to begin with! Your arrogance and complete lack of experience are what put them in danger by not being prepared, cautious, nor fully understanding your*' *powers, or how you could have actually helped them all! How you could have been helping each other instead of allowing yourselves to become separated. You were too busy reacting instead of thinking. You didn't even remember your telekinesis when you lost your melee weapon right at the beginning. I was proud that you thought of the rock wall, but you could have just summoned it back to you! And Merimer is connected with you; do not run for her when she will run for you. You are as reckless as a hatchling and just as experienced!'* Taking another deep breath, Turathyl tried to calm back down. *'It was not I that nearly got them killed today—it was you.'*

The words from the great dragon pierced through her as Laila crashed down to her knees, decimated, her mouth agape, wishing she could retaliate, but the truth of the accusations hit her hard. Her lip began to quiver, and suddenly, as she realized that Turathyl was right and she had nearly got them all killed, her eyes welled up, and tears streamed down her cheeks. She sobbed regretfully, realizing that she needed so much more than just a change in attitude if she was going to succeed in her mission.

Seeing Laila in pain, Turathyl's heart began to warm. *'I am sorry, young one, but I had to see how you all handled yourselves, and mostly, how you would manage under pressure. I suppose you could say that it was a test.'*

Sniffling, Laila looked up at the dragon, wiping her tears away. 'And I failed.'

Turathyl bowed her head in confirmation. *'Yes. You have much to learn. Perhaps we should reconsider going before my clan.'*

Laila shook her head, disappointed. 'Please, no. I will be ready. I will.'

The dragon looked down at her gloomily, not convinced, but was distracted as the others started to gather around her, with Davion still resting against the rocks, recovering. Nikolean gently placed his hand on Laila's shoulder, trying to comfort her. She stiffened at his touch, wiping her eyes with the backs of her arms.

"We're okay," he told her reassuringly. "We're all okay." Nikolean didn't need to hear the whole conversation to understand why she was so upset. He looked at Turathyl, wishing he could talk to her as well, say a few things of his own. The dragon glared back at him knowingly.

"Aye, lass," Hort chimed in. "Twas a close one, but we all worked together and were victorious! And ye saved me boy!"

"He is right," Salyaman added.

Turathyl admired the support Laila was receiving from the others and realized something as well. *'There are going to be times that you will have to face challenges alone, but...perhaps with their help, you will become ready. And with time and practice, you will become better and stronger as a team as well. I can see why you value their lives. They may have their purpose with you after all.'*

Blinking up at the dragon, Laila nodded appreciatively. "I was foolish," she admitted to everyone. "I can't promise it won't happen again, but I will do better." Standing slowly to her feet, she turned to face the others with humility. "I hope you can forgive me."

"Ah, nothin' ta forgive!" Hort exclaimed, and she smiled appreciatively at him.

"He's right," Nikolean said. "We are all with you until the end."

Salyaman nodded his agreement.

Laila walked to each of them, hugging them gratefully. "Thank you!" she exclaimed. "I will not be so proud. I will ask for help and continue to learn." She ran back over to Davion, who had been watching quietly, and threw her arms around him, kneeling on the ground beside him. "I am so sorry," she said remorsefully.

CHAPTER 27

He returned her embrace the best he could, considering his limited strength, and gave her a gentle kiss on the side of her head. "You never have to apologize to me, Laila," he said sincerely, glad to have his beautiful warm elf back. "You are doing your best."

'Now, no more tears.' Turathyl sent to her sternly. 'You must be strong if you are to be the Omi Méa.'

CHAPTER TWENTY-EIGHT

LOCHLANN

*H*umbled by the events with the orcs, Laila used the rest of the journey to Lochlann as an opportunity to learn from her companions. She knew how to hunt with weapons, both spear and daggers, but fighting against something that could fight back was proving to be much more challenging. The feel of Dragonsbane was also unusual for her, as well as converting it from one type of weapon to another. For the majority of their trip, her great dragon had stayed with her, keeping her safe and aiding with her practicing.

The dragon was right; the land had become overrun by the orcs this far north, but with Turathyl by their sides, the orcs would flee before the group could even approach, clearing a path for them all the way to the mountains.

Whenever they stopped for a break, Nikolean and Salyaman would take turns training her in melee skills with Dragonsbane. She was slowly gaining more confidence in all of her skills but still had much further to go before she would achieve mastery level or even just be competent enough to face the Silvers.

On the last night of their journey, Davion tried to teach her fire magic as they practiced around the campfire, but she still could not seem to grasp it. His way with fire magic didn't mesh with her own knowledge of magic. Instead of contacting the spirits or connecting with things around him, he used incantations, gestures, herbs, and potions for his skills, none of which made any sense to Laila. However, she never gave up trying, determined to find the fire spirit, and refusing to admit defeat. Each night she had hoped to confront the fire spirit in her dreams again, but he had not returned to her. *Perhaps it was all just a dream anyway...* she began to wonder.

As they scaled over the final hill, the Gorén River came to an end, pooling into a large body of water at the base of the mountains. Laila was, once again, enthralled by the architecture before her as when she faced the gates of Má Lyndor. A grand stone bridge crossed over the river, with a railing carved to resemble swords stuck into the earth, that led up to the entrance of the dwarven city, Lochlann. Several of the stone swords, however, looked recently demolished from an attack. Immense and battered, ironclad wooden doors were center stage, surrounded by tall stone parapets carved into the mountain's side, towering over a hundred feet at their peak. Laila admired the stone's carved structure and details, anxious to discover what wonders awaited them on the other side of those doors.

Davion was relieved to finally be back home—as was Hort—but instead of gawking at the grand entrance of Lochlann like their guests were, he chose to gawk at Laila instead. It made him smile to see such wonder in her eyes, lighting up her face. He maneuvered his mare up beside her and said just loud enough for her to hear, "Welcome to Lochlann, Lady Laila."

Glancing over at Davion for a moment, Laila smiled and nodded, then gave her attention back to the upcoming bridge.

'This is where I must depart,' Turathyl mind-sent to Laila. *'I will be listening for you when you are ready to head to my clan. You should*

be safe here with the dwarves until then. Take your time, young one. There is no rush, and you must be ready in body and spirit.'

Laila wished the dragon didn't have to go but understood and mind-sent back to Turathyl her warm affections and farewells.

"This be it, folks!" Hort called out to the group. "Hmmm... Keep behind me as we approach. They may not be too thrilled to 'ave all of ye here." He glowered briefly at Nikolean, not needing to state the obvious.

Nikolean caught up to the others and rode beside Salyaman. "Am I to be bound and imprisoned again?" he inquired of Hort, considering if he should stay outside.

Hort thought for a moment but realized he couldn't promise him anything and shrugged under his heavy armor. "Guess we be findin' out soon 'nuf." He snickered to himself for a moment at the thought of it, secretly hoping they'd take him off their hands. None of them understood Laila's insistence on his accompanying them, but they had all come to accept that arguing with her about it was fruitless. Davion and Salyaman both felt a pull towards the girl and correctly assumed that it was the same with her and Nikolean. Despite their hatred for the drow, they knew they were stuck with him for the meantime.

The five of them made their way across the bridge slowly, taking it all in as they approached the gates. Hort held up his hand and called out, "Whoa!" commanding them all to stop. Hort and Davion dismounted as their customs dictated, and the others joined them respectfully.

"Mond ta nöije!" *State your purpose!* came a gruff voice calling out in Dwarvish, but they couldn't see where it was coming from.

"Tis I, Hort Strongarm!" Hort responded in Onish, putting his fist over his heart. "And me boy, Davion Collins. We seek

CHAPTER 28

audience with Lord Kilgar Stonesplitter for these 'ere elves and drow. We've much ta tell 'im."

After a brief moment, the earth rumbled beneath them, pebbles dancing on the ground, as the grand doors trembled slowly outward. Four dwarves emerged through the gate, clad in heavy armor of bronze and gold, holding long spears upright and swords strapped to their backs. They lined up with two on either side facing inward, creating a path for the group to proceed through.

Hort and Davion were the first to step forward, elated to be home at long last, unlike Nikolean and Laila, who were nervous about what they could expect. Salyaman, although a stranger here, was confident in himself and his people, knowing no harm would befall him by the dwarves. Even though they tended to keep to themselves, the dwarf clans had been long allies to the elves. Nikolean dreaded another round of judgment, which could possibly cost him his life, knowing it awaited him upon passing through those gates.

Laila was merely unsure of what to anticipate. Her life had propelled into fast-forward the moment she left her home, and she was struggling to process all that was happening to her. All these places that she was getting to see and be a part of—while amazing— were quite overwhelming. She didn't know what to expect of yet another race looking upon the strange wayward elf, unlike any elves before her.

Taking a deep breath, she slowly took a step toward the dwarf guards, mentally preparing herself. Feeling her anxiety, Merimer kicked at the dirt beside her, echoing her nervousness, and Laila patted her gently, sending warm, reassuring thoughts to calm the hybrid.

The guards were all roughly the same height as Hort, and not much could be discerned past their armor except for four bulging noses and bushy beards, all groomed with braids and metal clasps, as they cascaded down their chests and bellies like waterfalls.

"Hail Hort Strongarm! Hail Davion Collins!" the four called out as they approached.

Davion looked back for Laila and became concerned when he saw a look of fear in her eyes. Immediately, he dropped Helna's rein and paced back to her, taking her hand firmly in his.

"It's alright, Lady Laila. This is my home. I promise they will love you here and what you...what all of us are here to accomplish."

Attempting a smile, Laila gripped his hand tightly and let him lead her forward. It wasn't as welcoming a sight as the grand elven city of Má Lyndor with its resplendent design and bright, open spaces. While the dwarven architecture was impressive, it conveyed the impression of being cold, hard, and overall unfriendly. Having only ever seen the mountains briefly when she had connected to the earth spirit, she had no grasp before now of how monumental they truly were. The earth spirit also failed to reveal what lurked inside the darkness.

Nikolean trailed behind the group dragging the old mare. Upon reaching the guards, two of them turned and walked alongside him, keeping a close eye on him the entire time. However, they neither shackled nor blindfolded him, and for that, he was not only grateful but was extremely surprised.

As they all stepped through the gates, the guards disappeared into the mountainside, returning to their posts. Everything grew darker, and the group was startled as the doors slammed shut with an echo booming through the cavern before them. A faint light appeared from a side entrance as another dwarf approached, riding an okullo and carrying a torch to light their way but only a few feet surrounding them were visible.

"Mount up," he said curtly. "And keep up."

CHAPTER 28

They did as instructed and remounted.

Once situated, Davion held his staff upright at his side and said quietly, *"Luminas,"* creating a glowing light at the tip, doubling the illumination they previously had. He held it out proudly for Laila, offering what little comfort he could, and she smiled, appreciating the gesture.

They all followed close behind their guide, Hort at the front, talking endlessly along with the old dwarf, and Nikolean at the tail end. The clip-clopping of their mounts echoed through the cavern, along with water dripping loudly from overhead pipes into small puddles on the ground. Laila felt a chill run down her spine as the air grew damp and cold around them, and Davion, monitoring her every movement, wished he could pull her close to him to warm her.

The guide told Hort all about the attack on Lochlann by a horde of orcs while he was gone. They managed to break through the front gate, but once the brutes reached the city, they were quickly exterminated one-by-one like the pests they are, until they were no more. Hort was relieved to hear that there wasn't much damage done to the city but saddened by the names of those lost in battle. Luckily, his Glondora was safe and well, relieving his biggest fear.

After what seemed like forever, walking in the near silence of the dark, dank cavern— although it was actually closer to three hours—they could finally hear a loud commotion coming from ahead where the tunnel slowly began to brighten. The heat emanating from the city just past the tunnel exit wafted over the group like a wave, relieving them from the damp coldness of their trek. The noises from the city were deafening with all the banging, clanging, clinking, clanking, clunking as they departed the tunnel, and Laila's mouth dropped when the vast underground city unveiled before her.

Incredible, the young elf thought, looking out over all the buildings and homes built into the mountain's rock, tied together by bridges and stone paths. Large gaping holes plummeted into nothingness beneath. It was a wonder to her how anyone could create such marvels.

From the magnitude of fires lighting the great city within the mountain's darkness, the heat radiated over them, quelling the damp frigidness of the tunnel. Further in, beyond what was visible from where they stood, were the mines and forges, all adding to the immense heat reaching throughout the city.

"Welcome to my home," Davion whispered gently to Laila, pleased with her transformation from nervousness to admiration.

The dwarf leading them hobbled forward down a path to the right.

"This way!" he commanded in Onish, and the group followed closely, traversing through the maze of paths toward a central building.

Laila was fascinated by the buildings' architecture, gawking at it all on the way, while the local onlookers were fascinated by their guests, whispering amongst themselves. The buildings were all built from the stone of the mountains, shaped with great precision and technique. Each building was unique in its shape or detail, but the homes were all small and clustered together and separate from the larger buildings. There were also several small shops and armories. Many, many armories.

After making their way through the maze of pathways, they stopped in front of a very official-looking building sporting the city's emblem over its entrance of two swords crossed over a burning fire, and everyone dismounted, eager to stretch their legs.

"Wait 'ere," the dwarf stated bluntly, then signaled to a couple of other dwarves nearby, who came to take the mounts to the stables, Davion and Hort assuring them that it was fine.

CHAPTER 28

Sensing Merimer's uneasiness, Laila held her, sending reassuring thoughts before the majestic creature would allow the dwarf to take her away. Then, their escort disappeared into the building.

Davion pulled Laila gently closer to him so he could tell her what was going on, and she gripped onto his arm, settling the knots in her stomach. "This is where Lord Kilgar lives. You should not be worried, Laila. He is a kind ruler and has no quarrel with the elves."

Laila nodded. "And Niko?" she asked, looking back to Nikolean, flushing uncomfortably as they locked eyes. Nikolean was distressfully awaiting yet another judgment of his fate and had nothing but hatred and contempt on his face for his current situation. Laila looked away again after a moment, a feeling of nausea sweeping over her at the sight of his guise. "What about him?" she asked quietly.

Clenching his teeth, Davion shifted in his stance slightly away from her. "I do not know how he will react to the drow," he responded truthfully.

Before either of them could say more, the door opened and out popped the head of their escort. "He'll see ye now," he said, smiling under his thick beard for the first time, and the doors opened the remainder of the way, allowing them to enter.

When they came upon Lord Kilgar, he was sitting alone at a large banquet table with several spreads of food before him, sampling bites from each plate. "Come, come!" he exclaimed, waving a meaty rib bone, signaling them to step forward. They complied, all piling into the room, but Nikolean kept back from the rest of them.

"Ah, Hort Strongarm! Friend! Good ta see ye!" He stood up from his table and went quickly over to Hort, grasping his forearm. "I see ye 'ave Davion with ye. How are ye, boy? All done with yer schoolin' then, are ye?" He stepped over to Davion and grabbed both his arms, and Laila stepped away uncomfortably. "Come now, let me look at ye. My, have ye grown another head?"

Davion smiled and replied, "Yes, I suppose I have grown since you saw me last, my lord."

"Good, good," Lord Kilgar said, placing his fists on his hips while looking around at the rest of the party. "Well now, ye all look ta be a sorted lot, don't ye?" He chuckled. "So what business do the elves and drow 'ave with Lochlann? I understand ye have much ta tell me?"

Salyaman, being accustomed to diplomatic dealings, opened his mouth to speak, but Hort stepped forward, eager to share the details of their journey and of Laila, the elf to end the war and unite the races. Lord Kilgar listened intently, rather confused by most of it.

Although he was amused by the tales Hort told, he kept looking over to Laila with disbelief. "I see, I see..." he commented several times throughout the story.

"...and we be lookin' ta stay here while we prepare for our journey up the mountain ta see the Silvers. We was hopin' fer yer patronage to the elves and drow while we do," Hort concluded.

Lord Kilgar stepped before Laila, looking her over for a moment while pulling at his beard. He showed no interest in the others, not even the drow. "Show me," he said, eyeing her.

Laila glanced at Davion, confused.

"Your powers, Lady Laila," Davion said quietly, even though they could all hear.

Nodding, she looked around for something to demonstrate with. Spotting a small potted plant with a single ruby flower set on the table, she stretched out her hand to it, making it grow and grow with vines and roots spreading out over the edges of the large tabletop and onto the floor. The plant used its vines to pick up two nearby chairs, high up into the air, and then put them down again.

CHAPTER 28

Laila then pulled water from a cup and had it swirl in the air before turning it into ice and sending it shattering to the stone floor. Next, she had the air blow throughout the room as though they had suddenly been caught in a strong storm, but only for a moment as the sconces began to extinguish, leaving them in near darkness.

"Okay, lass! I see, I see! Now light me sconces back up!" Lord Kilgar called out through the gale.

Embarrassed, Laila looked to Davion for help. He reached out to the sconces and whispered "*illioso*," igniting them all once again.

"I not find fire yet," Laila said insecurely.

"No worries, lass," Lord Kilgar replied. "Okay," he added, "ye be a better man than I, Hort Strongarm! Tis cause fer a celebration! We shall 'ave a feast tomorra' in yer honor. Ta think one of me fine men will be part of a legend of the lands! If ye are who ye say ye be, then we will all be rejoicin' soon. And if not...well, at least ye will have a grand meal before ye go out swingin'!" There was nothing the lord loved more than a good excuse for a party and the food that would come with it.

"Thank you, my lord," Davion said, bowing humbly.

"Aye," Hort added. "ye are most gracious, Lord Kilgar."

The dwarf leader turned to head back to his meal, which he was a little irritated had been getting cold, but Hort interrupted him. "Lord Kilgar?" he said hesitantly, causing him to turn. "What of the drow?"

Looking at Hort confused, Lord Kilgar echoed, "What of the drow?"

"Well," Hort continued, "he be permitted to stay as well?"

"Yes, yes..." Lord Kilgar said, waving his hand dismissively. "I don't fear the drow. Ye vouch fer 'im, then I trust ye will keep an eye over 'im."

And with that, Lord Kilgar signaled to the dwarf who had escorted them in to lead the group back out so he could return to his now-rather-disorderly table spread.

Nikolean's mood changed in an instant, and Laila excitedly wished she could grab his hand at that moment and share in his relief, but she stayed by Davion's side and instead offered him a simple nod and a grin.

As they made their way back out of the building, all came to a stop when they heard "Hort Strongarm!" being shouted by an angry female dwarf. "I dun suppose ye planned on tellin' me ye back anytime soon?" she demanded, but, before he had a chance to reply, she continued berating him, "No, I 'ad ta 'ear it from Dokgrebela, who 'erd it from Glarfaeni, who said she 'erd it from the Marblebeards, who said they saw ye come in wit' a bunch of elves and such! Do ye 'ave any idea 'ow I felt bein' da last ta know ye be back in Lochlann? Do ye 'ave..."

"Glondora!" Hort interrupted, reaching his arms out towards her. "Glondora, me love! I'm tickled under me beard at the sight of ye! I just got here, I swears ta ye!"

The stout female dwarf had dark rusty-colored hair, tied back in a lengthy thick braid down to her shins, hazel eyes, and was donning a short faded-blue robe with leather trousers and boots. She tried her hardest to be mad at Hort, but the smile she fought back made its way through as she let him kiss her cheek, then she embraced him warmly. "I missed ye, ye big oaf!" She punched him strongly in the arm, with love.

"And I missed ye too," Hort replied, rubbing his arm. "The gods would be jealous of yer beauty and brawn." Pulling her back for a moment, he motioned to the others. "Glondora, this be Lady Lailalanthelus Dula'Quoy, Salyaman Dula'Sintos, and Nikolean Den Faolin. They umm. Well, they be stayin' with us fer a few days."

CHAPTER 28

Glondora scowled at Hort briefly before examining the rest of the group, focusing mostly on Laila, a look of confusion on her face. "Well, we best be gettin' 'ome then," she finally said. "And Davion, my 'ow ye've grown!" Davion bent down to give Glondora a welcomed hug before they all followed the dwarves back to their home within the Gorén Mountain.

Hort had a modest home with a combined kitchen and living area and two small bedrooms, one for himself and one for Davion. Glondora had her own place back near the mines, where tunnels led to the farms where she worked, but normally when Hort was in town, she'd spend all her free time with him and only return home to sleep. Glondora stayed close to Laila all evening, chatting her up with questions, and Laila felt an instant bond with the quirky dwarf, enjoying her company.

After they had all eaten and were getting ready to turn in for the night, Davion offered Laila his room to give her some privacy. He also needed to keep her far from Nikolean, who continued to watch her, irritating Davion to no end. Hort had gathered some spare straw mattresses from friendly neighbors and laid them out in the living area for the others, along with some feathered pillows and blankets. Even with such meager accommodations, it was still a step up from living on the road for so long.

Alone in Davion's room after turning in for the night, Laila was feeling very isolated and missing her own home exceedingly; the comfort of her mother's soft fur and smell, of her siblings all piled in their den with her, of their familiarity compared to this bizarre place she had found herself in. Without them, she curled up into a fetal position on the bed, feeling very cold and forlorn. Pulling the blanket tightly around her, its fabric itched and irritated her skin, not at all like the wolves' soft fur.

Laying there in silence, Laila stared blankly at the wall across from her and wished she were back out in the forest with her great dragon, her mother, and her kin. She thought of them all lovingly, remembering all the perfect moments.

Longing for kinship, she reached out with her mind in search of Turathyl, the closest thing she had to the deep connection she shared with her mother.

As Laila stretched her mind out past the mountain, she couldn't feel Turathyl's presence anywhere and began to grow even more disheartened. After pushing her mind further and further beyond the mountain, she realized she had gone too far, and she tried to stop, but it was already too late.

Unexpectedly, there were dozens of voices filling her head at once, all so strong that they clobbered through her mind like hammers. The noise was so great that she cradled her head with her hands and tried to pull herself back. There were too many of them, and they were too powerful, coming through in a great big jumble, leaving her unable to make sense of any of it. As she strived to separate from the overbearing pain of the voices, her mind slowly began to release them. Easing back, she shut them out until she had completely withdrawn and was returned to her former silence.

What WAS that? Laila gasped.

Relieved that the voices and associated pain had stopped, she was left beyond intrigued, needing to know more but afraid to try again. *I must find out. 'Tury, where are you when I need you?'*

Feeling completely alone and displaced, Laila bundled herself in the sheet and stared blankly back at the wall until she inevitably drifted off to sleep.

CHAPTER 28

CHAPTER TWENTY-NINE

PARTY

*S*trapping her cloak around her neck, Laila looked around the room to ensure she had everything. Already exhausted from spending the day with Davion being shown around the great city of Lochlann, Laila was not eager about the event still yet to come. They had even ventured into the mines briefly, the city's most prized asset. It had been a wonderful day with him, but she was nervous about the grand feast celebration that Lord Kilgar was throwing in their honor, having little idea of what to expect. As they prepared themselves to attend, Laila allowed Glondora to fuss over her, helping her "look like a laiden" for the great event, attributable to much persistence from the dwarf.

"Are you nearly ready?" Davion called from the other side of the bedroom door.

Laila stepped out of Davion's room, wearing one of the beautiful elven gowns bestowed on her during her stay in Má Lyndor. It was green and white with gold trim and a thin gold cord wrapped like lace around her torso. Glondora had insisted on helping her style her hair into long ringlets with a red and white flower clasped above her right ear. She also let the elf borrow some golden bands and bangles for her arms and wrists, and Laila proudly displayed the chain with Turathyl's gleaming silver scale around her neck just above her bosom.

Davion could tell she was feeling nervous the way she kept fidgeting with her bracelets, so he stepped toward her, took her hand, and led her gently forward. "You look beautiful," he told her reassuringly.

Laila looked up to thank him, feeling foolish. Afterward, she looked around the room and saw that everyone was starting to head out the door, with Hort and Glondora leading the way, arm-in-arm. Only Nikolean stayed behind, staring at her, as he always did. They locked eyes for a moment, and he nodded to her as though to confirm Davion's remark, then she looked away and let Davion lead her out behind the others. However, when she didn't see Nikolean following, she turned back.

"Niko, aren't you coming?"

Nikolean smirked at her and shook his head, "no," then leaned against the wall, tucking his foot up against it with his arms crossed.

"Please, Niko," Laila insisted. "This is for all of us, and that means you too."

Sighing, he replied, "I doubt anyone would miss my presence, my lady."

"Come, Laila," Davion pressed. "He can stay here if he likes."

Hort overhearing the conversation, stepped in. "Actually..." he said, "I 'ave been entrusted with 'im, and I canna be watchin' 'im if I'm there and the drow's 'ere. So," he continued, "ye best be comin' along, drow. I won't be missin' the party."

Nikolean, defeated, stood up and replied, "Well then, I guess I shall join you after all."

Laila smiled, happy that he would be accompanying them and not remaining here alone. Then, they all headed through the door towards the great hall where they had met with Lord Kilgar the day before.

Upon arriving at the hall, they were astounded to see how many people had gathered, not aware that it was to be such a public event. Looking around, Laila realized there must have been at least a hundred dwarves running about, all busy doing something, whether they were serving or just gossiping with one another. However, as busy as they were, they all made sure to stop and take notice as the strangers breached the hall entrance and entered the room.

A dwarf standing guard announced, "We welcome Hort Strongarm, Glondora Emberforge, Davion Collins, Salyaman Dula'Sintos, Lailalanthelus Dula'Quoy, and Nikolean Den Faolin."

There was much cheering and clapping, along with steins of ale being raised towards them. "Oiy!" they bellowed. Laila blushed as she held Davion's arm shyly, ducking slightly behind him, feeling self-conscious from all the attention.

"Please, please!" they heard Lord Kilgar call to them as he pushed his way through the crowd. "This way! This way! Come sit with me, I insist!"

He then shuffled the group over to the head of the banquet table and motioned to where they were to take their places. Salyaman sat to Lord Kilgar's left, then Davion, then Laila, next to a young female dwarf with a large burn on the side of her cheek. On his right sat Hort with Glondora, followed by Nikolean, who looked across to Davion and Laila. Davion was less than thrilled with his view and that it would make it even easier for the drow to leer at his beloved all night. He tried to casually place objects about the table in front of them to block their visibility, subtle to no one.

As they settled into place, Lord Kilgar slammed a large mallet on the table three times, and the room grew silent. From the silence, Lord Kilgar began to hum something deep in his throat, and several other male dwarves joined in while others began to play instruments akin to a flute and violin. They began stomping in beat on the stone floor, and the room was quickly in an uproar as they began to sing:

(To hear this song online, go to https://youtu.be/4v6FV5y8j7Q)

> Deep in the core of mountain Gorén,
> We are all safe from dragons soarin'.
> The brawny orc and troll maul
> Can't break our mighty walls.
> We dwarves are tough, and we'll fight them off,
> And celebrate with some ale!
> (cheers-OIY!)
>
> Dark or high, the elven wars are nigh.
> But, we won't fall to their hate.
> For them, it's up to fate.
> We'll hold the line 'til the end of time,
> For our home, Lochlann!
>
> The fires burn, and foundries churn.
> Our hammers bang, and pick-axe clang.
> The gems flow from our great mines,
> The sacred and the rare.
> Our metals make for the finest wear,
> And let's not forget our ale!
> (cheers-OIY)

CHAPTER 29

Platinum, gold, and icen ore behold.
No greater weapons or arm'r
Possess a fiercer pow'r.
We'll keep the best, and we'll trade the rest,
For our home, Lochlann!

If it is writt'n that I should die,
My darlin' dear, please do not cry.
Tis my time. I must protect our kind.
No matter how far we trav'l,
Nor the peril of batt'l,
When ends the war pray ye'll see me more
In our home, Lochlann!

The room cheered wildly as they all raised their steins, clanking them with their fellow friends and patting each other on the backs. Laila was enjoying the cheer of the dwarves and beginning to relax.

Lord Kilgar talked incessantly while they ate, even as he took bites out of the flesh on his plate. Laila thought the lord's display worse than her kin back home and snickered a little under her breath. Davion quickly squeezed her hand, worried she would offend him, but the dwarf lord had not noticed.

While they ate the wonderful feast before them, they were all given a strong dwarven mead to accompany it. Laila was genuinely appreciative of the hospitality and to have such a spread of meat. Actually, most of what was before them was meat of some sort, quite the opposite experience from the elves. She looked thoughtfully over at Salyaman, who hadn't touched his plate.

"Thank you, King Kilgar, for this feast," Laila said when she could squeeze a word in.

"Oh, lass! It be *Lord* Kilgar!" He let out a belly laugh. "I wouldna' want the title of 'King.' My, can ye imagine? No, lass, the mighty King Brakdrath Lightsword rules all the dwarves from our capital city, Gortax, further west from 'ere. Tis a grand city it tis. We be the miners 'ere, but the best warriors come from the great Gortax. And ye'd think it'd look like Lochlann bein' in the same mountains, but no, tis a beautiful place covered in snow and ice. Its entrance is at the largest waterfall in Onis, Onis Falls if ye will, and through the mountains, ye step out ta see the great castle and city of Gortax, surrounded by mountains risin' up ta the 'eavens. Ye should go there! I bet King Brakdrath would be 'appy ta meet ye lot. Might even offer some warriors fer the cause." Lord Kilgar slapped Hort on the shoulder. "Hort Strongarm, that's a Gortax name, is it not?"

"Yes, Lord Kilgar," Hort replied proudly. "I hailed from Gortax as a lad with me mum who came fer work in yer great mines."

"Yes, yes," Lord Kilgar said. "Thought so. See, tis in yer blood to do this 'ere stuff. This quest o' yers, fightin' dragons, and whatnot. Better ye than me. I plan ta live a long time, safe in this 'ere mountain of ours. But, if ye warriors want to go off questin' and get yerselves killed, well, that be up to ye. Not me, though, no sir. Ye tellin' me ye want to go travelin' up the mountains to see the dragons, well, that be the dumbest thing I had tickle me ears, but if ye think ye can help, then so be it. Who am I ta stand in yer way?"

Lord Kilgar continued to prattle on, and the noise in the hall was loud, with the bustle of the dwarves sharing stories and asking questions about how they planned on ending a war with just a few people. Laila had no real answers to offer but tried her best to smile as Davion and Hort told tales of her unique powers.

Salyaman excused himself after expressing his gratitude toward Lord Kilgar but didn't get very far as several lady dwarves swarmed around the exotically tall and handsome royal elf, asking unending questions of him.

As the event wore on, Laila had stopped paying attention at some point and was starting to feel a little strange and sick to her stomach. She stared at the plate in front of her, trying to focus on making it stay still, then was drawn back to Lord Kilgar when she heard Davion's name.

"So, Hort tells me tis yer eighteenth glootendally tomorrow! Excellent! I understand that makes ye a man in human time. Tis that right, Hort?"

Hort nodded in confirmation. "Aye."

Laila's curiosity got the best of her, and she looked inquisitively at Davion. "Glootendally?" she asked.

"Yes," he blushed, "my birthday."

Laila recognized the latter term from before but still didn't quite understand. "What is it?"

"Why tis a celebration o' the day ye were born, lass!" Lord Kilgar exclaimed. "Do ye not know how old ye are?"

Embarrassed, she shook her head but remembered Anallee's story of when her mother was killed. "Sixteen years, I believe, but not sure."

"I see, I see." He pulled at his beard for a moment. "Jus' a babe then! Well, I s'pose ye could make any day yer glootendally then! Pick a good one! Now, let's celebrate our Davion becoming a man! More ale!" Lord Kilgar shouted to a serving wench. "And tomorra' I'll be sure ta have a right gift for ye, boy. Ye can count on that!"

Davion had several dwarves come to congratulate him on his upcoming birthday, demanding his attention this way and that, and Laila took the opportunity to sneak out for a moment to get some fresh air. Unfortunately, she regretted her decision as she left the hall and remembered that there was nothing fresh about the air here in this humid stuffy mountain with its industrial atmosphere. Her head was spinning wildly, and she was certain she had come down with some horrible illness as she grasped onto the ledge of the veranda railing to keep her balance.

Startling her briefly, she felt a gentle hand on her shoulder and was relieved that Davion had managed to find her.

"My lady, are you alright?" she heard Nikolean say.

Turning around a-little-too-quickly, Laila discovered that it was Nikolean who had found her, and Davion was nowhere to be seen. She wanted to lie, tell him she was just fine, tell him he could go back inside and not to worry about her, but she couldn't. Instead, she found herself grabbing his arm for support and trying to make the world stop spinning for just a moment.

"No," she admitted reluctantly.

Attempting to aid her as she stumbled toward him, Nikolean placed her arm over his shoulders, then wrapped his arm around her waist, supporting her.

"Shall I bring you back inside?"

She shook her head slowly.

"Then I think it would be best that we get you back to Hort's dwelling," he said. "Can you walk?"

Laila took a step forward and then another and found that she could. So, Nikolean escorted her back to Hort and Davion's house, supporting her the whole way. When they were inside, Nikolean brewed some tea and set up a pair of chairs on the deck out back where the air circulation seemed to be the best.

Laila took in the view overlooking the city, grateful to Nikolean for his help. She could see all the way to the mines from their elevated view even though the fires weren't burning quite so brightly being late at night. It was also much quieter now without all the banging and clanging from the mines and forges, with only the noise of music and laughter resonating from the party they had left behind.

"I am so sorry," she said as Nikolean brought her some tea, "I must be ill."

Nikolean laughed at her, perturbing her greatly. "You're not ill, my lady," he chuckled. "You've simply had too much dwarven mead." She looked at him, confused. "It will pass. The tea will help. Drink up."

After taking several sips of the herbal tea, she placed it on the glass table between them, already starting to feel some relief from the ale's effects. Laila appreciated the company as Nikolean sat in the chair adjacent to her, the world still slightly swaying from the effects of the party. She could feel his eyes bearing into her as she talked anxiously about their quest and how she still didn't feel ready. Feeling uneasy without understanding why, she looked out over the underground fortress for distraction while they conversed, trying to avoid his piercing eyes.

"I want to stay here longer—do some more training—before we head to Silvers. I need to," she told him matter-of-factly. "I still have not found fire spirit, and I need more help with using Dragonsbane." She cringed as she said the name *Drangonsbane*, feeling the need to rename her weapon. "Perhaps you show me skills with daggers. And..."

"My Lady," Nikolean interrupted, sensing her distress, "I will help you in any way I can, you know that." He reached over and took her hand gently in his. "I am here for you in any way that you need me." His words were soothing, and she believed he meant them.

Laila looked at Nikolean, warmed by his words, and was instantly captivated by the blood-red glare she had tried so hard to avoid. There was something about his stare that had changed, or perhaps it was always there, and she was just finally noticing, but it no longer seemed mischievous nor eerie to her.

Her heart began to race and pound hard against her chest. For a moment, she thought that the dwarven mead was affecting her more than she had believed as her stomach twisted into knots, and her breathing became heavy while staring back into his eyes. She clenched her free hand into a fist, trying to ground herself. As Nikolean squeezed her hand tighter, it sent a nervous tremor through her system, and she realized that, while some of it may be the mead, there was definitely something else causing her to feel a sudden surge of panic and confusion.

Nikolean, his enchanting eyes locked on hers, slowly stood to his feet and stepped forward before her while still holding her hand, tightly entwining his fingers with hers. He squeezed even more as though trying to fuse them into one and gently pulled for her to stand. Her body seemed to float up to him as she unwittingly let him guide her like a marionette.

"You are everything to me," he said softly, his words flowing soothingly into her slender pointed ears, and she closed her eyes as the world began to spin again. Nikolean pulled her forward, commanding her body with invisible strings, and wrapped his arms around her, steadying her. He pulled her against him in an amorous embrace.

Without his hard armor in the way this time, Laila felt his firm—but comforting—chest through his shirt as it pressed against hers. She wrapped her arms around him, reciprocating his embrace, still confused by the feeling she was having but not wanting it to stop. Burying her face in his chest, she inhaled every scent of him, her body tingling as his powerful musk filled her lungs, making her feel weakened.

"My life is yours to command, my lady," he whispered.

CHAPTER 29

With a tenderness not common among the drow, Nikolean gently kissed the top of Laila's head, then softly again on her temple, and finally on the tips of her pointed ears, sending a shiver down her spine. Having never been so overwhelmed by feelings that she didn't fully comprehend, she pulled back slightly, looking up into his face to see if it was all a dream or her imagination feeding off the mead. He gazed back down at her with a seriousness in his eyes that she hadn't seen before, then he suddenly leaned in close to her and pressed his lips firmly against hers.

At first, Laila was shocked, her eyes wide with surprise. However, even though she wasn't expecting it, she found herself instantly wanting it—no, *needing* it—as though he were breathing life into her. Her eyes fell softly closed as he gently placed his hands on the sides of her face, his fingers slightly tangled in her luscious golden locks. Parting his lips, he kissed her tenderly but passionately. Unfamiliar emotions overtook each of them. Not being able to hold back, she pressed her lips strongly back against his, giving in to him, gripping her fingers into his back as she pulled him enticingly against her.

Their hearts pounded in their chests as they let their passion consume them. He wanted nothing more than to touch her skin, to put his mouth over her body and feel her soft, naked frame against his own. The kiss continued to intensify, her body succumbing and yearning for him as he pulled her strings. She had never felt so alive holding onto him so tightly, not ever wanting to let go. Feeling his hands running over her, her heart felt ready to explode with the intensity and heat that she felt pulsating throughout her body.

In this moment, nothing else in the world seemed to exist except for the two of them. And, for that moment, Laila had forgotten about her quest, forgotten about her promise to herself not to be distracted, and forgotten about...everything.

Laughing at Hort's whimsical renditions of their journey home, Davion took another sip of his ale. He was so relieved to be back home among "his" people; he had forgotten just how much he had missed it. Being here again, this place, this city, the dwarves gathering around to hear the tales; this was his reality, as though the rest had all been a dream. But, what a dream it was.

"Come now, show us a flame!" cried out a lady dwarf, Nassirgith.

Davion rolled his eyes, pretending to be embarrassed, meanwhile loving the attention. And unlike after his graduation when he had started this journey with Hort, he actually felt confident in his powers now. He believed he had grown more in his powers on the road home than all the time he had spent at the magi institute.

Several other dwarves had joined in, begging to see some "tricks." The magic that the dwarves held was somewhat limited. Magic dwarf classes included paladins, hydromancers—like Glondora—and enchanters, which were rare. In Lochlann, there were only two gem-smiths Davion knew of that harnessed the power of enchantment. The dwarves were captivated by his fire magic, imagining how useful those skills would be in the forges. So, he complied with their imploring, and, after a whispered incantation, the flames of the candles lifted into the air and began to dance around the room high above their heads. The crowd cheered at Davion and raised their steins, clanging them together. Davion joined them, blushing from all the attention.

"Where'd that perdy elfie go?" Davion heard one of the dwarves ask. He looked around to see, and the smile slowly faded from his face as his eyes failed to find her in the room.

CHAPTER 29

Glondora responded, "I saw 'er step out a bit ago. Didna' look too good, that one. Couldna 'andle 'er ale, tis my guess from the looks of 'er. Not like a dwarven lass. Am I right, laidens?"

The females all raised their steins and shouted, "Oiy!"

Concerned for Laila, Davion went and thanked Lord Kilgar again, clasping his arm and bowing his head gratefully, then he left the hall in search of her. Salyaman followed Davion out, having been ready to go for some time and also concerned for Laila.

When they reached the great hall's veranda, they looked around but did not see her anywhere.

"Perhaps she went back to your dwelling," Salyaman offered.

"Yes," Davion responded, "perhaps." He immediately headed for his home, with Salyaman accompanying him. When they reached the dwelling, they went inside in search of Laila, but she was not there. Davion went to his room to see if she had fallen asleep, but she was not there either.

Salyaman noticed the tea kettle by the stove that was still warm. "Someone was here," he pointed out as Davion returned.

Just then, Davion thought he heard something out on the back deck and made his way through the rear door, where he went from being concerned to being enraged within an instant. Davion could not believe his eyes as he saw Nikolean kissing and grabbing at his beloved.

Nostrils flared, fists and jaw clenched, head pounding, Davion darted over to Nikolean and grabbed him with strength beyond what he knew he possessed as he pulled the drow backward away from Laila.

"GET OFF OF HER!" he yelled.

Whipping Nikolean around to face him, Davion threw his clenched fist hard across Nikolean's jaw, but it wasn't enough. All he could see was red and fire before him as he continued to throw punches, Nikolean trying his best to dodge the attacks without fighting back.

"I'LL KILL YOU!" he roared. "HOW DARE YOU HURT HER!"

Laila screamed for Davion to stop and was tugging on his arm, trying to get him to listen. Tears were streaming down her cheeks as guilt overtook her, and she feared for Nikolean, seeing him battered, his face bloodied.

"Stop! DAVION, STOP!" she yelled hysterically. But he would not listen. He had gone mad with rage.

Finally, Laila pushed her way between them and raised her hand to Davion. Forcing him with her mind, she sent the enraged human flying backward into the wall, knocking the wind out of him. She looked at him with sadness and remorse, tears on her cheeks, and a quivering lip. It was then that Davion realized that he had seen it all wrong; Nikolean hadn't been attacking her and forcing himself on her. His worst nightmare had come true—he had lost her—just not in the way he had anticipated.

Salyaman helped pull Davion up, but he jerked his arm gruffly away from him after standing, not wanting to be touched. Knowing how Laila cared for Davion, Nikolean continued to stand behind her, not wishing to provoke the human further.

"I see," Davion said bitterly.

Salyaman stepped forward and cautiously put himself between Davion and Laila. "I suspect everyone is too full of spirits from the party. I believe it would be best if we all retire for the night, and perhaps a new day will bring more light."

Without another word, Davion turned and left them all on the porch, back through the house, and grabbed his sack. He headed out the door with no intention of spending the night there, yet unsure of where he was going.

CHAPTER 29

Salyaman looked to Nikolean, waiting for him to depart as well. The drow gazed at Laila, who nodded for him to leave, holding her hands tight around her torso, shutting herself off from him. He bowed to her gracefully and said, "My lady," before leaving.

"Are you alright?" Salyaman asked, concerned.

Laila nodded to him as well, and then she was alone. Her head was overflowing with confusion and self-loathing. *What have I done?* She looked out and saw Davion in the distance heading away from the house at a brisk and heated pace, her heart aching as she watched him steadily fade from sight. *Please forgive me.*

CHAPTER THIRTY

GLOOTENDALLY

*I*t's dark, too dark to see, but Davion preferred it this way for now. Today marked his eighteenth birthday, and his head was still spinning from the night before. Davion's heart ached throughout his whole chest, and he wished it had all been a bad dream. There had been so much that he wished was all just a bad dream.

After he left Laila and the others, he had headed back to the great hall and caught up with Hort and Glondora, bitterly drinking away his pain. There was a lot of drinking and dancing, and of course, music. Not that the dwarves' music was quite to his taste, but it brought his spirits up regardless—if only for a moment. His Uncle Hort insisted he stay at Glondora's place near the mines after hearing what had happened. So, now Davion was close enough to hear the clanging with each swing as it echoed tormentingly through his skull, his hangover doing him no favors.

As much as Hort disliked Davion's fondness for Laila, he understood heartbreak and hated to see him so dispirited. He also knew what a particularly hard time of year it was for Davion, making the situation even worse.

Wow, has it really been twelve years? Brushing his hand through his light brown hair while lying on Glondora's couch, he closed his eyes and wished for sleep to return before his inevitable thoughts could. He was quite cramped on the small couch but would have been just as cramped had he taken the bed. His own bed was the largest in all of Lochlann to compensate for his exceptionally long body—for a dwarf—but he was grateful to call this great city his home, despite the reason he came to be here...

The candles flickered on the dining room table in the dim light of the old house. A gentle breeze came through the cracks of the wood frame stirring up the musty smell from the damp spring Amillia had been having. The quiet ticking of a brass heirloom clock on a shelf against the far wall was the only sound that Davion's mother, Aleta, could hear as she continued waiting for her husband's return.

"Don't play with your food," she said sternly to Davion.

He put down his fork on the plate and looked across the table at her. "Yes, Mum," he replied, looking at her quizzically. She seemed nervous and had been acting very unusual since Papa had left. Davion did not know what was going on, but, even at only six years old, he knew enough to realize that it wasn't good. His older brother of fourteen, Torrence, had left with his father two days prior, carrying weapons and shields in such a hurry that they did not even say goodbye.

"Eat your greens, sweetie," said Aleta, tucking her long copper bangs behind her right ear. "They'll help you grow strong like Papa." Forcing a smile, Aleta had to look away to hide a tear from Davion's sight. She knew she had to stay strong for him.

Davion picked his fork back up and poked at the steamed spinach on his plate. "Mum," said the soft young voice, "when's Papa coming home?"

Aleta forced another smile, "I don't know, dear. Soon, I hope." She stood from her chair, the wooden legs scratching noisily across the floorboards. "Finish up, and we'll send out a prayer to Kyrash for him and your brother." She took her plate and mug and headed for the kitchen basin. "Don't forget we still have birthday cake."

The last comment made Davion smile, and he quickly finished his spinach as he admired the cake his mother had baked for him, waiting tauntingly on the counter. She had even written "Happy 6th Birthday Davion!" in blue sweetberry jam on it.

Aleta had prayed for her husband and Torrence to return before this day and had tried holding off on the celebration but feared the worst had happened. She went over to Davion and scuffled his shaggy hair with her delicate-but-blistered fingers. They were the hands of a worker, not soft like those of the fair maidens of court. Smiling warmly at him, she hugged him after he stood from finishing his meal. "I love you, sweetie," she said tenderly to him. "I'm so sorry they won't be here for your birthday, but it's okay that it's just the two of us, isn't it?"

As much as Davion wished that his whole family was together for his birthday, he could sense her sadness and smiled for her benefit, "Yes, Mum. It's okay."

Davion was small for his age and much more slender than his brother. He had the same light-blond hair that his father had had as a boy, which would grow darker with each passing year, but he had the petite facial features of his mother. His childhood had been different from the other boys in the village, refusing to play swords with kids his age and preferring to play in the gardens instead. Davion loved learning about the different kinds of herbs from his mother. His father, Laut, was a large muscular man and the town's blacksmith. Laut blamed Davion's "girlish ways" on Aleta, accusing her of pampering and encouraging the boy because she had a still-born daughter two years prior to Davion's birth. Aleta, of course, did not agree with Laut and insisted that Davion was just different and should not be punished for being thus.

As Davion held his mum, and she brushed her fingers lovingly through his hair, something started pounding frighteningly on the front door, the whole house quaking in response. He looked up and saw his

CHAPTER 30

mother panic-stricken, shaking her head and trembling. She swiftly grabbed him by the arm, practically dragging him through the house behind her into a back room without a word. The banging persisted, and strange guttural sounds were heard with the sound of each clunk. The wooden door let out a loud crack as whatever-it-was tried to break it down.

Throwing aside a rug from the middle of the room, Aleta flung open a secret door and whisked Davion down into a small dark space under the floor.

"Whatever happens, don't make a sound and be still...be STILL." The door slammed shut over Davion's head, and he tried to peek through the cracks between the floorboards to see what was going on. His mother unlatched a tall armoire at the top and grabbed an axe clumsily from within. A heap of other weapons fell out, clanging on the floor, as she dashed out of the room.

With a final strike on the front door that knocked it down off its hinges, Davion heard what sounded like a pig snorting, followed by his mother yelling while running through the house. Davion thought he heard some men shouting far in the distance but then heard a squeal followed by another as his mother shouted furiously at whatever had breached through the door. Davion tucked himself into a corner, pulling his knees against his chest, rocking back and forth, terrified of what was happening, but did as his mother had said and didn't make a sound. The shouts of the distant men grew closer, but then he heard his mother scream high-pitched and unnatural, and Davion covered his ears, trying to block it out. Immediately after her screaming stopped, the sound of a man's voice and clanging of metal-on-metal followed. The pig-like squealing grew loud, and then it too came to a stop, followed by a loud thump as something substantial fell to the floor. Davion released his ears as the house became quiet again.

After a brief moment, loud clunking boots echoed through the floors, and Davion looked up through the cracks, hopeful that his father and brother had returned just in time to save the day. He crawled towards the door, ready to be lifted out by his father. Then, when the trapdoor was opened, Davion's look of happy-anticipation changed to nervous-confusion when he saw a strange man staring back at him.

"Come lad!" said the rugged, long-bearded man reaching down for Davion to take his hand. "You canna' stay 'ere."

Davion took the man's hand somewhat hesitantly. He was lifted out of the hole and lowered until his feet touched the floor. To Davion's surprise, although beastly in appearance, the man was not much taller than he was and was heavily clad in armor with a large axe strapped to his back.

"MUM?!" Davion called out, looking down the hallway.

The beastly man kept his grip on Davion's hand, pulling him back. "I'm sorry, lad. I was too late." The man turned Davion around to look him straight in the eye. "She's gone, lad. She's..." breaking eye contact, the man looked off to the side and choked the words out, "she's dead."

Tears welled in the young boy's eyes as he ripped his hand free from the man's grasp. "NO!" he cried out and ran to the hallway. "MOMMA!!"

When he reached the end of the hall, he saw his mother lying on the floor, her olive green dress spread out around her petite frame, torn and covered in maroon stains. Davion fell to his hands and knees, crawling closer to her, and quietly called to her, "Mum?" Inching closer, he made his way around the bulk of her dress and saw her face surrounded by a pool of blood that covered her neck and shoulders. Her eyes were staring glassily at the ceiling, her mouth slightly open with a trickle of crimson blood running down her lip and chin. "Mum," Davion repeated, throwing his arms over her and holding onto her, his tears pooling in his eyes. "MUM! Wake up!" he pleaded as his body shook and the tears broke free, streaming down his face. "MUM, WAKE UP!"

With his limited six-year-old strength, he tried pulling her closer to him, searching for the familiarity of her heartbeat against his ear that he had listened to so many times in his short life. But, he could hear nothing except the sound of his own weeping. Holding onto her tightly, he sobbed into her dress, afraid to let go. "Mum..."

Suddenly, Davion became aware of the man standing behind him. He sniffled and pulled himself back from the still body of his mother, then turned and flung himself at the man, yelling angrily and beating his chest plate with his tiny fists. "YOU KILLED HER!! YOU KILLED MY MUM!!!"

The man grabbed the boy's wrists and looked at his tear-streaked face, the boy squinting and crying hysterically. "No, lad. Look..." The man turned him around and pointed past his mother.

Davion looked blurrily through his tears and saw a large mass of a monster, the color of dirt, heaped over on the floor. Wiping the tears from his eyes to get a better look, Davion saw that the monster's head had been split open, and a thick green goo was pouring out. It was the ugliest thing that he had ever seen or could have imagined. Its face looked squished with large nostrils and a snout full of fangs containing two tusks on either side. The thing's body was massive and covered with rippling muscles.

"What...what is it?" Davion inquired, backing up into the short man.

Putting his arms comfortingly on Davion's shoulders, he replied, "Orc. A horde o' them broke through the city gates, and I saw this one turn down the alley ta yer house. I knew yer folks, lad. Yer mum was a wonderful laiden. I'm so sorry, me boy." Turning Davion back around to face him, he added, "When I found yer mum, she had not yet passed and told me where ye were hidden. She asked I look out fer ye, that I take care o' ye, and I promised 'er I would."

Davion looked up at him, confused, "But... Papa..."

"He ain't comin' back, lad, yer papa was killed, and yer brother left to join the king's army." The man leaned over slightly to match Davion's height. "I'm sorry, lad, ye'll have ta come with me ta Lochlann. Me name's Hort. I'll be yer Uncle Hort, okay?"

"Lochlann?" *Davion questioned. His head was clouded as he tried to grasp what had just transpired. His mum, his papa, what was happening? The whole room began to spin and Davion, without realizing what he was doing, threw up his dinner all over the floor. Hort then took Davion's hand and led him to the kitchen where the front door had been bashed in, away from his mother's still corpse and her predator. Unable to grasp his new reality, not having any idea of what it meant or where he was going, he had never felt so empty. He wished his mother would wake him from this horrible nightmare.*

Hort half-smiled at the boy. "Lochlann tis a grand city in the northern mountains. Tis the home of me people." *Davion, pale as a ghost, looked woozily at the strange little man.* "Dwarves, lad," *he clarified.*

Releasing a yawn, Davion was exhausted from all the turmoil.

"I know, me boy, but tis not safe 'ere. We best be goin' fer now, and we'll give yer mum a right burial in the morn'."

Staring at his cake splattered across the floor, Davion let the man lead him out of his home, away from all he knew and loved, into the unknown as though walking through a thick fog.

Davion rolled onto his side, apprehensive about what today had in store for him, but he was confident that it would not be a "happy" birthday.

* * *

It had been a quiet morning so far. Davion had unavoidably made his way back home after helping himself to a quick breakfast at Glondora's. Hort and Glondora were excited with his return, boasting about how he looked like he grew another head tall in his sleep. They made sure all the surrounding houses could hear that it was Davion's "Glootendally!" in case they hadn't already known—which was impossible in Lochlann since everyone knew everything about everything that happened in Lochlann.

"Thank you, Uncle," Davion said with a forced smile while he indulged Glondora's overly-firm, dwarven birthday hug. He had been avoiding looking at Laila since he returned, but after Salyaman approached him to say "Happy Birthday" to honor his human tradition, he knew he wouldn't be able to for much longer. Salyaman grasped his forearm firmly and nodded to him, then stepped out of the way as Laila timidly approached.

Looking into Davion's eyes, she followed the others' lead and nervously said, "Happy Birthday, Davion."

He wanted to hate her. He wished he wanted her to get out of his sight, to tell her to pack up her things and just leave, but it simply wasn't so. Although the anger and hurt remained, he just could not bring himself to hate her or wish any ill will toward her. He did, however, wish he'd killed the drow back in the woods earlier when he had the chance. But instead, here he stood, broken and humiliated in his own home, trying to swallow his pain.

Standing there sternly, he finally met her gaze and saw the sorrow in her eyes. After taking a deep breath, he nodded to her and replied, "Thank you." He quickly looked away again, not ready to face her or what she had done, and Laila remained there awkwardly for a moment, looking dolefully at him before Hort interrupted.

The dwarf reminded them that Lord Kilgar was awaiting them at the mines with Davion's gift. Relieved with the interruption, Davion nodded to Laila, then prepared to leave.

"I come?" Laila queried hopefully. She thought that by spending more time with him, he might open up to her so they could move past what had happened.

Before he could decline, Glondora hooked her arm with Laila's and answered for him, "Of course, ye can!"

Nikolean, who had been standing in a far corner assessing the situation with Davion, gladly stayed behind with Salyaman to watch over him. Davion noticed that the drow's face was still badly bruised and sported a nasty slit on his puffy lower lip from the night before. He wondered why Laila hadn't healed him but was too pleased with his work to ask. Laila had actually offered to heal Nikolean that morning, but he refused to let her "waste the spirits' powers" on his face.

On the way to the mines, Laila walked with Glondora, the dwarf chattering up a storm to fill the quiet. There was something about the perky dwarf that she couldn't quite grasp but felt keen on her and was sad that she would be parting with her soon. Until then, she was grateful for Glondora's distraction and enjoyed her happy disposition—a nice contrast to the anger radiating off of Davion, who was walking alongside Hort ahead of them.

Laila felt, once again, that she needed to stop being distracted and focus on her task, and she didn't know how to do that until things were sorted out with Davion. There was too much at stake and too many lives relying on her to have such distractions.

When they reached the mines, a guard had them stand wait for Lord Kilgar to arrive. Laila took the opportunity to break the ice with Davion and inched her way over to him.

"Are you alright?" she asked him cautiously.

Davion, avoiding her gaze, wasn't quite sure how to answer. Of course he wasn't alright. But he didn't see what difference it made, not to her. To him, it was harrowing to his core, believing that the girl he loved was not just desiring another man, but a drow scum of all creatures.

"I am." he responded curtly.

"Please forgive me," Laila added, hearing what she misunderstood as hate for her in his tone and demeanor.

　　CHAPTER 30

Davion took a deep breath before responding, "There is nothing to forgive. It is I that misunderstood the situation." Although, he had no intention of apologizing to anyone. He wished she would just drop it so he could stop feeling his heart being torn out repeatedly.

After a long moment of silence, Laila asked, "Will you still come on quest?"

Gaping down into her eyes, Davion suddenly felt ashamed and also hurt that she would think that he would abandon his promise to her because of last night. As he looked fixedly into her eyes, his heart began to ache even more, reminding him of how deeply he cared for her.

"Lady Laila," he began, "I promised to be with you through this, and I intend to keep my promise. I am still very much committed to our quest and will protect you all that I can." He took her hand gently in his, trembling slightly from her touch, which felt different and cold to him now, then clasped his other hand overtop. "I only hope one day that you will see that drow for what he is, but I will be here for you no matter what." Letting go of her hand, he averted his gaze from hers, unable to stand to look into her eyes a moment longer for fear of showing weakness.

His feelings for Nikolean were never a secret, so Laila wasn't surprised by his comment. However, she was definitely appreciative of his commitment despite everything that had happened. Yet, she could also sense that things had changed between them, and she hated that.

Before Laila could reply, Lord Kilgar was approaching them from within the mines, followed by two miners at either side.

"Good day, my friends!" Lord Kilgar shouted as he drew nearer to them. "I hope ye have'na been waitin' too long! I wanted ta make sure I got ye the most perfect one that we had! Come, come... Come see! Oh, I'm so excited! I think ye'll love it, and it be perfect fer yer quest to see the dragons! Yes, yes. I got jus' the thing for ye!"

Hort clasped arms with Lord Kilgar in salutation as he finally reached them.

"Okay, okay! Let's get on with it then! Come now, Stantul, come, come!"

The male miner, Stantul, stepped forward and held out a pouch to Lord Kilgar, a little larger than a dwarven fist (which is roughly that of two human fists.) He snatched it up and advanced to Davion. "Here ye go, lad. I was askin' meself, what ta get fer such a fine lad as yerself and especially fer this quest ye be goin' on. I says, 'self? What think ye for this 'ere boy?' and lo and behold! Come, come, open it, boy!" he exclaimed excitedly.

Davion smiled, taking the pouch from him, and tilted it to his palm. As a very large stone fell heavily into his hands, he forgot for a moment all of his pain and troubles, and his eyes lit up.

"This is incredible!" he exclaimed to Lord Kilgar.

Davion admired the stone glistening in his hands. It was an exquisitely shaped and polished, deep-red garnet—the most perfect gem for pyromancy staffs.

"Oh, I'm so glad ye like it! I will have it infused to yer staff right away! It will make a grand addition ta yer powers!" Lord Kilgar clapped his hands twice, and Stantul stepped forward, taking both the garnet and Davion's staff from him. "Ye'll be the best pyromancer yet! I just knows it!"

"Thank you so much!" Davion replied as he bowed humbly.

"Of course, of course! Tis me honor to help ye out, lad. I knows 'ow 'ard ye worked ta get 'ere, and I wish ye all well on yer journey. Me 'opes this wunna' be the last time we will enjoy yer company!"

Davion and Hort expressed their gratitude and pleasantries to Lord Kilgar before the dwarf lord took his leave, heading back into the mines. The young mage was glowing, finally feeling like he was becoming a true fighter mage and hoping he could live up to the expectations of everyone to be deserving of such a fine gem.

"Now, who be up fer some glootendally pie?" Glondora asked cheerily, leading the way back to the house.

"Hmmm... Lady Laila, yer in fer a right treat now! Ye thought the honeyed bread was good, but ye ain't tried nothin' yet! Did ye get the one I likes with the baskaberries and wine, me love?" Hort asked as he scurried up to Glondora, taking her hand. She laughed and nodded at him, and Davion and Laila joined them as the dwarves skipped down the gray brick road.

CHAPTER THIRTY-ONE

READY

The fire flickered brilliantly in the dim light, and perfect round donuts of smoke erupted from the dancing flames. Laila watched quietly as Davion effortlessly honed his connection to the fire in the tall sconces and wished she could feel its power in her hands as well. They were outside the barracks, preparing themselves, as much mentally as physically, for what was to come. Laila was already sore from the morning's practice and wished desperately for some fresh air.

Salyaman had been growing impatient as the days grew into weeks since they arrived in Lochlann. He was anxious to move on, but Laila still felt ill-prepared. She spent a lot of time at the barracks working on improving her melee skills and powers. Her comrades all fought so differently, and she found it helpful to learn how to fight and defend herself against the different skill-sets, but none of them were dragons. Glondora even used her water magic attacks for Laila to practice against, but it was still not the same magic as the Silvers would be using.

Although her skills were improving, she had no idea what to expect when she was to come face-to-face with a horde of dragons. She prayed daily to Kyrash and Jayenne that she would not need to use any of her skills or powers against the reigning ancients of the land.

Turning to go back into the barracks, a chill ran up Laila's spine, giving her goosebumps, as she heard ever-so-faintly a voice that she had missed dearly, '*Lailalanthelus.*'

'*Tury?*' she reached out with her mind.

'*Laila,*' came Tury's mind voice again.

'*Tury! Where are you? You are so faint!*'

After a long pause with no response, Laila pushed out again, searching for her friend, and could finally feel her like a tiny spark of light in the distance.

'*I am here, young one.*' Turathyl finally sent clearly. '*I have been trying to reach you for weeks. I worried the mountain was too great.*'

'*I've missed you so!*' Laila responded, wishing she could reach out and hold her long snout. '*I have been trying to find you as well, but when I reached out for you, I found so many voices all at once! They were much too loud and shot into my head so painfully!*'

After a few moments of silence, Turathyl replied, '*You must have reached my clan. Incredible. We are all linked and feel each others' thoughts, but they are much further than I am from you.*'

Laila thought for a moment. '*So, will it be like that when I face them? All of them talking at once?*'

'*I would suggest you let Aeris speak to you directly and not open your mind to them all. I didn't even know you'd be able to, but it does not surprise me after what I've seen. It should be alright. We know how to dampen our mind-touch when needed, such as with hatchlings, which are much more sensitive. I do the same with you, except for now when trying to reach you through so great a mountain.*'

Relieved, Laila nodded mentally.

'*When are you leaving Lochlann?*' asked Turathyl.

Laila looked around her. She really didn't know. All the practicing she'd been doing with melee and her powers, all her attempts to find the fire spirit, she had been waiting for some sign to guide her, to direct her. She always had her mother, or now Tury, telling her she *wasn't* ready, but no one telling her that she *was*. How would she know when that would be?

'*I don't know,*' she finally said honestly.

'*I must go for now, but I will try to stay close,*' Turathyl said. '*Let me know when you are ready.*'

Laila sent a mind-touch of affection to Turathyl, and the link was severed. Once again, she felt alone in the quietness of her own mind.

"Laila?" Davion interrupted her thoughts. "Is everything okay?"

Smiling at him, she nodded.

Davion stepped closer to her, feeling the wedge that had formed between them. He missed being close to her as before and had convinced himself that Nikolean had taken advantage of his angel in her intoxicated state that night. Wishing to move past it, he had been striving to return to where their relationship had been before; he just wasn't sure how. But, he noticed that she had been keeping her distance from the drow as well, which gave him hope.

"You look like something is bothering you. If I can help..." Davion took her hand in his and stepped forward again, closing the gap between them.

"I'm okay, really," Laila told him.

"Laila," Davion started, "you don't have to carry this burden alone. We are all in this together." He held her hand against his chest, then gently brushed some hair away from her face. "I hope you know that."

Nodding, Laila replied, "I do." She felt a little nervous with him being so close to her, still adamant that she needed to stay clear-headed and not lose her focus on the mission again. However,

CHAPTER 31

she had been missing him also and the warmth and comfort she felt when he was near. Was it so wrong to want that again?

"Good," Davion said. He leaned toward her, wanting to forgive her for her indiscretion, to move forward, and desiring so much just to hold her. He wondered if he should dare try to kiss her, believing that the kiss would show her it was *he* that she was meant to be with. His heart was racing in his chest, his palms growing sweaty against hers, and his stomach tight with nerves. Davion opened his mouth, wanting nothing more than to tell her how much he loved her and to kiss her, but they were interrupted when Nikolean emerged from the barracks.

"Are you ready?" the drow said to Laila.

"We were talking, drow." Davion retorted, scowling at him.

"I'll be right there," Laila interjected.

Nikolean hesitated, not wanting to leave them alone, fully aware of what he had walked in on, but took his leave after a brief moment.

"Thank you for your words," Laila said to Davion while gently taking her hand back. "I am glad to have all of you."

Before Davion could react, Laila turned and followed Nikolean into the barracks for another round of melee practice with her daggers. Watching her go, Davion was crushed at the missed opportunity, and he felt the fire growing hotter within him, unaware of the sconces behind him also burning hotter and higher, feeding off of his anger and hatred toward the drow.

After another grueling day of drills, they all gathered at Hort's home for supper and listened as he told humorous and embarrassing stories of previous adventures. Davion loved watching Laila laugh at the dwarf's tales. He watched her closely, trying to devise a way to get his angel back, but was overly aware of the lurking drow in the corner, who also never took his eyes off of her.

Laila had been avoiding both of them that night, not wanting her feelings to interfere with her mission. She wasn't even sure what those feelings were, but it didn't matter—she told herself—they were merely a distraction that needed to be quelled.

After the laughter died down, Hort stood up and raised his stein in the air to the others. "This may be an unlikely lot, but 'ere's ta what tis bound ta be the greatest adventure or the biggest mistake of our lives!" Everyone raised their steins and took a sip.

Hort then turned to Glondora at his side and added, "And, if I'm ta be off fightin' ta save the world, it would give me strength and courage ta know that I'd be comin' back ta the most beautiful, toughest, and best lass any dwarf could ever 'ave 'oped fer, waitin' ta be me wife."

Hort pulled out an ornate necklace with shining yellow gems and presented it to Glondora, who had clasped her hands over her mouth, tears welling in her eyes. "Glondora Emberforge. Ye 'ave put up with me fer nigh six years, always off on me adventures and comin' 'ome, just ta see yer smile. I couldna wish fer a better lass than the one standin' before me right now. When I 'eard that our great city 'ad been attacked, I feared the worst and realized I didna' wanna wait no more! So, I ask ye, if I be so lucky as ta return from this quest, will ye make me the 'appiest dwarf by bein' me wife?"

Glondora looked at him, everyone eagerly anticipating her to say "yes," but her look of excitement suddenly turned to vexation. "So's I'd jus' be waitin' 'ere fer ye once again, prayin' ta Kyrash that ye return someday? Be promised ta someone I may never see again?" she barked at him, "No, Hort Strongarm, ye canna ask me ta wait 'round no more!" Everyone shifted uncomfortably, looking at one another, wondering if they should leave. "But," she continued, "if I am ta be yer wife, then I will want

CHAPTER 31

ta spend every last minute with ye. We will wed in Lochlann, and then...ye be takin' me on yer quest!" she said absolutely.

Hort gasped at Glondora. "No, me love! Twill be far too dangerous! I couldna' bear the thought..."

"Ye think I've been workin' the farm me whole life? I can fight. I have magic, and I can heal. Ye all could use me. I won't be no bother to no one, but that is my final answer. If ye want ta marry me, then I'm comin' with ye. AND..." she raised her voice, "ye must promise me tis the LAST adventure! Ye already said twill be the greatest. So, twill it be enough?"

Hort grasped Glondora's hand and replied without hesitation, "Twill, me love, I promise. If ye agree to become me wife, I will never leave yer side again so long as I live."

Glondora smiled and threw her arms around him. "Then, yes, I will marry ye!" They kissed, and Hort put the necklace on her while everyone applauded. "Besides, who else would put up with ye?" Hort chuckled and kissed his fiancé again.

Looking around at the group and bowing her head humbly to Laila, Glondora said, "I promise I won't be no bother ta ye."

Laila stepped forward and took Glondora's hand. "You are welcome to come, of course."

For a moment, Laila felt strangely relieved, as though Glondora was meant to be with her, just as Salyaman, Davion, and Nikolean were. However, she now felt even more weight on her shoulders as another life was being put at risk for her, making it increasingly hard to breathe. Not being used to feeling so confined for so long and now the added pressure of being responsible for Glondora's life, Laila suddenly felt an overpowering urge to escape, to find a moment away from it all to clear her head. So, while everyone was distracted and congratulating the happy couple, Laila made her way outside into the gloomy evening lighting of the city.

Sensing someone following her, she turned to find Nikolean standing before her. He said nothing and just stood, staring at her with his piercing eyes, as always. Turning away again with a quiver, Laila was aware of the drow coming closer to her, so close that she could feel his breath on her shoulder, his warmth emanating from him, but still, he remained silent. She could perceive his presence, even without touching him or seeing him, and found herself wishing he would just reach out and hold her again as he had before. Closing her eyes, Laila relived that moment, that feeling of longing for him, that all-consuming kiss, the feeling of his hands over her delicate frame. She wished desperately to feel it all again, desiring for him to just grab her and pull her against him in a passionate embrace. Her heart was racing at just the thought of it, her breathing heavy.

However, her promise to herself was still sharp on her mind, causing her to fight those urges, especially with Davion so near. She still didn't understand her feelings but knew she couldn't hurt Davion like that again. There had been a clear connection to him, which was undeniable, but now she was faced with having these thoughts about Nikolean that she couldn't deny nor comprehend either. With the weight of the world looming over her, it was all just too much to bear, and she knew she had to push her feelings and desires aside—no matter how much she craved the taste of his lips again.

After several moments of silence, while lost in her conflicting thoughts, she began to feel chilled. As the coldness washed over her, she turned to face Nikolean again but found herself standing there completely alone. Her heart instantly sank. Then, within the blink of an eye, Davion appeared in the doorway.

"There you are! I was wondering what happened to you. I saved you some barden cake. It's the sweetest thing you'll ever taste!" He held out his hand, praying for her to take it.

CHAPTER 31

Laila nodded, taking his hand and let him lead her back inside while Nikolean watched silently from the shadows.

The blackness was vast, and Laila could feel the ground rumbling as a large being made its way closer to her. She wasn't scared. It was different, but not new. She knew who lurked out in the darkness and was determined to make him face her this time.

"Hello, Fire Spirit," Laila said with indignation.

Through the dark, she could hear the dragon breathing deeply; he was quite close to her now.

"You keep coming to me. What is it you want? Will you ever let me find you?"

"You are looking in the wrong direction," the dragon boomed out loud.

Laila looked around confused but could still see nothing. Suddenly, she heard the dragon inhale a very deep rumbling breath, and she feared what was to come next. In a moment, the darkness was lit up as a column of fire headed straight toward her. The flame burned hot, ready to scorch her. Instinctively, she raised her hands, closing her eyes in terror, and screamed out against the blaze.

When Laila didn't feel the blaze upon her skin, she opened her eyes and saw that she had parted the flames, pushing them out from her like waves. Delighted with herself, she smiled smugly before she heard the dragon inhaling again, and her victory was short-lived as another flame came forcefully toward her. This time, she wasn't able to react quickly enough and instead dove out of the way.

"Why are you doing this?!" she screamed at the dragon while trying to get back to her feet.

The dragon continued to blare fire at her, and she dodged again and again, and she grew angrier and angrier from each attack. She wasn't sure how much more she could take and wished she could just wake up.

"STOP!" she finally screamed. "STOP TORMENTING ME AND JUST TELL ME WHAT YOU WANT FROM ME!"

After a moment's pause, the dragon inhaled again, but this time, Laila had had enough. As the fire bellowed toward her, she raised her hands against it again and screamed as before, but this time did not close her eyes. Fueled by her rage, a wave of fire erupted from her fingers and plummeted against the dragon's, exploding with light as the two flames collided between them. She held onto the fire, continuing to push it harder and stronger, and took one step, then another, toward the dragon who was maintaining his fire as well.

Finally, her strength gave out, and she collapsed to her knees, the inferno fizzling out around her. The dragon also stopped, but Laila could still feel the heat of the fire spirit within her. Then, Laila was illuminated as the flame walls ignited around her once again, and as she raised her head, she saw the dragon.

Looming over her in all of his magnificence and regalness, the dragon was much larger than Turathyl by at least twice. The young elf's jaw dropped as she marveled at him, pushing herself up to her feet, watching in awe how the flames once again danced in his reflective ruby scales, and his eyes glowed with the blaze.

"Great Fire Spirit!" she said, bowing her head to him.

Gazing down upon her, he replied, "You flatter me but are mistaken. I merely helped you find the spirit within yourself when you were ready."

Laila felt her chest tighten. She couldn't believe it. She had finally found the fire spirit. "But how?" she inquired of the great dragon.

"Fire is unlike the other spirits. It stems from a dark place within. You were only light when first we met, but things have changed. You have changed. However, beware of this gift, for fire cannot be trusted. Heed my warning. Things are not always as they appear. If you trust the fire, you will be burned." The dragon bowed his mighty head before her. "Our paths will meet again, Omi Méa. You have grown strong."

CHAPTER 31

The dragon turned from her and began to walk away, the ground protesting with each step. Laila realized the Great Red Dragon had called her Omi Méa from the prophecy; Great Spirit. So, it must be true—she is the one. The validation from him filled her with hope.

"Wait!" she cried out after him. "Please! How will I know when I'm ready to face Aeris?"

Without stopping or looking back, the dragon responded, "Never will you be more ready, nor less ready than now. The question is, are you prepared? What must be, will be; when, matters not. Be brave, be well, and when all seems lost, you will find me."

Laila stopped and stood in her tracks, dazed and confused. "What does that mean?!" But the dragon was already gone.

Blinking, Laila took a moment to remember where she was. Then, jumping up out of bed in Davion's room, she realized she had finally discovered the last spirit and could still feel her connection to it. She knew exactly who she had to tell first.

"Davion!" she cried out, bursting out of the bedroom, finding everyone together waiting for Glondora to finish preparing breakfast. In her excitement, she jumped into his arms, and he grabbed her happily. "I finally found it!"

Sharing in her joy and enjoying the warmth of her touch, Davion asked, "What did you find?"

"The fire spirit!" Laila declared. Davion, stunned, lost grip of her as she darted off to each of them, hugging them in turn ecstatically. "The final spirit!"

As she reached Nikolean, he grabbed her firmly and whispered in her ear before releasing her, "I never had any doubt," and Laila's heart fluttered.

This was real. It was all happening and coming together at last. "I am finally ready to face Aeris!"

CHAPTER THIRTY-TWO

MOUNTAINS

*T*he following week after Laila acquired the final spirit, Hort and Glondora were wed in a small temple to Jayenne with their closest friends and several of Glondora's family members, none of whom were happy about her leaving, but all of whom were happy about the union. Davion and Hort were the only family each of them had left. Hort had tried to insist on something grander for his bride, but Glondora wouldn't hear of it. She knew that everyone was eager to start the adventure, and now that she was a part of it, she was just as excited, even though she wasn't entirely sure what she had just signed herself up for. However, she did know that she loved Hort and wished to be with him always and that some unknown compulsion was telling her that this is where she's meant to be.

Laila thought the whole concept of marriage and the wedding celebration rather intriguing and loved every moment of it. Of course, she had nothing to compare it against either, so she had no idea how small and quaint it was for a dwarven wedding.

Following the ceremony, they all headed over to their favorite tavern, The Stone Stein, and celebrated with much drinking and dancing. Laila, however, declined to partake in the ale in Lochlann. Aside from her experience at Lord Kilgar's party, she was also anxious to get up early and prepare for their departure.

After the celebration, the happy couple spent the night at Glondora's, leaving Laila awkwardly alone with Nikolean, Davion, and Salyaman. She had come to enjoy Glondora's company and didn't really understand why she and Hort wished to be alone. So, she turned in quickly after making just enough idle chit-chat as to make everyone unaware of her nerves.

In the morning, they had gathered the necessary supplies in town; rations and water, feed for the mounts, some climbing gear, and warm clothes of thick hides and furs to protect them from the icy chill up the mountains. Glondora had an old cart that they loaded up with the provisions and were grateful for it. They had left Hort and Glondora alone for as long as possible until they were ready to head back out through the mountain tunnel.

Of course, Lord Kilgar was there to see them off and fared them well. The dwarf lord, although gracious, wasn't overly pleased about Glondora's departure, leaving his farms with only one remaining hydromancer to tend the crops. Glondora had assured him that she'd be happy to go back to her work once she returns from their journey. Although no one was willing to voice their thoughts, it wasn't unreasonable for them to believe this was to be a one-way trip for the group, but the lord accepted her offer nonetheless.

Several curious sorts were beginning to gather around, waving goodbye to the group as they prepared to depart. Salyaman was in the lead, enthused to resume their quest and be back in the sunshine with fresh, un-recycled air.

They had to wait for the dwarves to retrieve their mounts and were happy to be reunited. That is, except for Nikolean and his old mare. He half expected the animal to be dead by the time they left and was almost disappointed, watching as it slowly hobbled along toward him while being dragged by a dwarven stablehand.

Mounts were kept at the farms in a separate part of the mountain with all the livestock, and Laila had only been able to visit with Merimer on a few occasions since they arrived. The hybrid easily broke free from the dwarves and dashed over to Laila, prancing joyfully around her before nuzzling her face with her snout.

"I missed you too, girl," Laila said happily as she mind-sent her affection to Merimer.

"Orbek!" Hort shouted, hurrying to meet him as though running to a long-lost love. Glondora rolled her eyes and snickered at her husband.

As the stablehand approached Nikolean with the old horse, Lord Kilgar called out, "Oiy! Drow! Ye be keen on that old mare?"

"Not at all, my lord," he replied.

"Aye, tis what I thought."

Lord Kilgar let out a loud whistle toward where the mounts had emerged from. Then another stablehand, struggling greatly, brought forth a large horse unlike any Laila had seen. It was a beautiful steed with jet-black hair and a shiny dark-gray coat. What caught her off guard was the red eyes that almost glowed, reminding her of Nikolean's. It was a strapping beast full of vigor as it fought the stablehand, trying to hold it steady. Other dwarves gathered hastily to assist, but it was no use. Finally managing to break free of the dwarf, the horse reared and bucked, squealing emphatically, threatening any who tried to approach. It pranced clear of the dwarves and stomped at the ground several times while looking for an escape.

As it prepared to bolt, Nikolean shouted out with raised hands, "Annaksula!" *whoa-there!* and the beast steadied, eyeing the drow. "Where did you get him?" he asked Lord Kilgar.

CHAPTER 32

"Best ye not worry 'bout that. Come now. He be yers now if ye want 'im. We canna' do nothin' with the beast anyways. Not fer lack of tryin', mind ye."

Nikolean nodded. "Thank you, kind lord. I am indebted to you."

"Nay, lad! Ye are off ta end the war! Tis the least I could do fer ye."

Bowing humbly to the dwarf lord, Nikolean claimed his steed, and it accepted him readily, clearly more familiar with the drow than it had felt with the dwarves.

The group readied their mounts and headed for the tunnel, which would lead them back out into the sunlight and fresh air once again. Waving and shouting their goodbyes, it seemed as though half of Lochlann had gathered to see them off on their journey.

While towing the cart full of supplies behind them with Orbek, they made the painfully long walk through the extensive mountain tunnel. When they finally reached the other side, they squinted as they emerged from the dank cavern and the sun gleamed blindingly into their eyes. Everything seemed much brighter than before after having been pent up within the mountains for so long.

Just as the gang breached through the massive doors of Lochlann, the dwarven guards started shouting abruptly in fear as they quickly took a defensive position.

"DRAGON!" they yelled in a frenzy while preparing to fire long javelin spears, and a shadow was cast over them when a great Silver approached from the skies.

"NO!" Laila called out, riding Merimer out quickly before them. "Don't hurt her!"

"HOLD!" shouted the guard master, as he looked confusedly between Laila and the great dragon.

Turathyl landed gracefully by Laila and stood poised for the dwarves, showing no aggression nor fear.

"But how?" the guard master muttered, his mouth agape.

"She is my friend," Laila replied. "She will help stop the war."

To Laila's surprise, the dwarf guards readily withdrew their weapons, and they all cheered for the elf and her dragon. Their eagerness to believe that dragons and man could together find peace gave her hope in herself and in her mission. She only prayed that she would not disappoint.

The companions traveled east along the mountain base, Laila riding in the lead atop Merimer and alongside the great dragon. The rest of the group held back, watching in amazement at the sight. Glondora, more than anyone, was in utter shock since she hadn't yet witnessed the phenomenon for herself. She rode with Hort atop Orbek, holding her husband firmly around the waist, chattering his ear off most of the way. After several hours, everyone slowly began to feel more at ease but still maintained their distance back from the dragon, not wishing to provoke its tolerance for their presence.

'I will not be able to stay with you when we reach the Silvers' Mountain,' Turathyl told Laila. 'You are going to have to face Aeris alone so that she can see your strength and gifts for herself. I do not see how she could deny that you are the one that the prophecy speaks of, the Omi Méa, after what I have seen in you.'

Even with Turathyl's words, Laila began to start doubting herself again. She had been feeling confident since her dream with the Red dragon but believed that she would have Turathyl by her side to at least foster the strength she would need before the Silvers.

'I also fear Aeris would see my bringing you to her as a betrayal against our kind. It would most likely end any chance we would have of

CHAPTER 32

gaining her audience before we even begin.' Turathyl could sense Laila's energy shifting uneasily, fear now emanating from within her. *'I will still be with you. I will meet you there and appear as a neutral third party. Have faith, young one.'*

Laila nodded to her, but they both knew she was still frightened. They were getting closer, and it was becoming more real. She looked up into the skies and saw in the far distance a dragon's form disappearing into the clouds. Taking a deep breath, she tried to pull herself together. She had to stay strong.

Along the way, Turathyl tried to impart some knowledge about the Silvers to Laila but wasn't sure how much it would help. She mostly warned her of Aeris's stubbornness, how she will be looking for her weaknesses, and always to address the monarch respectfully. To never, EVER look straight into Aeris's eyes; to never look into any dragons' eyes, or she will become defenseless against them.

When Turathyl left for the night to keep watch from above, Nikolean was the first to ride up beside Laila, his mount much swifter now atop his muscular drow steed. Davion had noticed all too late and was ready to move between them, but Hort held up his hand, wordlessly telling him to hold back and give them space. He could see the jealousy in Davion's eyes and actions and worried for him that he would take it too far and ruin any chance he might have to gain Laila's affections, as the human so desperately desired. Davion scowled as he fought his urges and watched the two of them riding ahead.

"Are you prepared?" Nikolean asked her.

Are you prepared? The voice of the Red dragon echoed in her mind. *What did that mean, anyway?* She started to get lost in the memory of her last encounter with the great dragon of her dreams.

"My lady?" Nikolean interrupted her thoughts. "Are you okay?"

Looking at him blankly, she came back to the present and glanced around at the others, apprehensive about what fate she was leading them into. "I am okay," she responded. "I am not sure how I can be prepared to face Aeris, though."

"I understand," Nikolean said.

"How can you?" Laila snapped bitterly. How could anyone understand the weight of the expectations that had been put upon her? All that she had wanted was to see what was outside of her little den. This is not at all what she had in mind and definitely not what she wanted. She wished beyond wishes that she and Merimer could simply ride off, far away from it all, and run full speed all the way back to her cozy, safe little den by the river. Oh, how she wished she could see her mother again. It all just seemed so far away and out of reach now.

"I suppose I can't," Nikolean replied sympathetically. "Only you will know if you are ready for this. It is your choice. I will follow you whether we go before Aeris or wherever else you wish to go."

Laila looked over at him, bewildered. "Where else is there?"

Nikolean let out a soft chuckle, irritating her as she once again assumed he was laughing at her. "My lady, I wish we were going anywhere apart from before an irate dragon. I would much prefer to take you to a place of beauty bereft of hate, danger, or prospect of dying. It would contain only that which would bring a smile to your lips."

Laila pondered on the thought of his suggestion, wondering if such a place even existed, apart from her home. "Would that even be possible before the war ends?"

Letting out a sigh, Nikolean responded, "Perhaps not. But, perhaps one day…"

Before he could continue, their conversation was interrupted by a band of orcs stampeding over a rock ledge heading straight for them, weapons drawn. Laila instinctively looked to the sky and reached out for Turathyl, but she was nowhere in sight—or mind.

Like a dance, the party gathered wordlessly in a circle, facing outward toward the orcs as they prepared for the battle. The yelling and snarling of the beasts echoed through the rocky surroundings, and they held fast as the first one approached. When it reached ten paces out from Laila, it slammed into an invisible wall and bounced backward from Merimer's forcefield, landing on the ground with a great *THUD* and a growl.

Glondora began mumbling incantations, and Laila realized that she was casting enhancing spells on them, causing her to feel more invigorated. "*Raniculym!*" the dwarf cast, and Laila's mind was suddenly sharp and clear.

A second orc began to get close, and a fire-bolt shot past her from Davion, causing the orc to squeal in pain. Laila reached her hand out toward a large boulder the size of Orbek and flung it with her mind at the orc, swiping it off its feet. The force propelled the orc away as both orc and boulder plummeted to the ground, and the orc was pinned under its considerable weight. Salyaman landed the final blow with an arrow shot straight through its eye.

Three more orcs came rapidly toward them, but Laila was becoming infuriated. She was fed up with everything trying to get in their way. Her task was challenging and stressful enough without all of these constant irritating interruptions trying to foil her plans and kill her before she's even had a chance to begin. Feeling her hatred boiling up for these nuisances attacking them for no reason, she charged Merimer out toward them. The others followed, concerned she was being heedless again.

Merimer veered sideways, clearing her line of sight, and Laila's hands became aflame as she let out a fierce outcry, summoning a pillar of fire that blazed out from both hands toward the orcs. The others froze in their tracks, shielding themselves from the immense heat emanating off of her flames and covering their eyes from the blinding light. The orcs' screams pierced through the mountains, causing everyone to cringe at the horror of the sounds and smells until the beasts could scream no more.

When the brilliance died down, and they could uncover their eyes, the group looked to find nothing but three piles of ash left in the petite elf's fiery wake.

"How...?" Davion murmured, completely aghast.

"That was AWESOME!" Glondora yelled excitedly. "OIY! Take that ye tardubs!"

Nikolean made his way back to Laila's side while Davion was recovering from his shock.

Salyaman also rode up to her and said, "I suppose that was the fire spirit you had been seeking?"

"How did you do that?!" Davion finally managed to ask, confused.

Laila glared at what was left of the orcs she had incinerated. "I didn't do it. The fire spirit did this. I only asked it to."

Wryly, Nikolean responded, "I'm sure it has a lot to do with who's doing the asking. You were incredible, my lady."

Blushing, she was starting to realize that her potential—now that she had all four spirits—was boundless. Maybe she really was ready to face Aeris after all. She only wished Turathyl had been there to witness it.

'I am here,' Turathyl assured her. 'I was always here.'

'Another test,' Laila realized.

'You truly are the one, Omi Méa.' Turathyl told her respectfully.

On the fourth day along the Gorén Mountain base, calls of dragons could be heard from all around, and their silhouettes flying through the skies to and from the mountain was beyond intimidating as the group approached the Silvers' Mountain. Turathyl had left the group that morning as they departed their camp, and Laila led them east while spending much of the day conversing with Davion, the others following behind. Over the last few days, he had been fanatically asking a hundred questions about her fire abilities while sharing his own experiences. He couldn't comprehend how she managed to cast such a powerful spell so quickly after finding her "spirit." Laila wasn't able to offer him any of the answers he was looking for. She really didn't know how to explain it or why it came to her so powerfully.

Maneuvering the group closer to the Silvers' Mountain, Laila dismounted, and the others did the same.

"I will need you all to watch Merimer while I climb the mountain," Laila said to the group.

"Whoa!" Hort exclaimed. "What are ye sayin', lass?"

"You are not going alone, Lady Laila," Salyaman insisted.

"No. You aren't," Davion added.

Laila looked at them, seeing that they had no intention of letting her leave without them. "But, this is my burden," she explained. She didn't know if she could live with the guilt were she to lose any of them.

Nikolean stepped toward her and took her hand; Davion clenched his jaw.

"My lady, we did not pledge ourselves to this quest only to leave you when you need us the most."

Laila took a deep breath. "Merimer and the others will not make it up the mountain," she stated.

"M'lady," Glondora said nervously. "Ye all can leave them with me. I will watch 'em 'til yer return."

"It is settled then," Salyaman said without hesitation, taking his elkah, Friet, over to Glondora. "We shall go the rest of the way by foot."

"Will ye be safe here, me love?" Hort asked, concerned. "What if some orcs or a dragon finds ye?"

'*She will be safe,*' Laila heard Turathyl mind-send her along with some instructions.

"Turathyl said that she will be fine," Laila relayed to the group. "Glondora, take them through that passage over there. You'll find a spot you will be safe until our return. It's flat enough for the wagon to pass." She pointed to a gap between the Silvers' Mountain and another. "Orcs will not come so close to the Silvers' Mountain, and the Silvers will have no interest in you." They all complied and turned over their mounts to Glondora, only taking what would be necessary for the climb, including heavy furs for the cooler air further up.

Gazing up at the pinnacle full of Silvers from the base of the massive landmark, Hort instantly felt woozy, his acrophobia kicking in as he realized how high he would be climbing.

"Goddess Mother, Jayenne, and Kyrash," he moaned, looking up at the grandness of the mountain. "Hmmm... Maybe I should stay behind after all and keep me wife some company."

Davion patted his uncle on the shoulder. "Uncle, you've done plenty of hiking. It'll be just like riding a horse."

"That's what I be afraid of," Hort replied woefully, then pulled up his britches and sauntered closer to the mountain. "Well, let's get on with it then!"

As they began to make their way up the side, they found it rather easy at the beginning since it wasn't steep along the bottom. Nikolean was the quickest and lightest on his feet as he stealthily and effortlessly scaled his way over the mountainside but had to keep holding back for the others to catch up. Laila and Salyaman were also pretty adept at climbing. Hort was strong and sturdy, making his way along grumpily, trying to keep up to the elves, and doing well so long as he remembered not to look down. However, Davion was struggling, clumsily following along. It was definitely a very foreign terrain and skillset than he had much practice with.

After spending the greater part of the day climbing, they were all fatigued but could see that they had finally reached the halfway point. However, it was apparent that they would not complete the climb in a single day. The mountain was becoming steeper and harder to scale, and slippery with ice. Each of them had taken a turn losing their footing here and there along the way—except for Nikolean, who was always a ways ahead of them. Davion had taken more than his share of stumbles but had been very lucky thus far, only needing help from Hort once, who had grabbed his arm to keep him from falling.

As the sun began to set behind the mountain peaks, the comrades quickly found a crevice to tuck themselves against, hoping they would not be spotted by the dragons during the night. Laila crammed herself between Salyaman and Hort, and they all took turns keeping watch until morning.

Laila had been trying to stay focused, scared of how close and real this was all becoming, and so preferred to keep her distance from the feuding human and drow for the time being. It would be quite soon before this whole journey, all the stress and training, everything that all of this had been for, would be over. So many uncertainties were mulling over in her mind: What would she say to the great dragon, Aeris? What would come next after she won over the Silvers? Would she ever get to have a life for herself? Would she ever get to explore her feelings for Davion or Nikolean? She shivered as the frosty cold hit her, and pulled her fur coat tighter over her shoulders, her mind racing until she eventually managed to drift off to sleep.

Resuming their trek when the day broke, they had reached the point where snow and ice had begun blanketing over the mountain stone. The group was still sore from the day before and anxious about inevitably having to face the dragons that day. They all remained silent as they scaled the mountain, afraid of attracting any attention from the dragons that were all too close at this point.

Coming around another narrow corner, Laila grabbed hold of a rock jutting out to step up onto, but her hand slipped on a patch of ice that had formed, and she lost her grip. Sliding down past the ledge they had been walking along, she reached frantically, grabbing at whatever she could. She was skidding down the mountainside in a panic before finally managing to catch herself on another rock.

"Laila!" Davion yelled, frightened.

Everyone rushed to see where she had landed and found her dangling below the ledge, barely grasping on.

"Hold on, my lady!" Nikolean cried, swiftly scaling back down to her.

"Take my staff!" Davion shouted, reaching it out toward her, holding tight to the other end, but the staff was still two feet shy of her reach.

"I can't hold on much longer!" Laila hollered, terrified. She reached out mentally, calling for the earth spirit, seeking any life or seedlings that she could grasp and forcefully grow to secure her, but there was none; nothing but lifeless dirt and rock beneath. Her arms began quivering, and she could feel her fingers slipping, getting ready to give.

And then it happened; her fingers failed her, her powers failed her, and she found herself falling away from the mountain ledge, away from her friends, away from her destiny.

"LAILAAAAAAAAAA!"

CHAPTER 32

CHAPTER THIRTY-THREE

CONFRONTATION

"*L*AILAAAAAAAAAA!"

As she fell from the rocky ledge, Laila's heart stopped, and everything went quiet. The air blew past her as she slipped away, falling in slow motion. Frantically, she sent her mind out in all directions, searching for help, searching for anything. '*TURY!... MOTHER!*' But, there was only the sound of the wind howling past her ears. She couldn't even hear the screams of her friends as they cried out to her in terror.

This couldn't be the end! It couldn't have all been for nothing! But, Turathyl did not answer, and her mother was nowhere near. *Mother...* She thought about all of the Great Wolf's warnings of not being ready, of all the training and preparing. She had foolishly been in such a hurry to prove that she was ready for whatever her destiny had in store. Laila closed her eyes, rolling over in the air, facing downward, memories of her mother's loving mind-touch racing through her thoughts as she wished she was still back in the Sacred Forest.

'*LAILA!*' she heard Turathyl's mind-voice break through, waking her up.

Then, like a shot, it hit her. The air spirit grasped onto her before she could even pursue it. She felt its intense power and force against her, followed by a moment of tranquility and clarity—she was not alone. Giving over to instinct, Laila stretched out her arms, thrusting them through the air, summoning a great gale beneath her. The air bent to her will, pushing back up against her fiercely until it felt as though she were floating in water. She pushed for the air again, plummeting her hands toward the earth, and her body became more stable as the air pushed back even harder.

The next thing she realized, she was gradually ascending back up the mountain toward the ledge with the force of the wind spirit surrounding her. She could feel the spirit pulling from her energy, from her life force, could sense the magnitude of power and sacrifice it was requiring from her, and she gave herself over to it willingly. The air spirit and Laila became as one, her eyes glowing white from its power.

The gale beneath her increased in intensity as it sent her swiftly back to the others, up and over the ledge. She braced herself, landing with great force against the mountain's surface, impacting the ground as she slammed down into a crouched position before her friends.

Laila slowly stood, blinking the white glow from her eyes as the air spirit withdrew from her, leaving her frail and weakened while she looked around at her companions gaping at her.

Davion was the first to leap forward and grab her in a firm embrace. "Don't ever scare me like that again!" he exclaimed.

After he let go, Salyaman took her hand and led her further away from the ledge. "I have never seen anything like what you just did, Lady Laila."

"I nearly whizzed meself when I saw ye slip, lass! I canna believe ye flew like a blastit bird!" Hort declared.

CHAPTER 33

Nikolean stepped toward her, looking in her eyes with reverence, trembling, and said, "My lady," his eyes speaking more than his words. She could discern from them his immense fear and his relief—and something else that made her unable to look away.

Laila gazed at him, still in shock herself, when his eyes unanticipatedly became blurry to her, and darkness loomed across the edge of her vision, making everything turn pitch-black. It immediately became apparent how weak she had become from the exertion and connection to the wind spirit as her knees quivered and abruptly gave out under her. Nikolean, catching her as she collapsed, lifted her into his arms, and the fear returned, flooding his eyes.

"There is a widening up ahead. Look there," Salyaman pointed out. "Let us get her where it will be safer to rest."

"I'll take her," Davion said, stepping forward.

"I have her." Nikolean snapped sternly, following Salyaman further up the mountain's edge toward the landing, while Davion bitterly followed behind with Hort.

As they made it to the clearing, Nikolean knelt down with Laila, holding her in his arms while setting her gently on the ground. He leaned her against him for support, sensing that she wasn't doing any better, and tightened his arms around her.

"My lady," he said again, praying for her to snap out of it, but then her whole body began to quiver in his embrace, and he tried to hold her steady.

Laila, half-conscious, unthinkingly reached out with her arms, scratching her fingers into the dirt, searching for life from the earth that she could draw from. After a moment, her quaking slowly subsided as she began to feel her strength returning. Energy flowed into her, coursing through her veins, and she gradually became stronger and stronger. Keeping her eyes shut, she concentrated on pulling the energy and forcing it into her body to heal herself. Oddly, she found the life source on the mountain unfamiliar from the roots and plants she had become accustomed to below.

"My lady!" Nikolean gasped in distress.

"Laila, stop!" she heard Salyaman shout.

Laila opened her eyes and saw Nikolean on the verge of unconsciousness when she realized she had been siphoning his life force by mistake.

Jerking away from him to break the link, she cried out, "Niko! I'm so sorry!"

In his weakened and drained state, Nikolean still managed to smile wryly at her and reply, "It's nothing, my lady."

"What happened, Laila?" Salyaman asked.

Davion stepped forward, taking her arm to help her stand and steady herself. She remembered then that she wouldn't have been able to siphon any life from the mountains because there wasn't any to be had. *But, a person?* She knew this was not the earth spirit's doing, and it scared her. Moreso, she was scared that she had hurt him and could have killed him.

"There was no life in the mountain. I didn't mean to," she replied with remorse.

"Ye canna heal on the mountain?" Hort said, and Laila shook her head in response. "Hmmm... This isna' good."

Davion held her close. "You're freezing," he pointed out, rubbing her arms to warm her while also making his actions clear to Nikolean. He watched for his reaction, unconcerned with his state, but Nikolean never took his eyes from Laila's nor wiped the smirk from his face.

"I hate to interrupt," Salyaman said, "but if the dragons did not know of our presence before, they certainly do now."

Everyone followed his gaze toward the sky as they watched three Silver dragons descending upon them.

CHAPTER 33

Stretching out her mind, Laila could sense the hostility in their thoughts and quickly told them, *'FRIENDS! Please, we are here to speak with the Great Aeris!'*

Disoriented, the dragons landed on the platform instead of killing the intruders where they stood. Laila noticed that they were significantly smaller than Turathyl was, with hardly any quills protruding from their necks and backs. They appeared quite lean and young in comparison and built for speed instead of brawn. The largest and eldest of the three dragons landed closer than the others and looked around dumbfoundedly for the voice that had spoken to him.

"It was I!" Laila said aloud as well as in his mind. *'Lady Lailalanthelus Dula'Quoy, here for an audience with the Great Aeris.'* She bowed her head humbly at the dragons.

They responded with growls and snarls. *'What is this?! You puny elf cannot speak with Aeris.'*

Maintaining a subservient posture, Laila continued to plead with them in the language of the ancients. *'Please. We have come very far to speak with your great Aeris so that we may all find peace and put an end to the war.'*

The dragon reared his head and puffed out his chest and wings. *'How dare you ask such a thing after what you elves have done!'*

'She will want to hear what I have come to tell her, I promise you. She would not be happy if you killed me before I had that chance,' Laila begged.

'Aeris would never bother listening to any lies you elves would spit at her. You have wasted your time, and now your life!'

The dragon stomped his foreclaws into the dirt, startling Laila to look upon his face. He instantly locked her in his glare, his deep-onyx eyes hypnotizing her not to look away. And as he took a step toward her, his teeth in a snarl, he knew he had her.

Although not having heard the exchange between them, the others realized the shift in energy and knew they were in trouble. Salyaman recognized the dragon's entrancing glare, knowing that Laila had been captured by it. He called out for her to look away, but she couldn't move, staying frozen in place like a statue.

"Prepare yourselves!" Salyaman ordered to the others, arming himself with his bow.

Nikolean darted in front of Laila, blocking the dragon's glare, and breaking the hold it had over her. Blinking out of her trance, Laila tried collecting herself as she recovered from the enchantment. The dragon came at Laila and Nikolean, and the drow clenched his daggers tightly, ready to attack.

Davion held out his staff, waving it as he shouted, "*Andrea enférot!*" casting a large fireball that shot forth from the new gem in his staff and exploded against the dragon's scaly hide. The dragon's shrill yowl echoed through the mountains as it was knocked back from the jolt of the fireball; its scales scorched.

Salyaman began to bombard the dragon with his arrows, but they were merely deflecting off its armored hide. He then cast his thorns spell on himself, grabbing his swords and preparing to attack.

Axe held high, Hort let out a battle cry, challenging the dragons, who were not at all intimidated by his feeble threat.

Joining the leader's advance, the other two dragons lurched forward, ready to kill the puny two-leggeds. The group placed themselves between Laila and the dragons, shielding her from the oncoming attack. The comrades were most certain that there was no way they were going to survive this, but it didn't matter. Their primary goal was to protect Laila for as long as possible.

For just a moment, Laila closed her eyes and opened herself to the spirits, begging for their guidance. The crisp air began to blow forcefully through her hair and all around her. She opened her eyes and felt the air spirit strong at her fingertips. Feeling as though she were part of the air itself, she reached up to the sky and stretched out her hand. Responding to her command, the skies quickly darkened, and thunder rumbled through the mountains. Before the lead dragon could reach the group, Laila sent a bolt of lightning, scorching down right between them and the dragons.

'*Your arcane magic is no threat to us!*' the dragon laughed at her. '*You are in the belly of the beast now, you insignificant worm. If you wish to see what true power is, then I shall be happy to demonstrate!*'

The dragon sat up on his hind legs and began to beat his mighty wings towards them repeatedly, stirring up all the stones and dust. Laila watched as a small tornado began to form before them. Trying to dissipate the twister before its formation, she reached out, gusting wind toward it, but wasn't sure how to make it stop. When her attempt failed, she grasped the earth spirit next and pulled from the mountain beneath, bringing forth four large stone spikes, piercing up through the surface, blocking the dragons.

The great beasts still weren't impressed with her efforts. They pummeled through the rock spikes as easy as knocking down a tower of sand. However, it had distracted them long enough that the tornado formation had been thwarted.

With another beat of his wings, the dragon sent the two-leggeds all flying backward, cannoning hard against the mountainside.

'*Tury...*' Laila tried again weakly, jostled by the impact. '*Where are you?*'

As the dragons moved in toward the group, who were all struggling to stand, Laila looked around at her friends and realized there was little hope of them defeating three dragons, even if they had trained for decades. She had been so naive to think that she could change anything. To think that she could get through hate that had been boiling up for thousands of years just because she could speak to dragons. Why did anyone think she could do this?

Standing back on her feet, she felt anger and disappointment in herself seeping in. With the roar of the approaching dragons, her wrath grew, knowing that in moments, all of her friends would be dead, all because of her. Taking a step toward them, she felt her body burning inside, screaming to be released, so she raised her arms and screamed at the dragons, casting out the fire from within, towards them in an unholy inferno.

The fire filled the area, but she wasn't trying to kill the beasts; she knew that would defeat her goal of seeking peace. Instead, the fire burned out and around the dragons in a wall reaching up past their scaly backs. The crackling and intensity reminded her of the firey walls from her dreams.

'ENOUGH!' roared the commanding voice of another dragon that had arrived, her fierce screech echoing through the mountains. It was a voice that was familiar.

Seeing Turathyl there in the clearing with them, Laila felt great relief and the walls of fire began to fall slowly, fizzling out as the flames died against the hard stone ground.

'What is the meaning of this? Griton?' Turathyl addressed the lead dragon before them, barely looking at Laila and the others.

Bowing his head slightly to Turathyl, he explained that he was simply getting rid of some pests.

'Please. I just want to speak with Aeris,' Laila tried again, sending out her mind-speak to all four of them.

Standing strong and tall to assert her dominance, Turathyl stepped forward, looking thoughtfully at Laila, then back to Griton. 'An elf that can speak with us?'

'It's a trick, Elder,' he replied with hostility toward the two-leggeds.

'And the earth, air, and fire magic she displayed; is that a trick also?'

Griton looked at Laila, then glanced over at the rest of the puny creatures, who had all managed to get back to their feet. He wasn't sure how to respond, but he didn't doubt his hatred and desire to kill them all.

'Aeris has been watching and would like to see the young elf. The others are to remain here, guarded, until she can decide their fates.' Turathyl ordered, 'Griton, take the elf girl to Aeris. Dailan, Coryln, watch over the two-leggeds. They are not to be harmed.'

'Yes, Elder,' Griton said obligingly.

With a quick nod to Laila, Turathyl leapt off the mountain and flew back toward the top, where the Silvers perched.

Laila quickly looked at the others, yelling to them so they wouldn't be alarmed. "It's okay! You will be okay!"

Griton glared down at the little elf before him, hatred in his eyes, then grabbed Laila roughly in his claws before leaping over the side himself. Laila vaguely heard the others screaming out her name, but before she could explain to them what was going on, they were gone.

CHAPTER THIRTY-FOUR

PROPHECY

*I*t was frigid on the mountaintop, not just from the ice and snow, but from the aura emanating off of the dragons, sending shivers up Laila's spine. She could not have prepared herself for the number of dragons she would be faced with, nor the hatred radiating from them. Dozens of Silvers glared at her, showing remarkable restraint, as she stepped slowly through the pathway they were creating for her, assembling on either side. They watched as she traversed the path before her, like a prisoner running a gauntlet, a random dragon snapping its jaws threateningly at her every few feet. Her body trembled as she tried to keep calm, holding her head high, exerting a false appearance of confidence. The beasts emitted low growls, baring their teeth as she passed, eagerly anticipating the finale.

Laila tried desperately to look straight ahead and not be intimidated by the fierce creatures surrounding her, but she couldn't help glancing to and fro as she'd catch some of their thoughts floating around between them. None were good thoughts. All the dragons seemed to want her dead, with many confused about why Aeris would even tolerate meeting with her at all. The dragons ranged in size and age as she progressed through the masses. She even noticed a very young dragon not much larger than herself tucked behind her mother's wing, full of curiosity.

As she reached near the center of the mountaintop, the final dragons parted, revealing before her a great Silver perched on a large jagged platform. The colossal dragon stood tall and proud with its head held high, staring down at her, studying her. She was by far the largest of all the Silvers, and the quills cascading down her neck were like a thick thatch of fur. Her once-shiny silver scales appeared dull and darkened with time, and her face was even wrinkled and sagging through her scales with age.

Laila had practiced in her head a hundred times what she planned to say to the monarch dragon if she should be so lucky as to be granted an audience. However, standing here now, she couldn't remember a word of it. The thoughts of the dragons were crowding her mind as she tried to block them out.

When the great dragon before her heaved a low rumbling breath impatiently, she realized it was now or never.

"Great Aeris," Laila began. She spoke aloud in the Ancient tongue, speaking firmly in an attempt to show bravery, even though she felt very little of it at this moment. She recalled Turathyl had warned her not to mind-speak directly to the monarch unless she permitted it, so believed it best to address her this way. Kneeling down, she bowed her head in obeisance before continuing. "I have traveled very far to speak with you about the war that rages between your kind and the elves." Laila looked up at the great dragon towering over her, searching anxiously for a reaction. Aeris continued to stare at her apathetically. "I have come to beg your forgiveness for the wrongs of the past and plead with you to put an end to the war. I wish to speak of peace among our races and all of the races of Onis."

For the first time, Aeris reacted to the young elf, but it was not as Laila had been hoping for as the monarch erupted with a loud rumble of dragon laughter. She shifted on her platform, her old bones and the rock beneath echoing their struggles, and she brought her massive head closer to Laila to get a better look at the strange little elf.

The young girl kept her eyes averted from the blackness of the dragon's intimidating stare and remained still. Aeris was so close Laila could hear the air flowing through her nostrils, could smell her foul breath as it wafted over her face, could hear her saliva drip against the ground as she wet her muzzle with her tongue. Laila winced as the dragon sniffed at her hair, realizing that at any moment, the monarch could easily snatch her up in her jaws. Although only a few seconds had passed, it felt like an eternity as Laila stood her ground, feeling the judgment and hatred of the old dragon pouring over her.

After Aeris's amusement and curiosity had ceased, she glanced nonchalantly over at Turathyl, her next in command, and ordered, '*Kill it,*' then began to turn away, the other dragons all roaring and cawing with excitement.

Having heard her command, Laila disobeyed Turathyl's advice and shouted with her mind to Aeris as she dropped to her knees, '*No! Please! Give me a chance to explain!*'

Startled, Aeris whipped her head back around and glared at the elf with disdain, '*How is this possible?!*' she boomed toward her. '*No elf can commune with dragons!*'

Laila grabbed the sides of her head as the voice came blaring into her mind. When it eased, she looked back to Aeris.

Attempting to display a little more courage, she slowly brought herself back to her feet and said with conviction, '*I, Lailalanthelus Dula'Quoy, born of Lady Leonallan Dula'Quoy, have come before you, aided by the spirits of the land, to ask for your help in putting a stop to the war.*'

CHAPTER 34

'The spirits?' Aeris asked apprehensively. 'I am not naive, little elf. Only dragons can invoke the spirits. You are nothing. You have come to my home, attacked my children, and now further insult me by speaking nonsense.' She took a step aggressively toward the edge of the platform, scowling down at Laila, digging her claws in over the side. The young elf grew more nervous under the gaze of the resentful dragon but tried her best to hold her ground.

'I was curious to see what was causing such a disturbance to my mountain. Now that I have seen you for myself, I am no longer impressed. You have no right to ask of me what you do. You are too young to even grasp what it is that you are asking of me. This is not a war that I started, it was the elves that started it, but it will be I that finishes it when I rid the land of you all!' Aeris growled, enraged.

Turathyl took a slight step forward, her head bowed in homage. 'Monarch,' she interjected, and everyone turned their attention to her. 'Great Aeris. I sense something different in this elf. Does she not remind you of anything? One of our own cubs, perhaps?'

Indulging Turathyl for a moment, Aeris glanced over the elf with scrutiny. Looking upon her golden locks, pointed ears, and tiny form, she saw an arrogant elf cub standing before her and nothing more. However, she was reminded of something else...

'Dula'Quoy? Is that your name?' Aeris asked, more calmly.

Laila nodded.

'Lady Leonallan Dula'Quoy. Yes, I remember now.' She looked over to Turathyl. 'Did you not extinguish the life of Lady Leonallan some sixteen years past?'

As though struck through the heart, Laila whipped her head around and stared at Turathyl in shock. Turathyl felt her eyes bearing into her but dared not return her glare, afraid to blow her cover if she showed her emotion and guilt over that act. Instead, she looked only at Aeris and replied, 'You did issue that command, Great Aeris.'

'Yes, I did. But as I recall, it was you that carried it out, was it not?'

Turathyl ached as she nodded her head in confirmation.

Aeris let out a chortle of dragon laughter. 'So, that is what this is? You thought you might fight your way up the side of my mountain and have your revenge by toying with me and killing my kind?' She laughed again. 'Be my guest. There is the slayer of your mother. I heard she mangled her up very well to send a clear message to your people. Go ahead, let us see you, little elf, slaughter the dragons and win the war!'

The mountaintop was filled with dragon laughter at the notion, and Laila's heart began to pound hard in her chest. She clenched her fists at her side, fighting back her anger.

Turathyl looked at Laila, seeing the pain and hatred filling her eyes as they glistened, filled with tears. She shook her head slowly to the girl, hoping that she would stay focused and not be overcome by emotions. Laila clenched her jaw, wanting so much to lash out at Turathyl, to call her out on everything, to scream at her for her lies, but she didn't. Rather than succumb to her anger, she closed her eyes and took a deep breath. And then another.

As she stood there completely still, trying to calm herself, she felt the spirits surrounding her, dancing about her, taunting her to grab them. Ignoring their taunts, Laila hoped that she could reason with the ancient beings without the aid of the spirits' powers. Instead, she mind-sent out for all the dragons to hear, 'I am not here for revenge. I am here because I believed in the prophecy that was told to me. I believed that I could make a difference and that you could find it in your great heart to forgive and take pity on the other races. They are no match for your greatness, but they deserve to be here.'

'Prophecy?' Aeris inquired, slightly intrigued. 'Of what prophecy do you speak?'

Turathyl stepped in again, making sure all could hear, 'I believe she speaks of the Omi Méa.'

CHAPTER 34

The mention of a Great Spirit called the attention of her kin and monarch, and she reminded them of the prophecy from long ago, nearly forgotten by all.

'*Following the death of the Earth Mother, the One Mother, of Onis Caelis, the land of Onis will endure a great suffering. Valleys and streams will dry, becoming cracked and barren. The soil will spoil the harvests, leaving wilted crops and famine throughout. The hatred and anger between the races will grow as they struggle to survive, blaming one another for the destruction of the land, and the Reign of the Ancients will be like no other, full of wrath and vengeance.*' As Turathyl recited the words, the interest of the other dragons piqued, particularly that of the younger generations who had not yet heard the prophecy.

Laila again felt the spirits tugging at her, insisting that she surrender to them. So, ignoring them no longer, she opened her arms and tilted her head back, letting all four spirits enter her one after the other until her body surged with their power.

Turathyl continued, '*When the land of Onis and its people have endured their suffering, there will be born of an elf a Great Spirit who will unite the races. That spirit will engage all of the races and will know no boundaries between them.*'

The air on the mountaintop stirred as a slight gale began to form. Laila stretched her arms out while keeping her eyes shut, pulling from the air. It whirled around her, lifting her as it had before, but only a few feet off the ground, and more controlled. The dragons watched the young elf curiously as Turathyl continued reciting the prophecy.

'*That spirit will confront the ancients of the land and ask forgiveness for the two-leggeds' past actions. The Great Spirit, the Omi Méa, will be guided by the earth, the air, the fire, the water, and the phantom realm to bring forth peace among all the evolved races.*'

Thunder rumbled through the sky, and rain began to shower lightly over them. The rain was warm from the spirits as it quickly gained in intensity and melted the snow, wetting the mountaintop with a glossy finish. The dragons' interest was piqued by her display and by Turathyl's tale of the prophecy, but they were not yet impressed—having similar control over the air spirit.

The gold spirit shone next within the elf, and she let it flow forth readily, as it caused the mountaintop to quake and crack. Then, a spiked wall erected around Laila, pointing outwardly towards the dragons. They jumped back from the sharp points, becoming uneasy of the elf, and looked back and forth between each other, unclear of what to do. Those nearby flew away from her while still staying close enough to watch, enthralled with the story and the strange little being.

When the ground ceased quaking, Laila brought down the rain harder, then summoned the droplets with the blue spirit. The raindrops pooled and swirled, dancing throughout the sky in unison like a large flock of birds, creating a beautiful mural of shapes and patterns. The ancients watched the beautiful display, slightly soothed by its hypnotic movements.

'The Omi Méa will bring about a new era and replenishment of life over the land, changing all that was, and all that will be.' Turathyl bowed her head toward Laila upon concluding the prophecy.

As the elf closed her fist to the sky, the rain became bright like little lights, and then each droplet burst into fire, showering down toward them like miniature meteors. They all ducked low, becoming frightened of the display, cawing out their displeasures. Laila held her hands out toward the dragons, and the tiny fires fizzled out right above their heads before they could make contact. After the fire stopped, the rain continued to pelt down over the dragons, their wet scales sparkling like gems in the storm.

Never before had any of them seen such a spectacle involving all four spirits by a single two-legged. Several of the dragons were growing nervous, unsure of the elf or what the prophecy was predicting, while others had become captivated, eager for it to be true, and tired of the war themselves.

Seeing the demeanor of her dragons shifting as they watched the elf curiously and cautiously, Aeris grew worried of their intrigue, whether being reminded of the prophecy or hearing of it for the very first time. The great monarch dragon's displeasure increased, unable to see past her enmity for the elven race.

'Enough of this!' Aeris roared hellaciously, and Laila floated slowly back to the ground, staring up at Aeris, frightened and confused. 'I recall the prophecy of a Great Spirit, but you are merely an elf. I care not for what show you can perform. You are not the Omi Méa and will not be changing what was nor what is yet to come! I tire of your games!' Aeris looked again to Turathyl, infuriated, and ordered, 'Kill the girl!'

Looking back at her monarch, Turathyl did not move from her post. 'I will not,' she replied firmly, lifting her head high.

All the dragons filled the skies with their roars, echoing through the mountains. No dragon had ever disobeyed a direct order from their monarch. None of them could believe the audacity of Turathyl, especially Aeris.

'How...DARE...YOU!!!' Aeris huffed outraged with a loud dragon roar, 'You insolent lizard!'

'You are wrong about the girl, Aeris, just as we have all been wrong about the death of Onis Caelis. We must hear her out!' Turathyl pleaded.

'Who do you think you are to tell me what I must do?!' bellowed Aeris as she raised her massive wings, stretching them out wide. 'You are not monarch yet, Turathyl, and now you never shall be!' She let out another fierce roar that made Laila shake in her spot, terrified of the direction her confrontation had gone and wishing more than anything to flee. However, looking around her in fear, there was just nowhere to go. She was completely surrounded by dragons, all going wild in an uproar, ready for a fight. Those near Turathyl leaped and flew quickly away, afraid of being caught in Aeris's wrath.

The monarch thrust her wings powerfully toward Turathyl, slamming her with a fierce blast of wind, knocking the large dragon to her side. Turathyl raised her head and snapped her jaws at Aeris instinctively, roaring back while she regained her footing.

Forgetting her anger toward Turathyl over Lady Leona, Laila couldn't bear to see her dragon in trouble as Aeris raised her wings again, ready for another attack.

"Please, stop!" Laila cried out, grabbing Aeris's attention.

Aeris turned her head toward the girl and took a step forward, aiming her gale at the elf instead. As the strong force came toward her, Laila raised her hands hastily, and a wind of equal force struck back against it, canceling the dragon's out. This, of course, only angered the monarch further. She began to beat her wings faster, roaring and cawing furiously, and Laila felt as the air was being pulled from her lungs. She gasped and grasped for breath that she simply could not catch.

'Kill her!' Aeris called out to her children.

Weakened, Laila almost didn't see the two dragons coming from behind her on either side but turned just in time to pull the spikes from the earth that had protruded around her and hurl them toward both dragons, knocking them out of the sky and onto their backs against the ground. More dragons came at her, but she was still losing breath when, out of the corner of her eye, she saw Turathyl lunge for Aeris, snapping her jaws on her neck and clawing at her wings. Aeris's spell was broken. The great monarch screeched out in pain and rage as she was knocked to the ground by Turathyl, and Laila felt her breath returning to her just in time. She pushed a continuous gale towards the oncoming dragons, casting them backward and disabling them from approaching.

CHAPTER 34

Turathyl continued to attack Aeris, distracting her from Laila while she was left to handle the horde of dragons alone. One of the younger dragons decided to attack her on foot from the right while she tried to keep the ones in the air at bay using their own magic class against them. However, she turned quickly when she spotted him approaching.

Her own anger now building as she fought for her life and Turathyl's, and for all of Onis, her hands became aflame, her eyes glowing red. She felt no heat from the flames but could feel the fury of the fire spirit boiling up inside of her, ready to erupt. Laila pushed out toward the dragon coming at her on the ground, and a large fireball shot from her palms, slamming into the dragon with an explosion. It reared back, screeching out, scorched from the flames before they sizzled out from the falling rain.

The tempest raged on around the young elf, as did the dragons. When another group went to strike at her, she froze the rain into ice shards, propelling them down on the enclosing beasts. The dragons let out their piercing cries as the shards cut through their vulnerable wings. Unfortunately, the ice was not sharp enough to cut through their scaly hides, and the Silvers continued to charge at her.

Screaming as the monsters drew near, fire streamed out from Laila's hands in a blast around her, forcing the dragons back temporarily. She held onto the fire as long as she could, but it died away too quickly from the storm, and they were closing in on her again.

Laila grabbed her Dragonsbane daggers just as a dragon lunged for her with its claws. Diving out of the way, the dragon's talon grazed across her calf while she simultaneously slashed at the beast. The blade easily sliced through its protective scales, slitting its shoulder, and dark-blue blood sprayed out from its wound. They both screamed in agony, and then the dragon turned, resuming its pursuit, with others joining it.

As the beasts continued to come at her again and again, she pulled from each of the spirits, whichever she could grab to protect herself, combined with stabbing and slashing at those that came within reach, but she was quickly becoming drained. She had never used so much magic for so long and felt it diminishing her, especially with no life in the earth to draw from. The dragons could sense her weakening and continued their attacks against her, with her barely evading each one.

Laila was slowly being backed toward the battling Turathyl and Aeris. Then, one of the beasts used her own rock spikes against her, striking it with its tail, sending the spike soaring through the air. Laila dodged to the side, but the rock scraped across her arm, and she cried out in pain.

Out of the corner of her eye, as she recovered from the last attack, Laila saw Aeris grab Turathyl by the neck in her jaws and toss her ruthlessly toward the mountain ledge. Her great dragon skidded across the wet-stone platform and stopped just shy of tumbling over the side. Turathyl was losing and battered, covered in streaking blue blood, unable to get up.

"TURY!" Laila called out to her.

As a Silver descended on Laila from the sky, she used what little energy she had left to shove at the oncoming dragon, using telekinesis to send it flying into three others, knocking them all back clear of her. She turned and ran limping and bleeding over to Turathyl, with Aeris stomping supremely toward them both.

'*Impressive*,' Aeris said to Laila as she approached them by the mountain's ledge.

Looking back at Aeris, for a split second, Laila let her guard down as she looked into her pitch-black eyes. The moment she did, Aeris had her. The monarch locked around the young elf's mind as she was entranced by the eyes of the dragon, holding her there, defenseless.

'*But, not impressive enough,*' she sneered.

Then, Aeris whipped around and thrust her tail hard against Laila, mightily slamming her entire body, breaking bones, and slashing her with the tail's sharp quills.

Laila flew backward, far beyond the edge of the mountaintop, the impact of Aeris's tail reverberating throughout her broken body. She let out a scream that couldn't be heard. Her heartbeat pounded loudly in her ears, and her head throbbed with intense pain. *Tha-thump... Tha-thump...* Her vision became tainted red as blood spots filled her eyes. She flailed her arms and legs frantically the best she could, pain shooting through her body, reaching out for the air spirit as before. But she had grown too weak from the battle. *Tha-thump... Tha-thump...* There were no bright little lights left for her to grab onto; she was alone. She stopped flailing, the pain too great, knowing there was nothing she could do to stop it. *Tha-thump... Tha-thump...* As she reached her peak, terrified beyond measure, Laila began to descend powerlessly through the sky, and she felt time slowing down. *Tha-thump... Tha-thump...*

She blinked. There was Aeris, smiling smugly at her, haunted by her hatred that had been reigning over the land, poisoning all against forgiveness or mercy—hatred Laila had hoped to abolish so the land could begin to heal...could become united.

She blinked. There was Turathyl, watching her in horror, unmoving, mouth agape. Her great dragon that was covered in blood and gashes from trying to defend the young elf—the majestic Silver that had saved her, guided her, protected her...believed in her.

She blinked. There was the side of the mountain, quickly rushing past her. The side of the mountain where the fierce monsters guarded her comrades in arms who were waiting for her, depending on her—who would now all surely die because of her; her Davion, her Nikolean, her Salyaman, her Hort...her friends.

She blinked. There was nothing. There was no light. There was no sound. There was only darkness. Even her heartbeat no longer pounded in her ears. Laila wondered if her mother would ever know what had happened to her, how sorry she was for leaving the way she did, or how much she loved her. She could see her mother's face in her mind, hear her loving words, and wished she could nuzzle into her, feeling her soft mane once more. But all she could feel was the wind whipping across her face as she plummeted toward the surface...toward her end.

She could see all of her friends, the memories flooding her thoughts, memories of the journey with them, of how they all believed she would be the one to save them all, risking their very lives for her. Closing her eyes one last time, with a heart full of remorse, a final thought whispered through her mind as the darkness ultimately consumed her, *I failed you all.*

CHAPTER 34

To Be Continued...

HERE ENDS PART ONE

OF

REIGN OF THE ANCIENTS

GLOSSARY

PRONUNCIATIONS:

Aeris [AIR-iss]
Aleta [ah-LEE-ta]
Amillia [ah-MILL-ee-ah]
Annallee [ah-NAW-lee]
Ballat Sueda [bal-LET SWAY-dah]
Brakdrath [BRAK-drath]
Coryln [cor-ILLN]
Dailan [DAY-lin]
Darton Dula'Quoy [DAR-tin doo-lah-COY]
Davion [DAYV-ee-uhn]
Drakka [DRAH-kah]
Duep Nordor [doo-EP nor-DOR]
Elkah [ELK-ah]
Glondora [glon-DOR-ah]
Gortax [GOR-taks]
Griton [GRYE-tin] (GRYE rhymes with try)
Helna [HEL-nah]
Hort [HORT]
Ignisar [IG-nih-sar]
Jayenne [jay-EN]
Kilgar [KILL-gar]
Kyrash [KEE-rash]
Lailalanthelus (Laila) Dula'Quoy [lay-lah-LAN-thuh-luss (LAY-lah)
    doo-lah'COY]
Laut [LOWT]
Leonallan Dula'Quoy [lee-OH-nah-lan doo-lah'COY]

Lochlann [LOK-len]
Lupé Caelis [LOO-pay KAY-lis]
Lyson [LYE-sin]
Má Lyndor [maw lin-DOR]
Merimer [MAIR-ih-mer]
Mira [MEER-ah]
Neremyn [NAIR-ih-min]
Nikolean Den Faolin [nik-OH-lee-en den FAY-oh-lin]
Nikososo Den Faolin [nik-oh-SOH-zoh den FAY-oh-lin]
Onis Caelis [OH-nis KAY-lis]
Orbek [OR-bek]
Othsuda Theora [oth-SOO-dah thee-OR-ah]
Port Iyos [port EE-ohss]
Rath Almon Dula'Ertha [rath AL-mon doo-lah'ER-thah]
Rath Beldroth Dula'Sintos [rath BEL-droth doo-lah'SIN-tohs]
Rathca Saelethil Dula'Sintos [RATH-cah SAY-luh-thill doo-lah'SIN-tohs]
Rathelle Saelihn [rath-EL say-LEEN doo-lah'SIN-tohs]
Roco [ROH-koh]
Salyaman Dula'Sintos [sal-YAM-in doo-lah'SIN-tohs]
Shakiera Nesu [shah-KEER-ah NEE-soo]
Silex [SYE-leks] (SYE rhymes with my)
Stantul [STAN-tul]
Thas Duar Moran [thas dew-AR mor-AN]
Thorgru [THOR-grew]
Thornton [THORN-tin]
Torrence Collins [TOR-entss]
Turathyl [tur-AH-thul]

ANCIENT LANGUAGE:

anna [AH-nah] — no

caelis [KAY-lis] — mother
elo [EE-loh] — I
ess [ESS] — you
fetian [FE-tee-ehn] — prophecy
lupé [LOO-pay] — wolf
méa [MEE-ah] — spirit
melo [MEE-loh] — my
numat [noo-MAT] — never
omi [OH-mee] — great
onis [OH-nis] — the one
pavula [pah-VOO-lah] — child
reliensa [ree-lee-EN-sah] — go
únethera [yoo-nee-THAIR-ah] — know/understand/familiar

DROW LANGUAGE:

anaksula [ah-NAK-soo-lah] — whoa-there/settle down
Den [den] — high ranking or honored family title

DWARF LANGUAGE:

baccat [BAH-cat] — a curse
barden cake [BAR-din cayk] — a very sweet dwarven cake
blastit [BLAST-it] — damned/darnit
blockendarf [BLAWK-en-darf] — popular dwarven meal similar
    to a meatloaf
dumbest thing I had tickle me ears — slang, dumbest thing I've
    heard
glootendally [GLOO-in-dall-ee] — birthday/birthday celebration
    ("t" is silent)
glootendally pie [GLOO-in-dall-ee peye] — traditional birthday
    dessert ("t" is silent)

hobbit's uncle — slang, monkey's uncle
Ignisar's lair [IG-nih-sars LAY-er] — Red monarch's lair, slang for hell
laidens [LAY-dens] — ladies
mond [MAWND] — state
nöije [NOYZSH] — purpose
okullo dung — slang, bull crap
shut yer pie hole — slang, be quiet
son of an elf — slang, darn it or scoundrel
tah [TAH] — you/your
tardub [TAR-dub] — another word for scoundrel
tickled under me beard — slang, very happy
what a load o' okullo dung — slang, what a load of crap
what in Ignasar's lair was that? — slang, what the hell was that?

ELVEN LANGUAGE:

aimiadal [ay-mee-ah-DAL] — friend
annalsa [ah-NUL-sah] — cancel spell
areta [ar-EH-tah] — please
dimisna [dim-IZ-nah] — extinguish
Dula' [DOO-lah] — Lord/Lady/Royal
ekia [EE-kee-yah] — seek
elfah [EL-fah] — elvish
enférot [en-feer-OT] — inferno
essa [ESS-ah] — calm/easy
excassida [ex-CAH-sid-ah] — multiply
helna [HEL-nah] — horse
illioso [ill-ee-OH-soh] — ignite
iret [eye-RET] — go
lacarté [lah-CAR-tay] — bolt
lat [LAT] — the

lingaithio [ling-GAY-thee-oh] — language/speech
luminas [LOOM-ih-nas] — illuminate
mall [MAL] — I/me/my
malléalan [mal-EE-ah-lan] — my love
malva [MAL-vah] — my name is
méa [MEE-ah] — spirit
naiht [nay-ET] — no
norn [nORn] — black
omine [OM-ih-nay] — fire source object
ominus [OM-ih-nus] — fire
ono [OH-noh] — one
onsilith [UHN-sih-lith] — council
Ranchetal [RAN-cheh-tal] — Elven ritual display of powers
ranicúlym [ran-IH-que-lum] — tranquility
Rath [RATH] — Ruler/King
Rathca [RATH-cah] — Ruler/Prince
Rathelle [rath-EL] — Ruler/Queen
salvath [sal-VATH] — hello
sithio [SIH-thee-oh] — know
solas [SOH-lass] — light
suliath [SOO-lee-ath] — great
ta [TAH] — what
unasceiry [OO-nah-sair-ee] — orb of death
vall [VAL] — you
veriness [VAIR-ih-ness] — forcefield
verte [VAIR-tay] — increase

To hear Distant Lover on youtube.com go to:
https://youtu.be/KO1_5yfNQ4c

DISTANT LOVER

Written for the novel "The Onis Chronicles, Reign of the Ancients: Part I"   R.E. Davies

To hear Home Lochlann on youtube.com go to:
https://youtu.be/4v6FV5y8j7Q

HOME LOCHLANN

Written for the novel "The Onis Chronicles, Reign of the Ancients: Part I"

R.E. Davies

ABOUT THE AUTHOR

R.E. Davies is a Canadian-American author who moved to Florida from Canada in 2001. She has since completed her Bachelor's Degree, found and married her other half, and had five incredible children. In 2012, all her future plans changed with the birth of her first son, who was born with a rare genetic disorder, Cornelia de Lange Syndrome (CdLS,) severely affecting both his mind and body. Through her adventures of learning how to be a special needs mom, she has also battled and won against both thyroid and skin cancer, motivating her to cherish every day that she has with her family. No matter where fate took her throughout life's adventures, there has always been one thing that she came back to; writing. She began writing as early as elementary school when she wrote and directed her first play to perform for her classmates. Whether it was plays, poems, short stories, novels, or songs, she always loved sharing her stories and fantastical lands with those she loved and is now even more excited to be able to share those tales with others.

Connect with R.E. Davies (@REDaviesAuthor) on Facebook for news about upcoming books, links to songs, maps, and other great information!

ACKNOWLEDGMENTS

More than anything, I would like to thank my husband and children for their patience and their encouragement while I pursued my dreams of introducing others to the land of Onis. While writing a book with five children 8-years-old and younger through a pandemic with a combination of remote learning and homeschooling a special needs child and a 1-year-old crawling all over me and pulling my hair had its challenges, they all (the two old enough to understand) knew how much this meant to me and never doubted me. Or, if they did, they never let me know it! When my husband said, "You should finish that book series you've been working on for the last twenty years," I don't think he realized that it meant staying up until after midnight every night, or using every free moment I had to work on it, or that he'd hear me talk about it endlessly as I excitedly shared every detail! I feel very blessed to have such a family stand beside me in my dreams and help me do whatever it takes to get there!

I would also like to thank my parents for always encouraging me that I could do whatever I put my mind to and for believing in me more than anyone. To my mom, for being my emotional support throughout everything life has thrown my way, both great and terrifying. To my dad, for supporting me with every direction my life has turned and for loving my writing even though there were no cowboys or planes! Thank you both for pushing me whenever I was ready to give up or was having doubts in myself.

Thank you so much to my proofers! To my step-dad, who took on the challenge of helping me to proof my first book. It was a bumpy start, but we both learned a lot during this process, and you were such a tremendous help! To Dawn, your positive feedback brought happy tears to my eyes to know how much you enjoyed the story and the characters.

To the several teachers I had from grade school through high school that encouraged me in my writing, even during class time, just so they could read it, thank you! To my Creative Writing teacher at the University of West Florida, thank you for all of your positive feedback on my writing, including Davion's memory of his mother that I had added as a "short story" for your class. You were right; it really was just "a small part of a much bigger picture!"

And, of course, I am so very grateful to you, the reader! It touches my heart to have you buy and read my book, helping turn this dream into a reality! And, if you loved it, or are still loving it, don't worry; the rest of the series is well underway!

Thank you all SO much, from the bottom of my heart!

Printed in Great Britain
by Amazon